"YOU ALL RIGHT?" VIGHOLF ASKED.

Rhona nodded. "The universe began to spin, so I decided to sit until it stopped."

"Good plan."

Since he didn't know how long she'd need to sit, Vigholf sat beside her. He carefully took her raised finger and tucked it back into her fist.

"Thank you. I didn't seem to have control of that talon."

"Finger."

"Whatever." She smiled a little. "You can let go of my hand."

"I could, but probably won't. What with your universe spinning and all."

"Any opportunity. You Lightnings take any opportunity."

"There's truth to that, I'm afraid."

"You are, however, surprisingly light of touch."

"Pardon?"

"The way you're holding my hand. I always thought you'd be more of a mauler. Like a diseased wolf chewing the knuckles off me fist."

"That's very nice."

"Not really."

"I was being sarcastic."

"Oh. I see." Rhona gazed off for a moment, then asked, "Where are we?"

"Okay. That's it. I'm taking you to bed . . ."

More from G. A. Aiken

DRAGON ACTUALLY

ABOUT A DRAGON

WHAT A DRAGON SHOULD KNOW

LAST DRAGON STANDING

And find her stories in this anthology

SUPERNATURAL

Published by Kensington Publishing Corporation

THE DRAGON WHO LOVED ME

G. A. AIKEN

ZEBRA BOOKS
KENSINGTON PUBLISHING CORP.
http://www.kensingtonbooks.com

ZEBRA BOOKS are published by

Kensington Publishing Corp.
119 West 40th Street
New York, NY 10018

All Kensington titles, imprints, and distributed lines are available at special quantity discounts for bulk purchases for sales
promotion, premiums, fund-raising, educational or institu-
tional use.

Special book excerpts or customized printings can also be created to fit specific needs. For details, write or phone the office
of the Kensington Special Sales Manager: Attn. Special Sales
Department. Kensington Publishing Corp., 119 West 40th
Street, New York, NY 10018. Phone: 1-800-221-2647.

Zebra and the Z logo Reg. U.S. Pat. & TM Off.

ISBN-13: 978-1-4201-3289-2
ISBN-10: 1-4201-3289-X

First Printing: September 2011

10 9 8 7 6 5 4 3 2

Printed in the United States of America

Prologue

The girl slept. Not hard, though. She no longer slept hard—or without a weapon. Too many times there were attacks on their camp in the middle of the night. Too many times she'd found fellow soldiers trying to sneak into her bed, hoping to get out of her what they couldn't afford to buy from the camp girls. Those who survived were usually sent back to their homes. Not because of what they'd done, but because the body parts they were now missing made it impossible to expect much out of them during battle.

Yet she'd never be able to say whether it was her light sleeping or her much-more-honed instincts that told her she needed to be awake and moving. Silently stepping past the other sleeping squires, she eased into the night and followed where her instincts led, to a copse of trees right outside the camp. That's where she found her. The woman sneaking out of the camp without her guards, troops, or horse, carrying only one travel bag, her two swords strapped to her back. Going alone. Because she was brave. Because she was desperate. Because, on a good day, she was more than a little crazy.

Without saying a word, the girl ran back to her tent and grabbed her own travel pack, her own sword and battle-ax, her warmest boots and cape. She returned to the woman's side, smiled.

"You didn't think I'd let you go without me, did you? My place is by your side."

"And your death may well be by my side if you come with me. I can't allow it."

"You leave without me—and in seconds rather than days everyone in this camp will know that you're gone."

Bright green eyes glared and, after five long years of seeing that look on a daily basis, the girl no longer recoiled in fear. Then again, over the many years this war had been going on, she'd learned how far she could push—and how far she couldn't.

"I'll not be responsible for you, little girl. You'll have to keep up."

"When don't I?" the girl lashed back.

"And watch your tone. I'm still your queen."

"Which is why you need me. No war queen should be without her squire."

"Squire? When was the last time you washed my horse?"

"When I couldn't get anyone else to do it for me."

The queen grinned, the scar she'd received in battle four years ago crinkling across her face. It went from her right temple, down across her forehead, the bridge of her nose, her cheek, finally slicing into her neck. The blade had missed major arteries and, with stitches, had healed well enough. But the scar remained and the queen left it there. To the enemy, it seemed to suggest that the rumors of her being the undead were true—for how could someone survive such a cut? As for how the queen felt about her scar . . . well, she never looked in a mirror that much anyway.

"Let's be off then, squire, before they realize we've gone."

They headed deeper into the forest surrounding their camp, but were forced to stop after a few minutes when they found the human body of a young dragoness passed out in front of them, the victim of too much drink.

"What should we do with her?" the queen asked.

"Can't just leave her here. Besides, it would be good to have a dragon by our side should we need one."

"Good point." They picked the dragoness up, let her vomit up whatever she'd drunk, then began walking with her until she could walk on her own.

After some time, the dragoness asked, "Where are we going?"

"Into the west," the queen answered.

"Our enemies are in the west."

"Aye."

"They'll kill us all if they find us."

"Aye."

"But torture us first."

"Aye."

"So I'm guessing you have a plan."

"Not really."

The dragoness let out a sigh. "I kind of knew I'd regret drinking with the Eighteenth Battalion tonight—I just had no idea how much."

"Don't worry. We'll either stop this war in its tracks or become martyrs to it."

"I'm a dragon, my lady. Dragons don't become martyrs. We create them."

"Well then . . ." Annwyl, the Mad Queen of Garbhán Isle, patted the She-dragon on her back as they headed farther into the west. ". . . now you have a goal."

Chapter 1

She watched them move through the trees. They nearly blended in, but not quite. Not to her eyes.

For these enemy dragons, the Irons, trying to sneak into their camp had become a weekly occurrence. Not that she could blame them. After five years of a standstill war in this valley called Euphrasia, both sides had become tired of it all. The constant but ineffectual skirmishes, the occasional attempts to poison each other's water supply. When would it end? When would this war become something they all talked about in the past tense?

Rhona the Fearless certainly didn't know. She was merely a soldier in Her Majesty's Army. She received her orders from commanders and made sure those orders were executed. She killed whenever necessary, and protected those who needed it. What she didn't do was play politician. She was never involved in decisions that affected anything beyond the general safety of her troops. As a sergeant that was all she *needed* to be responsible for, and she was good at what she did.

Then again, she was one of the Cadwaladr Clan. Low-born warrior dragons of the Southlands who many said were born to kill. To destroy. Rhona's mother, Bradana the

Mutilator, would say those many were right, and to prove it, she expected all her offspring to become elite Dragonwarriors of Her Majesty's Army. And almost all Bradana's offspring did. Except her youngest daughters, triplets who had a few more years of battle training ahead of them before they were ready, and Bradana's eldest. Except for Rhona.

Ahhh, nothing like thinking of a mother's disappointment to keep one warm during watch in the Valley's winter months. Yet those were deep, slightly bitter thoughts for another day. Right now, she had to deal with what was at hand—Iron dragons.

She'd grown up hearing tales of the Irons. Steel-colored fire breathers with white horns that curved toward their mouths who believed they should rule all under the banner of the one and only god they worshipped—Chramnesind, the Sightless One. In their estimation, the entire world should be their empire and all others—dragon, human, or otherwise—should be their willing slaves, bowing down before the Overlord Thracius, sacrificing only to Chramnesind. It was a philosophy Rhona's kind didn't much like. They barely tolerated having a queen and Elders, much less an overlord. So the Southland Dragon Queen's armies and the Northland Hordes, once great enemies, had joined forces to stop Thracius and his soldiers. There was just one thing none of them had planned on: that the Irons had a huge army. More dragon soldiers than Rhona had ever seen before at one time. And fresh troops kept coming. Did they have a dragon factory pumping out full-grown soldiers, ready for battle? Rhona had begun to think so. For while the Southlanders and the Northlanders had battle skills on their side, the damn Irons had numbers and the regimented, disciplined attacks of their troops.

Thankfully, though, those currently trying to sneak in didn't have large numbers on their side. There were about ten of the enemy dragons against Rhona and her triplet sisters. The siblings had been heading to the safety of the nearby Hesiod Mountains, where the Southland and Northland dragons had set up a stronghold, when Rhona had spotted the Irons. Now the siblings stood next to trees, the four of them blending in as Rhona had been taught to do by her mother when she was still too young even to fly. It was a skill she'd passed on to her siblings.

While the Irons moved closer, Rhona raised her hand and readied to give the signal. Her sisters gripped their weapons and shields tighter, a small identical smile on each of their faces as they eagerly awaited her next order. And Rhona was moments from giving that order, her arm about to slash down in an arc, when something big and not remotely subtle crashed through the trees. A small group of Lightnings must have caught sight of the Irons as well, about three of the purple-haired and purple-scaled bastards tearing from the opposite direction, pushing the enemy dragons right into Rhona and her sisters.

Rhona waited another beat, then gave the order. Her sisters moved quickly, silently. Unlike the Lightnings, there was no inelegance. No stomping or crashing like their Cadwaladr cousins either. Rhona had trained her sisters to move with methodical precision from the day they'd fought their way out of the egg. And that's what they did now, cutting into the contingent of enemy soldiers.

Edana, as always, struck first. Her broadsword slammed through the snout of the first dragon charging right into her. She cut through nostrils and bone, right into brain, twisting her blade once before yanking it out. Nesta spun around Edana and used her mace to crack the faceplate of the next Iron, following that up by ramming the tip of her tail into his skull while simultaneously cracking the breastplate of another and finishing him off with her mace. Breena, however, enjoyed the close-up kill. And although she had a sword, ax, and mace on her, she still used her long, curved slashing knife to finish off the job once she'd tackled her victim to the ground. Breena reminded Rhona the most of their mother.

While the triplets did what they did best, the Lightnings rushed forward—to help. To help the poor weak females.

Because after five bloody years, the Northlanders all still seemed to think that having females on the battlefield was too great a risk. A risk to the females, of course. Poor pathetic females that they were. Although after several bar fights with quite a few of Rhona's female cousins and siblings at the heart of them, the Lightnings were now smart enough to keep that sentiment primarily to themselves. Except in situations like this when they felt females were in "grave danger."

Yet Rhona didn't rush in to help anyone. She knew her sisters could handle themselves. So, she waited. And, as she had come to expect lately, three Irons silently slipped through the trees on the opposite side of the fracas while the rest battled it out. These were the Elite Iron warriors. Much better trained than the foot soldiers. Smarter, faster, and excellent at ambushes.

It was too bad they made this particular move with a Cadwaladr nearby, though. As smart, fast, and sneaky as the Iron Elites might be, they still hadn't been raised by a mother who'd taught Rhona to fly by sneaking up behind her while she quietly stood on the highest mountain in the region, grabbing her by her still-developing wings and flinging her off while yelling, "Whatever you do, luv . . . don't look down!"

No. You'd have to be a lot craftier if you hoped to sneak by one of the Cadwaladr Clan.

Gripping her favorite spear, Rhona followed after the three Elites until she was only a few feet away from them. That's when she allowed her tail to drag, just a little bit, behind her. The three males stopped and so did Rhona. She knew she shouldn't enjoy this. As a soldier of Her Majesty's Army, she should simply do her job and get back to her siblings. But she so rarely had any fun these days.

The one closest to her spun around and Rhona shoved her spear into his eye. While he screamed, she pulled the weapon out and used it to block the sword aimed for her neck. She slammed the sword to the ground and headbutted the one who wielded it. She ducked as another sword swung at her head, then slashed her tail across his face. While that one stumbled away and tried to wipe the blood from his eyes, Rhona was shoved back by the other. She hit the ground but quickly rolled to her claws, raising her spear, ready to strike.

The Iron charged forward, swinging his blade in an arc. Rhona leaned back, the blade slashing at the breastplate of her armor, but doing little more than denting the metal. But the Iron had overcompensated in his haste, his body stumbling forward. Rhona helped him along by wrapping her tail around the claw holding his sword and yanking him down.

Rhona didn't waste time doing anything fancy once she had him on the ground. Instead she rammed her spear into the back of his neck to finish him off. Once done, she quickly moved back. Good thing too. The one whose face she'd slashed realized he hadn't been hurt that badly and was now on the attack. She warded off his blade with her spear, but while she moved back, she didn't have time to step elegantly over the bodies of the two others. She tripped, falling. The Iron took the advantage, coming in quickly to run her through. But Rhona shoved her tail into the ground, halting her descent, and with a good shove, she was back on her claws, her spear up and ready to strike.

But then she was falling again. A big, purple claw slamming against her chest and forcing her back.

Rhona hit the ground hard, the breath knocked out of her. But she didn't allow herself to sit there. She forced herself up, her spear still gripped by her talons. She watched the Iron come toward her and she lifted her spear, waiting for the strike. Then she saw the giant warhammer coming from overhead. The Iron saw it, too. Caught hold of Rhona's spear and yanked her and it forward. The hammer, so heavy it would not be easily stopped, kept coming, and Rhona quickly leaned back. But she was unable to move her spear in time and, to her absolute horror, that big, inelegant hunk of Northland steel crashed into her favorite weapon, breaking the shaft in half.

Rhona stumbled back, part of the wood shaft still clutched in her claw. The Iron fell to the ground and the Lightning turned on him, bringing his warhammer up, over, and into the head of the enemy dragon. The Iron's scream begging for mercy quickly silenced, the Northlander slowly faced her. Dark grey eyes gazed at what was left of her weapon, and then he said with all seriousness, "And this is why females shouldn't be out here trying to fight. That could have just as easily been your head."

Vigholf the Abhorrent slammed the head of his warhammer into the ground and leaned against the handle.

Poor thing. She looked positively devastated by the damage to her cute little spear. Gods, a spear? He hadn't used one of those since he'd started training at the age of six winters. His father, a bastard of a Northlander, didn't believe that his sons should wait until they were a little older. He believed they should be able to kill with their own claws and weapons before they could even fly. In case, according to Olgeir the Wastrel, "I ever need to throw one of you little bastards into the fighting pit to make a bit of coin." But Vigholf had grown out of that spear by the time he was ten winters, moving on to a mace, then a sword, and finally his favorite weapon, the warhammer. He had two hammers. One that he could use whether in his natural form or as human, the entire thing extending with a good slam to the base. The other hammer, which he used only when dragon, had a head big and heavy enough to crush a dragon's skull with a single blow. Sometimes, if Vigholf was in a bit of a rush, he'd work his way through a battalion by swinging his hammer from side to side until every soldier was dead or broken enough that the rest of his troops could finish them off.

But a spear? Only a female would use that for anything other than first-wave attacks by an entire legion.

Since she was still just sitting there, staring at him, stunned by nearly being killed, Vigholf held his claw out to her. "Come on, Rhona. Let's get you inside."

She took his claw and he helped her rise. But halfway up, she stopped and whispered something, her pretty brown eyes downcast. Vigholf leaned in, thinking she'd been hurt during the skirmish—and that's when the treacherous little bitch head-butted him!

Gods-damn Cadwaladrs! None—absolutely *none*—of them could be trusted!

Vigholf released her and brought his claws to his forehead.

"What was that for?"

She was up now, the broken staff of her spear pressed into his throat. "If you get between me and a kill again, you overbearing ox, I'll tear out your eyes!"

"I was trying to help, you unbearable she-demon!" he snapped, fighting his desire to shove her back to the ground.

"Well, don't! Don't help! Don't assist! Do *nothing*!"

She reached down and swiped up the other end of the

spear. "My father made me this," she told him, holding the pieces up to him. *"My father!"*

"Oh, Rhona." Another Cadwaladr female, one of the pretty triplets, stepped forward. "Your spear. What happened?"

"This idiot—"

"I was trying to help!" he cut in.

"Shut up!" She cleared her throat, looked down at the ground. Vigholf knew what she was trying to do. Get control. She was Rhona the Fearless after all. The perfect soldier. Or so she believed. In her female mind, soldiers didn't lose control, they didn't get angry, they didn't shout unless it was to relay an order. And all of that was true—in battle. But Rhona was like that *all* the time.

To be honest, he was enjoying seeing her lose control for once. Even if it was just a little bit.

Wanting to see her pissy for a few seconds longer, Vigholf helpfully added, "I'll have another adorable little spear made just for you."

Brown eyes locked on him. "And you can take that spear and shove it up your—"

"Rhona!" all three triplets cried out, their green eyes wide, their attempts not to laugh weak.

Snarling, black smoke snaking from her nostrils, Rhona the Fearless stalked off.

"Bring those bodies back for the commanders," she ordered over her shoulder.

"You're very adorable when you're angry," he told her.

"Shut up!"

"She's going to kill you while you sleep," one of her sisters—Edana, maybe?—warned once Rhona was out of earshot. "Daddy made her that spear."

"We're relatively sure she slept with it," another said.

"And you went and broke it. While getting between her

and a kill and taunting her." Another observed. "It's like you wish for an early death."

"I was really trying to help. You lot shouldn't be—"

"If you say as females we shouldn't be out here—"

"—we'll cut off your legs while you sleep—"

"—and let the forest animals have 'em for dinner."

One of them patted his chest—Nesta? Gods, who knew—"We like you, Lord Abhorrent. Don't make us regret that."

And having been curious about the answer for the last five years, Vigholf asked, "Rhona likes me too, yeah?"

"Gods, no!" one said, laughing, dragging two of the bodies away by their back claws.

"And if I were you, I'd stay away from her until she gets over the loss of that spear," said another. Vigholf honestly couldn't tell the three She-dragons apart. "Otherwise, she just might take those pretty grey eyes."

"I'm a Northlander," he reminded them. "I don't have pretty eyes."

The triplets laughed.

"At least you have them, Lightning. Keep getting between me sister and her glory in battle and you won't for long."

Vigholf grinned, watching the three females drag six of the bodies away.

"You better get her a new spear," a low voice muttered behind him.

Vigholf glanced over at his cousin Meinhard. "Why?"

"Because I don't feel like leading you into battle because you're missing your eyes."

"She wouldn't hurt me. She's too nice."

Meinhard studied the bodies the female had left behind. "I think, cousin, that she'd cut your throat, then go have ale with her kin and not give you another thought."

"The Babysitter?" It was his nickname for Rhona the

Fearless, who seemed to make it her lot in life to watch out for anyone under the age of one hundred and fifty.

"Babysitter to those she cares about." Meinhard grabbed hold of several bodies by their tails. "But a cold-blooded soldier to those she doesn't. And the gods know, Vigholf, that female doesn't care about you."

"Wrong. Right now she hates me. That is a form of caring, which could easily, with some skill, turn to love and eventually adoration."

Shaking his head, Meinhard headed off. "My mum was right. You are thick as two planks."

"Your mum loved me, too."

"Only 'cause she felt sorry for you."

"See?" Vigholf laughed. "With some skill, comes the love and adoration!"

Chapter 2

For five long years the war had raged on. For five long years, Rhona had been dealing with the Lightnings on a daily basis. But not as the enemy she was raised to loathe. Instead they were now the allies of her kind. Strange how everything could change so. Rhona's mother and her aunts and uncles had made their names and reputations by decimating the Lightnings in battle. Her royal cousins, the Dragon Queen's three eldest sons, Fearghus, Briec, and Gwenvael, had also faced the Northlanders in war, earning them respect beyond their royal titles. So Rhona had always assumed that one day she'd go talon-to-talon against the Lightnings just as her kin had before her.

Instead, Rhona was forced to endure their presence as allies. Forced to forget how Lightnings used to kidnap Southland She-dragons and force them into being their mates. The more difficult ones losing a wing to keep them trapped in the harsh lands of a foreign country with males they loathed. Yet, as the Northlanders were quick to remind anyone who mentioned their past, that had been a long time ago. Now that the older, more heartless Horde leaders had died off, the new regime didn't allow this practice anymore.

They were a new, kinder Horde that still couldn't manage to believe a female could protect herself during battle.

And, honestly, on days like today, tolerating the Northlanders' new and kinder image was nigh-on impossible. Then again, maybe Rhona's problems weren't with tolerating the Northlanders as a whole but tolerating *one* of them. Vigholf the Abhorrent or, as she liked to call him, Commander Pest.

Yet by the time Rhona had made it deep into their mountain stronghold and she knew she was officially off duty for the rest of the day, she pushed all thoughts of annoying, closed-minded Northlanders from her mind and decided she desperately needed a bath. She'd found a lovely little lake with a waterfall deep inside the mountain. Only a few of them knew about it and they kept it secret from all the others.

Yet Rhona found that her plans rarely if ever played out exactly as she saw them because something—or someone—always got in her way.

"Oy, Rhona."

Rhona stopped, her body tensing at the sound of that voice, rough-hewn thanks to a knife to the throat a few centuries back, and faced one of the commanding officers. "General, sir!"

"Can't you just call me Mum?"

Gods. When her mother said, "Can't you just call me Mum?" it was a warning to Rhona. As bright and clear as a battle cry from a mountaintop. The first time Bradana the Mutilator had asked Rhona to call her Mum she'd shoved a freshly hatched Delen the Blue into Rhona's arms and said, "You're not too busy to take care of your new sister, are you?" Then Bradana went to war—for nearly four years.

Rhona had been mostly responsible for raising her siblings ever since.

"Mum."

"Heard you ran into a spot of trouble."

"Aye, but nothing we couldn't handle. Had the triplets with me."

"They're growing into right little brawlers, my girls, eh?"

Rhona cringed at the description because she didn't raise brawlers. She raised warriors. Yet her mother saw it as a compliment, so Rhona didn't argue with her.

"They are. Getting better every day."

"Your Uncle Bercelak will probably want them to go to Anubail Mountain next year."

"Great. I can't wait for them to go." All right. She was outright lying now. And it wasn't that she didn't want her sisters to go and follow the path of the Dragonwarrior as their other siblings had. But of all Bradana's offspring whom Rhona had raised over the years, she'd become closest to her youngest sisters. Of course she'd actually been there when they'd battled their way out of their egg, head-butting and biting and lashing each other with their tails. Her mother usually stayed around for the hatching, but just before the triplets came along she'd rushed off to raid some traitor dragon's fortress, thinking she'd be back in time—she wasn't.

"And," her mother continued, scratching the vicious scar across her throat with the tip of her tail, "you can go with them. You all can train together. Won't that be fun?"

Tricky. Her mother was definitely tricky. Bradana knew how much the triplets meant to Rhona and clearly she wasn't above using that love to get what she wanted. And what she wanted was for Rhona to take the path of the Dragonwarrior. Like all her other offspring and like most of the Cadwaladr Clan. There was just one problem with that plan—Rhona had no desire to become a Dragonwarrior. Much to her mother's annoyance, Rhona was perfectly satisfied with what she was doing. She was a soldier and a damn good one.

Why did her mother have such an issue with that?

So Rhona said, "I'm sure they'll be fine. Without me."

"Your Uncle Bercelak is offering you an opportunity."

"And I appreciate that. But I don't need it."

Rhona turned to go, needing that bath more and more.

"I didn't dismiss you," her mother snapped and Rhona rounded on her.

"Which is it, Mum? Are you my mother at this moment or my commanding officer? Because I can walk away from me mum!"

"I'm both!"

"Can't be! One or the other! Pick!"

"Don't snarl at me, you viperous little—"

Rhona raised a talon, cutting her mother off, and looked behind her. "You lot," she snapped at the three soldiers standing behind her, one of which was nursing his right forearm. "What happened?"

"His arm. It got crushed in the tunnels."

Turning away from her mother, Rhona went to the young soldier. "That's broken. You." She pointed at the gold dragon. "Take him to the healer. And you"—she pointed at the Lightning—"back to the tunnels. The commanders need all available troops working there. Now go."

Rhona faced her mother and asked, "So where were we? Oh. Yes. I'm a viperous little . . . what was the rest of it?"

Slamming down her tail, her mother marched off. Rhona knew this argument wasn't over, though. Not when it had been going on since the first time Rhona turned down her Uncle Bercelak's offer to train at Anubail Mountain. As consort of Her Majesty, the Dragon Queen, and commander of the Queen's armies, Bercelak the Great did not offer the chance to be one of the legendary Dragonwarriors lightly. In fact, Rhona's mother had actually left mid-battle to seek out her daughter and tell her what an idiot she was being by turning Bercelak down. But Rhona would not let her mother bully her, cajole her, or finesse her into changing her mind. Rhona prided herself on knowing her strengths and weaknesses. Her strength was being as stubborn as her mother. And her weakness was not wanting to be a Dragonwarrior. All right. Perhaps not a true weakness, but her mother seemed to think it was.

"You all right?"

Rhona looked at her younger sister Delen.

"Aye. Just the same damn argument. How can she never get bored with it?"

"The beauty of Mum is that she never gets bored. She can kill and kill for days at a time without ever feeling boredom. I think that's a foreign word to her. Like rational. Or caring."

Rhona laughed with her sister, putting her arm around her shoulders. "Excellent point. And how are you doing?"

"Fine. I'll be working in the tunnels the next couple of days with my troops. I'm hoping to push them along to get the tunnel done. Sooner we can get under those mountains, the sooner we can wipe out the Irons and go home. Unlike our mother, *I* do get bored. Now"—her sister patted Rhona's shoulder with her tail—"why don't you go on and take your break. You've been working nonstop for days. You're no use to any of us if you're asleep once we hit the other side."

Rhona chuckled. "Good point."

"You going for a bath?" her sister whispered.

"Trying to."

"Take that exit." She pointed at a narrow tunnel cut through the cave rock. "You'll have to go outside for a bit, but you'll avoid Mum."

"Thanks, luv."

Rhona slipped away without being noticed and eased

through the narrow tunnel until she found herself on the mountain's summit. She stopped, gazing out over Euphrasia Valley. A stretch of land caught in the middle of the Northland territories, the Western Mountains, and the Southlands. A rough and dangerous valley with thick, almost junglelike forests during the summer and brutally cold winds and ice storms during the winter. It was surrounded by a ring of mountains in varying sizes. They'd made the Hesiod Mountains their stronghold while the Irons were directly opposite from them using the Polycarp Mountains as their protection. Could be worse, though. At least they had access to fresh water and supplies.

"Nice, yeah?"

Rhona's shoulders slumped, her eyes closing. "I can't get a break," she sighed.

"Now what did I do?"

She didn't bother facing the Lightning. What was the point?

"Nothing." She started to walk across the ridge of the summit, but the Lightning cut in front of her.

"What if I bought you a long sword?"

"What?" What was he babbling about? Gods! She only wanted a bath!

"A long sword. To replace your spear."

"I don't need you to buy me anything. Especially weapons." She took a step, but he stepped with her.

"I can teach you to use it if that's your concern."

Rhona's front claws curled into fists. "I don't need you to teach me how to use a sword."

"You shouldn't use one unless you know how."

"I know how."

"Then why were you still using a spear?"

"Because I like them. Because my father made it for me. *And why am I discussing this with you?*"

She took another step and he stepped with her.

"What about an ax?" he asked. "A small one. With a weight you can handle."

And that's when Rhona became a little cranky.

Gods, she was such a pretty little She-dragon. A bit scarred for his usual tastes but still . . . very pretty. He'd thought so from the beginning, from the first time he'd seen her all those years ago. A brown-scaled She-dragon with shoulder-length brown hair that she kept in simple warrior braids, and dark brown eyes that were bright and lively— when they weren't glaring at him. Something that had become rare these days. She seemed to always be glaring at him. He could only imagine it was the strain of the war on her. She was a Southlander and a female, after all. Northlanders knew nothing *but* war, so five years in battle was no real strain for them.

Although she wasn't just some Southland She-dragon, was she? She was a Cadwaladr. They bred nothing but unstable females from that bloodline. But Rhona wasn't much like the others. She'd kill, but it didn't seem as if she enjoyed it too much. Not like Rhona's mother, who only smiled when she was sawing someone's head off. No. Rhona the Fearless was different, so Vigholf had taken it upon himself to keep an eye on her. A sweet thing like her could easily fall prey to the more forceful of his brethren, which was why he'd warned them off. Strongly. And it's not like he followed her around or anything. Just . . . watched out for her.

Although it seemed sometimes that the biggest problem in Rhona's life was that mother of hers.

Vigholf nearly shuddered at the thought of *that* particular female—if you could call her that. Yet she had mostly pleasant offspring. Rhona, the triplets, and a few of her other daughters and sons. Then again, Vigholf had heard that Rhona had raised the lot of them, which explained much in his estimation.

"I don't need an ax," Rhona snarled between clenched teeth.

"There's nothing to be afraid of. They're easy enough weapons to handle."

"I know how to handle an ax, foreigner. I don't need lessons from you. Why don't you just accept the fact that you destroyed a beloved weapon because you have so little control of that warhammer of yours."

"I have absolute control of my hammer, thank you very much. But once it's moving, it's not always easy to stop, my lady." He grinned, feeling cheeky. "I can say that about all my hammers, in fact."

"First off, ew. And second, I ain't a lady. I'm a Cadwaladr and a sergeant of Her Majesty's Army. You want to deal with a royal, go see my cousin Keita. She couldn't be more royal."

She stepped around him and he turned to follow, but her tail suddenly lashed out, aiming for his eye. Vigholf stumbled back and Rhona, glaring over her shoulder at him, snapped, "And stop following me around."

"I wasn't. Just . . . keeping an eye on you. These caves can be dangerous."

"The day a She-dragon can't move around a cave as she likes is the day she should climb onto the funeral pyre."

"Or you could just have an escort."

Her brown eyes nearly rolled to the back of her head, but before she could say another word, they both heard her name.

"What?" she yelled over him.

One of her sisters, he didn't know which, appeared in the cave exit. "They're at it again."

Rhona's snarl was so vicious that Vigholf briefly thought

about moving out of her way. He didn't, but it crossed his mind.

"By the unholy gods of piss and fire, I'll kill them both!" she nearly yelled. "And if not them . . . I'll kill *her*. Then maybe this centaur shit can end!"

Shoving past him, Rhona marched off in the direction her sister had motioned to, leaving Vigholf simply standing there. Instead of following her, he kept on the way she'd been going. After a few minutes, he came to the underground waterfall. This had been where she'd been going. The female did like her bath times. But, as always, the needs of others had gotten in her way. Unfortunate, really.

Rhona stormed through the chambers and caverns where the lower-ranking dragons resided when they weren't out on the field.

And, as Rhona's sister had said, her cousins were "at it again" while the rest of the young recruits stood in a circle around them, passing coin, taking bets, and cheering their favorite.

Seething and absolutely fed up with all of this, Rhona pushed past the troops and grabbed the wings of both males. With strength born of raising her siblings, Rhona yanked the pair apart, then slammed them back together again. Their hard heads collided and they stumbled around in stunned confusion.

"*That is enough!*" she bellowed, shoving them into the crowd surrounding them. "I am tired of this centaur shit!"

"He started—"

"You started—"

Rhona unleashed her flame, first at one, sending him careering into the wall, and then the other, forcing him to roll across the cave floor.

"I said *that is enough!*"

She leveled her gaze at the other recruits. "Out! All of you!"

And the lot scrambled out of there as if the gods of death ran behind them.

Once they were alone, Rhona said, "I don't believe you two. Five years I've put up with this shit. Five years I've watched you two go at it like pit dogs!" She shook her head. "That brat's pussy must be mighty for all this!"

Éibhear the Blue, her royal cousin and youngest of Her Majesty's offspring, stood to his lofty height. "Rhona! That's my—"

"If you say niece, I will rip your lips off! Because, you twat, we both know the real problem here is that Izzy the Dangerous is *not* your niece. She's merely the whore who's gotten between cousins!"

Her not even remotely royal cousin Celyn the Black suddenly grew balls, and stood tall before her. "Don't you dare talk about Izzy that way. If this is anyone's fault—it's his!" Celyn pointed an accusing talon at his cousin. "That overreacting harpy!"

"You took advantage!"

"That's a lie!"

"Shut it!"

Both males snarled and looked away from each other.

All this over a woman. Not a She-dragon but a human female. The adopted daughter of Éibhear's brother Briec had decided it was a good idea to take Celyn as her lover while the human and dragon troops of Annwyl the Bloody and Dragon Queen Rhiannon fought the Tribesmen of the Western Plains a few years back. And the rest of them had been suffering from that girl's idiotic decision ever since.

"Perhaps you haven't noticed," Rhona pointed out, "that we're in the middle of a gods-damn war. Perhaps you haven't noticed that every time you two idiots do this, you put your fellow soldiers at risk. Our troops risk their lives every day and yet you two peck at each other like angry birds! As if you have *nothing* better to do!"

"Rhona—"

"I don't want to hear it, Éibhear. Not a word!"

She rested her front claws on her hips. "I should just send both of you back to the Southlands. A few years' suspension while your kin earn glory or death would certainly get my point across."

As she expected, Rhona saw the panic in their eyes at the threat. And it was a threat she'd carry through on—if they could afford to lose the brute strength of either idiot. Of course as low-level privates neither idiot would know that.

"Please don't, Rhona," Éibhear begged. "It won't happen again."

"It won't," Celyn pleaded. "Just don't send us back."

"I don't know. . . ." she hedged.

"We won't fight again."

"Ever."

Rhona didn't bother making them swear to that. What was the point when they didn't even realize they were lying? But at the very least she was sure she'd put some fear into them.

"All right," she finally told them, watching their bodies sag in relief. "But if I catch you fighting with each other one more time—"

"You won't," Éibhear was quick to promise. "You won't."

"I better not," she warned.

And with that, she headed out of the chamber and to her gods-damn bath.

Éibhear the Blue glared across the chamber at his cousin. "This is *your* fault."

"My fault? You started it!"

"I started it? If you'd kept your cock tucked—"

"This again? Really?"

"Yeah! Really!"

"Let me assure you, cousin, that everything I did with Izzy the Dangerous was at her explicit consent!"

They were chest to chest again, Éibhear enjoying the fact he stood quite a bit taller than his cousin since his last few growth spurts.

"I know I don't hear more arguing. . . ." Rhona's voice called from outside the chamber. "I know I don't hear *that*."

Austell the Red rushed in and pushed his way between the pair. "No, no," he yelled out. "You don't hear anything." He shoved the pair apart as Rhona had. "Not a thing."

Austell, a fellow soldier and friend to both Éibhear and Celyn, scowled at each dragon. "What is wrong with you two? This fighting has to stop."

"It's this prat's fault," Celyn snapped.

"*My* fault?"

"Go." Austell pushed Celyn away. "Just go."

"I've got watch anyway," he said, stomping off.

"Don't die a tragic death while you're out there," Éibhear called after him.

"Fuck you."

Austell shook his head. "Cousins shouldn't fight like this."

"It's *his* fault."

"Over a woman."

"She's an innocent."

Austell shrugged. "Not from what I've heard."

And Éibhear had his friend by the throat and slammed up against the wall before either even realized it.

"At what point," Austell asked once he'd pried Éibhear's claw off his throat, "are you going to admit how you feel about—"

"She's my niece."

"Not by blood." He patted Éibhear's shoulder. "Just be smart, friend. There's no female in the world worth fighting over."

"I'm not fighting over anyone. I'm merely protecting one of my own."

"Do you really believe your own ox shit?"

Éibhear sighed and headed off to get something to eat. "Usually."

Vateria, eldest daughter in the House of Atia Flominia, walked into the room where her younger sisters prepared for their night out. There was a monthlong worth of games being thrown by the sons of the human ruler of these lands, Laudaricus, and Vateria's family would be blessing them with their presence on the royal dais. Family members would be going in their human forms as they often did, although they never allowed their human pets to forget who or what they were.

For they were the true rulers of these lands. The ruling Imperium of the Quintilian Sovereigns for the last six hundred years. The Iron dragons.

At one time, the Iron dragons were part of the dragons of the Dark Plains. But Vateria's grandfather grew bored at being ruled by another, so he and his allies moved their families far past the Western and Aricia Mountains and into what was the Quintilian Province. Unlike the Dark Plains dragons, Grandfather refused to hide his true form from the humans. Instead, he presented the small ruling body of Quintilian humans with a choice: Accept the Iron dragons as your rulers or watch your men burn and your women and children enslaved to the dragon's will. Weak, like most humans, the rulers quickly agreed. In their minds, they thought they'd let their invaders get comfortable in their underground cave homes and then go about destroying them.

But Vateria's grandfather had been much too smart for that. From the beginning he worked to make the Quintilian Province his own, without question. He kept actual killing to a minimum—he needed the humans as farmers, herders, and general labor—while using the *threat* of killing and much worse as the sword he used. When a senator dared question one of his decisions, the senator's children were taken and turned into slaves, his wife or wives turned into whores, his land burned to embers. The senator in question, however, was kept alive, so that all could see him, day after day, wandering the streets without a home and penniless. His enslaved family sometimes passing him on the way to do their duty, their bodies covered in whip marks, their faces seared with their owner's brand. Sometimes several brands if they were sold more than once.

By the time Grandfather handed over rule to his eldest son and Vateria's father, Thracius, the Irons' rule of Quintilian was without question and without challenge. That's when Thracius captured the mate of Adienna, the Southland Dragon Queen of that time, during the Great Battle of Aricia and took him back to Quintilian. While the queen sent messengers with offers of treaties and promises of no retribution for the safe return of her mate, Thracius held public games in his father's honor with the highlight being the crucifixion of the Dragon Queen's mate.

Once dead, the queen's mate was cut into pieces, boxed, and returned to Her Majesty. At the time, it was rumored the queen was planning an all-out assault on Quintilian, something Thracius hoped for since they'd be fighting on his territory rather than on hers. But that confrontation was put on hold for the queen had another problem—barbarian dragons from the north, the Lightnings. It had crossed Thracius's mind to attack Dark Plains then, but he didn't trust that the barbarians would automatically side with him. For enough gold or females to breed with—both of which the Southlanders had in abundance—the Lightnings could easily be bought. Besides, there was much to the west of the province that held his interest and Thracius had never been one to rush.

Now, centuries later, they were no longer simply the Quintilian Province. That was just the main city of what was known as the Quintilian Sovereigns, and the empire's territories stretched for thousands and thousands of leagues in all directions.

All directions, but one.

But that would change soon enough for at this moment her father and his vast army fought the current Dragon Queen's armies and the barbarian Hordes in Euphrasia Valley while Laudaricus's human armies fought the armies of Annwyl the Bloody, Queen of Garbhán Isle, in the Western Mountains.

The two-prong attack would be quite effective, especially with the enemy armies not having nearly as many troops as the Irons.

Columella, one of Vateria's four sisters, posed for Vateria in her dark red tunic. "What do you think?"

"You look well enough, I suppose."

"Don't overwhelm me with your flattery, sister."

"I hadn't planned to." Vateria studied one of her younger cousins, her eyes narrowing. "That's my necklace," she told her.

"Can't I borrow it?" The young dragoness glanced at Vateria over her shoulder, her tone teasing and playful due to the excitement of the upcoming evening. If Vateria remembered correctly, it would be her cousin's first event as an adult. "You do have to admit it suits me a bit better than you."

"It's true, cousin. It does," Vateria admitted. Then she

caught hold of the dragoness around the neck and unleashed her talons, breaking through the skin, blood pouring across her still-human hand. "That doesn't mean I gave you leave to take what's mine."

Her cousin slapped at Vateria's arms and chest, unable to scream or breathe. Vateria took her to the floor and waited until a nice pool of blood had formed beneath her cousin's head before she released her. She snatched the necklace off her cousin's throat and walked over to one of the cowering human servants.

"Let her bleed out a bit more. When it looks like she's about to die"—she grabbed a small jar and handed it to the shaking slave—"use this ointment on her. It should stop the bleeding and keep her alive." Something Vateria had discovered as she'd spent more and more time entertaining herself in her father's dungeons. For there she kept a great prize. Something so precious that another, more formidable foe was continually kept from the Province gates. Kept away at least until the return of the great Overlord Thracius and his army.

Vateria focused on one of the royal guards, a dragon. "She'll suffer more as human, so if she shifts to dragon, kill her where she lies."

He nodded and Vateria motioned to all the females. "Let us go. We need to take our seats so the games may begin." Because no one would dare start the games without the royal family in attendance.

Vateria headed off down the hall, the females falling in line behind her while a servant ran along beside her, wiping the blood off her hand.

"You could have just taken the necklace back, sister," Columella reminded her.

"That's very true. But what would have been the lesson learned if I'd done that?"

Chapter 3

The next morning Vigholf walked into his brother's war room and asked the question that had been plaguing him all night. "Know anyone who can fix a spear?"

"A spear?" Rágnar the Cunning glanced up from his scrolls. "When did you start fighting with spears again?"

"Not my spear." He sat back on his haunches and gazed over what Ragnar was looking at. "What's this?"

"The tunnel plans." For nearly seven months they'd had their troops digging out a tunnel that would lead them directly under the Polycarp Mountains and right into the Irons' stronghold. Once in, they could take the Irons unaware and destroy them. At least that was the current plan. Whether it would work or not was anyone's guess, but it was better than sitting around and waiting for something to happen. "It shouldn't be much longer now."

"Good. Because the Irons are getting bolder."

"Why do you say that?" Ragnar asked.

"Another attempt to get in here. Don't know what they think they'll find, though."

"How many were there this time?"

"About ten trying to get our attention and three Elites trying to sneak past."

Ragnar looked up again. "Only three?"

"Yes." Vigholf saw a pile of dried and smoked cows' legs in the corner and he went over and grabbed one. "Which is why I say I don't understand what they're doing. Coming to spy, maybe?"

"Perhaps." Ragnar sat back on his haunches. "Or they know about the tunnel or they've found a weakness here. Something we've missed."

"Don't be so paranoid." Vigholf ripped the flesh off the cow's leg with his fangs. "We didn't miss anything, we've got all the entrances and exits covered. And if they knew about the tunnels, Thracius would have destroyed them by now."

"You don't know that."

Meinhard walked in and Vigholf tossed him a cow's leg as well. "Ragnar's being paranoid."

"When isn't he?"

"We can't afford for anyone to get in here," Ragnar reminded them. "So do me a favor and see if we may have missed any more possible entrances."

"You're asking for a favor?" Vigholf said.

"Like we're old chums?" Meinhard added.

Fed up, Ragnar snapped, slamming his claws against the thick wood table. "Do what I tell you!"

"No need to get snappy," Meinhard muttered, and Vigholf hid his smile behind the cow's leg.

"Bastards," Ragnar complained with a snarl, but it quickly turned to a smile when the lovely Princess Keita walked in.

"Oooh," she cheered. "All these handsome males in one place. It makes a girl so happy!"

Ragnar held his claw out and Keita took it, allowing him to pull her tight against his side.

"The Irons tried to get in here again. It's making me concerned," Ragnar murmured to her.

"It'll be fine."

"Maybe, maybe not. But I'm glad you're going with Ren to Dark Plains."

"Ren's leaving?" Vigholf asked. Ren of the Chosen was what the Northlanders termed a "foreign dragon," which meant he was from somewhere none of them had ever been before. Specifically the Eastland territories across the sea. He'd turned out to be a helpful ally. Good fighting skills and he could work Magick as well. It helped during the heat of battle.

"He's needed in Dark Plains," Ragnar answered while he studied Keita's face. "And Keita's going with him."

"Your brother is trying to get rid of me."

"You know I'm not."

"And we like having you here," Vigholf volunteered. "You're the only reason Ragnar's even remotely pleasant."

"Thank you," Ragnar said flatly.

Keita petted Ragnar's neck. "I could stay. If you need me to."

"I do need you. But I'll feel better if you're far away from here." He squeezed her. "Go with Ren. He'll appreciate the company."

"About that . . ." Keita went up on the tips of her claws and began whispering in Ragnar's ear. Vigholf glanced at Meinhard, but his cousin was too busy sucking the marrow from that cow leg to notice anything.

"You sure?" Ragnar asked.

Keita nodded. "She's the best choice."

"Perhaps, but I doubt she'll be happy about it."

"She'll do it for me. Besides, I'm betting she'd like some time away from my aunt."

"I'll feel better if it's her. She's good."

"And you don't like the idea of me being alone with Ren," she teased. "But he knows that I'm *your* Battle Twat!"

"It's maid, Keita!" Ragnar complained over Vigholf and

Meinhard's laughter. "It's Battle *Maid*. Not Battle Twat or Battle Slut or Battle Slag. Battle. Maid."

She giggled and slipped away from him, silently walking out of the room.

"What was that about?" Vigholf asked.

"Protection detail for the flight back to the Southlands."

"Why would they need that? The foreigner can handle himself and Keita, quite well."

Ragnar began to say something, stopped. Thought a moment and finally said, "He might be distracted. It's best he has a guard. *Especially* with Keita traveling with him."

"Who? One of her brothers? Gods," Vigholf quickly added, "not the boy."

"No. Éibhear stays here. And I need Fearghus and Briec here as well. We're sending one of the cousins instead." He flicked his claws. "Keep this quiet for now, and we can discuss later."

"A Cadwaladr, though?" Vigholf pushed. "Willing to leave battle to be protection detail for a couple of royals?" He shook his head. "It will never happen."

"And you know Keita won't take no for an answer," Ragnar reminded him. "My dragoness always knows how to get what she wants. No matter how bloody annoying she has to be to do it."

Although Rhona had been unable to find time the previous eve to bathe after several additional things came up that needed her attention, she'd finally managed to sneak away during first meal. Now she stood under the waterfall and let the water pour down on her. It felt wonderful against her scales, pounding the tension out of her body and massaging her muscles.

Aaaaaah. Just what she needed. A chance to relax and simply enjoy the quiet and—

"Cousin!"

Rhona faced the cave wall, refusing to be interrupted. Refusing to let her kin invade what had become an almost sacred thing for her—a bath. A gods-damn bath.

"Rhona, you're so funny," Keita said, moving closer. "I know you can hear me."

Letting out a sigh, realizing she couldn't avoid this, Rhona faced her cousin, but she refused to be moved from her spot under the waterfall.

"What is it, Keita?"

"I wanted to see how you're doing. And to tell you how pretty you look with your warrior braids in your hair. Ever thought of adding ribbons to—"

"No." Rhona examined her cousin. She was buttering Rhona up for something. "I will never put ribbons in my hair. Now, what do you want, Keita?"

"Well—"

"If you dance around this any more, I'm going to get tense."

"All right, all right. No need to threaten. I just need a small favor."

"There are no small favors where you're concerned. So just get it out."

"I need you to escort me and Ren back to Dark Plains."

"No."

Keita frowned. "What do you mean 'no'?"

"I mean no. I mean you're up to something, Keita the Viper, and I'm not getting in the middle of it." Then again, Keita was always up to something. Although rarely mentioned, this particular war was, in fact, down to the actions of Keita the Viper when she'd lobbed the head of the Overlord's wife at him in the middle of the Province's main arena. After that particular move, the war was pretty much a foregone conclusion. And, as far as Rhona was concerned, all Keita's fault.

"Oh, come now," Keita pushed. "That's not fair. And I really need you to do this for me."

"We both know Ren can take care of himself, he needs no escort."

"I'm going with him as well."

"He's capable of escorting you, too." Confused, Rhona asked, "Isn't that something you two do all the time? Travel around the world with Ren as your escort?"

"He'll be busy."

"Busy with what?"

"Things."

"Forget it." Rhona began to turn away again, but Keita caught her forearm.

"Look, I can't really go into this. At least not here." Keita leaned in and whispered loudly so she could be heard over the rushing water, "The cave walls have ears."

"Those are called bats."

"Och! Why must you argue *everything*?"

"Because you're trying to pull me into your insanity. I won't go, cousin."

"I need you, Rhona. This is important."

Rhona grunted.

"If you don't believe me, ask Ragnar. He'll tell you."

Beginning to believe her cousin was sincere—Keita would never send Rhona to Ragnar the Cunning unless she really was telling the truth—Rhona asked, "Why do you need to go back?"

"Ragnar would feel safer with me in Dark Plains."

"So would I. This is no place for you, Keita."

"Then you best take me back to Garbhán Isle." The human queen's seat of power in Dark Plains.

"I can't," Rhona admitted, thinking of all she had to do. "But I'll see if the triplets—"

"No!" Keita barked, startling Rhona. "They'll be missed."

"What do you mean they'll be—"

"Everyone will notice if they're gone, and ask questions. I can't have any questions asked. So your brothers can't go either. Or any of your siblings. This needs to be done quietly."

Rhona put her claws on her hips and glared down at her much smaller cousin. "Did you only pick me because no one would notice if I was gone?"

"It's not that they wouldn't notice you're gone. . . . They'd just be glad you are."

"Well, thank you very much!"

Keita's tail slammed down into the water. "You're taking this the wrong way!"

"How else am I *supposed* to take it?"

"That's it!" Keita slashed her claws through the air. "I am Daughter of Queen Rhiannon, low-born cousin, and as a lowly soldier you'll do as I say!"

Without speaking, Rhona moved forward—and kept moving forward until her cousin had been backed into the far wall.

"All right! All right!" Keita brought up her claws to ward Rhona off. "No need to get testy!"

"Then watch that you don't irritate me, cousin."

"Please, Rhona. Once we're free of this place, I can explain everything. But not here, not now. And I'm asking you to do this because I trust you. Ren trusts you. And you know the pair of us trust few."

Damn her. Keita always knew how to get her way. Yet Rhona did have to admit that her cousin—for once—appeared sincere. And a bit worried. Keita was never worried about anything.

"Ragnar will know, yeah? That I'm with you? That I'm following orders? If it comes up. Don't need my kin thinking I'm a deserter."

"Of course they won't!" Keita again put her claw on

Rhona's forearm. "Trust me. When this is all said and done, you'll be seen as a hero."

Rhona chuckled. "Don't need all that. Just don't get me tossed into your mum's dungeons and we'll be fine."

Keita's grin was bright and pretty. "That I can manage!"

Vigholf looked up from his fifth cow leg when Keita returned to the chamber. Meinhard had headed out, but Vigholf, wanting to know more about what was going on, had stayed.

Keita smiled at Vigholf as she passed and sashayed her way over to Ragnar.

He'd admit it. Vigholf didn't understand his brother. Keita had been with Ragnar for five years now, even coming with him when they moved from their Northland home to this valley. And although she'd been forced to stay in this cave with cranky soldiers and pesky kin, she never once complained or seemed unhappy. And yet Ragnar still hadn't Claimed her. He still hadn't put his mark upon her that would let every dragon know that Keita's heart belonged to him and him alone. What the dragon was waiting for, Vigholf had no idea. The war gods knew that Vigholf wouldn't have waited if he had a She-dragon ready to be his mate. Good females were too hard to come by. And Keita was one of the best. Pretty, smart, charming, elegant, and very loyal. Those dragons who dare question Ragnar's rule as Dragonlord of the Hordes usually ended up with uncomfortable rashes under their scales, unexplainable hair loss, or coughing up blood. After several cases of that sort of thing happening, the rest of them learned to keep quiet or, at the very least, not complain about Ragnar in front of Keita.

"All set," she said, smiling.

"Good." Ragnar brushed his claw against her cheek. "I'll miss you."

"Of course you will. I'm amazing."

"You're leaving now?" Vigholf asked.

"Sssh," Keita whispered. "Not so loud. We're doing this quietly."

"Why?"

"I'll explain it later," Ragnar said. "Give us a few minutes."

Vigholf nodded and headed toward the exit. But he stopped, worried. "And your escort is not Éibhear, right?"

"You know, he's improved greatly in five years," Keita reminded him, always so protective of her oversized baby brother. Emphasis on the *baby*.

"Your escort isn't Éibhear, *right*?"

Keita let out a breath. "No. It's not. He'll be staying here with you lot. And I expect you to take good care of him."

"He's not alone, Keita." Ragnar glanced at Vigholf. "He has his brothers to watch out for him."

"And we all know they won't!"

Vigholf and Ragnar laughed. It was true. That poor Blue's brothers were harder on him than any of the Northland dragons ever were, but it was evident Éibhear was starting to get a little tired of it. That is, when he wasn't too busy fighting with his cousin Celyn.

When Keita began to tap one talon of her back claw against the hard floor, Vigholf stopped laughing even if Ragnar didn't.

"So who *is* going with you?" Vigholf pushed, not liking any of this.

"One of my cousins. But, as I said, let's keep this quiet."

"Why?"

"Ragnar can explain it later."

"Why can't he explain it now?"

"Don't be annoying, Vigholf."

"Then answer my question."

Keita's eyes narrowed and she took a step forward. To

do what, Vigholf didn't know, but Ragnar held her back by placing a claw on her shoulder.

"Keita and Ren are being escorted by the finest soldier Her Majesty's Army has . . . Sergeant Rhona."

Vigholf rolled his eyes. *"Her?"*

"What's wrong with Rhona?" Keita snapped.

"If you'd asked me that a couple of days ago, I would have said absolutely nothing."

"And today?"

"She's overworked and she whines."

"Rhona? Whine? I didn't think she even knew the meaning of that word. And why would she whine?"

"Because I broke her precious spear."

Keita gasped, eyes wide. "You broke Rhona's spear?"

"It was an—"

"Her father gave her that spear. He made it for her."

"The blacksmith, yes?" Ragnar asked.

"Uncle Sulien. He used to live in a volcano."

Frowning, Vigholf asked, "Why?"

"He was born there. His whole family was. They're Volcano dragons. All that heat and dwarves nearby . . . they've become excellent blacksmiths and glassworkers over the last millennium or so. He can make all sorts of incredible weapons. My father hates Uncle Sulien, though," she added offhandedly. "Have no idea why. But it's a deep, resentful hate. More hate than he has for most dragons." She grinned. "I like him, though. He always brought me warm treats like little lambs or newborn calves, still bleating away."

Ragnar shook his head. "Lovely."

"I think you should take someone else," Vigholf told Keita. "A couple of my cousins should work."

"Why? What's wrong with *my* cousin?" Keita briefly pursed her lips. "Or is the fact she's lacking a cock your main problem with her?"

"That sounds amazingly wrong," Ragnar noted.

Vigholf sighed. "She cries over a broken spear—"

"That a father she adores gave her!"

"—and can any Cadwaladr female say she doesn't have a cock?"

"Very funny."

"Besides, you need stronger protection than the Babysitter."

Keita gasped again. "Are you the one who started calling her that? She *hates* that nickname." She shrugged. "Although she was my babysitter for a time. When my nanny was off."

"Are you even listening to me?" Vigholf demanded.

"Not particularly, no. I know Rhona. She'll keep me and Ren safe. Of that I have no doubt."

"Well, I do."

"Then you can go with them."

Vigholf looked at his brother. "What?"

"If you're that worried, you go with Keita and Ren."

"I have a war to fight here."

"And while we get everything in place and finish the tunnel, you have time to go to the Southlands and get back before you're even missed."

"I'm a commander. I can't just wander off."

"You're not wandering off. I'm ordering you off." Which made Vigholf chuckle until his brother's glare stopped him.

"Besides," Ragnar continued. "You can check on Mother." Their mother, along with all the Northland She-dragons, had been sent to the Southlands for her own safety when they'd moved to Euphrasia. A decision that had confused all the Southland She-dragons. "Can't they fight?" Bradana had asked. "Most of 'em may be missing a wing, but not their claws or legs."

And although Vigholf could speak to his mother with his mind anytime he wanted, he still greatly missed her presence. "And wouldn't you feel better keeping an eye on the sergeant? Just to make sure she doesn't make any *huge* mistakes in her overworked, tired state."

His brother did have a point. And it wasn't like they were in the Northlands. Euphrasia Valley was much closer to all the borders. They could be in the Southlands and then Dark Plains rather quickly, drop off the royals, and be back in just a few days to finish off the Irons. Yes. That worked. And, while they were traveling, if he could find the Babysitter a new weapon, something a little more . . . appropriate for her age, all the better.

"All right then. When are we leaving?"

"Within the hour," Keita said. "But remember, not a word to anyone."

"And you'll tell me what's going on once we're on our way?"

"I will. Promise."

Rhona met the triplets in what they called their "safe place." The one place their mother would never be seen. In other words . . . the makeshift library.

She motioned them behind some tall piles of books and took another look around.

"What's wrong, Rhona?" Edana asked.

"Nothing. But I need your word that you'll not repeat what I'm about to tell you."

"Of course not," Nesta promised. "You know you can trust us, sister."

She smiled at the She-dragons whom, with her father, she'd raised. Of all her siblings, the triplets made her the most proud. They'd make mighty warriors one day and even better leaders.

"I'm off for a few days. Shouldn't be gone long."

"Off? To where?"

She couldn't help but roll her eyes a little at Nesta's question. "To protect the Royal Princess Keita on her way back to the Southlands."

Edana frowned. "And we can't repeat that . . . why exactly?"

"I have no idea. But Keita was adamant that I could tell no one."

"But you're telling us," Breena remarked, smirking. "Bad She-dragon."

"I know. I know. But this is Keita I'm dealing with. Who the hell knows what she's up to and why she feels the need to keep it quiet. But I at least want you three to know, in case something happens. Especially if Mum finds out. The last thing I need right now is for her to think—"

"You're a deserter?"

"Exactly."

Nesta shook her head. "Mum knows better than that."

"Well, she's a little pissed at me right now. So I don't want to test her."

"Good idea," Edana agreed. "So where exactly are you taking Keita?"

"Back to Dark Plains."

"Awww," the triplets said at the same time. "You'll see Daddy!"

That made Rhona smile. "Aye. I will." Her father had been working Annwyl the Bloody's forge since the war began. It was a huge forge and her father had many talented blacksmiths under him. Some dragon, others human. It was a good place for him to be since he didn't get along too well with those in Devenallt Mountain, the Southland dragons' stronghold. He especially didn't get along with Uncle Bercelak, as those two had never been friendly. "I'll make sure to bring you a few weapons from his collection."

Nesta and Breena clapped and cheered softly, still conscious of how sound traveled around cave walls, but Edana, always the more serious one, frowned. "Be careful, Rhona. I adore our cousin, but Keita is reckless and plays where she should not."

"I'm well aware of how our cousin operates, sister. I have my guard up. Now I need you to do the same."

"Don't worry, Rhona," Edana told her with a small smile, "we'll handle Mum."

Keita watched the big Lightning leave before she faced the dragon she adored—although she still hadn't told Ragnar that she adored him. It wasn't good to give a male that sort of information too early in the relationship. And yes! Five years was still too early in the relationship, no matter what her pesky aunts may believe.

"Why did you insist Vigholf go?" she asked.

"Because he would have driven me insane until Rhona returned. He won't admit it, but he keeps an eye on her."

"Whatever for?"

He smiled. She loved that smile. "Because he fancies her and has since the very beginning, I'd wager."

"That's unfortunate," Keita admitted. "She hates him. Calls him the pest. One should never be a pest to a Cadwaladr female. That never works out well."

Ragnar pulled Keita against him. "You shouldn't underestimate my brother. Besides, the more protection you have, the happier I'll be." Ragnar placed both claws on either side of her face, gazed deep into her eyes. "Please, Keita. Please . . . don't be stupid."

"Thank you very much," she said on a laugh.

"You know what I mean. You are, on your best day, foolhardy. You take dangerous chances. Especially when it comes to ensuring the safety of your kin."

"I won't do anything that will stop me from helping my kin."

"Are you sure we shouldn't tell your brothers?" Keita's three eldest brothers commanded their own troops with three generals reporting directly to each and the respective number of legions under each prince's banner. It had been many years since Fearghus, Briec, and Gwenvael had led troops into battle, but they'd done well from the beginning, impressing even the hard-to-impress Northlanders with their skills.

"If Fearghus and Briec find out, they will leave and take half of Mother's army with them, *and* the Cadwaladrs. You can't afford that right now and my brothers will not be stopped. Not when it comes to this and no matter the protection you think is in place in Garbhán Isle. But Ren and I can handle this without going through all that."

"And bringing your cousin?"

"Merely a formality to ensure our safety. Ren will be working Magicks, and his strength will be diminished. As will his focus. But Rhona will watch out for us like a ferocious demon dog from the underworld."

He finally smiled. "I wouldn't say that to her face."

"No, no," Keita replied with some seriousness. "She's not like her sisters and mother. She'd not find that a compliment."

Chapter 4

Rhona met Keita and Ren at one of the lower exits. As human, they'd take this tunnel out of the stronghold until they reached a safe distance and could finally fly. But seeing her younger cousin waiting patiently for her had Rhona remembering the last time she'd babysat Princess Keita when the Dragon Queen's centaur nanny had been away from Devenallt Mountain for a few months. A few months that had been the longest in Rhona's life. Yet Rhona loved Keita despite that past incident.

"Cousin!" Keita cheered when she saw her, running over to give Rhona a hug. "It's been absolutely ages!"

"I saw you less than an hour ago."

"Really?" Keita glanced off. "It felt longer."

Rhona's eyes briefly crossed before she asked, "Are you ready to go, cousin?"

"Aye. We are."

Rhona stepped away from Keita and went to Ren. Her smile warm, she hugged him. "Hello, old friend."

"Rhona. Are you ready for all this?"

"No. But to protect you from Keita, I'll be there."

Ren laughed and Keita pouted.

"Then let's get on the road," Rhona prodded, ready to be traveling.

Keita quickly sized her up. "You're being very pushy, cousin."

"The quicker this gets done, the quicker I can return to the battle."

"And glory?"

"What else is there for a Cadwaladr?"

Keita patted Rhona's shoulder. "You make me sad."

Ragnar, also in human form, wrapped his arms around Keita, pulling her into his body. He hugged her tight, whispered something into her ear.

Although unable to give them complete privacy, Rhona turned away—and faced Vigholf. She frowned, noting he was dressed for travel with his big, human-sized but adjustable warhammer and ax tied to his back, a thin fur cape around his shoulders, and a travel bag over that.

"Why are you here?" she asked Vigholf.

"I'll be coming along."

Her eyes narrowed more. So much she could barely see. "Coming along where?"

"With Keita and Ren, for protection."

Rhona slammed the butt of one of her emergency spears into the ground, her hand gripping the shaft tight. "They have me for that. *I'm* here to protect them."

"Of course you are." And the condescension came through loud and clear. She was surprised he didn't pat her on the head like a trusted but crippled mutt.

"New spear?" he asked.

"No. One of my backups."

"Have you thought about moving up to a short sword?"

"No."

"They're not hard to learn to work with. I could show you while we're traveling."

"I know how to use a short sword. As I've explained, I'm trained in all weapons."

"But you still use a spear?"

"I like it."

"For field use, I understand. But for this kind of mission . . . shouldn't you have something a little less . . . cumbersome?"

Rhona pulled the spear back to demonstrate on his neck how cumbersome her weapon was, but Ragnar stepped between them.

"Check outside," he told his brother. "Make sure it's clear."

Vigholf walked off and Ragnar faced her.

"I know," he said before she could speak. "I know."

"How can two brothers be so bloody different?"

"Let him do this," Ragnar pleaded with a smile. "He'll feel better and—"

"So will you?"

He shrugged. "She's my Keita. Knowing that both you *and* my brother protect her on this trip will give me nothing but ease. And you'll find out soon enough why this trip is so important. So for me—and my sanity—do this."

Dammit. If it had been anyone else . . . but it was Ragnar. From the beginning he'd impressed Rhona. Fair, smart, and a strong commander, he never questioned whether she or any female could or should fight. He simply assumed if you were in the army you could do your job. He was rare for a Lightning. His brother, however . . .

"Rhona?" Ragnar pushed.

She nodded, but with reluctance. "All right. But you'll owe me, Dragonlord—for putting up with him."

"Fair enough." Ragnar winked and motioned at Keita. "And you'll protect her?"

"She's blood, my lord. I'll protect her with my life."

"Good. Because she *is* my life."

Rhona smiled. "That I know."

Vigholf crouched low by the small cave entrance, big enough only for a human. He raised his arm, lifted his hand, and then he heard it. The signal from Meinhard letting him know that it was—as best he could tell—all clear. Vigholf waited another second, then two. When he was sure, he brought his hand down.

Rhona came out first. Her gaze swept the area. After a moment, she moved quickly and kept low.

Keita and the Eastlander rushed out behind her, keeping low, keeping quiet. He looked back at the exit one last time, his brother standing there watching them go. They locked gazes, the need for words and good-byes long gone. On this trip anything could happen to Vigholf, and during a war anything could happen to Ragnar. It was the way of the warrior and something they'd accepted long ago. But they wouldn't dwell on that. Instead, Vigholf nodded at his brother, took one more look around, but seeing nothing strange or out of place, he followed the others and headed to the Southlands.

Chapter 5

Talaith, Daughter of Haldane and Mate of Briec the Arrogant, also known as Briec the Mighty, walked down the stairs to the Great Hall of Garbhán Isle. She was tired. It would be the full moon in a few days and she had much to do before she performed the spells she was planning. For she was one of the Nolwenn witches out of the Desert Lands and for more than sixteen years her powers had been denied her by a bitch goddess she still refused to discuss in polite company. But Talaith had her powers back now and she was ready to truly master them. Not easy, though, when the only other witches who could help her were her most hated enemies. The Ice Lands' Kyvich.

The Kyvich were warrior witches out of the nightmarish Ice Land territories. They were known far and wide for many reasons: their incredible skills on the battlefield, their mystical powers as well as their connections to the gods. But what they were really known—and feared—for was that they built up their rank and file by taking newborn-to-toddler-age daughters. From peasant to royalty, it didn't matter whose daughter it was, nothing stopped the Kyvich once they'd decided a young girl was one of their own. Although they mostly stayed in the Ice Lands and took offspring from there, they'd been seen as far south as the Desert Lands and as far west as the Provinces. Only the Eastlands seemed to have kept them at bay, most likely due to the violent sea that separated continents. And from the time Talaith could walk, she'd been told by the Nolwenn witches who helped raised her that the Kyvich were no more than "murderous, low-level whores who should feel blessed that they're allowed to breathe the same air as us."

Or, as Talaith's mother so simply put it, *Those bitches.*

Yet Talaith could only complain so much about the Kyvich because they were here, in Garbhán Isle for a true and mighty purpose. To protect those who meant more to her than any words could ever hope to adequately describe.

They were here to protect the children.

"Good morn, Dagmar."

Dagmar Reinholdt, her sister-by-mating and Battle Lord of Dark Plains, glanced up from the letters and missives she received nearly every day. "Morn, sister."

Dagmar also came from the north like the Kyvich. The Northlands specifically. She was a mighty warlord's daughter but had earned the respect of Queen Annwyl by being what Annwyl could not . . . a rational, political force that many feared. Although Annwyl was feared, all she could really do was cut someone's head off and kill their soldiers.

Dagmar, when she set her mind to it, could do much worse—and often did.

"Everything all right?" Talaith asked her.

"Not sure."

"Anything I should be panicking about?"

"Not at the moment, no."

"Excellent." Talaith sat down at the large table. A servant placed a bowl of hot porridge in front of her and a basket of fresh bread beside it. She picked up a spoon, ready to dig in, but a door opened behind her and she heard that telltale squeal.

Talaith turned in her chair and opened her arms wide. Her youngest daughter charged into them. Her tiny body slamming into her mother's, her small arms wrapping around her mother's neck.

"There's my beautiful girl. How are you this morning?"

"Fine," Rhianwen said against Talaith's throat.

Rhianwen, Rhian for short—unless it was her sister, then it was Rhi—was an impossibly shy and sweet girl. Surprisingly not like her parents at all. Then again, Rhian wasn't even supposed to exist. For many reasons. Because her father was a dragon, her mother a human, and because as a Nolwenn witch Talaith was only supposed to be able to have one child in her what-should-be eight hundred years or so of existence. And that one child had been her Izzy, who was off risking her life as Annwyl the Bloody's squire. Izzy was the child Talaith had at sixteen. But then, it seemed, the gods had changed their minds and given Talaith Rhian as well. Her beautiful little Rhian. With the brown skin of her mother's people and her father's silver hair and violet eyes, Rhian had unparalleled beauty and thankfully no tail or scales. From what anyone could tell, Talaith's daughter was completely human—so far. And although strength and battle skills didn't seem to be Rhian's future calling, Talaith knew a fellow witch when she saw one. But not just a witch. The girl was unbelievably powerful, clearly blessed by the gods. Magicks swirled around and through her, and with one glance, Rhian could look right into your soul.

It was a little disconcerting at times. Even for Talaith.

"Where are your cousins?" Talaith asked her daughter— as always, afraid of the answer when the twins were not right by Rhian's side. Because Rhian, although younger, had a lovely calming effect on the brother and sister who also should not exist as the offspring of the human Queen Annwyl and Dragon Prince Fearghus. For while Talaith's dragon-human daughter may be sweet and innocent, Rhian's dragon-human cousins were definitely neither of those things. And, it was doubtful they ever would be.

"Playing with the dogs," Rhian said while tugging on her mother's long curly hair.

"Play . . . playing with the dogs?"

"In the fields. They brought their ax."

Dagmar's head snapped up and the two women looked at each other. They didn't need to read each other's mind to know what the other was thinking.

They were both up, Rhian still in her mother's arms, and near the back door when Ebba walked in. In each hand she carried a child. The girl, Talwyn, in her right and the boy, Talan, in her left.

"Got 'em," the centaur female said, smiling. After five years she still had patience with Annwyl and Fearghus's offspring, although none of them knew how she managed it.

"My dogs?" Dagmar demanded. Even with her duties as Battle Lord and Garbhán Isle vassal, Dagmar still managed to breed and train the most amazing but singularly violent battle dogs in the known world. Yet, surprisingly, they were also wonderful pets.

"Oh, they're fine," Ebba said, heading toward the stairs and the children's bedroom. "The twins were using the ax to chase the *cattle*, not the dogs. The dogs were simply tagging along."

"Somehow," Dagmar muttered to Talaith, "that doesn't make me feel better."

Talaith understood that.

"Well," Talaith said as the leader of the Kyvich legion in residence, Commander Ásta, walked by with two of her warrior witches behind her, "maybe if the Kyvich did their job and actually watched out for the children . . ."

Ásta stopped. She liked Talaith even less than Talaith liked her. "My job and the job of my coven is to keep

your offspring alive. Keeping them from hacking up the
cattle . . . that's *your* job, Nolwenn."

Talaith snarled a little, and Dagmar stepped in front of
her, cutting the sight of the tattooed bitch from her. "Stop it."

"She annoys."

"The world annoys you, Talaith. Stop acting like she's
somehow special."

Well . . . the Northland female did have a point.

"We have to stop," Keita said from behind them.

Rhona and Vigholf glanced at each other. They'd only
been walking for about four hours. Then again, Keita
wasn't known for exercising anything but her mouth and
her conniving ways, so perhaps she did tire easily.

"If you can't handle traveling a few miles on foot,
Keita—" But Rhona stopped talking when she turned and
saw that it was Ren sitting against a tree stump—panting.

"Ren?" She went to his side and crouched down.
"What's wrong?"

"Nothing." He tried to smile. "Just need a few moments."

Rhona looked to her cousin, but Keita was focused on
Ren, so Rhona stood, paced over to the Lightning.

"I don't remember the foreigner being so weak before,"
Vigholf murmured low so only Rhona could hear.

"That's because he's not weak."

"Then what's going on?"

"I don't know." Rhona faced her cousin. "But perhaps
it's time you tell us, Keita. Tell us what is going on."

"Tell them," Ren said softly. "So they'll understand."

Keita nodded and stood. "Ren is opening a portal. It's
taking a lot out of him."

"A portal? Why's he opening a portal? And," Rhona
went on before Keita could answer, "the gods know he's
opened portals before, so why should this one—"

"This one will take him and others into the Eastlands. That's not a short trip, cousin. And normally he'd take weeks to prepare for a casting of this magnitude. But we don't have that kind of time, so he's opening one as quickly as he can manage."

"He can't just"—Vigholf shrugged—"open one?"

"He can, but if it's not precisely done, it could dump them anywhere. It's too great a risk."

Rhona stepped closer. "Them? Who is he taking with him?"

Keita looked back at Ren.

"Tell them everything," he pushed. "You might as well."

Keita nodded and said, "As we speak, several of the Western tribes Annwyl tried to wipe out have teamed together and are riding toward Garbhán Isle. They know Annwyl and most of her army are not there and they want to destroy the castle and kill her offspring for revenge. And the reason we didn't tell you earlier is because we're hiding all this from Fearghus and Briec. Because you know what will happen if they find out their offspring are in danger. They'll rush off with most of the army to protect them and leave the Lightnings and the rest of my mother's army to fend for themselves. So I decided this was the best idea." Keita clapped her hands together. "But we've got it all covered and we've got you two to protect us all the way home . . . so there's no need to worry!"

Vigholf watched Rhona closely, ready to catch hold of her before she could grab Keita in a rage. But Rhona merely stared at her cousin until she said, "Yeah, all right." She sighed a little. "We should get horses then, for when we're not flying."

"Wait, wait, wait," Vigholf cut in, shocked Rhona was

just accepting what Keita had spewed. "How do you know all this, Keita?"

"Auntie Ghleanna—"

Vigholf held up his hand, stopping Keita, and asked Rhona, "Which one is she again?"

"General of the Seventh and Ninth Legions, sister to me mum. Likes to remove heads during battle by slamming two broadswords together against someone's neck."

"Oh! Right! Ghleanna."

"Anyway," Keita went on, "Auntie Ghleanna found a messenger sneaking through our territory to get to the Irons. She brought him back to me and I found out some . . . things."

"What does *that* mean?"

"Don't ask her that," Rhona warned him.

"Why wouldn't I ask?"

"Because she means she tortured him until he begged for death and told her whatever she wanted to know," Rhona replied, apparently accepting of all that as well.

He looked at Keita. "Does Ragnar know you tor—" Vigholf stopped himself. "Wait. Forget I asked."

"Forgotten," Keita happily chirped.

"But why are the Western Tribes attacking now?" Vigholf asked instead. "Annwyl's been out of Dark Plains for five years now."

"The messenger had a letter for Overlord Thracius from his daughter Vateria. While her father is in Euphrasia Valley, she rules Quintilian Provinces and the Sovereigns, and according to the letter she has paid the Tribesmen to attack Garbhán Isle and kill Fearghus and Briec's offspring."

"The messenger had a letter?" Rhona asked.

"Aye."

"That just happened to spell out Vateria's entire evil plan in detail?"

Keita grinned and Rhona shook her head.

"She's a piece of work that one," Rhona murmured.

"She wanted the messenger intercepted," Vigholf reasoned. "Thinking your brothers would find it, rush off to save their offspring, bringing the entire Cadwaladr Clan with them."

Keita nodded, laughed. "Leaving you poor barbarian Northlanders to the mercy of the exquisite military might of the Irons. He'd destroy all of you first and fly right into the Southlands to face a broken Southland army. Not a bad plan really. Because that's exactly what my brothers would do . . . if I hadn't gotten to the messenger first."

"But wait . . ." Vigholf studied the princess. "If you knew all that from the letter—why did you torture the messenger?"

The royal gave a very small shrug. "I was a wee bit bored. . . ."

"I keep telling you not to ask her questions," Rhona sighed out, "but you insist."

Annoyed Rhona was right, Vigholf snapped at her, "Have you nothing to say about any of this?"

"What do you want me to say?"

"She just told you that your cousins' offspring are in danger, that she has some ridiculous scheme involving portals and this foreigner, and that she might be taking us into the middle of a pitch battle with barbarians, but she hadn't warned us of that possibility before we left."

"Yeah . . . and?"

"I'd think a little rage or something would be in order. Some ranting, arms flailing." Vigholf needed some emotion from her. Something.

"And I do all that . . . what does it change?"

"Change?"

"Yeah. What does it change? Nothing. Will I still have

to follow orders and escort my cousin and Ren to Garbhán Isle anyway?"

"Well—"

"Of course I will. Will Keita ever stop being a spoiled, entitled brat who does whatever she wants and gets away with it because we're all terrified of her mother, who's a homicidal queen?"

"Uh—"

"Doubtful. So what's the point?"

"Well—"

"Exactly. There is no point. Now get those two fed and I'll get us some fresh water from the stream. We can decide whether it's safe enough now to fly or if we should get horses instead when I return."

She walked off and all Vigholf could do was watch her until Keita stood beside him.

"When she gets like that," Keita confided, "it's best just let her go. You can never win."

"She didn't even let me get a word in . . . and she answered her own bloody questions. Why ask them then?"

"That's Rhona's way. Don't let it bother you." Keita tugged the sleeve of his chain-mail shirt until he gazed down at her. "You don't think I'm entitled, do you?"

"Of course not," Vigholf lied.

"Because if I am, it's only because I deserve it! I deserve everything I want. Don't you agree?"

Rather than lying even more, Vigholf handed Keita his pack. "Here. There's beef in the bag. You two eat. I'll be right back."

Rhona filled up her flask with water and thought about next steps. Should they stay on foot or risk taking to the skies? After hearing the truth about this trip, she thought flying might be the wisest move. But she worried about

Ren's strength. Flying could be tiring, even for dragons and Ren didn't even have wings! He just sort of . . . flew. And if human forces on the ground attacked them while they were in the air, would Ren be able to dodge, much less fight?

Analyzing, she stood and asked the Lightning who'd been standing silently behind her. "Horses or flying?"

"What?"

"Should we get horses or fly?"

"I'm not good with horses."

"What do you mean you're not good?"

"I mean, they get my scent and they bolt." He shrugged. "I really like horse meat." He gazed off. "I'm so hungry."

Not having time for this, Rhona walked around him to head back to the others.

"So what's the plan?" he asked.

"Plan?" Rhona faced him, shrugged. "Do what we've been doing, I guess. Get those two back to Garbhán Isle."

"And?"

"And what?"

"We're heading into a war zone, Sergeant. Possibly. According to your cousin, we'll be caught between some pissed-off barbarian tribes and the Kyvich Witches. That is *not* a good place for anyone to be." He stepped closer. "And if you think the Kyvich are going to let that foreigner traipse off with those children after they've committed to one of their gods to protect them at Garbhán Isle—"

"All right, all right." Gods, he could ramble when provoked. "What do *you* suggest we do?"

"We need to find out what we're looking at with these Western Tribes. Are they bringing one legion, two, a thousand? We should escort these two past the Dark Plains border and then go off on our own. Head toward the west and see how close this army is."

"Okay," Rhona agreed. "We'll do that."

He scowled at her, but she didn't know why. "Or you can give me your opinion."

"My opinion?"

"Opinion. Suggestion. Ideas."

"Ideas?"

His scowl worsened. "You do have ideas, don't you?"

"I do, but you outrank me so—"

"First off," he angrily cut in, "don't pull that ox shit with me. We're not here with an army that needs to be controlled. It's just you, me, a weakened foreigner, and a poison-and-torture-happy princess. We can't afford for you to only take orders. I don't know this terrain and I think we both know you don't want your orders to come from Keita. So, Sergeant, we need to do this together—as a team. So I ask you again—what's your opinion?"

Rhona knew Vigholf had a point, no matter how rudely that point was made. And although she was completely unused to giving her opinion—only Dragonwarriors had that luxury during battles and missions—she did as he'd asked.

"I think our job is to get Keita and Ren into Garbhán Isle safely. That alone will be hard enough. The Western Tribes, the Tribesmen, are riders and nomads used to moving quickly all year round. They're not marching on Dark Plains, Commander. They're racing there, hoping to take advantage of Annwyl's absence. It's too risky to send Keita and Ren off on their own. And once we get them to Dark Plains, those two can also deal with the Kyvich."

The Lightning studied her for a long moment. Then he nodded. "You're right." She was? And he was admitting she was? "I didn't know about the Western Tribes. My Horde has never fought them. So you're right. We can't let those two off on their own. At least in Garbhán Isle they'll have some protection, and from what I remember of that territory, it will be easier to defend." He looked around. "We keep moving. I can carry the foreigner if need be."

Although Ren wasn't a large dragon, especially compared to Rhona's own kin, he would be no light burden for anyone. "And how long can you keep that up?"

Those clear grey eyes locked on her. "As long as I need to."

"Oh." She cleared her throat. "All right then."

"Let's get moving. There still may be Iron scouts out this far."

And without another word said between them, they walked back to Keita and Ren.

Chapter 6

They ended up risking the skies when the first set of wild horses they came upon stampeded at the first scent of the Lightning. A moment that he could only shrug at and mutter, "Sorry."

And although they made good time with only short breaks along the way, they were still forced to get some real sleep that night.

Rhona, though, feeling more awake than tired, took first watch. In her human form, she went up high in a tree, using its leaves for cover. She briefly thought about letting the triplets know what was going on, what had changed, but decided against it. She trusted them, but if they worried for Fearghus and Briec's offspring, they would most certainly alert the rest of the siblings and the rest of the siblings would tell Mum and Mum would make a straight line to Fearghus and Briec to complain about Keita using one of her soldiers—no, not her daughter, but one of her soldiers—for her "nonsense," which was what Bradana called almost anything that Keita did. So it was best to say nothing.

After a few hours, Rhona felt a tap and looked down at Vigholf. And with a lightness belied by his great human size, he pulled himself up until he sat across from her. The old tree groaned, but the limbs did not break under his weight as he settled in.

"All clear?" he asked, his voice low.

"Aye."

"Good." He handed over a cloth with meat and bread wrapped in it before turning his gaze to the land around them, grey eyes watchful. "Can you explain to me why the Tribesmen hate Annwyl so much?"

"Who says they do?"

"I doubt that just because a Quintilian monarch offers them payment they'll jump at the chance to take on Garbhán Isle."

"Well . . ." Rhona let out a little sigh, toying with the cloth holding her food. "Annwyl does not like slavery or slave traders, which is the Tribesmen's top means of income. She struck first a few years back, hoping to convince them, in her own way, to give up slavery in exchange for her not wiping them from the planet. They never took her up on her offer, and then this thing with the Irons and Sovereigns happened and she stopped worrying about the Tribesmen. Especially when she found out that most of the Tribesmen's patrons were Quintilians."

"And in Annwyl's mind, kill the ones demanding the product and the suppliers will go out of business?"

"Pretty much. For Annwyl it's not about power but about everything being what she thinks is . . . right. She thinks slavery is wrong, so she tries to stop it. She thinks the Sovereigns ruling everything is wrong, so she tries to stop them."

"You've fought by her side before?"

"More than once. As human. When the Cadwaladrs have no dragons to fight, we'll join human armies."

"Your royal cousins do the same?"

Rhona had to laugh at that. "*My* cousins? Direct bloodline from the House of Gwalchmai fab Gwyar? Hardly.

Even my Uncle Bercelak, their father, a true Cadwaladr, never had much use for humans except as a quick-moving snack. Then Annwyl came along . . ." Rhona shook her head. "Nothing's been the same since Fearghus found that female dying outside his cave about twelve or so years ago. Then there was Talaith and Dagmar. . . . Then the offspring were born and all bets were off."

Vigholf nodded slowly. "I see, but your cousin, Keita . . ."

"What about her?"

"She hides something."

"Keita hides much," Rhona admitted. "She is a Protector of the Throne. She will do all in her power to safeguard the throne of our kind, even to her death."

"She'd go that far? Even to risk her young nieces and nephew?"

"I doubt Keita thinks she's risking them. And she has and will risk her own life. I know now that's never a question." For tiny Keita had faced the wrath of their bitch cousin Elestren, who was anything but tiny. Elestren had believed Keita a traitor and, without orders, set about sending Keita to the salt mines on the Desert Land borders. All because Keita had embarrassed the Dragonwarrior by taking her eye during fair combat training. Unfortunate, perhaps, but Rhona's own mother had lost the tip of her wing while training with her sister Ghleanna. Something that affected her flying, but over the centuries she'd learned to manage it. And she'd never held it against her sister.

Yet Keita had faced Elestren bravely, proving what Rhona had always suspected about her cousin—Keita was *nothing* like she seemed.

Taking Rhona's word for it, he motioned to her food. "Eat."

"Thanks for this."

The Lightning grunted before asking, "And Keita's grand scheme—you all right with it?"

Around the dried beef she chewed, Rhona replied, "It is what it is."

"So you just accept it then?"

She shrugged, biting off a piece of bread. "Why wouldn't I accept it?"

"But you didn't ask anything. Push for more answers from Keita. What if this isn't what it seems at all? What if it's worse?"

"Then I'll adjust. Because that's what a good soldier does. I follow orders. I adjust. That's what I'll do now."

Vigholf didn't understand this female. She never asked questions, she never disobeyed, and she never did more than follow the orders given. Yet she was in no way lazy or stupid or incapable. Although female, she fought extremely well and deserved her title of sergeant. But Vigholf couldn't help but see more for her. Just like the rest of her siblings, who, to be honest, he didn't find nearly as capable.

So then what was it? Why did she seem happy to simply settle for being an order taker?

"Do you even like being a soldier?" he asked. "Because it never sounds like you do."

Her eyes widened a bit and he realized he'd surprised her with his question. Had no one asked her if she'd *wanted* to be a soldier? Then again . . . after knowing Rhona's mother, he doubted that anyone had asked Rhona anything. It was probably a given.

"I like it well enough," she eventually answered.

"Do you love it?"

She took an even longer time to answer that, slowly chewing her food and staring thoughtfully out over the land.

"I'm good at it," she finally replied, dark brown eyes focusing on him. "I am, point of fact, the best soldier you'll ever meet. The most loyal, the most dedicated, the most skilled. But I am no more than that. I am no more than the best soldier you'll ever meet."

"You make that sound like a bad thing." To be honest, he'd kill for a troop filled with nothing but soldiers like Rhona.

"Among my kin . . . it's a disappointing thing. So when I talk about it, what you hear isn't hatred over what I do. Just resignation."

She handed over half the meat and bread he'd given her. "You'll need to keep your strength up, too, Commander. We'll be back in Dark Plains in another day and a half," she added, expertly climbing down from her perch, "and I sense we'll need your Northland strength."

Then she was gone and Vigholf spent his watch thinking about brown eyes and the resignation he'd seen within them.

Chapter 7

They ended up taking several breaks because of Ren during the next day of travel. Whatever Magicks the East-lander was doing were quite strong and Rhona began to worry about him.

While Keita took a quick nap by the base of a tree a few feet away, Rhona crouched beside Ren. They'd shifted to their human forms and dressed in case any true humans stumbled upon them. The path they'd been flying above was often busy this time of year, and Rhona had no desire to kill some human because he simply stumbled into the midst of dragons and felt the need to warn his neighbors.

"What can I do for you, old friend?" Rhona asked.

Ren smiled at her. "Nothing. I'm fine."

"You don't look fine. You look like you've been out drinking with my cousins."

"Gods, do I really look that bad?" He grinned and Rhona felt better for seeing it. "I'm fine," he insisted. "Really. Exhausted, but fine. Once I get the children into the Eastlands, my father's strength and the power of my parents' home will get me back to my old self. I promise."

"Is there anything you need now?"

"Any food left?"

Her eyes crossed. "That barbarian's eaten what we've brought with us. He just sucks up all the food around him without caring about anyone else."

Ren chuckled. "It could be worse. He could be chatty."

"Good point. You know how I hate chatty." Rhona stood. "Let me see if I can track something down for you. I'll even roast it for you."

"That would be perfect. Thank you."

"Anything for you, Ren of the Chosen."

"Really? And why's that then?"

"Because you manage to control Keita and keep her relatively safe. For that alone—the entire Clan owes you."

Rhona lifted her head, sniffed the air. "Deer," she said and went after it.

Vigholf caught the deer by its throat and slammed it into a tree, snapping its neck, and tossed the carcass to the ground. His stomach grumbled and he reached for the animal, planning to tear it open and enjoy its still-warm insides.

But before his fingers could touch the animal's soft pelt, a blast of flame singed his human fingers.

"Gods-dammit! What was that for?"

"You have to be the most selfish dragon I've ever met," Rhona accused. "And considering *my* kin—that's truly saying something."

"What did I do now?"

"Ren needs to eat."

"So? Let him eat."

"You've devoured all the dried beef and bread we had. You haven't even asked any of us if we're hungry or not."

Vigholf shrugged. "I asked Keita. But she—"

"Keita? You asked Keita? Keita who's *not* doing any Magicks to protect her nieces and nephew? Keita who's *not* protecting anyone? Keita who's done nothing but talk about all the bloody dresses she plans to get—not buy mind, but get—when she arrives in Dark Plains? She's the one you're making sure is fed?"

Vigholf cleared his throat, scratched the back of his neck. "Well . . . yeah."

Rhona's eyes narrowed and she shoved him back from the carcass. "I'm giving this to Ren. You can bring your precious Keita something else that you caught or killed."

"That deer wasn't for her. It was for me. I'm hungry."

"Again?" Rhona gawked up at him. "How can you be hungry again? You've done nothing but eat all day. Now that I think about it, I've never seen a dragon eat while flying."

"Then clearly you're not putting in enough effort." Rhona's eyes narrowed again, and Vigholf, in no mood to fight with her, quickly put his hands up. "There's more deer over in that glen. I'll grab one of those."

"Good."

Rhona crouched beside the carcass and proceeded to skin it.

Vigholf watched her for a time until he asked, "How's the Eastlander doing anyway?"

"He's tired. To-his-bones tired."

"You're worried about him."

"Aye. I am."

"You two seem . . . close."

Rhona gave a good yank and removed the deer's pelt with her bare hands. "Aye. I guess we are."

"How close?"

She tossed the pelt aside and looked up at Vigholf. "What?"

"How close are you to the one your sisters refer to as the 'handsome foreigner'?"

"Why are you asking?"

"Why won't you tell me?"

"Because it's none of your business?"

"And what exactly is none of my business? What are you hiding from me?"

Rhona stood, flicking the deer blood and pulp from her hands. "I hide nothing from you, but my business and my personal life are my own. Even my *mother* doesn't ask me these sorts of questions."

"I'm not your mother."

"No. So you have even less right."

"Then answer me this," he quickly said before she could walk off. "Are you two . . . attached?"

She snorted a small laugh. "No. Not like that. We're . . . old friends."

"Uh-huh."

"Unattached old friends. So leave it be."

Except Vigholf wasn't sure he could.

Rhona blasted the deer with her flame, using the power of it to turn the carcass over and over until it was wonderfully roasted on all sides. She reached for it and lifted it onto her shoulder. That's when Vigholf asked, "Do you want to be attached?"

Rhona froze. All these questions were beginning to get strange. Then again, the barbarian was strange.

"Attached to what?"

"A mate of your own."

"Guess I hadn't thought much about it. Why?"

"No reason."

"How could you have no reason to ask me that?" Rhona snapped.

"Because I don't."

"Well, you don't have to snarl!" She turned away from him.

"But," he said to her back, "you're not against having a mate?"

Rhona faced him again. "Why are you asking me these questions?"

"Because I'm curious."

"Well, be curious with another female."

"Why? What's wrong with you?"

"Nothing's wrong with me except that I'd never settle for a male who wouldn't fight with me in battle."

"I've been fighting with you in battle for five years."

"Not willingly."

"That's ox shit. When have I ever said—"

"'Females . . . fighting by my side?'" Rhona imitated in her low, making-fun-of-Vigholf voice that she used to entertain the triplets. "'When did the hells come to earth?'"

He blinked. "Oh. All right. I may have said those words before, but—"

"But what?"

"But not when it's been you. I've never said those words about *you*. You've impressed me from the beginning."

"How very big of you," she snipped, again turning away from him. "You lunkhead."

Rhona took a few steps, but Vigholf cut in front of her. "I'll admit that my opinion of female fighters was that there were none. But," he quickly added when she hissed, "you and your sisters have changed my opinion on that belief. Shame I can't say the same about you believing all Northlanders are barbarians."

"You *are* all barbarians."

"Even Ragnar?"

"Well . . . no. But he's different. Special."

Vigholf's left eye twitched and she suddenly felt fear for Ragnar's safety. But, after a moment, Vigholf went on. "And has any of my brethren tried kidnapping one of you, forcing you into a Claiming?"

Rhona rolled her eyes. "No."

He took a step toward her, slowly closing the gap between

them. "Have some of us not proven ourselves to be excellent strategists in battle rather than berserkers you need to leash between fights?"

"I guess."

Another step. "Haven't we been polite and considerate to all the female warriors even when they're throwing ale, starting fights, and generally being a bit crazed?"

She let out a breath. "Most of you, yes."

"Then how about giving us a break? Giving *me* a break?" Another step. "Since we're all doing so well, that is."

They were nearly touching now, his grey eyes gazing down at her.

"I have to get this meat to Ren," she said. "He needs to eat before we can return to the skies."

"All right."

But he didn't move or stop looking at her that way. She couldn't explain what that way was—but it was *that* way. So Rhona forced herself to walk around him and slowly headed back to her cousin and friend.

Although to be honest, she really wanted to make a run for it. She just didn't know why.

Chapter 8

Morfyd the White, Eldest Daughter and Third-Born Offspring of Dragon Queen Rhiannon, Heir to the Queen's Magicks, and Battle Mage for Queen Annwyl's Army, tracked down her human mate.

She rode her horse around hurrying troops, cooks, riders, scouts, and all the others that made up a human queen's army.

"Morfyd?" Her human mate, Brastias, general of Queen Annwyl's army, pushed his men aside to stand by her. "What is it?"

"We move now for the Euphrasia Valley."

"So soon? I thought we had a few more—"

"The Sovereigns aren't pulling back. They've moved out. Heading to the Valley."

Brastias glanced out over what had been their battle-ground for nearly five years. His laugh was a little bitter. "I'd hoped they'd been running from our relentless on-slaught." He looked up at her. "But they're off to help the Irons."

"Aye. They're already heading there."

"You've seen it."

"I've seen what the gods have shown me."

"Could the gods be lying?"

"Of course. But we both know they aren't this time."

Brastias nodded. "So we follow."

"Take the Eastern Pass. If I remember the terrain correctly, you'll be able to cut the Sovereign army in half."

He nodded, turned to the commanders of Annwyl's legions. "We move. Now," he ordered. "Bring only what each man needs. No more."

"And Annwyl?" one of the commanders asked.

So Brastias wouldn't have to lie to his men, Morfyd quickly answered, "I go to her now. But everyone is moving at this moment. Understand?"

The commander's eyes narrowed a bit, but he wasn't about to challenge Morfyd. Although her reputation was nothing like Annwyl's—Morfyd simply didn't have the body count to her name—they still knew Morfyd was a She-dragon not to be trifled with.

The men left to get their legions moving and Brastias wrapped his hand around her ankle, sweetly squeezing it.

"Anything?" he asked, his voice very quiet.

"No. Annwyl and the others are blocked from my sight."

"Also down to your helpful gods?"

"I really don't know. The west, past the Aricia Mountains, has always been blocked from my sight and my mother's. Whether that's due to the gods or a very powerful witch or mage . . . I do not know."

"Don't worry, luv. If there has always been one thing I've had faith in, it's been our mad queen."

Morfyd leaned down in her saddle and kissed Brastias. When she pulled away, she whispered, "Watch your back, my love. There are always those working against our queen and those loyal to her."

"Aye," he answered sadly. "That I do know."

She left him then, knowing she'd stay behind for a bit. She'd stay behind and wait. Although she had no idea why.

And watching Annwyl's men scramble to head off for more blood and death in battle under Annwyl's banner, Morfyd realized she no longer had any choice but to do what she'd been resisting since she'd realized Annwyl had gone off with Morfyd's cousin and niece.

She would now have to contact her mother.

When they were no more than three miles outside of Garbhán Isle, Ren suddenly stopped, bringing the rest of them up short. The Eastlander looked so tired that if Dark Plains had been any farther away, Vigholf would have had to carry him.

"What is it?" Rhona asked Ren.

"They know I'm here. The Kyvich. And they are not pleased."

"Why?"

"Perhaps they know what I'm doing. I don't know."

"You wait here." Rhona motioned to Vigholf. "Watch them while I let the others know we're here. The last thing we want is the Kyvich to panic over Ren's presence and all my cousins need to see is a bloody Lightning about before they—"

Rhona shoved him. A good thing too with that giant, steel spear shooting straight at him. But Rhona's brown claws caught it in mid-flight, the steel tip inches from Vigholf's throat. The pair stared at each other.

"Thank you," he murmured.

"You're welcome," Rhona replied just before a big fist slammed into the back of Vigholf's head, shoving him forward.

Rhona flew out of the way when Vigholf was suddenly moving toward her due to that silver-scaled fist to the back of his head. Then another fist, this time black, slammed into the Lightning, forcing Vigholf back. But it wasn't some enemy dragons who'd followed them to Dark Plains, but her Uncle Addolgar, the Silver—and good gods! Her father!

While both males mercilessly pummeled Vigholf within an inch of his life, Rhona shoved the spear into Keita's hands, ignoring the royal's squeal when it nearly dragged her to the ground below, and quickly flew between the battling males.

"Daddy! Addolgar! No!"

Her father stopped immediately, but Addolgar kicked Vigholf in the face, sending the Lightning flipping back in midair.

She cringed, feeling bad for the Northlander. But seeing her father again . . .

Heartless female! He was getting battered by the wench's kin, and instead of coming to his defense, she was busy hugging some bloody Fire Breather. Where was the loyalty?

The older silver dragon had his broadsword out, aiming it toward Vigholf's head. Vigholf yanked his hammer off his back, swinging it through the air, mostly to block the sword. But if he happened to hit the dragon's head in the process . . .

But before Vigholf's hammer could hit anything, it was caught and held in a strong claw, as was the older dragon's sword.

"My daughter," the big black dragon with red-tinged scales told them calmly, "said to stop. So you'll stop. Even you, Addolgar."

The Silver snarled and yanked his broadsword away. "Someone should have warned us you were coming here,

Northlander. Thought you were a threat. Didn't realize you were just more Lightning scum."

"I'm so glad we have that truce with you," Vigholf muttered, wiping the blood that dripped from his nostrils.

"Uncle Addolgar fought against Northlanders in at least three wars, including against your father," Rhona explained. "So you shouldn't take it personally that he sees you all as worthless scum."

Vigholf stared at the female. "How does that help the situation?" he demanded.

"I'll escort you back," the black dragon told them all, his smirk reminding Vigholf of Rhona, "so the Lightning can arrive without being accosted. Poor, weak little thing."

"Daddy," Rhona—barely—chastised.

The dragon laughed and, after taking the steel spear from a still-struggling Keita and tossing it back to Rhona, headed toward Garbhán Isle, Keita and Ren beside him. Vigholf caught Rhona's forearm. "Daddy?"

"Be glad he was here, Lightning. He's one of the few strong enough to stop my Uncle Addolgar from doing anything."

Rhona made her way back to the castle, flying over the gates and landing in the courtyard.

The castle grounds weren't at all like Rhona remembered. Instead of the cheerful place with all the vendors in the courtyard and outside the castle grounds, it had become a military outpost. Siege weapons lined the inside of the walls and someone had begun to build a moat. Only a small portion was finished, but already there was something alive and rather unfriendly looking swimming in the murky water.

No. This wasn't the place she remembered.

Rhona nodded at cousins, smiled at aunts and uncles,

but it was her father she ran to, her father whose arms she threw herself into.

"My girl," Sulien the Smithy whispered, gripping her tight. "My beautiful, precious girl."

"Oh, Daddy, I've missed you so."

"And I you." He stepped back, looked her over, and smiled. "So beautiful."

She handed over the stainless steel spear that had nearly impaled the Lightning. "Not one of yours," she noted.

"You know my work." He leaned in, whispered, "This is shoddy." He motioned to the emergency spear strapped to her back. "And where's your spear?"

Rhona glared over at the Lightning who'd landed behind her father. "It's in pieces," she complained.

"It was an accident," Vigholf shot back. "I told you I was sorry."

"But you didn't mean it!"

"Don't worry," her father soothed. "I have something for you anyway." His brown eyes sparkled. "Something better."

Rhona grinned, feeling real excitement. "What? Tell me!"

"Get settled in first. I'm sure you're here for a reason, so finish all that, then find me at the forge."

Her father smiled at her, his claw petting her cheek. "Glad you're back, little one. Will you be staying long?"

"I'll probably head back tomorrow."

"Then we'll make the most of our time today."

Chapter 9

"We're heading back tomorrow?" Vigholf asked Rhona once her father was gone. "You don't think they need us here?"

"Unless my orders change . . ."

"Right, right." Gods, this woman and her bloody orders. "I just don't want to leave this place undefended."

For a brief moment he saw the concern on Rhona's face, but then one of the Kyvich walked between them, ignoring the much bigger dragons surrounding her. The witch carried the head of some human male. It looked to be a foreigner, but still. . . . "Jesella," the witch called out and tossed the head to another witch. "You know what to do with that. Tonight's a full moon."

"Where's the rest of the body? You know I need the fingers and tongue as well!"

Rhona smirked at Vigholf. "I'm heading back tomorrow," she said, walking off.

He watched her, unable to figure her out. She could be such a babysitter, caring for everyone, and the next a cold, uncaring, "I'm only following orders, sir" soldier.

"Lord Vigholf?"

Vigholf turned his focus to the ground and smiled. "Lady Dagmar."

Dagmar Reinholdt. The Northland woman his brother Ragnar had taken under his wing, educating her and making her as devious as Ragnar could be. At the time Vigholf didn't know why. He'd found nothing very interesting about Dagmar Reinholdt with her plain face and small body. But he thought perhaps Ragnar wanted her as a pet. Not for sexual reasons—she was much too young for any of that and Vigholf wouldn't have allowed it—but for general amusement. Like a puppy or a kitten. Yet Ragnar had paid too much attention to her education, her health, and the inadequacies of her eventual—and worthless—husbands.

Over the last few years, though, Vigholf had come to understand what had drawn his brother to the child and then the woman and why the Northland men—hard, brutal men rarely scared or intimidated by anything—had without humor or irony called her The Beast. Because Dagmar Reinholdt was brilliant. A strategist and politician, she wore reason and logic as her armor, playing her political games with the highest-ranking monarchs and, it was rumored, the gods. Her mind was such a vicious and deadly thing that Vigholf now realized it was better to have Dagmar Reinholdt on their side rather than against it.

"You must be starving, my lord."

"I am, but I'd like to see my mother first."

"She's been staying at Devenallt Mountain with the other Northland dragon females. I've sent word, so your mother will be escorted here soon. Until then"—she motioned to the castle—"let's get you fed."

Vigholf knew that tone. He heard it from Ragnar all the time. "I don't have much choice in this, do I, my lady?"

Her smile was small—and cold. "No, my lord. You don't."

* * *

Naked and in human form by the lake where her kin had made camp, Rhona studied the many scars littering her body. "I'm like a bleedin' pin cushion," she muttered.

"Rhona?"

Rhona turned, smiled. "Hello, Talaith."

"Think we can talk?" her cousin Briec's beautiful mate asked, and Rhona could hear the concern in the woman's voice. The stress. Not surprising. Most of them gone for five years, with no visits from her daughter for the entire time and none from Briec after the first two.

Rhona looked down at herself. "Got any clean clothes I can wear? Mine are all a bit stinky at the moment."

Talaith laughed a little. "Maybe in Annwyl's closet."

"That'll do." She started to head away from the camp, but Talaith caught her arm, pulled her back.

"Here." Talaith took off the fur cape she wore and wrapped it around Rhona's naked body. "At least until we get inside. For the sake of the servants."

"Such a prude," Rhona teased.

"I'm worried," Talaith admitted when they were away from Rhona's kin but not quite at the castle gates. "I haven't heard from Briec in several days."

"You've heard from Briec?" Usually only immediate blood relations could contact each other directly and at long distances. Unless, of course, they were . . .

"Witch," Talaith reminded Rhona. One of those Desert Land witches, mortal enemies of the Kyvich, Rhona had heard. So having the scantily clad, tattooed females around must be especially hard for Talaith. "Learning to contact my mate was one of the easier things I've had to relearn since the return of my powers. And with a little more effort and a lot less complaining, Briec could be an amazing mage, so it's been quite easy. I don't hear from him every day, but he's never gone this long. . . ."

"When I left all was well. We're at a standstill." Although

Rhona was well aware all that could change in a moment. But what was the point of worrying her?

"Can you check with your mum?" Talaith asked.

Rhona stopped walking, tightened the fur around her body. "Uh . . ."

"Uh? Uh what?"

"No one's supposed to know I'm here."

"Why the hells not?"

"Keita—"

"Och! That female!" Talaith raised her hand to silence Rhona's immediate defense of her cousin. "What is she up to now?"

"Maybe you should ask—"

"Forget it." Talaith caught Rhona's hand, pulling her along with a surprising amount of strength. Then again, Rhona did often forget that Talaith was once an assassin. A very good one.

With a little snarl, Talaith said, "Let's find that damn female."

"How is everything going?" Dagmar asked while Vigholf tucked into a heaping bowl of delicious-smelling beef stew.

"Fine."

The bowl suddenly disappeared, his spoon dangling in midair.

"You'd get between a dragon and his food?" Vigholf asked, only half seriously.

"When he insists on answering my question like a true Northland male—yes." She lifted the bowl, holding it in both hands. The scent of it wafted to his nose and Vigholf couldn't help but growl a little. "But unlike most of my countrymen, you can and do create and execute full and complete sentences. So I ask again . . . how is everything going?"

"I see my brother has taught you very well." Honestly, during the last five years, Vigholf had been forced to stretch his opinion on what was right for females to be involved in and what was not.

"Yes. Your brother did train me well," she replied. "And he told me I could trust you as I trust him."

Those words meant much to Vigholf because his brother would have never said them to Dagmar unless he'd meant it. "You can, my lady."

"Dagmar. Please."

"First off, Dagmar, your mate is well. Mean. But well."

"Mean?" She placed the bowl of food back in front of him. "Are you sure you have the right—"

"Gwenvael the Ruiner, yes?"

She nodded, eyes wide behind those spectacles his brother had made for her many years ago.

"He is quite . . . loyal to you, I'm afraid," Vigholf explained. "And has been for the last five years. But for someone like him that is not easy. Especially since, like his brothers, he has not returned here for the last three years. He's turned impatient, mean, and nasty; and he takes it out on the rest of us—and the enemy. The Irons call him Gwenvael the Defiler."

The woman burst into laughter, something Vigholf never thought he'd hear from the dour little human. She stuttered to a stop. "Sorry. Private joke. And . . . uh . . . why do they call him that?"

"He has a tendency to dismember the bodies. Sometimes while the owner of that body still breathes. I told you . . . he's become quite mean without you."

"I see."

"As to the war itself . . ." Vigholf sighed. "That's a bit more complicated, I'm afraid."

* * *

Rhona pulled on a sleeveless chain-mail shirt, brown leather leggings, and knee-high black leather boots. Thankfully, Annwyl was close to Rhona's size. The height of the boots covered up that the leggings were a tad short, and the fact that the human queen had larger tits gave Rhona more room in the shirt for her bigger shoulders.

And while Rhona pulled on the queen's clothes, the queen's sisters-by-mating argued like two angry harpies.

"How could you not tell them?" Talaith demanded of Keita. "You should have told Briec and Fearghus."

"And give Vateria exactly what she wanted? You seem to forget, sister, that I am a Protector of the Throne."

"Blah, blah, blah!"

"I made the decision to tell my brothers nothing, but I'm here to protect my nieces and nephew myself with the help of Ren. So please . . . *get over it already!*" Keita looked at Rhona in the mirror. "And you should have kept your gods-damn mouth shut."

"I'm off duty, cousin, which by Cadwaladr law means I *can* beat you ugly."

Talaith blinked. "There's Cadwaladr laws?"

"When necessary," Rhona said, and picked up her sword and the remnants of her beloved spear. "You two argue this out. I'm off to find my father."

"You're leaving?" Keita demanded.

Rhona faced her cousin. "You asked me to escort you and Ren here safely. You're now here safely. What you do from here is up to you." She walked to the bedroom door. "I'm off at dawn," she told them and walked out, closing the door behind her.

Talaith watched her mate's cousin leave the room. "Is she all right?"

"She's Rhona."

"What does that mean?"

"It means what it says—she's Rhona. Now let's get something to eat. I'm starving for *real* food."

Talaith locked her gaze back on Keita. "Don't try to change the subject—Ren's not taking my daughter any-bloody-where."

Keita pressed her fingers to her temples. "If you'd only listen—"

"No. She and her cousins are perfectly safe here, Keita. I'll not risk sending them to a country I know nothing about with Ren. Or anyone that's not me, Briec, or Izzy."

"But—"

"No. And that's the end of it. And just so we're clear, don't think for a second you'll get the twins past the Kyvich. I know that coven. They'll hunt Ren down and rip the scales from his hide. So if I were you, sister, I'd let this go."

Dagmar and Vigholf walked into the Great Hall from the kitchen. "When are you leaving?" Dagmar asked.

"Tomorrow, I think. I'm traveling with Rhona and if I don't keep an eye on her, she'll scurry off without per-mission."

Dagmar stopped and looked up at him. Vigholf was as handsome as his brother, but in a different way. Maybe it was the scar across his jaw. Because nothing about him looked as innocent as Ragnar the Cunning. "Keep an eye on her?"

"Someone has to."

"You do know she's a—"

"A Cadwaladr. *Yes.* I'm quite aware of her blood ties since everyone keeps reminding me," he finished on a mutter. Although Dagmar only thought of Vigholf as her friend's brother, she still felt the need to make it perfectly clear to him how things were with many Southland females.

"I wouldn't crowd, my lord. I've found the females of this clan and this territory hate that."

"I'm not crowding. I'm . . . helping."

"I'm a Northlander, too, Vigholf. I know how the males of my country 'help' females. It can be smothering for some of us. I don't know Rhona well, but if she's like the rest of her kin . . ."

"I'm careful. It just seems like she watches out for everyone else but no one watches out for her. Besides . . . I think she likes it."

"Really?"

"Yes. She just hasn't realized it yet."

"Aaah," Dagmar said at the same moment Rhona bounded down the castle stairs, her weapons strapped to her back and wearing what appeared to be the clothes Annwyl had left behind.

"Did you eat?" Vigholf demanded as she headed out the Great Hall's big front doors.

Rhona's answer was to flick two fingers at Vigholf and keep going.

"See?" Vigholf pointed out with a shocking amount of confidence. "She likes it."

Now Dagmar knew. When it came to females, Vigholf was nothing like his brother—but he *was* a true Northlander.

Sulien held up the broken spear, one piece in each hand. "A warhammer did this?"

"You saw that hammer the Lightning almost hit Addolgar with. And that's not even the one he uses during battles. That one is bloody huge. Nearly as big as the bastard's head."

Her father chuckled and stepped around her. "The only

purpose of this spear was to protect you—and it did. Its job is now done."

He started to throw the pieces into a bin he kept for trash.

"Don't you dare throw that out."

"Why not? It's broken, and repairing it would be useless. It'll only break again."

"But you made it for me."

"You cling to what is meaningless, child. Just like your mother sometimes, only with her it's mostly grudges."

He tossed the spear into the trash, and Rhona had to fight every instinct she had to not dive into that bucket after it.

"Besides," her father continued, "I have something better."

Sulien crouched in front of a trunk, opened it. "I was going to give it to you when I saw you back at home, but this is even better."

Her father stood and handed her a small metal stick. She'd guess it was only three feet long—and that was it.

"Oh . . . a stick. How . . . uh . . . nice."

"Don't be foolish, Rhona. It's more than a stick."

He took it from her, held it in his big hand. And Rhona smiled when a sharpened tip suddenly appeared at the end. "Oh! It's a long knife."

Then it extended another four or five feet, turning it into a metal spear. "Oh, Daddy! That's—"

It extended again and grew wider, stretching to and through the opening at the top of the tent.

Eyes wide, Rhona grinned. "That's . . ." She simply didn't have words for what it was. There were quite a few weapons among their kind, many of them created by her father or his kin, that could extend from small to big and back again, so that the dragons using them wouldn't have to constantly switch weapons depending on their current forms. Usually banging the weapon at a certain angle on its base extended it or a shield and they were easy enough to make small again.

But this . . .

"No matter what form you're in, you've got a weapon."

"What do I press?"

"Nothing." The spear quickly slipped into its original size, and her father handed it to her.

"But . . ." After years of training by her father's side, before she'd joined Her Majesty's Army, Rhona knew what was needed for their weapons to work. "Don't you need a chant? A spell? Something?"

"Only in the creation of it." He leaned in. "Want me to show you?"

"Are you joking? *Yes!*"

He laughed. "Go on and try it first. See what it can do."

Rhona held the weapon in her hand. It seemed so . . . ordinary. A metal stick. Nothing more. But then she called for the tip and it was there. She used her free hand to touch it.

"Careful," her father warned. "It's bloody sharp."

It was. And Rhona was delighted.

She called forth the spear, and the weapon lengthened and grew. It was the perfect height for her, too. As tall as her with the tip extending just past her head.

Rhona dropped into a crouch, one leg stretched out to the side, the weapon now in both hands. A low attack.

Her father stood back and watched her, his smile warm. When she was younger and home more, they often did this. He'd create new weapons and she'd try them out for him. It was the main reason she had proficiency with more weapons than most Dragonwarriors.

She thrust the spear, stood, and swiped it through the air.

"Daddy, I love the weight."

"Light, yeah? But combined with your strength . . . deadly just the same."

"I love it," she gushed. "I absolutely love it."

"Call its full length. You can still handle it while human even at that length and width."

Excited to try, Rhona aimed the weapon toward the exit and away from her father. She called forth the dragon-sized weapon and happily watched as it grew in her hands, the length of it reaching past the tent flaps and—

"Owwwwww! *Gods-dammit, female!*"

With a thought, Rhona retracted her weapon. A few seconds later, the Lightning stumbled into the tent, blood flowing from his shoulder, lightning sparking from his body.

"I told ya!" he bellowed *"What happened to your spear was an accident!"*

They shoved Vigholf into a chair and the two Fire Breathers leaned down to get a better look at his wound. Without much effort, he could see the resemblance between father and daughter. Although Rhona was much prettier.

"He'll live," the male said, appearing quite disinterested in Vigholf's wound.

"Why is it when I come to this bloody kingdom by invitation, I'm nearly killed?"

"Luck?" Rhona asked.

Along with Ragnar and Meinhard, Vigholf had escorted Keita and Éibhear to the Southlands five years ago just before the war with the Irons began. He'd had his first introduction to the infamous Annwyl the Bloody when she'd charged him and Meinhard. Then, while they tried to keep the crazed monarch at bay, she'd gone for Vigholf's head— and took his hair instead. When it happened, it had been humiliating. A shame he was sure he'd never recover from. But as Vigholf got to know Annwyl better, he quickly realized that he was lucky to have kept his head at all.

Rhona's father leaned in to take a closer look at the wound. "I can fix this." He reached for him, and Vigholf couldn't help but scramble out of the chair that held him.

"No offense if I'd rather not be tended to by a blacksmith."

"Don't be such a baby," Rhona chastised. "Me da's good with a needle and thread."

"Your da can keep his needle and thread to himself, thanks."

Rhona folded her arms over her chest. "So what are you going to do? Wander around all evening bleeding like a stuck cow until you pass out and die and we're forced to quickly burn your remains so the stink of your corpse won't bother the children?"

"Your concern for my well-being overwhelms me, Sergeant."

"You shouldn't have been following me, *Commander*."

"Who said I was?"

"Common sense?"

"I don't know who that is," he muttered, turning away and looking over the blacksmith's work area.

"If you're not going to let my father tend your wounds, at least see the healers by the lake. They'll help you."

"No need." Vigholf, pulling off his chain-mail shirt, walked over to the forge and picked up a poker that still sat in the burning coals.

"Wait—" Rhona cried out as he pressed the poker to his open wound, sealing it closed. It hurt, but nothing he couldn't handle. Once he knew he'd stopped the bleeding, Vigholf pulled the poker away, ignoring the bits of skin that went with it, and tossed it back into the forge. When he faced father and daughter, he found them gawking at him. Rhona's mouth was open, but her father was grinning, even laughing a little.

"You are a mad bastard," she whispered.

"What? It's done, isn't it?" He pulled his shirt back on. "Now—" Vigholf began until that familiar scent caught his attention, and he moved quickly toward the tent opening, ignoring the way Rhona scrabbled out of his way as if he was some dangerous animal.

Such an odd female.

Rhona watched the crazed male walk out of her father's forge and she couldn't help but follow, curious to see what had caught his relentless attention. She was taken by surprise, though, when she saw the Lightning put his arms around an older She-dragon in human form.

"Mum," she heard him whisper.

"My dear, sweet son," the female whispered back. "Oh, how I've missed you so."

All right. That surprised Rhona. Not that the Lightning had a mother, but that he'd treat her so . . . tenderly.

Rhona's father tapped her shoulder and she stepped back into the tent.

"You want to tell me what's going on? Why are you *really* here?" her father asked, and all Rhona could do was shrug.

"You know me, Daddy. I follow orders and don't ask questions. Especially when it's all coming from the royal side of my kin."

"Not like your mother at all."

"As she likes to remind me."

Her father put his arm around her shoulders. "She just doesn't understand you. But it's not your job to help her with that."

"But—"

"No time to discuss." He laughingly pushed her toward the forge. "You've got work to do, child. And I have much to teach you in a short amount of time. So to work with you!"

"What are you doing here, Vigholf?" his mother asked, her hand reaching up and stroking his jaw. "Is everything all right?"

"Everything's fine, Mum. I promise."

"Then why—"

"It's complicated. But you," he asked, changing the subject, "are you all right? Are you safe?"

"I've been treated like a princess since I've been here." Davon the Elegant leaned in and whispered, "I'm considered a returned prisoner of war, so they're all very gentle with me and give me lots of things. It's been nice."

"Mum."

"Well, if it hadn't been for my wonderful sons, it would have been horrible living with your father. But you all looked out for me. So it's easy for me to sit back and enjoy the pity."

"As long as you're safe, Mum. That's all Ragnar and I care about. That's all we've ever cared about."

She pushed long gold hair behind her ear. "I'm fine. I promise."

He stepped back and took his mother's hand. "Then I want you to meet someone."

"Oh?"

"No. Nothing like that," he laughed and pulled her toward the tent, lifting the flap so he could escort her in. But Vigholf stopped right at the entrance, his eyes on Rhona as she worked at her father's forge with a skill he'd only seen in blacksmiths who'd been working for hundreds of years. She swung a hammer, working away at some weapon.

Yet it wasn't just the skill that startled him. It was the joy on her face while she worked and laughed with her father. It was that *thing* that had been missing when he watched her following orders and flying into battle.

"My," his mother murmured. "She's quite . . . hearty." She glanced up at him. "A Cadwaladr, I'm assuming."

"We traveled here together."

"And you like her."

"Not really," he blatantly lied. "She just needs protection and like a true Northlander, it's my duty to protect helpless females."

"Helpless?" His mother looked over at Rhona. The Fire Breather lifted the sword she worked on, still glowing bright from the heat. The grin on her face, the light in her eyes . . . it was a beautiful sight to behold. Rhona put the blade in water to cool and caught another weapon her father tossed at her. A good-sized battle-ax. She swung it a few times, then threw it, the blade imbedding into the stuffed head of the practice dummy standing in the corner.

His mother nodded. "Oh, yes. I see now, my son. She's *extremely* helpless."

Chapter 10

Rhona stopped not far from the Garbhán Isle gates. The gates lined with Kyvich witches keeping watch. She'd forgotten how imposing the human females could be.

In one lone line, they snaked around the top of the gate walls, a shorter spear called a pilum gripped in each witch's hand. Considering it was winter, they wore little clothes. Mostly animal skins and bits of armor covering the important areas and arteries. But it was the black tattoos that marked their faces and/or necks. There was no uniformity in those markings or in the way the females dressed or looked—and yet there was no doubt they were a unified army. A deadly and well-trained one that had no mercy, no heart, and no loyalty but to those their gods had chosen for them.

"Disturbing to look at, aren't they?" the Lightning asked as he stepped up beside her. She'd lost track of him while she'd worked in her father's forge, learning all sorts of new and wonderful blacksmithing techniques. "They've been around for at least a millennia in the Ice Lands and they've been feared since the beginning."

"Can they really be trusted?"

"They follow the dictates of their gods without question."

"So then the answer is no. They can't be trusted."

Vigholf laughed. "Not a fan of the gods then?"

"I call them if I need them, but I'd be a fool to trust them."

"I like the war gods."

Rhona crossed her eyes. "Of course you do."

"So"—Vigholf faced her—"would you like to have dinner tonight with me and my mother?"

"No."

He scowled. "Why not?"

"Well, first off I'm having dinner with my father, and second . . . no."

"You don't like my mother," he accused.

"I don't know your mother."

"And you never will . . . unless you have dinner with us." His grin was wide . . . and a tad ridiculous—in an annoyingly adorable way. "Bring your father."

"You're getting stranger every day, I just want to make that clear."

"That's not a no to my dinner invitation."

At that point, Rhona was going to walk away, but that soft sound caught her attention first. A sound they both heard.

After so much combat, it wasn't surprising they both moved quickly, turning to face the small storage building on the left side of their path. Rhona dropped to a crouch, the tip of her wonderful new spear pointed directly in front of her. Vigholf stayed tall, his warhammer held high in one hand, a battle-ax in the other. She'd seen him use both at the same time to devastating effect for the enemy.

Vigholf motioned to her with a dip of his head and Rhona, keeping low, moved forward, the Lightning guarding her rear.

Then it came at them from the brush that lined the side of the building. Teeth snapping, small blade slashing. Reacting without thought, as Northlanders had been trained to do in combat, Vigholf stepped in front of Rhona, hammer raised high, but she slammed into his side, sending him stumbling a few feet away.

"What the holy hells—"

Rhona reached out and caught hold of their attacker, lifting it in the air, and holding it up so the Lightning could see it.

"It seems my cousin's offspring takes after his Great-Grandfather Ailean. He liked the surprise attack as well, according to me mum."

The boy, seeing he was well and truly caught, burst into dramatic tears and Rhona sighed. "And, sadly, he takes after his Uncle Gwenvael. This is Talan," she reminded Vigholf. "Fearghus and Annwyl's son who we've rushed here to protect."

"I remember. But where's the girl? Talwyn?" Vigholf demanded, his gaze searching, an air of anxiety rippling around him. "Where there's the boy, there's his sister."

Rhona shook the boy she still held. "Where is she, little snake?"

He wailed louder and Rhona glanced up at the Kyvich to make sure they weren't taking any of this seriously. And although they watched her and Vigholf closely, they made no moves to step in. Good. They knew their place. They may be protectors, but Rhona was family.

"For the love of the gods," a voice said from behind them, "stop the wailing."

Rhona smiled and faced the centaur. "Hello, Ebba. How's the nanny business going for you?"

"I won't say they're unmanageable," the pretty centaur told them as they slowly made their way back toward the castle. "But they are the reason I'm paid so well." She smiled. "I've already bought land near the ocean. Lovely view."

She walked a few more feet and stopped next to a tree with a large hole beside the base.

An empty hole.

"Uh-oh."

Vigholf didn't like the sound of that at all. "Uh-oh?"

"I left Talwyn here."

"You left a child buried in the ground?" Rhona demanded.

"She was just buried up to her neck. Besides, I didn't put her in there. He did." The centaur pointed at the boy. "Didn't you, little monster?"

Still held by the back of his trousers by Rhona, Talan grinned.

"Of course," Ebba observed. "She's loose now. And she'll be coming for you, little monster."

The boy's grin faded.

"Are you staying long, Rhona?" Ebba asked as they continued heading to the castle.

"No. I'm leaving in the morning. Back to the Valley."

"Good. The sooner this war ends, the sooner these little monsters get their parents back." She lovingly smiled at the boy. "And I can finally take a bloody holiday."

Rhona had known Ebba for years. She'd met her mother, Bríghid, when she'd taken over the care of Keita for that short time. It was strange how the much smaller centaurs made such good caregivers for young dragons, though their powers were legendary and they tolerated no fools. Although Rhona had never seen it, she'd heard that an army of centaurs could devastate kingdoms when pushed too far. *Anyone's* kingdom. The problem, though, was to get centaurs as a group to agree on anything. So there weren't many times that they challenged any kingdoms but their own.

They neared the steps that would lead into the Great Hall, and Rhona glanced around and said, "All this . . . preparation?"

"Our Battle Lord is quite cautious," Ebba explained, speaking of Dagmar. "The local merchants have all been moved to nearby towns and only those who live here, are invited by those who live here, or are part of the Queen's army are allowed entry. Everyone takes the children's safety very seriously." They walked up the stairs to the castle's Great Hall. "Although I don't know why."

Rhona stopped right in the doorway. "Why would you say that?"

Ebba had only a chance to raise a brow before the boy was ripped from Rhona's hand by his dirt-covered sister. She attacked silently, only growling once the pair had hit the floor in a flurry of fists and sibling rage.

The girl, glaring like Rhona's Uncle Bercelak, got her brother on his back and head-butted him. Twice.

"Awww," Rhona observed, feeling nostalgic. "Just like our Aunt Ghleanna."

"I need to eat," Vigholf announced, apparently not feeling nostalgic at all.

"He constantly needs to be fed," Rhona complained, watching her young cousins rolling across the floor.

"Should I starve instead?"

"Yes." She watched the twins a bit longer. "Should we separate them?"

Ebba pulled a red dress over her now-human form. "If you'd like."

Rhona reached down and took hold of the siblings, yanking them apart. It didn't stop them from trying to rip each other into shreds, though. "Are they like this all the time?"

"Only when they're not torturing others."

"Do they speak?" Rhona had yet to hear anything from the pair but snarling, snapping, and growling. It was disconcerting.

"Only to each other and only in whispers." Ebba brushed her long, reddish brown hair from her face. "We try not to be terrified by that."

"I need to eat," Vigholf said again.

Rhona faced him, shaking the snarling children for emphasis. "Can you not see we're talking?"

"About babysitting." And he grinned at her when he said it. "Shocking."

Her eyes narrowed, daring him to call her that blasted nickname.

There were screams from the courtyard and panicked humans running. "How nice." Ebba took the children from Rhona's hands. "Queen Rhiannon's here."

"Oh," Rhona said. She glanced at Vigholf, but he was already staring at her. She nodded and said, "I have to go. Need to clean up, meeting my father for dinner."

"Me too," Vigholf chimed in. "What I mean is . . . meeting *my* father. Wait, no, he's dead."

"Your mother. You're meeting your *mother*."

"Right, right. Mum."

And with that, they scattered. It wasn't dignified or remotely brave, but it was necessary because neither of them wanted to face the queen.

"Ren can have the portal open in a day," Keita explained to Dagmar, Talaith, and the Kyvich leader, Ásta.

"And then what?" Dagmar asked.

"I'm not going to—"

Dagmar raised a finger, stopping Talaith's potential tirade. "And then what?" she asked Keita again.

"He takes them to the Eastlands. They'll be safe there.

His parents will be happy to help." She smiled. "They adore me."

"I'm sure they do. But that doesn't mean they'll adore the children."

"While I appreciate your eagerness to help, Princess," Ásta cut in, "I will not allow you or this foreigner to take the children from our care."

Keita's eyes narrowed and Dagmar warned, "Don't you dare unleash flame in this room, Keita."

"It won't matter if she does," Ásta smugly boasted. "A dragon's flame means nothing to a Kyvich."

Ren stepped forward; the handsome Eastland dragon looked so very tired that Dagmar worried about him. But Keita had come here with her grand ideas about rescuing her nieces and nephew, so whether she noticed the wear on her friend was anyone's guess. "On my word and the honor of my family, those children will be protected with the dying breaths of my kin, if need be."

"I believe you," Dagmar said. "But Commander Ásta—"

"Their leader's Magick is strong, but not as strong as mine." Ren said, sounding surprisingly cocky—Dagmar assumed that was because he was too tired to hide his natural dragon-based arrogance. "And she knows it."

"What I know," Ásta warned, stepping closer to Ren, "is that I do not fear any dragon. Even the Snow dragons out of the Ice Lands stay out of the path of the Kyvich—and I can assure you they are stronger than you could ever dream, foreigner."

"*I'm* the foreigner?"

Dagmar raised her hands. "If we could all calm down—"

Ásta slapped her hands together. Dagmar saw nothing, but the way that Talaith's eyes grew wide and she pushed away from the table, Dagmar knew something Magick-related was happening in front of her. "Perhaps it's time you learn your place, foreigner. And remember that no one takes those children anywhere without our permission."

Ren raised his hand and Talaith scrambled to her feet. "Stop it! Both of you!"

Dagmar still couldn't see anything, but that didn't mean she couldn't be affected by it. "I'd like us all to calm down," Dagmar began. "Before this gets out of—"

The war-room door slammed open and the Dragon Queen of the Southlands swept in. She held Talan in her arms and had Talwyn hanging from her neck. The queen seemed to be the one being who could calm the children down without doing anything. None of them, however, had figured out how she managed that.

"There you all are. I've been searching for you for at least two minutes! The only ones to greet me were Ebba and my darling grandchildren." She grinned at the boy in her arms. "So adorable!"

"Mother—" Keita began.

"What's going on?" Rhiannon asked, her eyes seeing what Dagmar's never could. "Oh, honestly. You *children*." She flicked the fingers of her left hand and Ásta flew back, hitting the wall hard. Ren gasped, dropping to his knees.

"Ren!" Keita ran to her friend's side, putting her arms around his shoulders.

"It's gone," Ren said through hard pants. "The portal. It's gone. She's closed it."

"Opening a doorway in my territory without *my* permission?" Rhiannon accused. "You should know better, Ren of the Chosen. But I'm assuming it was my daughter's idiotic idea."

"I was trying to help, you crazed viper!"

"Don't bellow at me, demon spawn!" She pointed at Ásta. "And you! Don't threaten anyone without my permission, barbarian witch."

"Is there a reason you're here, my lady?" Dagmar asked,

knowing the Dragon Queen hadn't come down here to simply entertain Dagmar. And gods, Dagmar was quite entertained. "Or just dropping by for your weekly torture?"

The queen smirked and answered, "We have a problem, little barbarian."

"Bigger than the Western Tribes descending upon us as we speak? Which they are, according to Keita."

"Aye. Bigger than that. I heard from Morfyd. . . . Annwyl's gone."

Keita pressed her hand to her chest. "Annwyl's . . . dead?"

"Did I say dead? I don't think I said dead."

"Then what the hells did you say?"

"Again with the yelling?"

"My liege . . ." Dagmar pushed.

"She's gone," Rhiannon said again. "As in Morfyd woke up one day and Annwyl was gone."

"Kidnapped?" Talaith asked.

"No. Just gone. Along with Izzy and Branwen."

Talaith's eyes grew wide in panic at the mention of her eldest daughter. "That crazed bitch took Izzy?"

Rhiannon pursed her lips. "Ooops. Bercelak warned me not to tell you that part."

"But you did! You did tell me!"

"Now *you're* yelling at me?"

Dagmar stood. "Everyone stop. Right now." She motioned to Ásta. "Commander, if you would excuse us."

Trying to shake off whatever Rhiannon had done to her, Ásta got to her feet and walked to the door.

"And could you take the children back to Ebba please?"

The children jumped down from their grandmother and charged out of the room, Ásta following and closing the door behind her while Keita helped Ren into a chair.

Once all had calmed down, Dagmar looked to the She-dragon queen in human form. "Now, my liege. Perhaps you could explain what the battle-fuck is going on."

Rhona kissed her father good-bye and left him at the base of the large hill he called home. He didn't like staying at Devenallt Mountain, had no desire to reside by the lake with the Cadwaladr Clan, and he didn't like sleeping in a bed like a human. So he found and dug out his own place in a hill no more than ten miles or so from the Garbhán Isle gates and was as happy as any dragon could be. Her father was an uncomplicated male, easily pleased but just as easily annoyed. And, like most of his volcano-loving kind, he was even more solitary than the Fire Breathers.

Walking through the nearby town, desperate to get to sleep, she passed a pub. It sounded as if everyone inside was having quite a good time, but she kept walking. She wanted to be up early tomorrow and on her way before the two suns were high in the sky.

And Rhona knew what would happen if she went into that pub. Well, what would happen besides the drinking.

The pub door slammed open and Rhona picked up her step, hoping to get past before she was—

"Rhona!"

Strong hands grabbed hold of her and hauled her into the pub. Her aunts and uncles were nowhere to be seen, but the majority of her cousins, mostly the females, were in attendance.

Rhona was forced into a chair and a pint of ale shoved into her hand.

"Drink!" one cousin cheered. "And tell us all about the violence at the front!"

"Nothing happens here," another cousin complained. "For five years, no one's done anything and Mum won't let me go to the Valley. 'You're needed here,' she says. Here for what? Watching those demon spawn twins grow taller and meaner every day?" She leaned in and drunkenly whispered—which was really screaming—"And by the gods those two are so bloody mean!"

"Any new scars?" another asked.

"That Lightning you came in with . . . he's a big buck. You fuck him yet? If you didn't, are you going to? 'Cause . . . you know."

Rhona lifted her ale to her lips and drank it all in one gulp. Then she motioned to the barmaid and demanded another, her cousins cheering when she did.

Vigholf escorted his mother to the front steps outside the Great Hall. They'd had dinner in his room, had gone for a walk around the grounds, and during all that had talked for hours. Tonight she'd stay in the castle so they could enjoy breakfast together in the morning before he left.

With so many sons, Davon always managed to show each of them how much they were loved. Although they'd all known she had a special place in her heart for Ragnar. But Vigholf had understood that. Since Ragnar had hatched, their father had made it his business to crush Ragnar's soul rather than harness the dragon's power. Perhaps because Olgeir had known from the beginning that of all his offspring, Ragnar would be the one to bring him down.

"I'm so glad we had this time together," Davon told him before they went up the stairs.

"Me too. But this should all be over soon enough." Vigholf glanced down at his feet before asking the question that had been bothering him and his brothers. "And once this is over . . . will you come home?"

Davon blinked wide blue eyes. "Of course! Why would you think any different?"

He shrugged. "You weren't with the Horde of your own free will, Mum. I know that. So I can understand if you'd rather not come back."

"But I will. Because my sons are there. My grandsons. And you, your brothers—you've made it different now."

"It's really been Ragnar."

"He wouldn't have been able to do any of it without you and your brothers and Meinhard. And I've never hated the Northlands. I love it there. I merely hated your father—and he's dead now." Gods. She sounded so . . . perky.

"If you're sure."

"Of course I am. Now"—she took his hands into hers—"stop worrying about me. I'm perfectly safe here. I just want you to go back and help your brother win against those awful Irons."

"I will, Mum. Promise."

"Good. So . . ." His mother looked off and frowned.

"What's wrong?"

"I think your weak little friend could use some help."

Vigholf looked across the courtyard, and there was Rhona, leading her female kin toward the side door that would lead them back to the nearby lake. It wasn't an easy task, though, when She-dragons kept breaking off from the group and trying to make a run for it.

"Give me a moment, Mum."

"I'm going to bed, so take your time," she laughed.

Rhona caught hold of another cousin and yanked her back to the group.

Gods, she didn't have time for this. She should be in bed, getting a few hours' sleep before the suns rose and she returned to the armies in the valley. What she shouldn't be doing was dragging her kin from a brawl—that *they* started—in the middle of the nearby pub and trying to get them to bed.

When did that become her job?

Once Rhona got one cousin back in line with the others, another cousin made a run for it. Where were they running to? Most likely back to the pub for more drink and more fights. But before her cousin could get far, the Lightning was there, swooping up the She-dragon in one arm.

"Need help, Sergeant?" he teased.

Although Rhona would like to tell him no, she couldn't afford to at the moment.

"I just need to get them back to the lake. The aunts will take care of them from there."

"I can help with that. But what will I get out of it?"

Annoyed, she snapped, "Not to get my fist shoved up your—"

"Now, now. Let's not get nasty, Fire Breather."

"Are you helping or not?"

He picked up another one of her straying cousins in his free arm and motioned to her. "Lead the way, Babysitter."

"I hate that nickname."

"I know you do," Vigholf laughed. "I know you do."

Rhona may hate the nickname Babysitter, but she had to see how it fit her. At least that's how Vigholf felt as he watched the She-dragon chase down one of her cousins and tackle her to the ground. Once Rhona had her pinned, she grabbed her by the hair and dragged her back to the lakeside.

"Now stay!" she ordered the female, brown eyes fierce.

Vigholf chuckled until a hand reached up and gripped his crotch and twisted.

"Owwww!"

Rhona ran over and desperately tried to pull another cousin's hand off him.

"Let it go!"

"It's *huge*, Rhona! You should give it a feel."

Rhona dropped to her knees in front of him, one hand trying to pry the other female's fingers off him, the other pulling at her wrist. "I will. I promise. But you need to let go!"

The she-viper finally released him and Rhona flung her kin's arm away. Dropping back on her heels and panting, she looked up at Vigholf.

I am so sorry, she mouthed at him.

Vigholf nodded and forced himself not to rub his poor cock.

It took some time, but eventually they got all the females in their bedrolls and asleep. Once done, Vigholf and Rhona headed back to the castle.

"Well," he muttered, "that was fun."

"I'm sorry," she said again.

"No need to apologize. But I'm surprised you didn't keep your promise."

"Promise? What promise?"

"The one to your cousin to give it a feel." He glanced down at himself, gave her a wicked grin. "So you can see how huge it is."

"What are you talk . . ." She shook her head and laughed. "Gods, you're pathetic."

"I'm merely trying to help you keep your promises to your kin."

"Of course you are. Look, a few of my cousins may not be able to hold their liquor, especially when a male is around, but I assure you that I can."

Vigholf stopped, studied her when she faced him. "You drank tonight?"

"Drank more than any of them, that's for sure."

"And yet you're . . ."

"I'm what?"

"Sober."

She chuckled. "I'm my father's child, Northlander, and he can hold his liquor."

"Considering how badly off the rest of your cousins are, I have to say I'm impressed. You don't seem even a little different."

"What can I say? It's a gift." Rhona suddenly held up a finger as if to silence him—although he hadn't said anything—and then she sat down hard on the ground. Still holding up that one finger.

Vigholf crouched next to her. "You all right?"

"The universe began to spin, so I decided to sit until it stopped."

"Good plan."

Since he didn't know how long she'd need to sit, Vigholf sat beside her. He carefully took her raised finger and tucked it back into her fist.

"Thank you. I didn't seem to have control of that talon."

"Finger."

"Whatever." She smiled a little. "You can let go of my hand."

"I could, but probably won't. What with your universe spinning and all."

"Any opportunity. You Lightnings take any opportunity."

"There's truth to that, I'm afraid."

"You are, however, surprisingly light of touch."

"Pardon?"

"The way you're holding my hand. I always thought you'd be more of a mauler. Like a diseased wolf chewing the knuckles off me fist."

"That's very nice."

"Not really."

"I was being sarcastic."

"Oh. I see." Rhona gazed off for a moment, then asked, "Where are we?"

"Okay. That's it. I'm taking you to bed."

"No, no," she protested as Vigholf got to his knees. "I'm fine. I can walk."

"Is the universe still spinning?"

"No. Now it's just the trees."

"Right." He reached for her, put his arms around her. "I'll put you to bed and you'll feel better in the morning."

"I'd rather stay out here. Sleep under the stars."

"You don't like beds much, do you?"

"They're all right, I guess. But I'm just as happy on the ground, looking up at the sky."

"Then we'll do that."

Vigholf picked her up and carried her over to a big tree. With care, not wanting to bash her head against the ground, he set her down.

"This is nice," she said, smiling. "Can't see the stars, though. With all those branches and leaves in the way."

"I'm not destroying a tree so you can have a view of the sky. You'll have to imagine what it looks like."

"Such care about foliage."

"We don't have much in the way of lush trees and plants in the Northlands. So the ones strong enough to survive, we take care of."

Vigholf stretched out next to her, lying on his side and propping his head up with his hand.

"So you must be glad the fighting moved to Euphrasia," she said.

"I am. Especially the way you Fire Breathers just blast everything in your way." He smiled. "We have much more finesse with our lightning than you have with your flame."

"Yeah. Right," she laughed. "Finesse." Rhona looked at him. "You don't have to stay out here if you don't want. I'll be safe. My kin's right there." She pointed in front of her, then off to the side. Then she sort of flitted her hand about. "They're around."

"You act like I have somewhere to go. Besides, I want to stay here. Keep you company." When she frowned a bit, he added, "I like you. You and your little spear . . . cute."

She gazed at him for a long time before she asked, "Do you actually *like* me, or is any unattached female worth your time? You Northlanders do seem a bit hard up and I do have a pussy available. And it's been pretty unused lately."

It took a lot for him not to laugh. Mostly because he *knew* she'd regret all this come first light. And they had at least two and a half days of travel together back to Euphrasia during which he could absolutely torture her over it.

It was wrong, wasn't it? That he couldn't wait for the torturing.

Yeah. It was wrong.

The Lightning glanced off for a moment, probably trying to come up with some appropriate and smooth-worded lie. Males were all alike, weren't they? They'd say or do anything to find a warm hole for the night. Worthless. The lot of 'em. Bloody worthless.

Thankfully, Rhona wasn't like her cousins and most of her sisters. She didn't have what they all termed "needs." She could—and often did—go ages without a lover. Unlike Delen, the slut, who became right cranky when she'd gone for more than a few months without a cock, Rhona found better uses for any additional energy she may have stored up. She prided herself on that. So the dragon could just get that bloody look off his face.

"What look?"

"What?"

"You told me to get that bloody look off my face."

"Oh. Yeah." At least she hadn't said anything else out loud.

"That was after you mentioned you can go long periods of time without a bit of cock unlike your slutty sister Delen. Although I've never thought of her as slutty. Maybe a bit forceful—"

She slapped her hand over his face.

"Ow."

"If you even *think* of repeating anything I've drunkenly said here tonight—"

He pulled her hand away. "Not a word. Promise."

"I think I'm going to sleep before I say anything else about my sisters that they'd cut out my tongue for."

"All right."

"And we leave tomorrow, head back to the Valley, end this war, get all the glory we can stomach, and never see each other ever again. That's a plan we can both live with, right?"

"Possibly."

"And I'm sure I'm only saying this because of that last ale I had, but your human form . . . quite attractive."

"Thank you."

She lifted her hand, fingers sliding across his chin. "The scar on your jaw is a very nice touch."

Vigholf's eyes closed, he let out a breath. "You're killing me, Sergeant."

"Well, it's not like I haven't tried before. If it'll make you feel better . . . I have scars, too." She started to lift her shirt. "Want to see?"

He caught her hands, held them. "Another time."

"That's right. You lot don't like scars on females."

"That's not the problem at all."

"So it's just my naked human body you find hideous."

"I have no problem with your hideous human body." He scowled, but she didn't think it was directed at her. "That's not what I meant to say."

"That's all right. Among my mum's offspring, the triplets are the ones considered pretty."

"Then no one's looked at you at all."

"You're only saying that because you're a desperate Northlander that's forced to steal She-dragons and mutilate them so they'll never leave you. You'd think anything with a pussy was pretty."

The scowl this time . . . for her. "First off, we don't do that anymore. Second, not all Northland males did it in the first place. And third, I have no idea how pretty your pussy is, but I do like your face."

Rhona reached up, patted his cheek. "You're sweet." She closed her eyes. "And I'm tired. Can we have sex another time?"

"Were we planning to have sex?"

"I was. But I'm too tired. So another day, yes?"

"All right." The Northlander lay down and snuggled in close, his nose tickling her ear. "Another day of lots of sex," he murmured, his breath warm against her neck.

"I didn't say anything about lots."

"No. You didn't." And she could feel him smile. "But I did."

Junius Bato Toranius of the House of Toranius knew he was one of the most powerful dragons in the Quintilian Sovereigns. Only Overlord Thracius held higher rank. But when it came to actual power . . . well, that was one area the good Overlord never tested Junius on.

Yet, as with all things, there was a price to pay for his power, for his skill as a mage. It wasn't too high a price, though. Junius merely had to ensure that all Irons worshipped one, and only one, god. And that as the power of the Irons spread throughout the world, this worship of one god would spread along with it.

Not easy. Some were quite attached to their multiple gods. But the Quintilians knew many ways to get and keep the loyalty of those whose countries they invaded and eventually conquered.

The lands to the east of the Provinces would be no different.

Junius stood alone in the dry riverbed and waited. Like his father before him, he was very good at waiting, patience being important for any mage.

The hard earth in front of him stirred and cracked and the one god pushed his way up and through.

Chramnesind. The Sightless One. A name he'd received because he had no eyes, for Chramnesind saw well enough without them. In fact, he could see everything.

"My god," Junius said softly. "You summoned me."

"I did, Junius Toranius. Good fortune has shined upon you." He smiled. "And my true reign is about to begin. . . ."

Chapter 11

A fist slammed into his chest twice, but he wasn't surprised to open his eyes and find a scowling Rhona staring down at him. He'd had a feeling she'd be dealing with some remorse this morning, and he'd be facing her wrath. But he'd been more than willing to risk all that because he really liked Rhona. A lot. And he was willing to risk a little Fire Breather rage if it meant getting closer to her.

"I know you're mad, but—"

She held her finger to her lips, silencing him. Then with the same finger, she pointed to a spot in front of them.

Vigholf raised his head, blinking hard.

There was an early morning mist over everything, the suns just peeking over the low hills in the distance, and yet Vigholf could see her. She stood there. Alone. Watching them. One hand gripping a stuffed toy dog, the tips of her fingers from the other hand stuffed in her mouth. Curly silver hair surrounded full cheeks and stark violet eyes stared at them.

Vigholf sat up, looked around. There were no Kyvich. None of Rhona's kin. No nanny. No one was watching a girl who was never alone. How had she gotten out here on her own . . . ?

"Hello, darling girl," he said softly, resting his arm on his raised knee. "You all right?"

"They're here," the girl whispered.

"Who's here?" Rhona asked, keeping her voice equally soft, unchallenging.

"She sent them. From the west. They're here."

"We better get her inside," Vigholf said, getting to his feet, but the girl stepped back.

"It's too late for us. We're in it. But not for her. Not for *them*. They still have a chance. But someone has to help them before it's too late."

"Do you have *any* idea what or who she's talking about?"

"Not at all," Rhona admitted. "But that doesn't matter right now." Rhona walked toward her. "We need to get her inside before—" The sudden call from the Kyvich cut off the rest of Rhona's words.

"Damn." Knowing how the Kyvich could easily over-react to Rhian being outside the castle walls without the usual protection, Vigholf quickly picked the girl up.

There was another call from the Kyvich and, scowling, he locked gazes with Rhona. They both knew a warning call when they heard it and he was sensing it had little to do with them and the girl.

"Let's move," he ordered while running, knowing Rhona would follow.

But Rhona called out, "Vigholf!"

He stopped. Looked at the girl in his arms. "They're here," she said again, her expression much older than her six winters in this world would suggest.

Realizing what she meant, Vigholf dove behind a cart, Rhona landing right by his side mere seconds before everything went dark from the onslaught of arrows.

* * *

"We need to get her inside," Rhona said once the arrows stopped.

"I know. But we have a bigger issue than getting her inside."

"What?" Rhona demanded.

"Catching them before they clear the fence."

With small swords in hand, the twins charged past them, shooting around the gate.

"Piss and fire!" Rhona snarled, scrambling to her feet and running after them. "Get Rhian inside!" she yelled to Vigholf.

Despite their size the twins were fast. Yet she thankfully had longer legs. She neared them, her arms almost around them when horses charged their way, the riders aiming their bows at them, arrows nocked.

Rhona shifted, gripping her weapon in her claw and immediately lifting herself up so she didn't crush the children in the process. But before she could release her flame or use her spear to stop the riders, Talan dropped to his knees but continued sliding forward. Using his sword, he cut the tendon of the first horse he passed. The horse screamed, his damaged leg buckling, his rider flipping off. The rider's neck snapped on impact and Talwyn ran up and onto his bent body. She used the momentum of her run and the extra height from the corpse to launch herself at another rider. The blade of her sword slammed high into the rider's leg, the rider screaming as she used both hands to yank the blade down his calf.

Not knowing what else to do, Rhona caught hold of both children and took to the skies. The girl yelled and punched at her claw, trying to get loose while her brother did nothing but patiently wait until Rhona landed in the courtyard. Of course that's when he slammed his sword into a spot between her talons.

"Aaargh! You vicious little—"

"Talwyn! Talan!" Talaith tore down the courtyard steps, her beautiful face streaked with tears. "Where is she?" the witch demanded. "Where's Rhian?"

"Here." Vigholf landed beside Rhona, carefully handing over the child to her mother. "She saved our lives, my lady. Thank you."

Talaith nodded, holding Rhian tight to her. "Don't you ever do that again," she told her daughter. "Never sneak out again." Fierce brown eyes locked on the twins. "And you two . . . get your asses in that castle. *Now!*"

The twins charged up the stairs and came face-to-face with their livid nanny. She picked them up and went back inside.

"Go, Talaith," Rhona ordered the witch. "We'll take it from here."

With a brief glance at Vigholf, they both flew up and landed on the castle gates.

"It seems your cousin was right," the Lightning admitted, gazing down at the number of Tribesmen riders charging and surrounding the castle gates.

Rhona, her new spear clenched in her claw, nodded. "She was."

The Kyvich rode out of the gates on their horned steeds, their bloodthirsty dogs by their sides. The first sound of clashing weapons rang out.

Smiling a little, Rhona asked Vigholf, "Still mind having a female fighting by your side, Northlander?"

"Not when it's you, Southlander." He grinned at her. "Not when it's you."

Dagmar sent the commanding castle guards out to their troops with the warning, "Whatever you do, don't get in the way of the Kyvich."

She headed back into the castle, her faithful dog Canute

by her side and the stray puppy she'd recently found right behind Canute. Running soldiers moved out of her way as she quickly came down the hallway, stopping when she reached the Great Hall. Several of the Kyvich surrounded Talaith and Ebba, escorting them to a safe place that had been built beneath the castle walls. Dagmar didn't try to stop them, but was glad to see they were all right.

Thinking of nothing more than getting as many as possible through this alive, Dagmar coldly examined everything. And that's when she saw the Dragon Queen walk down the stairs and out the Great Hall doors. Dagmar hadn't even realized the queen had stayed last night. The discussion over what should be done about Annwyl's disappearance had lasted late into the evening, but usually the queen would return to her Devenallt Mountain home at any hour. Yet she didn't last night. She'd stayed.

Normally Dagmar wouldn't worry about it, but she couldn't ignore it this time. So Dagmar followed Rhiannon.

Rhona swooped down on the advancing troops, unleashing a line of flame while she dodged arrows, axes, and more spears. As always when she flew into battle, Rhona was more pissed off at being attacked than she was afraid. It gave her an edge she normally didn't have in her day-to-day life.

She picked up horses and their riders and threw them into their own troops. Lashed her tail from side to side, sending the Tribesmen behind her flying and flipping through the air and across the ground. While her tail handled what was behind her, she used her spear to decimate what was in front. Tribesmen rode at her from all sides, using only their knees to stay seated while their hands were busy inundating her with arrows. Many struck home, imbedding past scales, but she ignored the pain as she always had, as she'd always been taught, and kept up her onslaught.

But she wasn't alone. She had her kin striking from the air, sending down wave after wave of flame, burning human flesh from bone. The Lightning nearby battered and crushed and hacked with that hammer and ax of his. And the infamous Kyvich unleashed something. She thought they were those unholy horned dogs of theirs. They weren't. They were men. Or what were once men, but were now no more than slavering beasts, broken by the heartless females they'd once challenged.

Younger witches clad—barely—in animal skins and bits and pieces of armor ran out to meet their enemy, combining weaponry and Magick to create a nightmarish whirl of blood and death. Tribesmen torn apart by nothing more than air, skin peeled from flesh by trees come alive. Some Tribesmen dragged underground, screaming all the way, by hands appearing from the earth beneath their feet.

Not willing to watch any more of that, Rhona focused on the enemies closer to the forests.

Rhiannon made her way to the top of the battlements, watching as her warriors and the human witches fought the Tribesmen. For human barbarians, the Tribesmen were dangerous foes, used to fighting not just Annwyl's armies but Rhiannon's dragon army as well.

"You shouldn't be up here."

Rhiannon glanced at Dagmar. "Neither should you, Battle Lord. You should be with the others."

"These battlements are mine until Annwyl returns. I'll not hide like I'm one of the children."

"Such a Northlander," Rhiannon murmured.

"Maybe we should have listened to Keita and sent the children to the Eastlands with Ren," Dagmar told her, watching Ren join the fight in his wingless golden dragon form. She'd never noticed he had paws before—and antlers.

"If we ship them away every time there's a problem, they'll be raised by strangers all their lives." The queen watched the Kyvich cut down man after man, while their dogs and horses ate the remains. "They stay here."

"What about Annwyl? Who will we send out to find her?"

"That's a bigger issue. Especially now. The Tribesmen won't back off simply because the Kyvich's pets have eaten a few of their friends."

"So what do you suggest?"

Rhiannon leaned against the railing, watching the battle raging beneath.

"Normally I'd send out one of my Dragonwarriors to find her."

"Can we afford to lose one of them now?"

"Can we afford to lose Annwyl?"

"We both know that if Annwyl left her army it was for a damn good reason."

Rhiannon nodded. "I know that. She headed deeper into the west, Battle Lord. And there's only one thing in that direction."

"The Provinces." The heart and home of the Irons. And getting into the Provinces was one thing. Getting out . . .

"This could very likely be a one-way trip for whoever we send." Rhiannon shook her head. "But it can't be avoided. We need to send someone to find Annwyl and bring her, Izzy, and Branwen back to their troops. So any suggestions, Battle Lord?"

Dagmar stepped closer to the rail. "One of your Dragonwarriors, yes?"

"They are my strongest and mightiest."

"But they can also be unpredictable."

Rhiannon smiled. The Northland woman her son had chosen as his mate was a quick learner.

"Exactly. They do what they *think* is right. If that means leaving Annwyl to die while they rescue lost urchins . . ."

"So then what?"

Rhiannon studied the battlefield. Of all who fought, there was one who stuck out to her eyes. "Which one is that?"

Dagmar adjusted her spectacles and squinted. "The Brown? Your niece. Rhona."

That name sounded familiar. "Rhona? Rhona?" *Oh, yes!* "Bradana's eldest. She babysat for me once when Keita was still a hatchling."

"How did that go?"

"She recovered from the poisoning quite well and her hair grew back, but her mother wouldn't let her babysit for us again, after that." Rhiannon pointed at her niece. "What is she now? A captain? Or a general?"

"Sergeant."

"Just a soldier then?"

"Just a soldier."

They watched the soldier spear a Tribesmen and his horse with one thrust, and crush another with her shield.

Rhiannon and Dagmar looked at each other—and smiled.

Chapter 12

Finally, the Tribesmen pulled back, disappearing into the forests that surrounded Dark Plains. But Rhona had fought them long enough to know they weren't gone, merely regrouping, using the trees and their forest-loving gods to shield them.

Rhona landed by one of her wounded cousins and pulled her forearm over her shoulder. Rhona walked-carried her kin toward the castle gates. Halfway there her load abruptly lightened, and she realized Vigholf had taken her kin's other arm, allowing the She-dragon to get off her wounded leg.

Once inside the gates, Rhona handed over her burden to the healers and searched out her father. She found him rounding up weapons. He would work through the night with his apprentices to repair the damaged ones and sharpen the rest so that when the Tribesmen attacked again, they'd be ready and armed.

"Rhona," he said when he saw her, wrapping her in a hug. "Good work, child."

"Sergeant Rhona!" Addolgar called out. "You've been summoned by the queen. Dress and meet her in the war room."

Sulien caught Rhona's forearm and held her. "What

does the queen want with my daughter?" he demanded of Addolgar.

But Rhona pushed his claw off. "Daddy, when the queen calls, I go."

Addolgar motioned toward the castle with a jerk of his head, patting Rhona's shoulder as she walked by.

"Don't do anything foolish, child," her father called after her.

Vigholf tended to a few dragons who couldn't reach the swords or arrows embedded in their backs.

Once done with that, he was about to go in search of Rhona when her father stepped in front of him.

"You," he said and, for a moment, Vigholf was sure Sulien had heard about Vigholf and Rhona cuddling under a tree all night. He was a ridiculously large dragon with forearms the size of large bulls. It would not be a fun fight. "Go with her."

Vigholf blinked. "Go with who?"

"Rhona. She's been called to talk to the queen—don't let her face that alone."

Vigholf quickly shifted to human and yanked the clothes off some poor, large-boned soldier who'd been walking by, and demanded, "Where is she?"

Rhona pulled out any arrows she hadn't dealt with on the field, shifted, put on clothes, and went into the castle. The Kyvich took up most of the Great Hall, healing the few of their number who'd been wounded. As she passed, they watched her but said nothing.

"Where are we going?"

Rhona stopped, faced Vigholf, who she'd had no idea was behind her. "I'm going to see my queen."

"All right."

Confused, but too tired to fight about it, she kept going.

She arrived at the door of the war room and knocked. Dagmar Reinholdt opened it. "Sergeant."

"The queen asked for me?"

"Yes." Dagmar glanced behind Rhona. "And you brought a friend."

Rhona didn't bother to turn around this time; she merely rolled her eyes. "No. I didn't. He follows me."

"Well . . . some dogs are hard to shake," Dagmar murmured. "You both may enter. And as Ragnar's brother," Dagmar said to Vigholf, "I depend on your honor not to repeat what you hear here, my lord."

Vigholf stooped a bit to clear the doorway. "On my honor, Lady Dagmar."

Dagmar closed the door and Rhona walked up to the table. The Dragon Queen stood on the opposite side, Talaith and Keita on the right, Ren—finally getting his color and strength back—behind the queen.

"I have a mission for you, Sergeant."

"Of course, my queen."

"I need you to—"

The door swung open again and Rhona's Uncle Bercelak, whom she hadn't seen since she'd arrived, stomped in. He sneered at Vigholf as he passed him until he reached Rhiannon's side. "I need to talk to you."

"Can't it wait?"

"No." He took her hand and pulled his mate out of the room, leaving the rest of them all standing there. It was, to say the least, an awkward moment.

That's when Keita said, "Lovely battle today, you two. You both kill so nicely. Oh!" She snapped her fingers and cheerily added, "And don't drink the water from the lake on the south side."

"Why—"

Rhona tapped Vigholf's chest with her hand, cutting him off. "Again I have to say, don't ask. Just do what she says."

"Choose someone else!" Bercelak bellowed from the other side of the closed door, startling them all.

"I will not, Low Born! I choose whom I like from *my* army even if it is *your* niece!"

"Choose one of my other nieces, Rhiannon. But a Dragonwarrior. One who is ready for this. Not Rhona!"

"Who says she's not ready?"

"Me! Addolgar! Her *mother*!"

No one looked at Rhona. Not that she blamed them. And when she heard the door open and close again, she wasn't surprised that Vigholf had made his escape.

But then she heard, "Oy!" And realized it was Vigholf. *Oh, no. No, no, no.*

"First off, you two," he nearly roared, "we can hear you through the bloody door. And second, she *is* ready."

What?

"How would you know, foreigner?" her always-welcoming Uncle Bercelak snapped.

"Because I've been fighting by that female's side for five bloody years. Can you say the same, Fire Breather?" he sneered and silence greeted the question. That's when Vigholf finished with, "She's ready. Now let's get this over with."

Vigholf walked back in, slamming the door behind him, and stood behind Rhona once again, his arms crossed over his chest. She didn't look at him. She didn't dare. She wasn't sure what her response would be. Rage at how he'd spoken to her queen and the queen's consort? Gratitude for having faith in her skills? Or mortification that he'd had to fight her battle for her?

Honestly, her feelings and response could go in any direction, so she silently stood her ground when the queen and her consort returned. Bercelak looked more annoyed than usual—which said much, since looking annoyed was his usual state.

Standing to Rhona's side, Bercelak snapped, "Soldier!"

Rhona straightened her back, raised her chin. "Sir."

"You are to head into the west, leave tonight, on foot, let no one see you. Especially since it seems that bitch Vateria has some sway over the Tribesmen."

"Aye, my lord."

"You are to find the missing queen—Annwyl." Gods, Annwyl was missing? "And return her to her troops. Her legions are heading to the Euphrasia Valley as we speak to join with our dragon forces. Do you understand your orders?"

Although Rhona wanted to immediately answer, "Aye, sir," as she always did, she knew she had one question. A question she felt the need to ask.

"Sir . . . I'm traveling into the west. Do you mean the Quintilian Provinces?"

Bercelak paused, then answered, "Aye, Sergeant. It's believed that's where Annwyl was headed. Morfyd can tell you more. She stayed behind while the army advanced without her. Stop at the camp first. Anything else?"

What was there to ask? To say?

"No, sir."

"For your own sake, Sergeant, I'd keep as low a profile as possible. Travel as human as much as you can, and do nothing . . . foolhardy. You have one mission—bring Annwyl back. Alive or dead. Understand?"

"Aye, sir. I understand."

"Then go. And may the gods of war protect you."

With a quick bow of her head to the queen, Rhona walked out of the room in search of her father.

* * *

"They're sending you to do *what*?" Sulien demanded of his eldest daughter.

"Don't make me repeat it, Daddy," she muttered, digging through his chests of excess clothes, uniforms, and armor. "Just help me find something that will let me blend in with other travelers." She motioned to what she wore. Standard protective gear with the Dragon Queen's colors and seal on it. "Can't blend in this, now can I?"

"Not in the bloody Provinces you can't."

"Scream it a little louder. Don't think they heard you in the Desert Lands."

Sulien gripped his daughter's shoulders and turned her to look at him. "Why are you doing this?" he demanded.

"It's my orders."

"To head into the Provinces and end up crucified?"

"Not if I can get in and out without being noticed."

"If you're going to rescue that mad bitch, you'll be noticed all right."

"Those are my orders—"

"Gods, girl! Stop saying that!"

Rhona sighed. "What do you want me to say? Do you want me to lie to you? Tell you what you want to hear?"

"That would be a start."

Rhona smiled and he saw himself in that smile. Of all his offspring, Rhona was the one who took so much after him. She had his face, his strength, and his skills. From the beginning he knew her place was behind a forge of her own, not fighting wars to prove something to her mother. He adored Bradana more than words could say, but if there was one thing they'd always fought over, it was his Rhona.

It wasn't that Sulien thought his daughter didn't have what was necessary to be a soldier or even one of those bloody Dragonwarriors. But having what was necessary and having your heart in it were two vastly different things. From the time Sulien had met his mate, he'd known what she was. A warrior. Without a doubt. It was in her eyes, in the way she walked, in the way she lived. She was a warrior and would take no less from this world. And that same look and attitude had been in all their offspring—except Rhona.

Rhona's skill with weapons was so that, like every good blacksmith, she'd know what was the right weight, what worked well during a fight, what could kill and what could maim.

But her mother had seen her skill as a calling to be a Dragonwarrior, and to this day it bothered her beyond reckoning that her eldest daughter had not gotten farther than a "mere soldier." Cadwaladrs, in Bradana's mind, were supposed to be Dragonwarriors, leading the way into battle. Making orders, not taking them. So round and round mother and daughter went. Rhona never going further than a good soldier because her true calling was to be a Master Blacksmith. And her mother still trying to prove that her eldest just needed a little push in the right direction.

A push right into death, it seemed.

Rhona held up a chain-mail shirt. "What about this?"

"No." He snatched the shirt from her and slapped it back into the trunk. "You've got your mother's"—Sulien awkwardly motioned around his daughter's chest—"assets."

"Assets?"

"Here. Wear this." He handed her a chain-mail shirt that he'd spent years perfecting.

"Daddy, I can't take—"

"You will and you'll wear it under your traveler's clothes. Here are the leggings that go with them."

"But this is—"

"My best work and I can't imagine who else you'd think I'd be saving it for if not for me own daughter."

Rhona smiled at him. "Thank you, Daddy."

"Don't get weepy on me. Don't think I can handle it."
He turned from her, unable to look at that beautiful face.
"By the time we're done, you'll be the most well-armed
traveler ever known."

Once he'd equipped his daughter as best he could, Sulien
walked her outside his tent and there they said their good-
byes. He hugged her tight, kissing the top of her head and
making her promise she'd at least *try* to be careful. Assur-
ing lies given, he watched his daughter walk off into the
busy crowd of warriors and guards and witches preparing
for another assault from the Tribesmen. At the right moment,
Rhona's kin would create a diversion that would give
Rhona the time she needed to slip out undetected.

Releasing a heavy sigh, Sulien walked back into his
tent, coming to an abrupt halt when he saw the Lightning
standing there, arms crossed over a chest nearly as big as
his own.

"What do you want?"

"Do you really think for a second I'd let her go into the
Provinces without *me*?" The Lightning lifted his giant—
even when it was fit for a human—hammer and dropped it
to the ground. "I need one of those fancy hammers of
yours, blacksmith. I have to blend, don't I?"

Grinning, Sulien helped the Northlander find just what
he needed.

Chapter 13

Rhona crouched beside the discreet door. It was built into the gate hidden behind trees on both sides. And that's where she waited to hear the signal that would tell her it was time to move.

Dressed as a traveler, she still had weapons hidden in every available place she and her father could think of. She was as ready as she could ever hope to be. Would she rather be doing something else? *Anything* else? Aye. But that desire didn't change anything.

Weapons clashed and she knew her kin had attacked the Tribesmen who'd been regrouping on the other side of the forests. There were so many of them, they'd ringed the castle gates, but Rhona just needed the ones near this door to be drawn away.

She eased the door partially open and watched, ready to make her move at any—

Rhona's entire body tensed and she slowly looked over her shoulder at what was crouching right behind her.

"What are you—"

A call went out and Vigholf shoved her forward. "*Go,*" he whispered.

Unable to confront the dumb ox at this moment, Rhona

scrambled out the door, keeping low and moving quick. She used the trees for cover, pausing every few feet to stop and make sure she was still unseen. The Lightning was right behind her, keeping up with her as he always managed to do.

She stopped by an old tree with a massive trunk. Peeking around it, she saw two Tribesmen on horseback. Just sitting there while all hells broke loose nearby.

Rhona held up her hand to Vigholf and he stopped. She pointed at the men, then drew her thumb across her throat. Vigholf nodded and they moved out.

The man Rhona ran up to never heard or saw her coming, and his horse gave no warning. She yanked the man off, slapped her hand over his mouth, and jammed a blade into his throat in such a way that he couldn't speak or call out. She pulled the blade out, rammed it back in, and this time yanked it from one side to the other.

The man Vigholf moved up next to was warned of the Lightning's presence by his horse rearing up in panic. To silence him, Vigholf punched the horse. It went down and Vigholf used his ax, cutting off the Tribesman's head before he could speak a word.

How Rhona would travel on horseback with Vigholf terrifying or punching the poor animals at every turn, she really hadn't figured out yet. But she could worry about that later.

She and Vigholf dragged the bodies of the men to a spot behind that big tree and slapped the rump of the horse that wasn't unconscious so that he'd take off. The other horse, Vigholf picked up and carried over his shoulder until they reached the river. He dropped the horse by it and together, they followed the river until they could cross it and make a run for the Western Mountains.

* * *

Edana and her two sisters Nesta and Breena were going through their daily weapons check, counting all their weapons and looking for any weaknesses in the steel or grip. Nothing worse than having your sword break on you when you're in the middle of a battle. It was a lesson that had been well taught to them by Rhona. She'd been the first face that Edana had seen when she'd crawled out of her broken egg, one eye swollen shut from being pummeled by Nesta, her back leg weak because Breena had nearly bitten the damn thing off. Their mother had rushed off to some battle before they'd made their entrance into this world, so it had been Rhona who'd raised them even though she hadn't been a grown adult herself yet.

Most dragons didn't have so many hatchlings in such a short span of time, but Bradana had put off breeding far longer than her mated sisters and being the competitive female that she was, she'd gone out of her way to make up for it. The only problem was, she wasn't much for sticking around when there was killing to be done. So off she'd gone before her triplets had hatched, leaving it up to Rhona to do the bulk of the work. Just like she'd expected Rhona to do with all her offspring.

Done with their own weapons, the three sisters changed places and examined each other's weapons. An unnecessary step, their mum called it. "Don't you know your own weapon?" she'd demanded when she saw the triplets do this. But often Edana's sisters saw something that she'd missed and she saw something that they'd missed. And what was the point of taking the risk? If they had the time, might as well do the extra steps. Couldn't hurt.

"Oy, you two!"

Edana didn't bother to sigh anymore. "There's three of us, Mum. Unless you're ignoring one of us for some reason."

"Don't back-talk me, little miss. Where's that sister of yours?"

Nesta snorted. "You'll need to be more specific than that."

Their mother snarled. The only one of them she ever checked up on was Rhona and all of them knew it. Yet it was still fun to toy with her.

"Rhona. Where is she?"

"Around somewhere," Breena said. "Just saw her, I did. Not more than ten minutes ago. Went"—she pointed at some random spot across the cavern—"that way."

"Gods-dammit. That *girl*," their mother griped before she marched off.

Edana waited until Bradana was out of earshot before she asked the other two, "Any word from Rhona?"

They both shook their heads. "But we can't let Mum know she's gone. You know how she gets," Nesta reminded them.

"And if Rhona wanted her to know, she'd have told her," Breena added.

Nesta nodded. "And if she was in trouble we'd know that too."

"Besides," Breena sighed out. "We've got bigger and *dumber* problems to worry about right here."

All three looked over and watched their cousins roll around on the cave floor, trying to damage the other. Over some female no less! A *human* female!

Normally Edana would never get in the middle of something so ridiculous, but Rhona wasn't here and Rhona *would* get in the middle. More important, if they were going to keep up the illusion that their sister was about, they'd have to manage these things themselves because that's what Rhona did when she was here. If things got out of control, their mother would know in an instant that something had changed.

"I'll take Celyn," she told her sisters while getting to her claws. "You two take Éibhear."

"Why do we always have to take Éibhear?" Nesta

whined. "He's as big as a mountain and don't pay attention to where he's swinging those big meat hooks of his."

"Yeah," Edana agreed. "That's why I have you two do it. Now move your asses before Mum notices."

Rhona crouched beside a small brook and took off her glove to scoop water to her mouth. It was cold and bracing, and revived her after such a long run. She was still in Dark Plains but far from the battle going on at Garbhán Isle, giving her time to think.

Hard snow and ice cracked behind her and Rhona, still crouched, turned, thrusting her spear up. The warhammer created by her father slammed into it, moving it aside but not knocking it from her hands.

"It's me," Vigholf told her quickly.

And Rhona replied honestly, "I know."

"What do you mean you know? Then why did you attack me?"

Rhona stood to her full, tall, human height, but she still had to look up at the Lightning to see his face. "Why do you think? And why are you here?"

"Why do *you* think? Did you really think I was going to let you go off on your own?"

"So you lied to my uncle then? You don't think I can handle—"

"Before you even finish that idiotic statement, let me make something very clear to you. If I'd been assigned this mission . . . I'd not want to go it alone. I'd need someone to watch my back. Someone I know would keep an eye out for me no matter what I may have gotten myself into. So I didn't lie to your uncle or anyone else. I know you can do this, but since I can afford to be here watching your back, I will."

"What about your brother?"

"What about him?"

"If Annwyl's army is on the move then they're gearing up for the final assault. The one that will end this bloody war and get us back to our normal lives."

"War *is* the Northlander's normal life, Sergeant. Once we're done sorting out the Irons for you Fire Breathers, we'll be focusing on the Spikes out of the Ice Lands. They've no doubt moved into our territory, thinking we're gone forever. So it's not like there won't be killing aplenty for me when I return home."

"But—"

"That's it!" he cut in. "I'll hear no more. I'm going with you. Just accept it."

"Fine. Then let's make a few things clear before we go any farther." She placed the butt of her spear in the ground, gripping it tight. "I know this will be hard for that thick Northland head of yours to get around, but I'm a soldier of the Dragon Queen's army and I've survived more than two centuries without you stepping in to protect me during every battle that comes my way. That I won't tolerate. Watch my back, yeah. But that's it. Understand?"

"You watch my back, Fire Breather, and I'll watch yours. And I'm not about to get in the middle of any of your fights if I don't have to." He motioned to her spear. "You've stabbed me enough with that thing."

"Yeah, but that first time was an accident. Can't promise that if I do it again."

"Fair enough." He looked around, shrugged. "So what do we do now?"

"Keep moving. The quicker we get to Morfyd, the better. We'd do better on horseback, but with you and your problems with horses . . ."

"What's that mean?"

"You just knocked one out."

"I was keeping him quiet."

Shaking her head, Rhona crouched down again and filled her canteen with fresh water. Once done, she stood and started running again. "Come on, Lightning," she called back to him. "Move that ass. We haven't got all night!"

She heard him sigh and mutter, "I hate running," and then he was by her side, keeping pace with her as they headed deep into the border territory between the Southlands and the Western Plains.

"Where is she?"

Eirianwen, goddess of war, stepped over the bodies of the fallen and went to her mate, Rhydderch Hael, father-god of all dragons. As she walked toward him, Eir, as she'd done since time began, admired the beauty of his form. A black dragon with scales that glistened in the dying light of the two suns; twelve bright, white horns atop his head; black mane of hair with the shades of every color in the spectrum streaked throughout, long and sweeping along the blood-soaked ground. She couldn't see his tail, it reached too far back at the moment, but it always reminded her of her favorite broadsword. Big, wide, with a blade of a tip that could destroy anything it touched.

Yet Eir's love of the dragon didn't mean she'd take his centaur shit. "And hello to you, my love."

"Don't play me about, Eir," he lashed back. "Where is she?"

"Who? Who are you going on about?"

"Annwyl the Bloody."

"Oh. Your pet." Eir put her sword back in its scabbard. "I have no idea where she is."

"Eir—"

"I don't! She's not my concern. She's *your* concern."

"Don't start that again. She was dead and *you* brought her back!"

"I did that for Dagmar Reinholdt."

"*Your* pet." His gaze moved around the battlefield. "You've been busy, I see."

"The beauty of this world is that there are so many wars for me to choose from."

"So what's going on in Euphrasia Valley . . . ?"

"That is not my war, lover. Although I have been entertained. Such strategists both sides have." She crossed her arms over her chest. "You know who this comes down to, Rhy. He's always wanted your power. To emulate your reign."

"How far do you think he'd go?"

"Do you mean do I think he'd abscond with your little pet?"

"Feel free to stop calling her that."

"No. I don't think he has the guts to do that."

"But?"

"What makes you think Annwyl would only attract you or someone out to get you? As far as the rest of the gods are concerned, you've tossed her aside. That means she's available to any god who can entice her to join forces. She's a powerful ally among the humans." Eir pressed her hand against her consort's neck. "Do you want me to look into it?" She grinned. "Wars *are* my area."

"What about the carnage here?"

"Eh." She shrugged. "When you've seen one battlefield with corpses, you've seen them all."

Rhy looked off, then shook his head. "No. You're right. She's no longer my concern."

"As you wish." She kissed his snout, walked away.

"Where's Nannulf?" he asked her as she stepped over the corpses in search of souls to take.

"No idea. Nannulf the wolf-god may be my traveling companion, lover, but we aren't joined at the hip. But I'm sure he's around somewhere. . . ."

Chapter 14

It was midafternoon when Morfyd finished putting the last few things into the bag that held her most important Magickal items.

At least she hoped it was the last few. She looked around the tent she'd called home for five years now and searched for anything she might be leaving behind. She could be forgetful that way. Especially when she was under a lot of stress. And since Annwyl had decided to go off on her own, Morfyd had been nothing but stressed.

She heard the tent flap pull back and she said to her apprentice, "Lolly, are you sure I have everything?"

"Cousin."

Morfyd looked up and blinked in surprise. "Rhona?" She went to her cousin, who, like Morfyd, was in human form and dressed. She hugged her. "Gods. What are you doing here?"

"Your mother sent me." Her cousin frowned. "Didn't she tell you?"

"No, all I knew was that she was sending help."

Of course Morfyd thought the help would be more like Ren or one of her mother's apprentices. Not . . .

Oh, hells. Did it matter? At this point, did anything matter but getting that damn female back where she belonged? With her bloody troops!

Morfyd went to the middle of the tent, raised her hand, and unleashed a small spell that would seal the area around the tent with a barrier, giving them some privacy for a few minutes. That's when she heard a small roar and a "Gods-dammit!" from outside her tent. Her cousin cleared her throat and smirked. It was nearly a smile.

"What's going on?"

"I'm not alone. But you've just entertained me greatly."

Morfyd released the spell and a few seconds later, a purple-haired dragon in human form stumbled into her tent. A Lightning, rubbing his big Lightning head.

"You could have told her I was out there," he accused Rhona.

"I could have. . . . Didn't though, did I?"

"Viperous . . ." He gritted his teeth and nodded at Morfyd. "My lady."

It took Morfyd a moment, but then she asked, "Vig-holf?" It was hard to tell with his hair grown back—the hair he'd lost to Annwyl's sword. Annwyl, as usual, had attacked first upon seeing the Lightnings on her territory. By the time she was done, Vigholf had lost his hair—luckily not his head—and his cousin Meinhard had a broken leg. In fact, Annwyl still had the Lightning's hair sprouting from the top of her battle helm.

Morfyd looked to her cousin. "Why is he here?"

"Because I apparently can't do anything on my own."

"I didn't say that. *When did I say that?*"

"Do not screech at me."

"I do not screech!"

Morfyd held up her hand. "Stop it. Both of you." She put

the spell that would protect them from the outside world back in place. "Let's try this again, shall we?" She pointed at Rhona. "You're here to help me with my problem. Yes?"

"Aye."

"And you"—she pointed at Vigholf—"you're here to . . ."

"Help her help you with your problem."

Morfyd flapped her hands impatiently. "Oh, whatever. Whatever way you two want to do this is fine by me. But I need you to get Annwyl. Even now her army asks where the hells she is."

"They can't function without her?" Rhona asked, appearing a tad disgusted at Annwyl's troops.

"Of course they can. But if fighting the Sovereigns these past years has proven one thing it's that if we want to win, Annwyl needs to lead them into battle." Morfyd began to pace. Something she'd done a lot lately. "Not only that, but if her troops arrive in Euphrasia Valley without Annwyl, my brother will leave my mother's troops to go looking for her. Followed by Briec *and* Ghleanna once they find their daughters have gone with Annwyl. I don't know how to explain it any better," she told them. "I just need Annwyl back and—"

Rhona stepped in front of her, took Morfyd's hands in her own. Morfyd hadn't even realized she'd been wringing them.

"Listen well to me, cousin. I've been given my orders. Find Annwyl. Bring her back. And that is exactly what I plan to do. Even if that means razing the entire Provinces and leaving no Sovereign or Iron alive. That's what I'll do."

And gods, Morfyd knew the truth of that. Give this She-dragon an order and she followed it like her very life depended on it—and gods protect those who dare step in her path.

* * *

The pretty witch suddenly wrapped her arms around her kin, giving her a desperate hug. What no one wanted to say out loud, but Vigholf knew the truth of, was that they didn't need Annwyl back to lead her troops. Instead, what they needed was not to have the remains of a crucified Annwyl lobbed at her armies. Nothing ruined morale more than having the head of your leader tossed at you.

"It'll be all right," Rhona soothed, rubbing her cousin's back. "I promise. I'll find her."

"When will you leave?" Morfyd asked, pulling away from her kin.

"Now."

"Do you need anything?"

"Can you afford to spare anything?"

Morfyd shook her head. "Not really. The troops took the bulk of our remaining supplies for the trip."

"Then we'll get what we need on the road. Now what I need to know from you, cousin, is where you think Annwyl went."

Morfyd eased farther away from Rhona, eyes downcast. "Uh . . ."

"Uh? Uh . . . what?"

"That's a little tricky."

"Right. She headed into the Provinces. We know that."

"No. I mean, yes."

Rhona glanced at Vigholf.

"Where is she, Morfyd?" Rhona pushed.

"She headed into the west, yes. Toward the Provinces. But I think—I'm not sure—but I think she's not heading *into* the Provinces."

"Then where is she headed?"

"Around the Provinces. I think she's gone to find someone. Someone she *thinks* can help her."

"Who, Morfyd? Spit it out."

Morfyd faced her cousin. "Gaius Lucius Domitus."

Again Rhona looked to him and all Vigholf could do was shrug.

"Who is that?" Rhona asked.

"The . . ." Morfyd cleared her throat. "The Rebel Dragon King of the Septima Mountains."

Rhona folded her arms across her chest and told her cousin plainly, "Then I guess we're a wee bit fucked, ain't we, cousin?"

The Rebel King? The bloody Rebel King? *That* was who Annwyl was after?

The Rebel Dragon King of the Septima Mountains was known for two reasons—he was nephew to Overlord Thracius and he was considered the cruelest bastard in the known world.

There'd been others who'd approached Gaius Domitus before. Most of them never came back. Those who had often missed bits of themselves. Arms. Legs. Wings. He and his army lived outside the Provinces, hiding in the caves of the Septima Mountains, it was said, waiting for the day when he could take Thracius's rule from him.

"Why," Rhona had to ask, "would Annwyl do this? Why would she go to *him*?"

"I don't know. I honestly don't. She never mentioned a word to me. Then she was gone."

"Then how do you know—"

Morfyd reached into the pocket of her witch's robes and pulled out a small piece of parchment. She read out loud, "Went to see the Rebel King. Wish me luck."

Exhausted to her bones, Rhona sat down in the closest chair, hooking her leg over the armrest. "Mad cow your queen."

"Perhaps," Vigholf said, taking the parchment and staring at it. "Maybe not."

Rhona gawked at him. "How do you figure?"

"Imagine if the mad bitch can get the Rebel King on our side? If she gets him to fight with us . . ."

"Or," Morfyd reasoned, "she could turn him against us by . . . oh, I don't know . . . *cutting off his hair while trying to cut off his head*?"

Vigholf flinched and handed the paper back to Morfyd. "Point taken." He looked at Rhona. "So what do you want to do?"

"What can I do? I have to get her. Maybe, if I'm lucky, she hasn't found him yet. Of course, never really been lucky," she sighed out.

"Hopefully that'll change." Vigholf motioned her up. "Let's go, Fire Breather. We've got miles to make."

"On foot?"

"Is this about the horses again? I'm a *dragon*, female. Horses are supposed to be terrified of me."

"Well, that terror isn't bloody helping us now, is it?"

"I have something for that," Morfyd said. She dug into a bag she had lying on her bed and pulled out a necklace. A talisman probably, but a boring one. Just a simple black stone hanging from a plain silver chain. "Wear this."

Vigholf reared back from the necklace Morfyd held out to him. "That's all right."

"You scared, Northlander?" Rhona couldn't help but tease. "Scared of a little necklace?"

"It's nothing dangerous," Morfyd promised, ignoring the way Vigholf glared at Rhona. "It'll simply help you with horses. Make them a little less afraid of you. Here. Take it."

When Vigholf didn't, Rhona got to her feet. "Honestly!

You'd think it was a snake, the way you're acting." She snatched the necklace from her cousin and went up on her toes to get the silver chain over his head.

"The chain's too small," he complained. "When I shift it'll choke me to death."

"If only," Rhona muttered, earning another glare.

"It'll grow with you, Vigholf," Morfyd promised, which just seemed to upset Vigholf more.

"How is that normal?" he demanded.

"Stop it," Rhona told him while she tucked the necklace under his clothes. "You're worse than a hatchling."

Rhona faced her cousin. "Anything else you need to horrify us with before we leave?"

"I think Gaius Domitus is horrifying enough, don't you?"

"Aye, cousin, I do." She hugged Morfyd again. "Don't worry," she whispered against her ear. "I'll find Annwyl and the others. I'll bring them home."

Morfyd squeezed her tight. "Thank you, Rhona. Thank you so very much."

Rhona walked out of the tent and through the camp. The Lightning beside her, his hand against his chest where the talisman rested.

"Leave it alone."

"It's searing my skin."

"No, it's not. It's in your head." But he still kept fussing with his clothes, so she grabbed his hand and pulled it away while she continued to walk.

They were nearly clear of what was left of Annwyl's camp when she realized that she still held the Lightning's hand. She tried to release it, but his grip tightened and he smiled at her.

"You truly are pathetic, aren't you?" she asked.

"Not pathetic," Vigholf reasoned. "Sneaky."

"I've dealt with sneaky. You forget I babysat for Keita. *She's* sneaky."

He didn't bother to argue with that and they left camp—with Vigholf still holding her hand.

Fearghus the Destroyer took a break from working in the tunnel. He walked down to the cavern where fresh water was kept and grabbed one of the buckets. He took a long, satisfying drink and poured the remainder over his head. He shook his wet hair out of his eyes and that's when he saw his younger brother glaring at him.

"What are you doing?" Gwenvael the Pain in the Ass demanded. He'd gotten this . . . tone lately that none of them were too fond of. Especially Fearghus.

"What does it look like I'm doing?"

"We don't have time for you to be lounging around, sitting on your tail, doing nothing."

Fearghus looked at the bucket in his claws. "I needed water."

"But you didn't drink and go. You drank and sat around."

"For two seconds!"

"Look," Gwenvael snarled at Fearghus, "we have maybe another week on this bloody tunnel. The sooner we finish it, the sooner we can kill the Irons and go home. And I'm not about to let you or anyone stop me from going home!"

Fed up with his brother's whining—they were all missing their mates, not just him—Fearghus slapped his claw against Gwenvael's chest and shoved him back. "You need to calm the battle-fuck down, brother."

"And you need to get off your lazy ass and work!"

"Stop it! Stop it!" Éibhear got between them. "Brothers shouldn't be fighting this way!"

Fearghus and Gwenvael stared at their very sincere baby brother; then they looked at each other. That's when they started laughing and seemed incapable of stopping.

"What's so bloody funny?"

"You," Fearghus told him. "Telling *us* that we shouldn't fight? After all that's gone on between you and Celyn?"

"That's different," Éibhear growled.

Not really, but try to tell that to Éibhear the Blue.

Fearghus's baby brother had been a right bastard toward Celyn since he found out Celyn had gone where Éibhear was too afraid to go with their niece Izzy. Of course Izzy wasn't related to any of them by blood, but that didn't matter. As far as Fearghus, Briec, and Gwenvael were concerned, Izzy was kin. But poor Éibhear didn't know what to do with little Izzy. He was simply too young to sort out his feelings. So, instead, he beat up on his cousin. Constantly. And Celyn, being a right prat when in the mood, fought back.

Really, though, there was nothing to be done with either idiot. They were at that awkward stage for dragons. Not quite adults but no longer cute little hatchlings either.

But gods, it had been five years. Five years! Get over it already!

Briec entered the cavern and walked over to his brothers. "Anyone seen Keita?"

"Should we be looking for her?"

"No."

"Then why are you asking?" Fearghus wanted to know.

"Because I haven't seen her. She is our sister."

"She's probably off poisoning someone. I wouldn't worry."

Briec grunted until he asked a scowling Gwenvael, "Why are you glaring at me?"

"I'm wondering why you're all not *working*!"

"That is it." Briec pulled his sword and Éibhear immediately grabbed him. "I'm cutting off the rest of that bastard's tail!"

Chapter 15

By late afternoon they hadn't gotten nearly as far as Rhona wanted. Going on foot was tedious and she was anxious to find Annwyl. If there was even a chance the royal hadn't made it into the Provinces yet, Rhona might be able to get the wayward queen and drag her back to her troops. But if they kept moving like this, there was no hope that would happen.

"There's some horses," Vigholf offered while he chewed on *more* dried beef. At this rate, she'd have to find a vendor soon to replenish their supplies. If she were alone, she'd have enough beef to last her for at least a week. Maybe two. But with Sir Eats-a-Lot, she stood no chance that would happen.

"Those are wild horses. We're better off buying tame ones," she suggested.

"Buying them? Why?"

"They'll be more docile, less chance of skittering off at the first scent of you."

"But I've got this thing that Princess Morfyd gave me."

"True, but I'm sure that can only do so—"

"And I doubt your docile horses can carry me. I'm not exactly light."

"So I've noticed."

"We should try." And off he went.

Gods! Dealing with the Lightning was like herding rats. A useless enterprise that would do nothing but make her annoyed.

"Wait," Rhona called out while running to catch up.

"Shhhh. You'll spook them."

"*I'll* spook them?"

"You stay back there."

"You don't know *anything* about horses except how to turn them on a spit."

"But I have this talisman thing," he boasted, suddenly falling in love with that bloody necklace. "It'll *lure* the horses right to—"

Rhona stopped in her tracks, eyes wide, watching the enormous chestnut-colored stallion run right into and right *over* Vigholf.

Vigholf hit the ground hard, startled and clearly hurt.

"Gods-dammit! Demon beast!"

Rhona slapped her hand over her mouth to keep her laughter in. Especially when the stallion came charging back, knocking Vigholf back to the ground before he'd managed to get off his knees.

"Aaaaaargh!"

The horse came back again, but this time he began to pummel Vigholf with his hooves, pushing and shoving the Lightning away from the other horses.

"I don't think he likes you," Rhona informed her traveling companion, something that got her a lovely glare.

Finally getting his bearings, Vigholf knelt on one knee. The stallion turned, moments from raising himself up on his hind legs so he could pummel Vigholf some more with his front. But Vigholf slammed his hand against the horse's chest.

"If you kill him," she warned, "no horse will ever come near you again."

"I'm not going to kill him," Vigholf snarled. "I'm just going to teach the bastard a lesson." Vigholf shoved the horse back and finally got to his feet. There were cuts on his face and bruises on his neck, and he briefly rubbed his chest, which made her worry some of his human ribs may be broken.

Vigholf raised his fists and Rhona wondered if the dragon had any sense at all.

"You can't fistfight him!"

"He started it!"

To ensure that Rhona understood that, the horse slammed his hoof into Vigholf's head. The Lightning snarled and punched back with a double tap, striking the beast in the snout and throat. Unlike the Tribesman's smaller horse, however, this one wasn't knocked unconscious, but he was definitely more irritated.

"By the gods of forge fires," Rhona laughed. "Do we really have time for this?"

"If you want us to ride horses."

"He's never going to let you ride him now, you idiot!"

Vigholf lowered his bruised hands. "Why not?"

"Because he doesn't like you. Can't you tell?" She held up her hand before he could answer. "You're a hardheaded Lightning male. Of course you can't tell."

"What does *that* mean?"

A tall white mare stood by Rhona's side now and the two females looked at each other, shook their heads.

"I know," Rhona told her. "Pathetic."

Vigholf's eyes narrowed when he saw that damn stallion sneer at him. He was sneering at him! At Vigholf! A true Northlander and a commander of the Olgeirsson Horde

Armies was being sneered at by a prey animal! The damn thing should be roasted by Vigholf's lightning and torn to pieces by his comrades.

And what was the She-dragon doing? Chatting with the bloody stallion's female!

"I don't know what you expect," Rhona told Vigholf. "You've probably terrified the poor thing."

"He ran me over! How terrified could he be?"

"Well, you can stay here and fight if you like. I've got a ride." She easily mounted the mare, using the mane as reins, and headed off.

"Can you believe those two?" Vigholf asked the stallion. "It's like we don't even exist."

The horse shook his head, long mane tossed about.

"I'd let the ungrateful wench go off on her own, but she's female and inherently weak. Who knows what will happen to her if I'm not there to protect her. And we can't expect that mare to watch out for her either. Two females together? Could anything be so useless?"

Vigholf shrugged, sighed. "Guess we better follow them."

The stallion nodded and took off.

"Wait! This would be much easier if you let me ride on your back, you difficult bastard!"

Once they had the horses, they made excellent time. Cutting fast across the Western Plains and reaching the forests that would lead them to the Western Mountains.

It was late when they finally decided to stop by a fresh-water stream. And while Vigholf built a small pit fire and hunted down something to eat for dinner, Rhona found an apple tree and was able to feed the horses. When she returned to their campsite, Vigholf had already eaten his portion of the wild boar he'd slaughtered, but he'd left half of it for Rhona.

She walked over to the small pit fire and sat down hard with a sigh, her back resting against her travel bag. "They're settled for the night," she told him of the horses.

"Think they'll take us as far as the Provinces?"

"Perhaps. They're still wild, so they could decide they're done with us whenever they'd like. There's no point in trying to tame them, we'll just hold on as long as we can."

"How did you learn so much about horses?"

Rhona smiled, remembering. "My grandmother and grandfather. When you spend as much time as the Cadwaladrs do fighting as human, you need to learn how to ride and care for horses. My grandmother, Shalin, especially had a way. She used to breed the most amazing war horses." She frowned a bit. "Although all the males seemed to loathe my grandfather."

Rhona motioned to the carcass. "That's mine, yeah?" Vigholf nodded and Rhona blasted the carcass with her flame. When it was cooked to her taste, she began to eat.

"You don't eat your food raw?"

"Sometimes. But I prefer cooked. Besides, at least my face isn't covered with blood."

Vigholf touched his jaw, wincing when he felt the sticky remains of his meal. "Sorry."

Rhona shook her head. "Don't apologize. I like a dragon who enjoys his food."

After Vigholf finished cleaning off his face and clothes, he picked up his weapons and began examining them.

"You're like the triplets," she said with a laugh.

"Short, adorable, and vicious on the battlefield?"

"No. You check your weapons, I'm assuming, for any damage from recent battle."

"Do it every night."

"That's how I taught my siblings," she said. "To always check every night. Most do, too."

"You raised them all, didn't you?"

"What makes you say that?"

"I see how they treat you and how they treat your mother."

"Which is?"

"She's the general and you're their mother. A mother they adore."

She shrugged, pretending not to enjoy hearing that. Seemed a little disloyal to her mum.

"My father give you that?" Rhona asked rather than respond to Vigholf's observation.

Vigholf held up the good-sized steel warhammer. "Yes." He shook his head. "Your father . . ."

"My father what?"

"He does amazing work, Rhona. I've never seen anything like it."

She smiled, feeling a daughter's pride. "I know."

Holding the weapon between his hands, Vigholf said, "I saw you yesterday. At your father's forge."

She blinked. "Oh. Yeah. Well"—she shrugged—"it's good to have some skill there in case you have to fix your weapon and there's no blacksmith around."

Vigholf gazed at her, smirked. "I *saw* you, Rhona."

"You saw what?"

"You. Enjoying yourself."

"What are you talking about?"

"I saw the gleam in your eye. The excitement. You want to do what your father does, don't you?"

The question struck her like a physical thing.

"Wait," he said after a moment, "I didn't mean to upset—"

"You didn't. And you're right. The first ninety years of my life, when I wasn't raising my siblings, I was at my father's side, working the small forge he'd built me near his own. Without a doubt those were the best days of my life."

"Why did you stop?"

She blew out a breath and replied, "Cadwaladrs fight. They join Her Majesty's Army. They become Dragonwarriors. They do *not* spend their lives *making* weapons for Dragonwarriors."

"I see no shame in it. Plus your father does it."

"My father's not a Cadwaladr. He's not even a South-lander."

Vigholf sat up, gazing at her across the pit fire. "That's right. Keita mentioned something about that."

"He was hatched and raised deep in the Black Mountains, near the southern Borderlands."

Vigholf thought a moment and asked, "The Black Mountains? Near the salt mines?"

"You've heard of them?"

"They're volcanoes."

"Aye." She smiled. "Daddy doesn't breathe fire, he spews lava." She leaned in a bit and added, "So can I when I put me mind to it. But Mum hates when I do that. If I'm not careful, it sprays, ya see."

"To be honest, I didn't notice a difference between your father and any other Fire Breather."

"The other dragon breeds can't tell the difference either. All you lot scent is heat and fire. That's mostly what lava is made of. Well, that and some melted rocks." She smiled a little thinking of her father's kin. "They're not very friendly, my father's kind. But they've built whole worlds under those mountains and are some of the best blacksmiths and glass blowers you'll ever know. It's the alchemy, you see. They've mastered it."

"Alchemy?"

"Aye. For the Volcano dragons, it's in their blood. Those with the proper training can change one metal to another."

"Can you?"

"Can I what?"

"Can you change one metal to another?"

"When I have to."

He grinned. "Show me."

"I'm not a dancing monkey."

"Come on. Show me."

She held her hand out. "Give me a coin."

Vigholf tossed her a brass coin. Rhona placed it on the ground, cleared her throat, and unleashed a bit of lava at the coin.

"Ow!"

She cleared her throat again, but this time so she wouldn't laugh. "Sorry, but I warned you it sprays," she reminded him while he rubbed his eye.

Rhona held her hand over the coin and whispered the words only the best Dragonsmiths of the Black Mountains knew. The words her father had taught her before she could fly.

Grinning, she handed the coin back to Vigholf.

He stared at it. "That's it?"

"What do you mean that's it?" She snatched the coin and held it up for him to see. "I changed this from brass to glass."

"Yeah . . . but I thought you'd change it into gold."

She threw the coin at his head. "Glass is just as amazing."

"Is glass even metal? I don't think it is."

"Look," she cut in, annoyed, "I haven't been taught how to change anything into gold. But I can do amazing things with steel and I can turn gold into—"

"Not gold."

"Choke on that coin," she ordered him.

Vigholf chuckled. "You make it too easy. I could torture you with this all night."

Rhona tossed the bones of her meal out into the dark

forest behind her for any animals that may have use of them and tried not to pout. "Daddy wanted to send me to one of his cousins for an apprenticeship where I could have learned all sorts of things like changing things into gold."

"But your mother said no?"

"She figured it was a waste since clearly her eldest daughter would be a Dragonwarrior just like her mum."

"You need to tell her."

"Tell her? Tell her what?"

"That you want to be a blacksmith. That you want to follow in your father's footsteps." He held up the hammer, his appreciative gaze moving over every detail. "That you want to stay in the Northlands after the war is over and make me and mine steel weapons like this. That's what you need to tell her. What you *should* tell her. As soon as we're done with this current nightmare."

She fought hard not to smile, even biting her lip a bit before she said, "So this is all about you then, eh?"

"Not all about me, but my brethren. I'm thinking of the Horde, not just myself. That would be selfish and we of the North are never selfish. We have a Code."

"And your Code says not to be selfish?"

"Probably. I've never been one for a lot of reading and that bloody Code book is *huge*."

Rhona laughed and Vigholf loved hearing the sound of it. "You're not like the other Northlanders, you know?"

"You mean serious and boring and patiently waiting for my glorious death on the battlefield? Yeah. I know. But why go through life being miserable? What's the point of that?"

"There is none." She yawned. "Guess we better get some sleep. We have a lot of hard riding to do tomorrow."

"We're running out of dried beef," he pointed out.

"Because you don't pace yourself."

"I don't even know what those words mean."

"I realize that."

She turned on her side and rested her head on her travel pack.

"Shouldn't we sleep closer together?" Vigholf asked, working hard to sound at least remotely innocent.

"Why? Because we did it before when I was a bit drunk?"

Well . . . yeah. "Of course not! For safety. It can get dangerous in these woods at night."

"How would you know? You've never been this far west."

"True, but aren't all dark woods near mountains the same?"

"I guess you can sleep over—"

With his travel pack in hand, Vigholf clambered over the fire and settled in right beside Rhona.

"Do we really need to be this close?" she asked.

"Yes."

"And why is that?"

"Safety."

"Are you just going to keep throwing that word at me, hoping I'll ignore the fact that you're just using any excuse to snuggle up close to me again?"

"Yes."

She settled down, her back to him. "Well, at least you're honest. My male cousins would have outright lied." She looked at him over her shoulder. "*That's* the Cadwaladr Code, I'm afraid."

"Which is why I didn't bother lying to you. You can spot liars a league away." Vigholf stretched out, his hands behind his head, his eyes gazing up at the stars above his head. "Gods, I'm hot."

Rhona sat back up, gawking at him. "There's snow on the ground. I'm wearing a fur cape. I can see my own breath when I talk or just breathe. This is winter here."

"Northlanders would call this spring. Ice Landers, the Spikes . . . a miserable summer."

"I have nothing to say to any of that." She settled on her side again, and after a few minutes, Vigholf turned on his side and put his arm around her, snuggling in close.

"What are you doing?" she asked.

"Keeping you warm. Don't want you to freeze in the night."

"I'm a fire-breathing dragon. I'll never freeze in the night."

There was a painfully long pause, and Vigholf expected her to throw his arm off or, possibly, castrate him with her spear. But then she finally admitted, "But you do have an amazing amount of body heat. And my human form does get quite chilly."

Grinning, he snuggled in closer.

"Don't get too friendly, Lightning. Just keep me warm. That's it."

"It would probably be better if we were both naked and—"

"Not on your life," she quickly cut in.

"Then how about a kiss," he suggested.

"I can't believe the Northland balls on you."

"We might as well just get it over with."

"There's nothing to get over with."

"We both know you'll kiss me eventually, Sergeant. I'm irresistible."

"I've been resisting you for five years."

"Because you're stubborn and unreasonable. I thought we already established that."

Rolling to her back so she could look him in the eye, the She-dragon warned, "You just watch where you put those hands and keep your lips and your cock—"

"When did I mention my cock?"

"—well away from me or I'm going to use that ax my father gave you to start chopping things off."

"Fine, fine. No need to threaten the important bits of me."

"We have a long trip ahead. I feel it's good to establish boundaries now."

"Right. Boundaries. On our long trip together—alone."

"It can't be that long, Northlander. We have a war to get back to."

"And we will." Vigholf settled down again, tightening his arms around her since she didn't stop him from doing so. "I doubt it will go on without us. And before you say anything, *yes*, I think we're that important."

"Not quite as arrogant as my royal cousins," she murmured, already falling asleep, "but surprisingly close."

Chapter 16

Where are you, brother?

Ragnar's voice in his mind woke Vigholf, and he sat up, yawning, and scratching his head. *Another day and a half from the Western Mountains. Did you contact Keita?*

No. I've been unable to contact her or anyone at Dark Plains. In fact, I've been trying to contact you, but this is the first time I've gotten through. I think it's because you're neither in Dark Plains nor here. The areas are being blocked from one another, but I'm not sure why or who is doing it.

There's a problem, Ragnar.

What's wrong?

The Tribesmen attacked after we arrived, Vigholf told him, but quickly added, *The Kyvich are guarding the gate and the Cadwaladrs are kicking arse. All's fine.*

What about the children?

Queen Rhiannon was not happy with Keita's idea, so they're staying put. But everything is fine, including Keita.

Good, but . . . why are you in the Western Mountains, brother? I know you wouldn't just leave during an attack.

You're not going to like what I'm about to tell you.

Tell me anyway.

It's Annwyl. She's gone off.

Her nut?

Vigholf chuckled. *You could say that. She's gone off to find the Rebel King.*

Gaius Domitus? Ragnar sighed. *If that wench is killed and Fearghus finds out we didn't tell him or Briec about why we originally sent Keita back, giving Fearghus the chance to find his mate himself . . . I'm a dead dragon, brother. You do know that?*

We'll find her, Ragnar. I swear by the gods of war, we'll find her.

Are you traveling alone?

No. This was Rhona's mission. I simply tagged along. Why?

I figured I could do more good here than just being one of the troops at Garbhán Isle.

Is that the only reason? Ragnar asked, sounding curious.

No. I couldn't let her go alone.

Vigholf looked down at a sleeping Rhona. She slept on her side, hands tucked under her cheek. She'd let him hold her through the night, and he'd never slept so well before.

I've become . . . attached, he admitted.

And has she?

She will.

And even without being able to see his brother, Vigholf knew Ragnar was rolling his eyes.

How long will you be? Ragnar asked.

Don't know. But we won't be back until we find Annwyl.

But if Gaius Domitus gets his claws on her . . . Ragnar warned him.

We're hoping to reach her before she reaches the Rebel King. Stop her and bring her back to the Valley.

Let's hope you do. Gaius Domitus is not welcoming of strangers.

Neither is Annwyl.

Ragnar chuckled. *You do have a point. But there is something else—in the Provinces. Thracius has a Dragonmage. A formidable one. Avoid him at all costs, Vigholf.*

Why?

His power in that region is unmatched and he'll do whatever he must to protect Vateria.

Vateria? What does Vateria have to do with—

You know Annwyl. I know Annwyl. If she locks on a target in the Provinces, it'll be Vateria. In her mind, she'll be the one who will need to die.

But she's there for the Rebel King, not Vateria.

I have yet to know Annwyl to ever have one simple task, Vigholf. Trust me—she'll want Vateria dead. But considering the power of her mage, I'm sure Vateria—

—already knows Annwyl's coming, Vigholf finished.

Exactly.

Now it was Vigholf's turn to sigh. *Just wonderful.*

Junius opened the door to his lady's bedchamber. He motioned for his guards to wait outside and entered the room.

He stood well away from the bed and quietly waited. The servant went to her lady's side.

"My lady?" she said softly. "Lord Junius is here to see you."

Smiling and stretching, the suns' rays pouring through the floor-to-ceiling windows illuminating her naked body as she sat up, long silver hair framing her beautiful face, Lady Vateria greeted Junius with a large smile.

"My Lord Junius. What are you doing here so early?"

"We'll have a visitor soon, my lady."

"A visitor?"

"Someone I think you'll be quite pleased to see."

Vateria, grinning, eagerly slid out of bed, and walked over to him. "Are you sure?"

"Our god is sure, which means I am. I sent word to your patrols in the Western Mountains."

"Will the messengers reach them in time?"

"I am our god's chosen mage, my lady. I need no messengers for such a task."

Although all dragons could communicate with blood kin, at the Overlord's command and their god's agreement, Junius restricted that sort of thing within the Provinces. Only the messages *he* wanted to get through were allowed to leave or enter the region. It was how Junius had discovered the rebellion growing within the Iron ranks and was able to nearly snuff it out. Although not completely finished with that situation, it was totally under control. And it would stay that way.

"Of course, of course." She stepped closer to him, her excitement making her eyes bright, her nipples harden. "Could she truly be so foolish as to come *here*?"

"Desperate, I think is the word you want. Once your father and Laudaricus join forces—nothing will stop them. And chances are this is a test by whatever god is protecting *her*. Annwyl the Bloody will not get what she wants until she comes here and completes some task."

"You mean like assassinating me?"

"Most likely. But I plan to capture her before that."

Vateria wrapped her arms around Junius's neck, meaning he could now touch her as protocol dictated. He did, pulling her close and gripping her ass.

"Another toy for my collection," she sighed.

"You'll have to be a little more careful with this one I'm afraid. The humans break much easier than our kind."

"I know, I know. But I've grown bored with the toy I have. I yearn for another."

"You've grown bored, yet you still go to the dungeons to play. Nearly every day."

Her head dipped and she smiled. "Not every day." She briefly chewed her bottom lip. "When?" she asked. "When will she be here?"

"Soon, I'm sure. Then she'll be all yours."

Vateria went up on her toes, kissed him. "You do so endlessly please me, my lord mage."

"Shame your father seems to think that even with my connections and pure Iron bloodlines I'm so beneath you then."

"Don't worry about Daddy. He adores me and he always gives me what I want. And now"—she led him to her bed—"*you* can give me what I want."

"Morning!"

Rhona growled and covered her head with her arms. "Go away."

"We must get on the road, female. Now rise and bless me with your presence."

Laughing, despite her annoyance, Rhona let the Lightning pull her to her feet. But Vigholf was an extremely strong buck of a dragon and he yanked Rhona up and right into his chest, their bodies slamming together, startling them both. The pair stared at each other until Vigholf's gaze moved over her face, finally resting on her mouth. She remembered his push for a kiss the previous evening, and she knew he was thinking about that now. But was he truly attracted to her or was she simply available? And even worse . . . why the hells did she suddenly care? She shouldn't care! She should be punching that look off his face before he did something stupid, like actually kiss her.

Gods! Her own weakness annoyed her.

Rhona pulled her arms from Vigholf's grasp but tried to

keep things light. "It's too early for you to be this extremely ridiculous."

"It's never too early," he joked, stepping away from her. "Now, did you sleep well?"

She stretched her shoulders, desperately trying to forget how well their bodies fit together in that brief moment. "I did."

"So did I. I think we'll need to sleep together tonight to ensure that restfulness stays the same. It's in our best interest."

Shaking her head, Rhona walked around him. "I need food."

Vigholf examined the hills. After a moment, he unleashed a bolt of lightning and a ram with several burn holes in its side tumbled down the hill and landed at Rhona's feet.

Grinning, Vigholf said, "Food."

Keeping her laughter in, Rhona nodded. "Thank you." She adored how proud he looked.

"Welcome."

They ate and walked, the horses following behind them.

"I heard from my brother this morning," Vigholf said.

"Was he angry?"

That was *not* the question Vigholf had expected her to ask. "About?"

"That you haven't returned. That you're not on your way back to Euphrasia readying your troops to destroy the Irons. That you've foolishly followed me on a death march after an insane monarch."

"Uhhhh . . . no. None of that seemed to bother him. In fact, he understood."

"Understood what? That you have this rabid desire to protect every female you've come in contact with?"

"Actually . . . yes. Yes, he does understand that."

Rhona laughed and bit into another piece of meat.

"You should be more positive about all this," he told her. "I'm sure it'll all work out fine."

She stopped and gazed up at him. "Why would you think that?"

"One of us has to be positive," Vigholf explained while he kept walking. "Or we're both dead."

Keita gratefully took the goblet of wine her friend offered her and moved over a bit so that he could sit down beside her, their backs against the wall of the staircase that led to the castle bedrooms.

"It's disturbingly quiet, my friend," Keita remarked after sipping her wine.

Ren nodded. "I know. The Tribesmen would have had these territories well scouted before they came here. They will hide someplace and ready for their next attack."

"We should have taken the children, these idiot witches be damned," she said again, earning her a glare from one of the nearby Kyvich. Keita's response was to stick her tongue out at her like a three-year-old.

"I could have gotten past the Kyvich, I think," he reasoned. "But not your mother. And you won't like hearing this, but I think she had a point. Run now, and the children will be running forever. Might as well teach them now to make a stand."

"But if something happens to them and I didn't warn my brothers . . ."

"The children will be fine. They couldn't be better protected."

"I guess."

"What else bothers you, Keita?"

"I've tried to contact my brothers, just to—"

"Check on Ragnar, who you are deeply in love with but still refuse to admit it?"

"Whatever. But they don't respond."

"I think we won't be hearing from them until this is all over."

Keita looked at her friend. "Why do you say that?"

"From the beginning, before the children were even born, the gods have been involved with this family, Keita. I don't know why you all seem to fascinate them so, but there you have it. And I think cutting off lines of communication between us keeps this rolling along."

"You think one of the gods sent Annwyl into the west, don't you?"

"Would it really surprise you? Annwyl may have her moments, but wandering off into the west to martyr herself to *anything* . . . ? I haven't known that woman long, but that's not Annwyl." He took the goblet from Keita and took a sip. "No, my friend. I'm afraid the gods are playing their games . . . and we're all caught in the middle."

"I must say, Ren. I've become quite annoyed with these gods. I mean . . . other than to make me so enticingly beautiful, I have no idea what their real purpose is. Do you?"

Ren laughed, kissing Keita on the scalp and handing the goblet back to her. "No idea, Keita. None at all."

They found a place to get a few hours' sleep near a stream for fresh water, a cave should they need the shelter, and someone's livestock roaming around.

Full from all the lamb he'd eaten, Vigholf leaned back against his pack.

Rhona held her hands out. "Let me see that."

Vigholf held up his hammer. "This?"

"Aye."

He tossed it to her and she caught it in both hands.

"Why would you choose something so heavy and cumbersome?" she asked.

"Heavy? My old one was heavy. This one that your father made? Light as a feather."

"This is not light, Northlander." She stood with the hammer, but stumbled a bit.

"Sure you just don't need some help with that, weak female?"

"I'm fine, thank you very much. It's just that I knew I shouldn't have had any of that wine we got in town. But I needed something to silence the screaming in my head over what we're being forced to do."

Gods, she was adorable, swinging his warhammer around. Even if she didn't like the weight, she still handled it well.

"Now a hammer . . ." he told her. "*That's* a weapon. A weapon for adults anyway."

"Leave off me spear. It had served me well until *you* destroyed it."

"It was an accident!"

"Of course it was."

"I hear sarcasm," he complained as she stood over him and dropped the hammer on his stomach. "Ow! Evil wench!"

Rhona laughed and sat down next to him. "I'm not nearly as tired as I should be."

"Good. Then perhaps you can explain Annwyl to me." And Vigholf adored how wide Rhona's eyes grew.

"Why not ask me to explain water? The air?" she demanded.

"I don't understand."

"You ask me to explain the unexplainable. Annwyl makes sense to no one. A bastard daughter of a monstrous tyrant, she should still be living in the peasant village her father dragged her out of. I mean what monarch wants his bastard daughter around when he already has a proper son as heir? She's also the sister of an even worse tyrant who sold her off to another tyrant so they could unite kingdoms. She *should* be married to that second tyrant with a few royal heirs to make everyone happy. But she never even reached the wedding and ended up destroying the brother who'd tortured so many."

"So what does all that mean?"

"It means she's amazing—and terrifying. Annwyl kills without question, rules with an iron fist, and has little patience for anyone. She can be cruel, she can be loving, she can be heartless, and she can care too much. She is blindingly loyal, but demands the same loyalty from everyone and is devastated when she doesn't receive it. I can't explain Annwyl, Vigholf, so I never try."

"I guess then we'll leave it at that."

Appearing relieved, she turned her gaze up to the sky. "Are those clouds?"

Vigholf shrugged, studying every part of her, not caring about the sky or clouds. "No clue."

She looked at him. "That's probably because you're staring at me and not up there—you know . . . where the clouds actually are."

"I like staring at what I'm staring at."

"Yeah, right."

"What does that mean?"

"Nothing. We need to get some sleep. Long day tomorrow."

"All right."

Rhona got to her feet and went over to her bedroll. By the time she'd settled down, Vigholf was stretched out right beside her.

"What are you doing?"

"Giving you my warmth."

"I didn't ask for it."

"And yet I'm giving it to you because that's how wonderful I am."

"Yeah, but—"

"Ssssh. You'll wake the horses."

Rhona shook her head and settled down. "You just never give up, do you?"

No. He didn't. But when Vigholf put his arm around her waist—she didn't complain either.

Chapter 17

It was the lightning that woke Rhona up the following morning. Not *the* Lightning, but actual lightning. The stuff Vigholf's kind was made of, the way she was born of fire. And because of that lightning, she wasn't exactly surprised to find herself no longer entangled with the Northlander. She'd discovered after their two nights together that Vigholf was one of those dragons who liked to wrap himself around a female like a vine. She'd punched and kicked her way out of several situations like that in the past, but it hadn't bothered her so much with Vigholf. Perhaps because he wasn't also a twitcher.

Rhona dragged herself up and ran her fingers through her hair. Thunder rolled from the skies and big bolts of lightning cut across the land. Lightning that seemed to be getting dangerously close.

"Should I even be sitting next to you?" she asked.

"The lightning will pass. Just give it a few minutes."

She studied the dragon. "You look rather . . . concerned."

"Not concerned. Tense." He looked at her. "Have you ever been hit by lightning?"

"Only during battle."

"Well, we tend to attract lightning, seeing as we're made

of the stuff—and it can sting like hell depending on where it strikes."

"Interesting. I can walk through fire with absolutely no problems."

"Don't brag. It annoys me."

She relaxed her back against the tree, her shoulder pressed into Vigholf's.

"Sure you want to get so close?" he asked.

"If I had a problem with it, I would have said something last night."

His chuckle was low and soft, and Rhona added, "I can handle lightning." She raised her knees, resting her chin on them, and wrapped her arms around her legs. She peered out over the field. "Besides, I like watching it. The way it skitters and flashes. You never know where it's going to hit or how big or long it will be. I find it kind of . . . fascinating. And pretty."

"Do you find me fascinating and pretty too?"

"No."

Vigholf's laugh was louder this time.

"Oh," Rhona said, wincing.

"What's wrong?"

"I forgot about the horses. They're probably long gone."

"No, they're at the foot of the hill over there, where the cave is. They'll probably stay in there until the lightning passes."

Rhona looked at him. "I bet it's warmer in there than it is out here."

"Probably."

She stared at him some more until he blinked and said, "Oh! Do you want to go in there?"

"You mean rather than sitting under a tree during a lightning storm? That might make sense."

He shrugged, gave a small, embarrassed smile. "I didn't want to wake you up unless I had to."

"A tree I'm under, destroyed by lightning would have definitely woken me up."

"You use that tone with your siblings . . . and Éibhear."

"It's my 'don't be an idiot' tone." Rhona got to her feet, picked up her weapons and travel pack. "Come on, Northlander. Let's see if you can beat what you're made of."

Vigholf didn't beat what he'd been made of. In fact, he was struck at least three times, but thankfully it was mostly on his shoulders and arms. The worst was the head, neck, and ass. A Northland dragon couldn't help but screech a little when hit in the ass with lightning. Although Vigholf always felt invigorated after getting hit with a few bolts of lightning, the effect often lasting for days.

They ran into the cave, now both of them drenched since the skies decided to open up once they were clear of that tree.

"That was exhilarating, eh?" Rhona asked him.

"No, it wasn't. It was painful."

"Don't be weak, Vigholf."

He narrowed his eyes at her, and laughing, Rhona stumbled away from him. "Don't you dare!"

"I was hoping you could show me how to not be weak."

"You unleash your lightning, and I'm unleashing my flame!"

Vigholf moved toward her, arms out and reaching for her. "I think I'm willing to risk it."

"Wait, wait." She held up her hand to stop him. "Where're the horses?"

Vigholf took a quick look around. "They were right here a few minutes ago."

"Piss and fire. They made a run for it."

"I doubt they went back outside." Vigholf sniffed the air.

"That way," he said, pointing at a passage and walking toward it.

"Wait, Vigholf, I'm not sure we should . . ."

But Vigholf was already moving, going deeper into the cave. Rhona was right behind him, but she seemed a little nervous. He had no idea why. Now that he thought about it, he didn't think he'd ever seen Rhona the Fearless nervous.

They located the horses about a half mile in. The animals seemed uncomfortable with the thunder exploding around the cave walls, which probably explained why they ended up going farther in rather than running off. Rhona walked up to the pair and, with one hand for each, petted them on their necks.

"It's all right. The storm will pass. Sssssh."

Gods, the female really did have a way with horses. Something he found completely fascinating. Especially since he did get the feeling that she had, on more than one occasion, eaten horseflesh. But the animals still seemed to like her.

Then again, Vigholf liked her too.

"They'll be fine," she said to him while smiling at the horses. "This bad storm just spooked them a—"

The horses suddenly reared, and Vigholf grabbed Rhona around the waist, yanking her out of the way. Good thing too because the horses bolted, running back the way they'd come.

"What the hells was that?" he asked her.

"I don't know." Rhona pulled away from him. "Something scared them and it wasn't the storm." She circled around him. "I knew we shouldn't have come in here. I knew . . ."

She was behind him when her words faded out and Vigholf turned around to find her staring off into another dark passageway. "Rhona?"

"Shit!" Rhona screamed before she shoved him toward the exit. "Run!"

She took off, heading the same direction the horses went, but it slithered out of the darkness, moving faster than anything Vigholf had ever seen, and cut her off.

Rhona fell back, falling on her ass. And it reared up on its tail, leather wings spreading out from its scaled body to block the exit. It hissed, the sound bouncing off the walls.

Its head reared back and Vigholf rushed forward, grabbing Rhona by the neck of her chain-mail shirt and yanking her up. They ran seconds before a stream of green venom hit the ground where Rhona had been, sizzling as it burned into the rock.

Deciding he had to protect the female, Vigholf turned, lightning sparking off him as he began to shift.

"No!" Rhona grabbed his hand and yanked him after her. "Don't shift."

"Why the hells not?"

"You'll never fit!" At first he didn't know what she was talking about, but as they charged into narrow passageway after narrow passageway, the thing easily slithering behind them, he knew Rhona was right. These caverns and passageways had not been carved out for dragons to stand and fight in, but for them to die, along with anything else unlucky enough to find its way in here.

If Rhona had the time, she'd stop and kick herself. Because she should have been paying attention. If she had, she would have caught that distinct scent or seen the slither marks on the cave's dirt floor or simply known that they weren't alone. That like most of these low caves in the west, this wasn't empty. It had a low-cave wyvern. A godsdamn wyvern! And the ones this far west were the worst of the lot.

Her father said the wyverns resented dragons because dragons could speak, could shift to human, and had arms and legs. Then again, dragons were higher beings. They weren't snakes that had lived so long their bodies had lengthened enough to wrap themselves around castles several times and had sprouted wings.

But the venom . . . the venom was the worst part of it. No matter the breed of dragon, there were none who could stop the wyvern venom from melting the scales off their bodies. A most unpleasant experience. First it destroyed a dragon's scales; then the wyvern wrapped itself around the now-defenseless dragon prey and squeezed until the life had been crushed from its bones.

An experience that Rhona had no intention of going through. Not if she could help it.

"We'll have to fight him," she told Vigholf as they both suddenly took a tunnel to the right.

"As human?"

"We don't have a choice."

They took the next turn into another cavern and split up, Vigholf immediately dashing to the other side of the opening, his back against the cave wall. And Rhona went to the left, crouching behind a boulder.

She grabbed the spear her father gave her and held it in her hand. The tip appeared and it grew to be about three feet, but that was it, waiting until she called on more.

She heard the wyvern slither into the cavern, but she could tell it instantly stopped before going farther in.

Carefully, she peeked around the boulder. The wyvern had reared up, nearly reaching the ceiling even though still part of its body stretched outside the cavern. Its eyes searched the area, scales shimmering in the darkness, thankfully easy enough for Rhona to see. If she were truly human, she'd have been eaten by now after getting lost in the black.

Its gaze finally locked on the boulder Rhona stood behind, the sides of its mouth curling up at the corners.

Rhona had only a moment to think, *Shit*, and then she was diving back behind the boulder, crouching as low as possible. The venom hit the rock and she heard the sizzle, smelled that burning scent of putrid death. Gods, she'd have to make this fast.

She spun around to the other side of the boulder, stepped out, and grabbed one of the throwing axes hanging from her belt. She lifted and threw it. The trajectory was spot-on, flipping end over end across the cavern until it hit the wyvern in the chest—and bounced off, completely ineffectual at this distance.

The wyvern hissed in annoyance and slithered after her. Rhona planted her feet and waited, watching the thing coming right for her.

But behind the wyvern, back by the entrance, Vigholf ran from his spot against the wall, his battle-ax arcing through the air.

Rhona prepared her body, waiting. The ax slammed into the wyvern's tail, hacking the end off. The high-pitched roar the wyvern unleashed shook the cavern walls, and it pulled up to look, ready to strike Vigholf. That's when Rhona moved forward, dashing to within feet of the thing. She lifted her spear and it grew from three feet to five feet to six feet, on and on until it was long enough to reach the wyvern's neck. She rammed the spear forward and buried it between scales and into vulnerable flesh, not only ripping into an artery but blocking the thing's ability to unleash any more venom. Just as her mum had taught her, years and years ago.

The wyvern tried to turn, its body thrashing wildly, blood spewing from its tail and its throat. Rhona held on, refusing to release the desperate animal even though her human body was weakening faster than she'd like.

"Pull him down!" Vigholf yelled as he charged forward.

It wasn't easy, but she did as he ordered, stepping back and yanking the beast down with her. When it was still about ten feet from the ground, Vigholf climbed up on its back and up to where its head met its neck. He lifted his warhammer with both hands—the weapon her father made easily tripling in size—and swung. The heavy steel struck the side of the wyvern's head, something snapping inside. But still it fought. Still it tried to kill or get away or both. So Rhona gripped her spear tighter and twisted it, shoving the tip deeper in. And Vigholf raised his hammer and brought it down again and again directly onto the wyvern's head, smashing it until the thing finally slumped forward, the only thing keeping it up being Rhona's spear.

Vigholf stood there a moment, his hammer pressed to the back of the thing's neck, and his body leaning on it.

"This is not comfortable, Lightning."

"Oh. Sorry." He went down the beast's neck until he could jump off without breaking something important. And as he walked toward Rhona, he heard it coming up from behind him. Hissing.

"Rhona?"

She leaned over, her hands still clutching her spear.

"I think there's more," he told her.

She blinked, then quickly examined the one still hanging from her weapon. "Shit and piss . . . I was right."

"Right about what?"

"This is the baby." She retracted her weapon and took off running. "You better come on!"

Vigholf bolted after her, ignoring the angry sounds coming from behind him. Rhona raced through caverns and passageways, the only thing leading them both the scent of fresh air. When they finally saw the way out, they hurtled toward the exit together, diving through it and out into the much safer world of rain and painful lightning.

"Vigholf!" she ordered. "Close it!"

Vigholf turned, his eyes briefly widening at the size of the head he could see slithering forward, mouth gaping open to unleash more of that venom. Having no desire to experience that, he unleashed his lightning on the rocky area above. Boulders crashed down, blocking the cavern, but it didn't stop the scream of rage that followed.

Panting, the pair looked at each other and then over to a nearby tree.

"You two," Vigholf accused the horses. "Leaving us to die. *You couldn't give us a little warning?*"

The female at least had the good graces to look away, but the male sneered at him. Again!

And Vigholf was marching over there, his fists raised to teach the rude bastard some manners, when Rhona caught his arm, pulled him back.

"Can we fight about this later? It's not like those boulders are going to stop her for long, and I'd rather not be here when she finally digs her way out."

"Yeah. All right." But he pointed a warning finger at the stallion. "But this isn't over!"

Rhona rolled her eyes before she mounted the mare. "I swear, the both of you—pathetic."

The stallion allowed Vigholf to mount him, but Vigholf knew he wasn't happy about it.

Even though it was still raining quite hard, they rode off, leaving the cave and that damn wyvern behind. But after about fifteen minutes the rain let up, then stopped completely. Soaking wet, but not minding too much because he was still alive and not covered in green venom, Vigholf rode alongside Rhona. After a while he had to admit to her, "You were amazing in there."

"In where?"

"In the cave. With the wyvern. Have you fought them before?"

"No, but Mum has. So has my father. They have a lot of them in some of the caverns in the Black Mountains."

"Well . . . you handled all that brilliantly."

"You sound surprised."

"We were trapped in a cave with an animal you never fought, that you'd only heard about from your parents, and yet you knew just what to do, and you knew quickly. That's impressive, Rhona. I know I wouldn't have handled it as well if you hadn't been there."

"I've seen you handle the unexpected, Vigholf. You would have done fine on your own." She stopped the mare and Vigholf halted the stallion. "But your words mean much to me. Thank you."

He shrugged, feeling a bit foolish. "I merely note what I see. Nothing more."

"It's more to me," she said.

And, no longer feeling foolish, Vigholf moved the stallion closer until they were side by side.

Vigholf reached out and stroked Rhona's cheek. She tensed, her eyes blinking wide in surprise. She'd had the same expression when she first saw the wyvern. A look of panic she was desperately trying to control.

He should stop. He should pull back and they should ride on. There was so much going on in their world, they didn't have time for any of this.

But the honest truth of it was he couldn't help himself. Not with those beautiful brown eyes watching him.

Vigholf slipped his hand behind Rhona's neck and leaned in closer, the stallion beneath him surprisingly calm and unmoving. Holding the back of her neck loosely, Vigholf brought his face in a bit closer, brushing his forehead against her chin, her cheek; his fingers massaged her neck.

When she didn't pull away—or impale him with that damn spear—Vigholf pressed his lips against hers.

Her whole body immediately tensed, her fingers curling into fists gripping the mare's mane tight.

Vigholf tipped his head to the side, his tongue gently sliding against her lips, trying to coax her into returning the kiss without seeming desperate.

And gods . . . he was desperate.

He'd wanted to do this for five years. Five long years of being stuck in the same cave with a female who told everyone he was a pest while swinging that damn tail at him.

Yet there was nothing from her or her lips. No response. No reaction except those tight fists.

Too fast. He was going too fast. Like she'd warned him their night together at Garbhán Isle, she wasn't like her sisters or her cousins when it came to this sort of thing.

So he'd wait because, he knew, Rhona was a female worth waiting for.

Vigholf pulled back, but let the fingers that still rested on her neck linger as he sat up straight.

She watched him but said nothing, and he had no idea what to make of that. But he wouldn't apologize for what he'd done. Not now. Not ever.

Rhona began to speak, stopped, frowned, and with a short shake of her head, turned her attention to the road ahead of them and spurred her horse into a gallop.

And, after letting out a soul-deep sigh, Vigholf followed.

Overlord Thracius walked by his soldiers, watching as they worked hard to ready everything.

"Any word from my daughter?" he asked his next in command, General Maecius.

"No, sir. I sent out scouts to see if they could find the messenger."

"And?"

"They discovered his body beside a lake."

Thracius stopped and faced the general. "Accident?"

"Signs of poisoning and his body showed signs of torture. He was killed."

"So the message got to the Southlanders?"

"I would assume. But there's been no retreat. No exodus of troops."

"That's fine. If the princes had left to save their spawn, I would have only had to kill them later anyway." He walked on, but asked, gesturing at the work going on around him, "How far along are we?"

"Another two days. Maybe three."

"Then start the siege tonight."

"But my lord—"

"*Tonight.* We start the siege and prepare everything else while they're dealing with that. But"—he stopped again and faced the general, pointing his talon in his face—"the timing must be perfect, Maecius. Understand me?"

"I do, my lord. And it will be perfect."

"Good." He headed toward his private chambers deep inside Polycarp Mountains. "By the time we're ready to strike . . . those idiots won't see us coming."

Chapter 18

They rode most of the day until they reached a town about another day's ride outside of the Aricia Mountains. Crossing the mountains would be the challenge. Not only because of the terrain, but because of what lay on the other side. But until then, Rhona wasn't going to think about it. Instead, she only wanted warm food and ale.

She knew the horses would never allow themselves to be placed in a stable for the night, so she left them about a mile outside of town near the river that cut through the mountains. And, if the horses were still there in the morning, they'd hopefully take them into the mountains the following day.

As soon as Rhona and Vigholf reached the town, they separated. He didn't say why, and she didn't ask. They hadn't spoken a word to each other since Vigholf had kissed her. He didn't seem angry, which she appreciated, but she never saw that kiss coming. And when it did, it took her completely by surprise. So she'd ended up just sitting there, feeling confused and foolish and annoyingly warm. But . . . what else could she do? For five years the dragon had done nothing but obsess over her spear and get in her way. Now he was kissing her—while on horseback. Acting as if he meant that kiss. As if kissing her was the most important thing in the entire world . . .

No, no, no! She didn't want to think about this. She was hungry and had things to do. So she went and replenished their supplies and eventually settled down at a busy pub for that hot meal.

A few bowls of stew later, the Northlander arrived. He wore the hood of his cape pulled down far on his head, hiding his purple hair. But he couldn't hide his size. The males instantly fell into an uneasy silence and the women . . . well, no matter the species, Rhona could see lust miles away.

He sat down on the wood bench across from her and motioned to a barmaid. "Ale and stew. Some bread, too."

The woman smiled sweetly at him before turning to Rhona. "*More* food for you?"

Rhona sucked her tongue against her teeth in warning and the barmaid walked off.

"Get what we need?" Vigholf asked, and she was quite relieved that he was finally talking to her.

"I got enough to last me at least two weeks. But with you along, I'm guessing we'll need more food in another day or two."

He shrugged and began eating the bread she had left.

"What have you been up to?"

"Tell you later," he muttered, leaning back as food was placed in front of him.

"All right, but I was thinking we could—" Another bowl of stew was dropped in front of Rhona and it was filled to the brim.

"You seem so hungry," the barmaid said by way of explanation.

Rhona's eyes narrowed onto the bitchy little service worker, but Vigholf made her smile a little when he said around a mouthful of food, "I like a female with an appetite."

Once the barmaid had gone off, Rhona asked, "Want me to get us a couple of rooms for the night? They have space upstairs."

"No," he replied, completely focused on his food.

"No?"

"No."

"You want to spend another night outside when we have a perfectly acceptable pub? Why?"

"Because you'd rather sleep under the stars."

"What?"

"You're just as happy on the ground, looking up at the sky. Right?"

It took a moment for Rhona to understand what he was talking about, but then she laughed. "You're throwing my drunken words back at me?"

"Only when I like them. You don't mind, do you?"

"Not at all." Rhona had never really liked staying in pubs or inns. She always felt trapped by the walls, but her kin had always felt completely different on that point.

Rhona watched the dragon eat. Although it was more like inhaling than an actual act of putting food in one's mouth and chewing. Yet it seemed to work for him. And, knowing that one serving would never satisfy Vigholf, Rhona pushed her bowl of stew across the table and let him devour that as well.

Once Vigholf finished eating, they headed back to where they had left the horses. Separating from Rhona for a bit had been a good idea. It had allowed him to get his reason back. Although he didn't regret kissing Rhona, he now realized he'd have to handle this with much more finesse. Something he knew he could manage . . . with a lot of effort. But, still . . . manageable.

"So what did you do in town?" Rhona asked once they were well on the road.

"Got information," he said, finally able to pull the hood of his cape off his head. It had begun to annoy him.

"Information? I thought you'd never been to this town before."

"I haven't, but you can always find out information. You just need to know the kind of places to go and the kind of people to ask."

"I'm impressed. I always seem to be the last one anyone sends out for information."

"Because you're such a soldier that you can't help but look like you're interrogating someone."

She laughed. "Thank you very much!"

He bumped her with his elbow. "I didn't mean that in a bad way."

"You *didn't* mean that I'm a villainous soldier that terrifies the poor townsfolk with my intimidating demeanor?"

"Well . . . you're not villainous."

"So what did you find out?" she asked, surprised that hadn't been the first question out of her mouth. Gods, who knew the Northlander could be so bloody distracting? Especially when all she wanted to do was demand to know what the hells that kiss had been about.

"We're on the right track. Three females were seen coming through town, dressed as travelers, on foot, but they sounded so large and well armed, they had to be Annwyl, Izzy, and Branwen."

She laughed. "When the Cadwaladrs don't breed them big, they mate with the big ones. Usually." She adjusted the pack she carried. "How long since they went through?"

"Three days, give or take a day."

"Shit. They're way ahead of us."

"We'll find them."

"Because we have horses?"

"No. Because those three will find trouble, no matter how they're dressed or what they do to be ignored. Trust me. . . . We'll find them."

"Anything else?"

"It seems that more Sovereign soldiers have been seen around as well. More than the townsfolk are used to since the war began. And even more in the last few days."

"They causing any problems?"

"Not so far, but we should be careful."

To Rhona's surprise, the horses were where she'd left them, grazing on grass and nuzzling each other.

Rhona pulled out a burlap bag filled with fruit she'd picked up in town, but Vigholf took it from her. "I'll feed them."

"You will?"

"I think they like me."

"No, they don't."

"The stallion lets me ride him."

"Only because he's keeping an eye on the mare. He couldn't care less about you."

"I don't agree." And off he went.

"You can't be that oblivious," she told his back, but she realized that not only could he be that oblivious . . . he *was* that oblivious.

Shaking her head, Rhona walked over to a nice spot and pulled out her bedroll. She spread it out and sat down, letting out a weary sigh.

She placed the palms of her hands flat behind her, propping her up, and stretched out her legs.

But she wasn't surprised when she heard, "Oaf!" seconds before Vigholf flipped over her legs and slammed into a nearby tree.

"I told you they don't—"

"Quiet," the Lightning barked at her, getting himself up and stepping over her to march right back over there.

Two seconds later, he came flying back again.

"What is wrong with you?" Vigholf demanded of the stallion.

"He doesn't like you and he doesn't want you around his female," Rhona explained.

"I don't care." Vigholf stepped over her legs, heading over to the stallion again, but Rhona reached up and grabbed his arm. "You of all dragons should understand his position. Now sit." When Vigholf only glared at the horse, Rhona insisted, "Sit down. Now!"

"Fine!" Vigholf threw the bag of fruit in the horses' direction. "Here, you bastard!"

Rhona bit the inside of her mouth to stop from laughing and was pleasantly relieved that everything seemed back to normal again.

She pulled on his arm until he finally sat beside her. "You take things so personally."

"No, I don't."

"You do, but you need to let it go. For your sake." She released his arm and brushed the growing welt on his forehead. "Before that mean bastard cracks your skull open."

"I thought we could bond over the fruit."

"You're not going to bond with that one. Just be glad they've stayed with us this long."

"Bastard," he muttered while rubbing his abused forehead. "Just a mean bastard."

"You should be used to mean bastards."

"Don't talk about my kin like that."

"Actually," she told him, "I was speaking of my own."

"Oh. Then you have a point."

Rhona took another look at Vigholf's head. "That's swelling. I better get a compress for it." She leaned over

Vigholf to get a cloth from her bag. That's when she felt him bury his nose against her neck and take a deep breath.

Rhona froze. "Are you smelling me?"

"No," the Lightning replied, but the word was muffled by all the hair he had his face buried in.

"All right then."

She pulled a clean cloth from her bag and, after easing away from Vigholf, went to the river, and plunged the material into the cold water.

Looking around for some snow or, even better, a bit of ice, Rhona stood and turned—only to find Vigholf standing right behind her. She took a step back, startled to find him so close and asked, "What's wrong?"

"Nothing."

"What's that look on your face?"

"What look?"

"Like you're starving." Rhona briefly closed her eyes, exasperated, immediately realizing this had nothing at all to do with her. This dragon was a bottomless pit! "Gods of death, you cannot be hungry again. You just *ate*."

"I'm not hungry."

"But you have your hungry face."

"My hungry face?"

"I guess you never noticed it because you never look in a mirror, but you have this . . . hungry face. Like you're a starving man ain't seen a good stew in years."

"Well, I don't have that look for stew."

Rhona panicked a little and desperately whispered, "This isn't about the horses, is it? You can't go around eating our transportation."

Vigholf snatched the compress from her hand, inexplicably aggravated. "I have no intention of eating our transportation." He pressed the cloth to his head. She was guessing he had a headache. His own fault really, trying to feed the horses.

"You can't lie to me, Vigholf. You clearly want something to eat, but you're not getting it. Not tonight. We need to economize with our supplies."

"I'm not hungry," Vigholf growled.

"You need to find a way to control your appetite."

"I'm not hungry."

"We're going into enemy territory," Rhona felt the need to explain as she would to one of her cousins or siblings. "I don't know how regularly we'll be able to get you food. So you'll really need to—"

"I'm not hungry!" he yelled at her.

Rhona slammed her finger into his chest. "Don't yell at me, you Northland bastard. *I'm* not the one who looks like he hasn't had a meal in years."

"You want me to be honest with you?" Vigholf snapped. "You want me to tell you why I have my hungry face as you call it? Because of you. Because I'm hungry for you. If there's anything I want to eat—it's *you*."

Rhona stepped back, hands on hips, and accused, "You cannibalistic bastard!"

And that was when the mare charged Rhona and shoved her into the river.

Vigholf nodded at the mare. "Thank you for that. Because I'd been moments from doing it myself." Because no one could possibly be *that* oblivious. No one!

Gasping and desperately trying to push wet hair out of her eyes, Rhona got to her feet.

"What was that for?" she demanded, pulling herself out of the river.

"Because," Vigholf answered for both him and the mare, "sometimes you ain't half a dimwitted twit."

"Me?" she nearly screeched. "Me? *I'm* the dimwitted twit, O Great Feeder of the Horses?"

"I was trying to *bond*!"

"Well, bloody good job you're doing with that." Rhona held her arms out at her sides. "Look at me! It'll take forever for my clothes to dry. Arrrgh!" She glared at him. "I should set you on fire!"

"I wasn't the one who pushed you in. Although I *wanted* to."

"Oh, really? Well, I'd like to see you try."

And, with a shrug, Vigholf shoved Rhona back into the river. He took great satisfaction in hearing that splash.

The mare, shaking her head, walked back to the stallion.

"She dared me," he argued, holding his hand out for Rhona to grasp so he could help her out of the river. "I couldn't ignore a dare."

Then again, he couldn't ignore that fist to the jaw either. And gods-dammit that female had a mighty right hook!

"You're just lucky," Rhona told him as she got out of the river by herself, "that I respect your brother too much to bring him back your corpse!"

Vigholf rubbed his jaw. "The punch was unnecessary," he muttered.

"Shut up." She walked around him. "Just . . . shut up."

"We're not done talking, Rhona," he said to her back.

"What else is there to talk about? You're an insane Lightning and that mare has no bloody loyalty. All seems clear to me."

Fed up, frustrated, and out of ideas, Vigholf just admitted the truth.

"I want you, Rhona."

She stripped off her soaking-wet fur cape and put it over a low-hanging branch near her bedroll. "You want me to do what?"

At that point, Vigholf was at a loss. He raised his hands in defeat, his mouth open as he gawked at her.

When he didn't reply to her stupid question, Rhona

looked at him. "Why are you staring at me like . . ." She blinked. Twice. "Oh. You mean . . ." Her eyes widened. "Oh!" Narrowed. "Oh." Shook her head, appearing a bit disgusted. "Oh." Then she smiled a bit. "Oh." Then she sort of slumped and sighed. "Oh."

"What was all that?" he demanded.

"It means I'll not settle."

Vigholf felt rage suddenly explode through his veins. She'd said something like that before, and he hadn't much liked it then either. "And with me you'd be settling?" he bit out between clenched teeth.

"Well, we'd both be settling, wouldn't we?"

"What?"

"No need to bellow. But it's plain, yeah? I'm here. I'm unattached." She pointed at her crotch. "I've got a pus—"

"Yes," Vigholf cut in. "I'm well aware of what you have."

"That's it then. You have needs. I understand that. But I'll not let some dragon fuck me because I happen to be here. Get yourself a barmaid."

"Is that what you think?" Vigholf asked her. "That I only want you because you're here?"

"You expect me to believe a Northlander would be seriously interested in one of us?"

"Us? You mean a Southland female? The ones you constantly accuse us of stealing?"

"No. I mean us. The scarred-up, less-than-reputable, drink-too-much, curse-too-often Cadwaladr females. The ones you lot *never* steal."

"We did once. And do you know what happened?" Vigholf asked her. "While one of your bloody aunts was removing the lungs from her captors, your Uncle Bercelak was kidnapping and dismembering the eldest sons of all the Horde leaders . . . until she was returned. Soooo, stealing Cadwaladr females. Not something we do anymore."

"Oh." Rhona rubbed her nose, and he knew she was trying not to laugh. "Right. Heard about that. That was my Aunt—"

"Don't care," he admitted. "But if you want to know why my kin were specifically *not* giving *you* a second glance—that was because I told them not to."

"You . . . you told them not to?"

"*Strongly* told them not to. With great force."

Rhona shook her head, confused. "What does that mean?"

"It means I told them to stay away from what was mine."

Wait . . . what? "Yours?"

"Mine. I told them that if they wanted to keep their eyes in their heads and scales on their backs—they'd stay as far away from you as possible."

"But—"

He started walking toward her. "And, as my kind often does, my younger brother tried to test me. Kept looking at you. Growling inappropriately."

"How does one growl inappropriate—"

"Lusting after what was mine."

"I'm not sure I'm comfortable with you—"

"So I cracked his bloody head open with my hammer."

Rhona froze and focused on the seething male before her. "You did what?"

"He survived. His head was kind of flat anyway."

"He's your brother!" she yelled.

"Then he shouldn't have looked!" Vigholf yelled back at her.

Disgusted, she turned from him and returned to her bedroll. "You're worse than Éibhear and Celyn!"

"I am not," he shot back, insulted. "Unlike that Blue baby, I made it clear from the very beginning I had interest in you. The fact that my brother chose to ignore that was his own damn mistake."

"Oh, well, I guess that makes it all right then."

"As far as Northlanders are concerned, it does." He followed her. "You might as well accept that I knew what my intentions toward you were from the very beginning. And the fact that you're a Cadwaladr was simply my burden to bear."

"Your burden to . . ." No. Best not get into that or she'd hit him again. So Rhona took a deep breath and crossed her arms over her chest. "And when exactly was the beginning of this great want? An hour or so? Two? When you kissed me this morning?"

"No. Since that night you got drunk with your cousins at Garbhán Isle."

Rolling her eyes, Rhona reminded him, "That happened . . . what? Two *days* ago?"

"Not that time. The other time. When me, Ragnar, and Meinhard brought Éibhear and Keita back from the Northlands and Outer Plains."

Frowning, "What the hells are you talking about?"

"I was sitting up one night, staring out the window . . . missing my damn hair." And gods, the glare she got when she laughed. "When I saw all these dragons flying low— all of you for some reason wearing eye patches—when you suddenly dropped Keita like a sack of grain." Rhona winced at the memory. Although it was more about those ridiculous homemade eye patches than dropping Keita, but that involved a long explanation she wasn't about to get into.

"The others went up and over the building, but you . . . you flew right into the wall by my window. Damaged the stone with that hard head of yours."

"Oy!"

"But all I could think was, 'Look at the tail on that one.'

You know why? Because that was *my* tail. And since you seem to be the only one completely oblivious to that—even after that damn kiss—let me make it clear for you . . ." He stood right in front of her and yelled, "*My tail!*"

Rhona let out a breath and stepped away from him, turning her back.

Vigholf gritted his teeth, now angry with himself rather than her. This hadn't been how he'd planned things. But the female was just so damn frustrating and confusing he had no idea where she was coming from or going!

For instance who knew she'd slam him in the knee with the butt of her gods-damn spear, forcing him down? Then who knew she'd press the tip of that spear to his throat? But that's exactly what she did.

Vigholf gazed up at her, staring at the pretty face with the small scar on her cheek.

"All right," he said, trying not to move. "I'm a prat. That don't change how I feel, Rhona."

"Good. That makes this a bit easier then, don't it?"

Then she leaned down and kissed him—making Vigholf even *more* confused!

Chapter 19

All this would have been so much easier if Vigholf had been just a tad clearer. Complaining about her spear and calling her Babysitter were *not* acceptable ways to show interest. At least not for Rhona.

Because Rhona was not a subtle female and she didn't know how to read subtle either. How to understand it. She was a straightforward dragoness, and she expected that straightforwardness returned in kind.

And once she was clear on his intentions, understood them, well, then . . . the rest was quite easy. At least for her.

So Rhona kissed him. Hard. Her tongue sliding into his mouth, tasting and teasing, her lips desperately pressed to his, surprising herself with the intensity of it all. But there really was something about this dragon that she very much liked. Perhaps more than she was willing to admit. But now, out here, far away from wars and battles and troops and kin and all the other distractions that could ruin a day, all Rhona had to worry about, to *think* about—for once—was her and Vigholf.

And truly, it was the best feeling ever.

* * *

Vigholf never expected her to kiss him. And her kiss was desperate, demanding, which was exactly how Vigholf felt. How he'd been feeling since a tumble of brown wings, hair, and talons had slammed into the castle wall beside his room, damaging the brick and stone and his equilibrium.

Her tongue invaded his mouth and her hands pulled at his clothes. This wasn't what Vigholf had expected when he'd stood there staring at her ten minutes ago. Maybe another kiss he'd hoped for. A kiss that perhaps she'd return this time. One that she actually responded to. But this . . . this was even better. And completely surprising. Especially since this was not how things were done in the north. In the north it was kissing first, fucking later. Sometimes much later. The females of their Hordes were so protected that for them to have more than one or two lovers before their Claiming was rare. For many of the males it meant finding human pets to entertain them until they found the She-dragon they would mate with for life. But the courting process was relatively simple with actual physical contact not made until commitments had been sworn to. Even then, if there was more than one male interested—and often there was—then an event referred to as The Honour would take place. A battle until the death—or at least till a single dragon had beaten all the others into unconsciousness—so that the final dragon could claim the prize. Although since the death of Vigholf's father, The Honour rarely took place these days among the Olgeirsson Horde.

Still, all these were long and complex steps that one must take to secure themselves a dragoness. An average, everyday, run-of-the-mill dragoness.

Then the Cadwaladr females had come along and that all seemed to change. Since taking their place beside the Northlanders to fight the Irons, the Clan females had been known to fuck whom they liked, when they liked. After a particularly rousing battle, a Cadwaladr female might simply grab the tail of some unsuspecting Northland male and drag him off to a quiet alcove somewhere. None of this the Northland males minded in the least. But it was what happened afterward that they did not favor.

For once done with males, the She-dragons wanted nothing more to do with them. Although, if the male made a good impression, she may tell her kin and the male may find himself busy nearly every night between battles. Which would be fine . . . if the Horde males didn't have a tendency to get attached to females. Nothing was worse for them than to get lost in the scales of a female, only to find out the next morning the She-dragon wouldn't even talk to him. Sometimes wouldn't even acknowledge him. And gods forbid a male got a little pushy. A little demanding. The She-dragons, Vigholf had quickly learned, watched out for each other. A dragon became a little too pushy or demanding and he'd find himself on the wrong side of a Cadwaladr She-dragon attack. A "Tea and Kick Party" they all affectionately called it. It was never pretty and it was hard for the male to ever get his reputation back among his own kin.

Vigholf had seen Rhona dish out quite a few of those attacks in the name of one of her cousins or sisters. She didn't like pushy males, which was why Vigholf had never been pushy. Or at least not very pushy. Not *extremely* pushy, anyway. Just . . . sort of pushy. But only to keep Rhona safe.

The question for Vigholf, though, was what did he do now, with Rhona in his arms, her human body pressed into his? Did he hold off, wait to see if what she was feeling went beyond the mere physical?

Or perhaps he should shut up and let her grip his cock the way she was doing now.

Vigholf closed his eyes, let out a breath while Rhona

kissed a line across his jaw until she stopped and pressed her forehead against it.

Yes, all good intentions would have to wait. At least for a little while.

His eyes closed, his breathing shallow, Vigholf's whole body tensed when she gripped his cock. All those muscles going rigid. Taut, as if just one thing, one touch, one move would have him snapping like a tightly coiled line.

Rhona squeezed and air rushed out of him. Then his hands were on her, lifting her up, turning, and shoving her back into the closest tree. He pinned her there with his body, his mouth searching out hers and finding it.

Rhona returned his kiss, enjoying that desperation she'd never seen from him before. Because he was a Northland warrior dragon, desperation was the last thing one ever saw from Vigholf the Abhorrent. Unless, of course, it was the desperation to kill you. Never a good situation to be in.

And yet, even with his desperation, she could tell he was holding back. Afraid of what? Scaring her off? She had no desire to stop him from what he was doing, to push him away as she'd been doing for the last five years when she'd just thought he was being a pest. An annoying pest who had an unhealthy obsession with her spear. But that was yesterday, last week, last month. And this was now.

Knowing and understanding Vigholf's strength of will, Rhona knew she had to make what she wanted clear to the dragon. Yet she'd never been one for a lot of words. Especially during fucking. So she gripped his hand—marveling at the size of the fingers tangling with her own—and led that hand under her leggings and between her thighs. She pressed his fingers against her and released him, leaving the rest to him. Praying he wasn't as oblivious as some of his kin could be. As sometimes he could be—especially when it came to horses.

His hand relaxed and for a moment she thought he was going to pull away. But his fingers curled, teasing, gently scraping, and then he pressed his middle finger against her clit, making small circles against it.

With her legs wrapped around Vigholf and his other arm holding her up, Rhona was free to grip the tree behind her. She dug her fingers into the bark while Vigholf stroked her. Making her wet and squirm. He took her mouth again, silencing what had become persistent whimpers. When she moved her hands from the tree and wrapped her arms around his neck, he pressed hard against her clit, still making those damn little circles.

She ended up screaming into their kiss, her legs tightening around him, and her body shaking as Vigholf made her come with those ridiculously large fingers of his.

Before she even finished, her leggings were torn from her and before she could say a word, think about anything but how long it had been since she'd come like that, she felt his cock pressing against her, then in her.

She gasped, her arms tightening around his neck. Never before could she remember being so grateful to have a cock inside her, ramming its way through still-pulsating-and-grasping muscle. The entire time he never stopped kissing her. That demanding, desperate, and oddly sweet kiss that had her knees shaking.

His hands slid under her now bare ass and gripped her tight, holding her steady while he dragged his cock slowly out of her, both of them groaning at the feel of it.

Then Vigholf was plunging back in, Rhona unable to stop the little squeal that came out from him filling her up, nearly stretching her out. Gods, was it her imagination or had a cock never felt so good before? It was true, it had been a while, but the gods be damned, this felt so good.

And Vigholf's inordinately large body keeping her pinned to that blasted tree . . . aye, that felt *really* good too.

She held him so tight with her arms and legs and yet that was nothing when compared to the viselike grip she had on his cock. Did she train her muscles to do that? Whether she did or didn't, he knew he'd been right. This tail belonged to him. But how he would keep the one making his eyes cross and his knees weak was a thought for another day. Right now, right here—he had all he needed. Rhona in his arms, her hot wet pussy wrapped around his cock, and her breath in his ear as she panted and made this delightful little squeal every time he thrust into her. Gods of fire and death, he could listen to that sound until the end of time.

But when she squeaked rather than squealed, he knew she was about to come. Her arms and legs tightening even more, her body shaking and twisting in his arms. He sought out her mouth again, pressed his tongue inside and licked and sucked his way to paradise. He finally came when she squeaked one more time, the sound dragging him over the edge. And he was glad that she was right there with him. Unable to imagine anyone else but Rhona ever being there again.

He leaned his head back and found her peering at him, her cheeks flushed, her lips swollen. He nearly laughed, realizing that they'd been so busy ripping at each other's clothes, they didn't even think about or discuss whether to shift back. But that was something they could save for another time since he enjoyed taking her as human so much.

Rhona took in a breath, about to say something when that

large and round fruit slammed into the back of Vigholf's head, turning Rhona's words into a fit of laughter.

Vigholf glared over his shoulder at the stallion standing a few feet away.

"Jealous bastard," he sneered before he had to drop both him and Rhona to the ground, another piece of fruit winging its way right toward them.

Chapter 20

They were supposed to be sleeping. Mommy wouldn't be happy if they weren't sleeping. But it was all so fun! Like a picnic . . . in the dungeon! So how could they sleep? Instead they stayed awake and talked. Not out loud, though. Mommy wouldn't like it if they were chattering away. That's what she called it when others did it. Chattering.

So they talked to each other just by thinking. They did it all the time. It was fun!

They were so busy chattering and thinking and having fun that they almost didn't notice. But her cousin Tally did. Tally noticed everything first. "She's your first line of defense," their friend said about her. They had lots of friends. Friends Mommy and the others could never see. Except Auntie Dagmar, but she was never around when their friends visited. Not since that first time one of their friends had come to see her and Tally and Talan. She'd still been in her crib then. Not in her big-girl bed. And Auntie Dagmar had been so angry at their friend, he never came back while she was around. None of their friends did. They were afraid of Auntie Dagmar—but they pretended they weren't. But when they did come, they were all pretty and shiny, glowing like bright lights in the dark. Sometimes she had to look away, it burned her eyes.

But those creeping in through the back door, they weren't pretty and shiny. They were bad. They hurt the two guards watching the door while the witches had gone to investigate noises in the other hallway. With all the fighting outside the castle walls, the witches didn't think there was any real danger *inside*. But there was. There was danger and there would be until Daddy was home. Daddy and the others.

Tally got to her knees. Tally hated outsiders. Even worse, she'd liked those guarding the door. They were pretty too, but without the glowing. Tally liked pretty. But she didn't like these men creeping in. She didn't like them at all. And if she didn't like them, Talan wouldn't like them either.

These bad men would move fast and quiet, not even waking the dogs, sacrificing themselves to hurt her and Tally and Talan. She didn't know why. What had she ever done? What had Tally and Talan ever done?

Tally, as always, moved first. Without a sound, she charged forward. The men didn't see her coming. They didn't expect her. She was too little, they'd say. Just a little girl. But Tally landed on the back of one of the sleeping dogs that they played with every day, and launched herself up, spun, and rammed her sword into the chest of the first bad man. Tally released her grip on her sword and dropped to the ground, and the man fell back into his friend. That's when Talan threw his own sword, hitting the second man in his open mouth with it. Good thing, too, he was about to wake everyone up. Then Mommy would be upset. She'd cry and they'd have to go far away.

The men weren't moving now. None of them were. Not the bad men or the nice soldiers who made her smile and let Tally hit their shields with her sword.

She didn't want to see this anymore. She didn't want Mommy upset. When Mommy was upset, it made her sad. So she opened what Pretty-Ren called a "doorway" and sent the bad men back to their friends outside the castle gates and the nice men back to the nice soldiers who would take care of them. It wasn't a hard thing to do. Opening two doorways at the same time and making them all go away so no one would be sad. She wasn't sure why it wasn't hard for her because Pretty-Ren always acted like it was so hard.

But then her cousins turned and glared at her.

Our swords? Tally snapped inside her head.

Even though she wanted to cry, she knew Tally hated criers. So she did what Mommy always did when she passed some of the witches. Raised two fingers and flipped them up in the air.

"Are you three up?" Ebba asked. She'd also been asleep in the room. She could sleep while standing. Just like real horses!

Rhian wished she had four legs and hooves, too. Then she could run with the big horses and play in the sun all day.

"Back to sleep, little ones, before Talaith has my head." Ebba smiled at them and put them back to bed. Ebba was always so nice, even when she was angry.

Once she had them down, Ebba went back to the other side of the room and all her books. Ebba loved to read. Once she was gone, Tally snapped, *Now what are we going to do without our swords? What if we're attacked again? You're hopeless!*

That made Rhian mad so she punched her cousin right in the arm, which only made Tally roll her eyes and turn over, pulling the blanket over her head. And Talan was already asleep. He could sleep through pretty much anything.

But now that no one was speaking to her anymore, Rhian was able to get some sleep too.

* * *

The commander of the mighty Horsemen of the Western Mountains discussed with his men their next plan of attack. He wanted this place pulled down stone by stone in the name of their horse god. If the Southland queen ever came back here—and that was doubtful—he wanted to make sure she found nothing but rubble and the bodies of her friends and family.

He was debating with his men about a possible weakness on the south wall when a bright flash lit up behind him. He and his men lifted their heads and, slowly, turned.

The two assassins—two of his best—whom he'd sent in to find and kill Annwyl's demon children only a few hours before, were now lying in a heap behind them.

His next in command walked over to the bodies and pulled the small-sized weapons out of the assassins' bodies. He held them up. They were clearly swords rather than daggers, which led his next in command to ask, "They've got centaurs *and* dwarves in there?"

Chapter 21

Rhona was impressed when Vigholf ended up eating the fruit rather than chucking it back at the horse.

Those two would never be friends, but what was the point of wasting food?

And, as she'd feared, Vigholf was one of those who was always hungry after fucking. *Like feeding an empty pit.*

He handed her a piece of bread, and Rhona was at least grateful he was good about sharing.

"We need to do something about our hair," Vigholf suddenly announced. It seemed an odd thing to say with the pair of them sitting on the bedroll, naked.

"What?"

"We've got warrior braids in. Sovereign soldiers' hair may be too short for that, but they'll notice it on others."

He had a point.

Rhona shoved the last bit of bread into her mouth and wiped one hand against the other. "I'll do yours first," she said while she crawled around behind him. Resting on her knees, she grabbed a plait in her hand and began to unbraid it. As she finished more and more of them, she ran her hands through his hair, enjoying the way Vigholf relaxed against her each time she did.

It took some time, but it was a smarter way to go if they hoped to be even remotely ignored as they moved farther along the road and neared the Provinces.

"Your turn," Vigholf said, pulling her around and placing her in front of him.

To her surprise, he managed to unbraid her hair without any help. To be honest, she wasn't sure his fingers were nimble enough, but she was learning his fingers were quite . . . adept.

She laughed a little, and Vigholf asked, "What?"

"Nothing." Rhona rested her arms on Vigholf's knees, but his legs were so long that when he bent them her arms were too high, so she stretched them out wide and placed them on either side of his hips. It felt kind of decadent, lounging around like this while in the lap of her once sworn enemy. She liked it. She liked being a bit decadent.

Rhona patiently waited for the Northlander to finish with her hair, noticing how what he was doing felt more intimate than what he'd done to and with her body.

"Do you ever let your hair grow past your shoulders?" he asked.

"Not really. When it's too long, it's too easy to turn my own hair against me during a close-in fight. But I can't keep it as short as my Aunt Ghleanna's, though. She has the face for that, I don't." She patted her cheeks. "No sharp cheekbones like her."

"But you have dimples."

"Quiet."

"You do."

"I know, but be quiet anyway."

He chuckled, his fingers brushing against her throat as he picked up each braid. When he was done, he ran his hands through her hair and Rhona let out a deep sigh.

"You all right?" he asked while gently massaging her head. Something no one had ever done for her before.

"I'm what one might call . . . perfect. At the moment."

He kissed her throat. "Good."

Rhona closed her eyes, already planning their day to-morrow. So much travel, in dangerous enemy territory, in search of a mad queen. Not exactly what she'd consider a fun time for anyone. And yet . . .

"I'm glad you came with me." She looked at Vigholf over her shoulder. "It's nice someone's watching my back for a change."

"I do have your back. You don't have to worry about that."

She reached up, slid her hand into his hair, and gripped the strands tight. She pulled him closer and said, "Good. But don't get in my way."

"With you constantly trying to impale me with that bloody spear? Not a chance."

She grinned and kissed him hard.

Aye. She was very glad he'd come with her.

Rhona's kiss was hard and lusty, surprising him because Vigholf had always wondered if she'd be as military-like in bed as she was in battle. She wasn't. Not even a little. She took, she gave, and she didn't hold back. At least not with him. Not when she was busy pushing him to the ground and taking his cock inside her.

She smiled down at him, her brown hair loose around her face, those damn dimples making her look unbeliev-ably adorable.

Vigholf grabbed her hips, the feel of her pussy squeez-ing and releasing him nearly driving him insane. She rode him with her back arching, her hands gripping his thighs and digging into the flesh. Although she took him hard, she didn't rush anything. She wanted to enjoy this and he was enjoying her.

He reached up and gripped her breasts, teasing the nipples with the tips of his fingers. Eventually he needed more, and he pushed himself up, slid his arms around her waist and his mouth around her breast. He lashed his tongue across and around the nipple, then tugged with his lips. Rhona made that little squeal sound again as she wrapped herself around him, holding him tight against her chest.

He continued to suck and tease and nip while she squeezed his cock, tormenting him almost, because it felt so damn good.

Rhona dug her hands into his hair, pinning him to her breast. He gripped the other breast with his hand, the pair of them groaning and sweating even though there was snow under the bedroll they sat upon. If it was cold, they neither felt it nor cared.

Vigholf heard a sob catch in Rhona's throat, and he rolled her over onto her back, placing his palms flat on either side of her. He plunged into her as her body shook beneath his, the cries of her release echoing out, making the horses restless while they tried to sleep.

He came right after her, the power of it racing from his head to his toes. He roared in pleasure, his body draining into hers, until he could do nothing but drop on top of her, exhausted and sated as he never had been before.

With one good push, Rhona shoved him off, Vigholf groaning when his cock left her.

"You're not as light as a feather, Northlander."

"Neither are you," he said, which not surprisingly got him a punch to the ribs. A deserved one.

Laughing, he pulled Rhona into his arms and held her against him.

After a while, she stated, "We can't keep doing this, you know."

He decided not to overreact to that statement and instead asked, "We can't? Why not?"

"We've got to finish all this and get back to the Valley."

"We will. You act like we've deserted everyone."

"Maybe we have."

He pulled her in tighter and kissed the top of her head. "There's no reason to worry. I'm sure they're all sitting around, immensely bored, waiting for that damn tunnel to be finished, so we can finish the Irons. We'll be back in time."

"But—"

"The war's been at a standstill for five years, Rhona," Vigholf reminded her. "I doubt they'll even miss us."

Ragnar was going over the state of their supplies when Fearghus the Destroyer and Briec the Mighty walked in. Their royal armor no longer glinted shiny and bright as it first did when they'd headed out from Dark Plains that early morning five years ago. Now there were dents on the steel plate, blood in the crevices they no longer bothered to wash away. Briec sported a spear wound to the throat he'd barely survived. Fearghus had a limp that worsened during the winter months due to the spear tip still buried past scale, flesh, and muscle and deep into bone.

"Where's our sister?" Briec demanded. Ragnar had become used to Briec's arrogant and rude nature, but that didn't mean he liked it.

"She's returned to Dark Plains," he admitted.

"Alone?"

"With Ren."

"Why?"

"For her safety." It wasn't a lie. He'd agreed to Keita's return because he knew she'd be safe in the Southlands. But he needn't mention the rest of it, because Keita, as always—he'd grudgingly learned—was right. They couldn't afford to lose the soldiers and Dragonwarriors the two Fire Breather princes led, especially since most of the Cadwaladrs would go with them if they returned to Dark Plains to protect the children. For that Clan it was all about protecting their kin, especially the hatchlings.

So Ragnar kept his answers short and vague. It was the safest route when dealing with Keita's brothers.

Fearghus, the smarter of the pair—or perhaps the more devious—circled around Ragnar.

"She just let you send her back? Without question?"

"Yes. But I'm being careful with what I eat over the next few days." For good or ill, Keita was known for her vengeful nature and her method of vengeance usually involved slipping certain herbs in the offender's food. Even if that offender was kin.

"Probably for the best," Fearghus murmured.

"But why now?" Briec pushed. "Why send her back now?"

"Because we're almost finished with the tunnel. And once that's done, we're not going to wait before we move. I don't know about you two, but I want this done and the Irons out of our lives for good. Now if you two will excuse me . . ."

"Where's your brother?" Fearghus asked.

"Which one?"

"The only one that is around you constantly. I've seen your cousin Meinhard, but I haven't seen Vigholf in days. Where is he?"

"I asked him to accompany Keita and Ren."

"Ren doesn't need a Lightning for protection. Ren doesn't need any protection."

"*I'd* feel safer if my brother was with them. He'll be back in a couple of days, so I wouldn't . . ."

Ragnar's words faded out when he saw Fearghus's gaze straying to the ceiling.

Briec watched his brother. "What is it?"

Fearghus raised his front claw, lifted one black talon. "Don't you hear it?"

That's when Ragnar heard the distinct whistling sound, his body instinctively tightening, waiting for the impact as something large and extremely heavy hurtled into the cave walls.

"Siege weapons," Fearghus said, before he turned and charged out of the cavern, all of them following.

They pushed past scrambling soldiers and warriors, all of them speeding toward the north side, where a circle of mountains kept the Fire Breathers and Lightnings separated from the Irons.

They made it to the wide cavern opening. The forces that usually protected this important area were diving for cover as giant boulders hurtled over the mountaintops and rammed into their stronghold.

"Pull back!" Briec ordered, grabbing Fearghus by the neck of his armor and yanking him away moments before a boulder crashed where Fearghus had just been. "Pull back!"

Ragnar helped two of his kin to their claws and pushed them toward the entrance. "Inside! Everyone in! Now!"

The air around Ragnar changed and he used his wings to quickly drag his body back, away from the entrance. "*Briec!*" he called out, seeing the boulder hurtling toward the back of Keita's brother. But the dragon was busy helping others. He didn't see. And that boulder slammed into the back of the Silver with a mighty force, ramming his big body into the far wall.

Chapter 22

Dagmar followed the captain of the guards to the barracks. As they walked in, the guards and soldiers moved out of her way, none of them speaking to her or each other.

"We found them last night. Just . . . lying there."

Dagmar studied the soldiers. The morning light streaming in through the windows making it easy to see that their throats had been slit but no other damage had been done. There were no signs that they'd fought back. Perhaps they didn't have the chance.

"Did you see any signs of Tribesmen inside the castle walls?" Dagmar asked the captain. "Perhaps when they left the bodies. Because this is clearly the work of their assassins."

"That's just it, my lady. We don't think the bodies were left, as you say."

"One second there was nothing there," one of the soldiers volunteered. "The next second . . . there they were."

"They just appeared?"

"Aye, my lady."

Dagmar raised her hands, palms out, to silence them although none had said anything. "The fact that we have no idea how these bodies got here is irrelevant. All we do know is that assassins were inside castle walls. This cannot happen again."

"We'll take care of it."

"Deal with the bodies first. Quietly and quickly. We can give them a proper burial later."

"Aye, my lady."

Dagmar headed to the exit, her dogs by her side. She motioned to the captain to follow. "You won't discuss any of this," she told him. "They must all swear to it."

"Aye, my lady. But why?"

"Not sure yet. Just . . . let's keep it quiet, eh?"

"Understood. And the assassins?"

"Do a room-to-room search for them. If you find anything, inform me immediately."

"If we find assassins?"

"Kill them. Then bring their bodies to me. Discreetly."

"Aye, my lady."

Dagmar walked back to the castle and inside. The Tribesmen had been quiet today. Something that did not make her feel better.

"Commander Ásta," Dagmar called out when she saw the Kyvich witch with her troop leaders.

"Lady Dagmar."

"Is everything all right? Any problems last night?"

"No, my lady."

"You sure?"

"Did you hear there was a problem?"

"No," Dagmar lied. "Not at all. Guess I'm just a little nervous about all this."

The Kyvich smiled at her. "Something tells me, Lady Dagmar, that you don't get nervous over anything."

"Of course I do. My whole life is filled with worry." She pointed toward the gates. "Is there a reason you haven't followed the Tribesmen out into the woods and finished them there?"

"That's not our job."

"Pardon?"

"We're here to protect the children and only the children. We will not leave them to take on a battle that *your* people should be fighting."

"So if the Tribesmen get past the gates, wipe us out . . ."

"Not our problem. The children are our concern. Now if you'll excuse me."

Annoyed, Dagmar headed downstairs to where they kept the children.

"What's wrong?" Talaith asked as soon as Dagmar sat down at the small table with her.

"Nothing," Dagmar lied again. "Everything all right here?"

"Fine."

"No problems last night?"

"No. None at all. Why?" Talaith leaned across the table a bit. "Are you sure everything's all right, Dagmar?"

"Yes, yes. Everything is fine."

Talaith sat back. "How's it going outside?"

"It's being handled, but it's clear that Annwyl has made enemies of pretty much every Tribesman from here to the Desert Land borders."

"So they're not giving up?"

"No, but we'll be fine," she assured Talaith.

"As my guests keep reassuring me." Talaith looked over at the squad of Kyvich who stood on guard duty inside the room.

"Would you rather be down here alone?"

"Might as well be. They're not exactly chatty."

"I don't mean for your social life, Talaith. I'm talking about the safety of the children. So please, do me a favor and suck up the misery for a little while longer."

"Oh, fine. Here. Have some tea. It'll make you feel better."

While Talaith poured Dagmar some tea, Dagmar watched Ebba search among the children's bedding.

"Lose something, Ebba?" she asked.

"Can't find the children's swords. And you know how they get when they don't get in their morning training. Cranky doesn't begin to describe it." She winked at Dagmar and went back to her search while Talaith complained about the Kyvich. She didn't complain about anything in particular, just that they existed.

Slowly, Dagmar shifted her focus to the children. The three of them sat cross-legged on the floor in a circle. Rhian drew symbols on parchment and appeared much more worried than usual, her smooth brow pulled down into a very deep frown; Talan played with one of the dogs; and Talwyn read. To everyone's surprise, Talwyn was an advanced reader like her mother. Very advanced. She could read at least three languages that they knew of. The language of the humans in this region, the language of dragons, and now, according to Ebba, she could read the language of centaurs.

As Dagmar watched her, the seven-year-old girl lifted her head and looked at Dagmar through dirty, unkempt hair, black eyes like her father's and yet she seemed so much like Annwyl. Especially when the child suddenly smiled at her.

And it was at that moment that Dagmar realized . . . the captain of the guard would never find those assassins alive.

Fearghus watched Ragnar hover over his brother. Briec hadn't moved since he'd been struck, the healers working on him through the night, but no one had told the rest of them anything and he was beginning to get anxious.

After several minutes, Ragnar came to his side.

"Well?"

"It seems that—"

"I don't have time for one of your carefully worded replies, Northlander. Just tell me if my brother's going to live or die."

"I don't know. He's completely unresponsive, barely breathing, and . . ."

"And?"

"His spine's been split." Ragnar shook his head. "Neither I nor the healers know how to fix that. Perhaps your mother or Morfyd . . ."

"Will they even know what's happened to him?"

"No. We've been cut off. I can't contact my brother or Keita or anyone."

"Neither can I." Fearghus cleared his throat. "If he survives . . . will he walk?"

"I don't know. But I do doubt he'll ever fly again."

"Thank you," Fearghus said and walked out of the chamber. He went around the corner and tried to control his breathing. He couldn't allow the troops—or his kin—to see this.

"Fearghus?"

He looked up at his Aunt Ghleanna.

"It's bad, isn't it?" she asked.

"Nothing's definite. We keep it quiet for now. Just say he's recovering."

"That's all well and good for everyone else, but I'm asking as your aunt. How's me Briec?"

He shook his head, working hard to gain control. "It's bad. Ragnar, the other healers . . . they say there's nothing they can do."

"What about your mum?"

"She's his best bet, but we'll never get him out of here now."

"But if we finish the tunnels, strike the next blow . . . the *last* blow." She gripped his forearm. "Then we can get your brother back to Devenallt Mountain and let your mum heal him. Don't give up on him, Fearghus. Please."

"Of course I won't."

"I'll get the ones working on the tunnels to move their collective arses. We'll get this done." She pressed her claw to his cheek. "We don't give up on each other in this Clan, boy. Don't you forget that."

"I won't."

She nodded and stomped off, ordering recruits to get to the tunnel, while all around them the cave walls shook from the never-ending siege from the Irons battering them mercilessly, giving them no way to get out—to get his brother out of here and someplace safe.

Yet Fearghus knew his aunt was right. They didn't give up on each other, and he wouldn't start now.

Chapter 23

After a quick but lusty morning romp, Rhona and Vigholf bathed in the river, dressed, and were riding toward the Western Mountain Pass by the time most people were sitting down for their first meal.

They rode hard and made good time, stopping at a few small towns along the way so Vigholf could do what he did so well: get information from complete strangers. Rhona would have to admit, she was impressed. She simply didn't have an easy way like that with people she didn't know. And those she did know, she wasn't above threatening to get information. Vigholf never had to do that. She couldn't explain it; he just . . . had a way.

Yet Rhona wasn't completely useless, able to follow the queen's tracks once they got into the Karpos Forests that surrounded the Western Mountains. Then again it wasn't hard to differentiate Annwyl's tracks from the many others that ran into and around the area. The woman had *such* big feet for a human female. . . .

They rode the horses deep into the forests, Rhona keeping an eye out for any new markings that would show a change in direction. She was just pulling to a stop to get a closer look at something near a tree when Vigholf murmured, "Smoke."

"What?"

"Smoke." He pointed. "Over there."

Rhona scented the air. Aye, there was smoke—and fire.

She turned her horse and rode in that direction, Vigholf beside her. As they moved along, they could see the still-burning remains of a small village. Before they got too close, she dismounted and left the mare. Unlike Rhona and, to a lesser degree, Vigholf, the horses weren't immune to flame.

As she neared the village, Rhona could hear the wailing and cries of those who'd survived the fire that had gutted their homes. Worried it was the work of a pissy dragon, Rhona walked up to the first human she found not completely lost in grief.

"What happened here?" she asked.

The man looked up at her, his eyes red from the smoke and his own tears. "Soldiers. From the Provinces."

"They just burned your village? Why?"

And it was his next words that stopped her heart. "Because of the woman."

"The woman? What woman?"

The man blinked, let out a breath. He looked so exhausted. "The traveler. She came with two other females."

"She fought the soldiers?" Vigholf asked.

"Nah. She went with them willingly. Alone. I don't know about them other two. They weren't with her." He swallowed, wiped at his brow. "She didn't fight, yeah? Until the soldiers started burning the place. Then she fought, trying to stop them. That's when they hit her. Hard. Knocked her out." His voice caught. "That's when they set the entire place to burn. My wife . . ." He shook his head. "Guess I should be grateful, though."

"Grateful?"

"Rumor was they'd burned some other villages the past few days, but not before they . . . to the women . . ." He shook his head and blindly walked off.

"We need to go," Rhona said.

Vigholf looked around and, if these humans weren't already in a state of shock, they'd have been terrified by the expression he wore. "But these people, Rhona . . ."

"I know. But there's nothing we can do for them now. And Annwyl's alone with those soldiers. We have to move."

"Right. You're right." Vigholf took a step, then stopped. "They were looking for her. They knew she was coming."

Rhona headed back to the horses. "We have to move."

It was easy enough to track the soldiers. They were headed back to the Provinces and moving at a nice clip until late in the evening when they finally stopped for the night.

Vigholf crouched beside Rhona on a hill overlooking the campsite. Together they watched as the soldiers dragged Annwyl from a cage. When they started kicking and punching her, Vigholf had to catch Rhona and hold her.

"Not yet," he told her.

"We can shift."

"You don't think they know how to fight us? That Thracius didn't give his human soldiers enough insight to bring a couple of us down during battle? We wait."

A Sovereign picked Annwyl up by her throat. Based on the elaborateness of his armor and the horse-hair crest on his helm, he was the commanding officer. Motioning to at least twenty of his men, he walked to the only tent that had been set up, dragging a barely conscious Annwyl with him. The men, laughing, followed.

"Now do we move?" Rhona asked.

"Now we move."

They began down the hill, staying low, using the tall grass to shield them. They'd stay human to start and only shift if they deemed it necessary.

But, as they moved, a crow sounded behind them and Rhona instantly stopped.

"What?" Vigholf whispered. "What is it?"

Taking a breath, Rhona let out a similar crow caw and there was an answering response. With a nod, Rhona kept low but ran to her right and slightly up until they spotted a large tree. They went around it and Rhona instantly wrapped her arms around the young She-dragon standing behind it.

"Branwen."

"Cousin Rhona?" Branwen whispered. "What the hells are you doing here?"

"Come to get you and your wayward queen. Are you all right?"

"Yeah, fine. I'm fine. We're fine."

"Hello, Vigholf."

Vigholf smiled at the human girl who spoke to him. She'd matured a bit since Vigholf had last seen her. Grown into a right little cutie. But a cutie that could tear a head off with her bare hands based on the size of her. "Izzy. In trouble again, I see."

"Only a bit." She nodded and smiled at Rhona. "Hello, Rhona."

"Iseabail," Rhona said coldly, turning from her. "You two stay here. We'll take care of the—"

"We have our orders," Izzy said. "You can come with us or you can stay here and watch. But we're moving." She nodded at Branwen. "And we're moving now."

Rhona glared at the pair as they quickly and quietly headed off down the hill. "Damn brats."

"Damn *soldiers*," he reminded her. "We follow?"

"It's not like we have any choice," Rhona said, pulling out her spear and letting it expand until it was the size she wanted it. "Now let's go kill some murdering bastards."

Rhona watched her cousin and Iseabail attack first. Brannie seemed to favor the old standard—a sword and a shield. Iseabail, however, used an ax and a short sword. Together, the pair ran into the soldiers cooking their food over pit fires. The first men they encountered barely had time to call to their comrades before they were cut down by the young females.

Yet the next wave of soldiers had time to pull their weapons and attack, but the four of them ripped through the entire battalion without much effort. It would have been more of a challenge if Rhona and Vigholf had been alone or if Branwen and Iseabail hadn't been as well trained. But they had been, hacking and slashing their way through the troops, all of them quickly making their way to the tent Annwyl had been pulled into.

Rhona cleared her way through the soldiers first, giving her a straight run at the tent. She didn't want her cousin to see . . . Anyway, she thought someone from inside would have heard the screams and been out here to see what was going on by now. But perhaps they were too focused on what they were doing to Annwyl.

Disgusted more than she could say, Rhona charged the tent, but she stumbled back when the tent flap was yanked open. She raised her shield and spear, ready to strike, but it was Annwyl standing in that tent flap. It was Annwyl who was covered in blood and was dragging the moaning commander by the neck of his breastplate.

The queen stopped right outside the tent, eyes blinking slowly. "Rhona?"

"Annwyl?" Rhona looked her over. "Are you all right?"

"Nose is broken," she muttered. Then she walked off with the commander.

Vigholf stood by Rhona now, the pair staring after Annwyl before looking at each other. Without a word spoken, they entered the tent, but didn't get any farther than a few inches past the flap.

"Gods, Vigholf."

"All of them," he murmured in awe. "She's killed all of them."

Not just killed either. More like decimated. She must have gotten someone's sword or ax, because there were pieces of the soldiers *everywhere*. Heads, arms, legs . . . penises. Those pieces, along with all the blood, filled the entire floor and walls of the tent.

Rhona walked back outside and watched Annwyl shove the Sovereign commander against the cage they'd kept her in. Iseabail tied the commander's arms to the bars and Branwen handed Annwyl one of her two swords.

Wondering what the hells was going on, Rhona headed over to the three females.

Annwyl crouched down before the commander. She stared at him a moment, then broke out in a bright smile. "That was fun, eh?" She poked him in the chest with her fist. Not hard, but based on his reaction Rhona was guessing there were some ribs broken there.

"Now," Annwyl began, "tell me how you knew I was here."

"You were seen," the commander said through blood and broken teeth.

"Now, now. Don't lie. I am so very good at spotting liars. So don't lie to me. How did you know I was here? That I was coming?"

"You were seen," the commander said again, glaring at her through the eye not swollen shut.

Annwyl let out a sigh, stood, and slashed her sword. It

moved so quickly, Rhona barely saw it, but she heard the screaming of the commander, saw blood pouring from where Annwyl had hacked off the fingers of his left hand. She crouched in front of him again.

"Let's try this again. How did you know I was coming? That I was here?"

Panting, gritting his teeth against the pain, "Got a message from Lady Vateria's mage."

"She has her own personal mage? How nice. And what's his name?"

When he didn't answer, Annwyl began to stand.

"Junius," the commander said quickly. "Lord Junius."

Annwyl returned to her position in front of the Sovereign. "And how did he know?"

The commander shrugged. "I don't know."

"No. You probably don't." She reached over to him with her free hand and wiped a splatter of blood away from his jaw. Kind of ludicrous since he was covered in the stuff. His own and that of his men. "But I bet you know where I can find someone else." She briefly pursed her lips. "Someone important." She patted his chest. "Tell me where to find Gaius Lucius Domitus."

This time the commander didn't bother lying; he simply shook his head. "Never. I am a soldier of the Sovereign Provinces and I'll never—"

Annwyl hacked off the commander's arm at the elbow, ignoring the blood that splattered across her face. "Branwen," she murmured. And Rhona, becoming more horrified by the second, watched as her cousin unleashed a small stream of flame that cauterized the wound and stopped the bleeding.

Crouching in front of him again, Annwyl calmly asked, "Where can I find Gaius Lucius Domitus?"

The strength of will of this one human commander showed why the Irons and Sovereigns were not easily killed. The leader shook his head. "I'll tell you nothing, whore."

Rocking back and forth on the balls of her feet, Annwyl said, "I can hurt you . . . for *hours*. Just like you were planning to do to me tonight. So, let's not pretend you have any real choice in the matter. Tell me where to find Gaius Lucius Domitus. And tell me right now."

"No."

Without raising her voice, Annwyl said, "Izzy."

And Iseabail the Dangerous, Daughter of Talaith and Briec, used her battle-ax to hack off the commander's leg just below his knee, and Branwen quickly followed that up with a blast of flame.

The commander's screams echoed out in the night and Rhona stepped forward, about to demand Annwyl stop this, but Vigholf caught her arm, shook his head. She didn't know if he stopped her because he was all right with all this—or afraid of what Annwyl would do about the interruption.

"Where can I find Gaius Lucius Domitus?" And this time, the crazed bitch almost sang that question.

Shaking, the commander said, "He lives outside the Provinces. In the Septima Mountains. But he'll be no more welcoming to you than Vateria. He'll kill you, whore, and your friends."

"That is so considerate," Annwyl mocked. "Warning me of impending doom after I've done nothing but cut pieces off you. When you think about it, it's *very* considerate. I'm sure it's not that you just don't want me to find him because he's a real threat to your overlord and his bitch daughter. I'm sure that's not it at all. But thank you for not lying. I appreciate that."

Annwyl stood, re-sheathed her sword, and took her other sword from Branwen. She stepped away and came toward

Rhona and Vigholf, while behind the queen, Izzy finished the commander off, using her ax to remove his head.

Once Annwyl reached Rhona, she tossed her swords at her. Rhona jumped a little but managed to catch the weapons just the same.

"So," Annwyl said as she grabbed her nose between both hands, "are you two coming with us?"

"We're here to fetch you," Vigholf told her. "Your armies are moving through the Eastern Pass toward Euphrasia Valley. It'll soon begin, Annwyl."

"It's already begun. The Irons attacked last night. Siege weapons."

"What?" Vigholf asked. "How do you know this?"

With a good *snap* Annwyl put her broken nose back into place and retrieved her weapons from Rhona. "We don't have much time. Come with us or go back. Your choice. But I'm not stopping until I see Gaius Domitus."

"You'll never get to him," Rhona told her. "They already know you're here. Vateria sent out a search party for you. A raping, pillaging search party that's destroyed villages while they look for you."

"You're blaming me? For that?"

Not really, but still . . . "Annwyl, everything's changed. If the battle for Euphrasia has begun, you must go back."

"If I go back now, we all die or become slaves to that tyrant." She finished tying her swords to her back and patted Rhona on the shoulder. Rhona took it as a source of pride that she managed not to flinch or jump away from that pat. *Years of training, that is. Years of training.*

"I'll not think less of you if you return to your comrades in the Valley. But I'm going to finish this . . . with or without you."

Annwyl stepped between them and began to walk off. That's when Vigholf said, "The Western Tribesmen are attacking Garbhán Isle, Annwyl. Where your children are."

The queen stopped in her tracks, her body one rigid line of tense muscle. But she took several breaths and said, "With or without you, I'm going."

To Rhona's shock, the queen headed off into the forests, heading farther into the west. Rhona never thought Annwyl would leave her children to the whim of fate with Tribesmen at her door. But she was leaving them and, without question, Iseabail and Branwen followed her. Rhona didn't bother to call her cousin back. She knew Brannie's decision had been made. For whatever reason, she'd follow this mad queen on her insane quest, and there was nothing Rhona could do about it.

Well . . . there was one thing.

"You're going with her," Vigholf said. "I can see it on your face."

"What else can I do?"

"We could go back. Back to the Valley. Back to the war. Even death in battle is better than this insanity."

"I can't go back. She has my cousin. She has Briec's daughter." She put her hand on Vigholf's forearm. "But you can go back. Tell them what happened, tell them—"

"I'm not leaving you."

"Vigholf—"

"I'm *not* leaving you. Not with her."

"Then you're a fool." She glanced over at the queen as she marched into the forest. "We're not coming back from this, Vigholf."

"Well, not if you're going to be so negative."

Despite everything, she laughed a little. "What?"

"Think positive. You never know. We could survive. And then what will you do with me? Keep me is what you'll do." He winked at her and followed after the others, whistling for the horses they'd left on the hill.

Rhona took another look around the camp, her eyes resting on the mangled commander's remains.

Still disgusted by all that—Rhona had never been one for torture—she followed after the Mad Queen of Garbhán Isle and prayed that when her time came, it wouldn't be anything like this human commander's.

She'd hate to meet her Cadwaladr ancestors missing her leg and fingers. They'd mock her for eternity over that.

Chapter 24

Rhiannon stood on the castle walls and stared out over her territory. True, she allowed the humans to believe this was their territory too, but it actually was all hers. So the fact that these Tribesmen had invaded annoyed her. The fact that Annwyl wasn't here to pound these barbarians into the dirt as she'd been doing for years, much to Rhiannon's enjoyment, annoyed her even more.

And the Tribesmen were . . . slippery. Disappearing into the forests until they were ready to attack again. *They must worship those nature-loving gods.*

Even Bercelak with a squad of Dragonwarriors had been unable to find the bastards, although they'd been attacked many times with arrows. So it looked as if they'd have to wait until the Tribesmen struck the castle again, when they were out in the open, before Rhiannon's warriors could really do some damage.

Well, it could all be worse.

Rhiannon felt a tug on the skirt of her gown and she looked down to see her granddaughter Rhianwen standing there. Honestly! A brigade of Kyvich, a battalion of guards, a centaur, and dragons and absolutely *no one* could keep their eye on one small child?

"My sweet girl. What are you doing?" Rhiannon crouched in front of her grandchild. "Why are you up here? It's too dangerous for you to be up here."

"But it's begun," the little girl told her.

"What has?"

"The siege. Where Daddy is." Small hands reached for her, and Rhiannon pulled her granddaughter in close.

"What happened, Rhian?"

"Daddy's hurt," she whispered. "They can't help him."

"Are . . ." Rhiannon fought to hold back panic, devastated tears. She wanted to believe the child merely had a bad dream—a nightmare. But Rhiannon knew that the girl had *seen*. "Are you sure, luv?"

She nodded. "I'm sure."

"Is it very bad?"

"Yes. It's very bad." She held up a piece of parchment that she'd drawn on. "But I'm drawing this to help him."

Rhiannon forced a smile. "It's very pretty. I'm sure he'll love it."

"Don't tell Mommy about Daddy. She'll be upset."

"I won't." Rhiannon kissed the child's forehead, concern for her son nearly killing her. "Now I don't want you to worry about anything," she told the child. "This will all work out."

"Only if the monster helps."

"Monster?" Rhiannon asked. "What monster?"

"The angry one. The bad people hurt him. So he hates everybody now. He only has one eye. An *angry* one eye. Maybe Auntie Keita can send him eye patches to cheer him up."

Good gods, the child spoke of the Rebel King. But how . . .

"Will the monster help?" she asked her granddaughter.

The child toyed with Rhiannon's white hair as she liked to do when her grandmother held her.

"Probably not."

"*Probably* not?" Rhiannon asked. "So there's a chance . . . ?"

"Auntie Annwyl will have to get back what means the most to him." The girl's face turned painfully sad. "But she'll have to get it from the bad one. The bad one won't give it to her."

"And what means most to the monster?"

"The same thing that means most to Talwyn and Talan. If Auntie Annwyl remembers that, she'll know what to do." Rhian sighed and looked her grandmother in the eye. "When can I have pretty necklaces and bracelets?"

"When I'm sure you won't turn into your Aunt Keita."

The girl finally smiled. "Auntie Keita's funny."

"That's one way of putting it." Rhiannon hugged her granddaughter tight while her mind raced with how to get Annwyl a message. Any attempts she'd made to contact either Annwyl or the others in the west, and her offspring in Euphrasia Valley had been fruitless. She'd been blocked. Her! A white Dragonwitch! Damn gods and their damn meddling. And she knew it was the gods because only they could stop her from anything. But there might still be a way. Of course she'd need—

"Take my hand," her granddaughter told her.

"Um . . . can we play later, baby? I need to—"

"Take my hand. We can contact Auntie Annwyl together."

"No, I . . . we've been unable . . ."

Rhian held her hand out. "We can do it together," she said again. "But soon. I've got to finish Daddy's drawing."

"You really can help me contact your Auntie Annwyl, can't you, Rhian?"

"Yes."

"How do you know how to do that?"

She shrugged. "I just know."

Not sure what was going on, but only able to deal with one major crisis at a time, Rhiannon took her granddaughter's hand. "Let's do this together, but I'll do all the talking. I don't want you in your Auntie Annwyl's head. Ever."

Sadly, Vigholf and Rhona decided to let the horses go. The terrain of the mountains was so rocky and the group would have to be able to take cover so quickly, they didn't want to risk the horses' safety or their own.

Although, at first, Vigholf began to believe this was a bad idea on their part. What with all the walking. For miles. And the gods knew they had many more miles to go. This Rebel King whom Annwyl wanted to find was located clear on the other side of the Provinces. The Provinces they hadn't even reached yet. How Annwyl expected to get to where she needed to go in a timely manner, none of them knew. But the queen seemed fixed on her objective. No matter how much Rhona tried to tell her gently this was not a good idea, the queen didn't want to hear it. She didn't want to hear anything, which explained why the normally chatty Izzy and Branwen mostly kept silent.

They finally took a break the next afternoon by a stream. Food was retrieved from travel bags and water replenished from the stream. Each of them sat on small boulders or overturned tree stumps.

"It could be worse," Vigholf softly murmured into Rhona's ear. "It could be summertime. So miserably hot."

Izzy dug into her pack and pulled out several pieces of fruit, which she offered to everyone. Annwyl declined with a shake of her head, Branwen took two, Vigholf took one, and Rhona declined with a flat, "No."

With a shrug, Izzy returned to her stump and began to eat. While she did, she asked Rhona, "So how's my father?"

When Rhona didn't answer, Vigholf replied, "Rude."

"So he's fine then?"

They both chuckled.

"And how's the war in the north? Going well?"

"Rough, I'm afraid. Those Irons . . ."

Vigholf shook his head and Izzy said, "They just keep coming."

"That's it. How are there so bloody many of them?"

"We've thought the same thing. Right, Brannie? Because they do just keep coming." She ate some more fruit, then added, "But you know, I have to say, the way their army works . . ."

"I know," Vigholf immediately agreed.

". . . their organization, their discipline. And they're so bloody ruthless."

"You admire them," Rhona observed, watching Izzy closely. Maybe too closely.

"How could you not? There are things they do in their ranks that we could start doing. Changes we could make that would help us in the long run."

"Still planning to be general one day, Iseabail?" Rhona asked and Vigholf definitely heard a sneer in that even if Izzy didn't.

Izzy shrugged. "Why wouldn't I? I have as much chance as anyone. But I know it'll take hard work." Then she grinned and added, "Discipline. Organization."

They all laughed except Rhona, who continued eating and scowling.

Izzy offered Vigholf bread. "So you were at Garbhán Isle. How's my mother? Rhian?"

"They're fine and Rhian is adorable."

"I can't wait to see her. She's probably so big now."

"I think she'll be tall. Maybe not as tall as the twins, though. They're growing like vines."

That's when Rhona asked Izzy, "Aren't you going to ask about Éibhear and Celyn?"

Both Vigholf and Branwen cringed at that question, but Izzy only shrugged again. "Should I ask?"

Rhona sniffed in disgust—a sound Vigholf was well acquainted with—and went back to eating her dried beef.

Izzy placed her food down and swiped one hand against the other to brush off crumbs. "Is there something you want to say to me, Rhona?" she asked.

"No," Rhona lashed back. "Because why would I want to say anything to the *whore* who got between two cousins?"

"Rhona!" Branwen snapped. "Have you lost your mind?"

Before Rhona could reply to that—and Vigholf knew the female was going to reply—Annwyl suddenly yelled, "What the hell are you doing in my head?"

They all stopped, the four of them looking at the queen.

"Out! Out of my head! Fearghus said you'd never be in my head! *Why are you in my head?*"

Rhona leaned over and whispered to Vigholf, "By the cock of the gods, she's gone 'round the bend."

"Are you sure?" Annwyl asked no one. She reached down and pulled a scroll out of her travel bag. When she unrolled it, Vigholf saw it was a map. "Aye. I see it. But are you sure? Well, how the hells would she know? She's just a . . . oh, fine! And never do this again."

Annwyl rolled up the map and stood. "Let's go."

"Go?" Vigholf asked her. "Go where?"

"I don't have time for a litany of questions. Let's just move."

Izzy and Branwen scrambled to their feet, grabbed their things, and set off. Reluctantly Vigholf and Rhona followed. But Annwyl caught Rhona's arm and held her back a moment while the two younger females went on. Unwilling to leave Rhona alone with a woman he was sure was completely insane, Vigholf stopped as well. Gods knew what the Mad Queen would say to her.

But she seemed quite clear-eyed and level-headed when she told Rhona, "Call my niece a whore again, Cadwaladr, and I'll slit your throat."

And with that, the queen walked away.

Vateria returned from the dungeons, her servants busy wiping the blood from her hands, neck, and face.

"What is it?" she asked her mage.

"They're dead."

"Who is?"

"The platoon I told you last night would be bringing Annwyl the Bloody here."

"How do you know that?"

Her mage smiled, and she casually flipped her hands, slapping her servants in the face. "Forget I asked." She peered at the powerful Dragonmage. "Can't you just . . . get her?"

"She's protected from Magicks."

"By that bitch Dragon Queen?"

"No. By the other gods."

"Oh. I see."

"If we want her dead, it'll have to be the close-up kill I'm afraid."

"And how are we supposed to do that when she's already killed a platoon of Laudaricus's men?"

Junius smiled. "Wait until she comes to us."

"Wait." Vateria shook her head. "Are you saying that mad cow is coming *here*? To my palace?"

"I believe so."

She clapped her hands together, and cheered, "My toy is coming to me!" Which made Junius laugh.

* * *

They were climbing up and across the side of a mountain, following Annwyl. Rhona still didn't know why. In fact, she felt like they should put Annwyl out of her misery like a diseased animal. Then again, Rhona liked her head right where she had it. On her shoulders and securely attached.

Iseabail suddenly dropped, motioning them all down. After a moment, they saw them. Sovereign sentries, in formation and on the march. At first, Rhona thought they were coming out for them, but she saw they were merely guarding a nearby fort. Vigholf pointed to the ramparts of it in the distance.

To be honest, Rhona thought Annwyl would want to kill them all. It seemed to be her answer for everything. Yet she didn't move, she didn't give any orders. She simply waited. Rhona had never thought the queen had it in her to wait for anything.

When the sentries had moved past and they felt they could go without being seen, they got to their feet and, keeping low, started up the mountain again. Where Annwyl was going, though, they still didn't know. But she kept moving until she abruptly stopped and looked down at the ground.

"Oh, sh—" was all she managed before the earth beneath her feet opened up and swallowed Annwyl whole.

Chapter 25

Izzy caught hold of her queen's arm but barely. Lying facedown on her belly, she held on to Annwyl with everything she had. Unfortunately she felt the ground beneath her begin to give.

"Shit," she yipped, not wanting to alert any soldiers nearby but not exactly seeing a good ending to this situation. Especially when all she saw beneath Annwyl was nothing but blackness. A very deep-looking blackness. "Shit."

"Don't panic," Annwyl had the nerve to order Izzy as she dangled there.

"I've got you," Brannie whispered loudly while gripping Izzy's legs. "I've got you!"

Izzy almost believed her cousin, too, until the land gave way beneath both of them and they were plunging into darkness, the three of them screaming until forearms they couldn't see in all this black wrapped around Izzy and Annwyl and held them.

"Hold on," Vigholf told them; then he was diving straight down. She didn't know why, though, until she heard warning shouts from above and felt arrows shoot past their heads.

Sovereign soldiers. And they sounded really pissed.

But it was so dark. Could the Northlander even see? She hoped so. Because as fast as he was moving, if he hit a cave wall, her and Annwyl would be nothing but a flattened queen and her loyal, flat squire.

It felt like they traveled for miles, down and down, Vigholf moving with unerring skill, so Izzy was going to assume he could see just fine. After what felt like forever and a day, Vigholf landed. Someone unleashed flame and a row of torches roared to life, lighting up a ledge that overlooked another nasty drop.

Vigholf placed her and Annwyl on that ledge. "Are you all right?" he asked.

"Fine. Yeah." Izzy smiled a little. "Thanks for that."

He nodded and winked at her.

A few moments later, Rhona appeared, dropping a still-human Brannie next to Izzy.

"You're an idiot!" Rhona snapped at her cousin, and Izzy thought about punching Rhona in her snout. Gods, she was being a right bitch tonight.

"I forgot! No need to get nasty," Brannie told her.

"How do you forget you have wings? Who forgets *that*?"

"I was taken by surprise."

"You'd have never survived that drop if I hadn't caught you, do you know that, cousin?"

"Well—"

"Because you wouldn't have!" Rhona flew closer. She and Vigholf didn't bother to land on the ledge, simply hovered near it. "I seriously hope you're smarter in actual battle!"

"I am! It all just happened so fast!"

"It *always* happens fast! That's the point!"

Brannie's head dropped forward. "I'm sorry, Rhona."

"I don't want your apologies." The tip of a talon lifted Brannie's chin so they looked each other in the eye. "I want you to be careful. You can't always count on one of us to catch your ass before you fall to your death, now can you?" And then Izzy understood that Rhona was just worried for her cousin. Izzy's mum often yelled like that sometimes when she saw her eldest daughter leaping from dragon back to dragon back hundreds of feet above the earth.

"So no matter what form you're in, always remember what you are. Understand?"

"Aye, I understand."

"Good." Rhona flew to Annwyl, but as she passed Izzy she seemed unable to stop her wings from whacking Izzy in the face.

Brannie winced and mouthed, *Sorry.*

"I really hope this is where you wanted to be, Annwyl," Rhona said, hovering near her.

"I think it is. It's an underground shortcut to the Septima Mountains."

"How do you know that?"

"It is. Trust me on this."

How could Rhona trust the woman when she was convinced she was bat-shit insane?

"Move out," Annwyl ordered, grabbing one of the torches to help light the way. Iseabail and Brannie followed, also grabbing torches, again without question, which was really starting to disturb Rhona. Gods, was she this bad? Was this what Vigholf was always talking about? Of course, she'd never had someone completely crazed as a commander, but she'd like to think that even as a soldier of Her Majesty's Army, she'd at least question a clearly insane queen.

"Are you all right?" Vigholf asked her, brushing her hair out of her eyes. Now that it was no longer in braids, it had become unruly.

"I'm fine. Not happy, but fine." She nudged him back a bit and urgently asked, "What are we going to do? She's—" She touched the side of her head with her talon.

"But what if Annwyl's right? What if this is the way to Gaius Domitus?"

"Then instead of dying in these caves, we can be killed by the Rebel King? None of these options make me happy, Vigholf."

He moved in closer. "What would you have us do? Even if you were the type to put down an ailing queen—and we both know you're not—there's no way Iseabail or Branwen will let that happen."

"But—"

"You of all soldier dragons should understand this, Rhona."

"Aaargh! I knew you were going to throw that in my face."

"And Branwen is loyal to Annwyl. You can see that your cousin will protect the queen with her life. Would you kill your own cousin, too?"

"Of course not."

"Then we keep moving and hope Annwyl's right about all this. Pray even. Perhaps the war gods will shine on us tonight."

"And why would they start now?"

Austell the Red wasn't surprised to find that Éibhear wasn't in the tunnels. Although that was where Éibhear spent most of his time. He was a big, burly dragon, and he was really good at moving big, unmovable things. And he'd be moving up the ranks a lot faster than he was if he had his head on straight and wasn't so busy wasting his time on Celyn and past history.

But try to tell him or Celyn that. Two of the most hard-

headed dragons Austell knew. Yet they were good friends.
Loyal . . . at least to him.

Honestly, such worry and bother over a female. A
human one at that! They could *buy* a woman for all the
trouble they've been through over some . . . well, to be
blunt, some stray. In the big scheme of things, she was
nothing more than a dog that wandered in from the cold.
But that didn't mean one had to make her a pet.

Austell finally found his friend in a small alcove, far
away from all the activity of the bigger caverns. He sat
down next to him.

"You all right?"

"No. They're not saying it, Austell . . . but they don't
think Briec's going to make it."

"You don't know that."

"I know my brothers. The last time Fearghus looked like
that, Annwyl . . . and now he looks like that again!"

"So what are you going to do, Éibhear? Sit here, worrying about something you can't fix? Or get off your ass and
help the rest of us lowly privates finish that bloody tunnel?
The sooner we get that done, the sooner we can get your
brother back to your mum. I bet she can fix him up right."

"She couldn't save Annwyl."

Austell frowned. "But . . . *someone* saved her, right?"

"It's a long and complicated story." When Austell's
frown grew worse, Éibhear rushed to explain, "She's not
the undead!"

"All right, all right. No need to yell at me."

Éibhear let out a breath. "Sorry. That was rude."

And Austell almost laughed at him. To Éibhear that was
rude. To the rest of the dragons in this world? It was nothing. Gods, would Éibhear go through his entire life being
such a goody two-talons? How was he supposed to make it
in the military when he was always so damn nice and ac-
commodating? Unless, of course, you were Celyn. Then

you got nothing from the royal but punched in the face and called all sorts of names Austell didn't even realize that Éibhear knew.

Austell really wished that Cadwaladr cousin of Éibhear and Celyn was still around. The sergeant. She kept the pair of them in line, but now that she'd gone off somewhere, they were getting worse and worse by the hour. Those cute triplets kept trying to stop them, but they didn't have the same terrifying demeanor as their sister.

Well . . . what could he do? Except for what he'd already been doing. Trying to keep the pair separated. And when they did have to work together, trying to keep them from fighting every five minutes.

Honestly, he wished they'd both just focus. Austell hated that tunnel. He hated being in such a small place. True, it wasn't small by most beings' standards, but it was to dragons. It would allow for them to make it into the Polycarp Mountains two at a time. Hopefully, once they were in, they would find their way to the Irons and destroy them from within. At least that was the plan, but Austell liked being outside. Or in a much larger cavern. Tunnels, like bridges, were just things that could collapse in his estimation.

"Come on. You need to get back to work."

"Yeah, all right."

Together they stood, but Austell stopped to put his claw on his friend's shoulder. "Don't worry. I'm sure everything will work out with Briec. We get this tunnel done, kill all the Irons, and get him home. Easy and simple. We like easy and simple, right? *Right?*"

Éibhear rolled his eyes and recited their creed: "Only where women are concerned."

Austell laughed and slapped the Blue on the back. "That's the spirit! Now let's get this done."

Chapter 26

It felt like ages as they traveled through those tunnels, but Annwyl seemed to know where she was going and it had to be safer than cutting straight through—or even around—the Provinces. But still, Vigholf couldn't help but be extra vigilant as they all moved along. It wasn't like the Sovereign humans didn't have their own dragons who could bring human soldiers down here just as he and Rhona had with Annwyl and the others.

But it did feel like they were alone.

At least it did until they reached the smallest caverns they'd found yet since they'd been in these caves. They weren't tiny by any means, but they didn't give him much room either. Instantly Vigholf thought of the wyvern. And because he was already so tense and ready for anything to come slithering along, Vigholf caught the wood spear that came shooting out of the darkness seconds before it tore through Rhona's head.

Blinking her eyes wide, she gave him a quick nod. "Thanks."

"I owed you one anyway." He turned the large spear in his claws until it faced the other way. "You ready?" he asked.

"Aye. I'm ready."

Needing to hear nothing else, Vigholf sped forward into a wide cavern, the spear gripped tight by his talons. Rhona stayed to the right of him, her own spear in one claw, her shield in the other.

He pulled his forearm back, the spear high, and was seconds from pitching the weapon when Annwyl yelled, "*Hold!*"

It was a command Vigholf and Rhona had been conditioned to respond to and they did so immediately, both of them using their wings to pull them back in midflight.

Annwyl walked forward, both swords in her hands. Izzy held a torch. It didn't do much for lighting her queen's way, but Annwyl still kept going.

Then Vigholf heard it. He'd heard it in battle so many times, he sometimes heard it in his sleep. The sound of a Fire Breather taking in a big gulp of air.

"*Annwyl!*" he bellowed. Yet the queen did nothing but shove her niece aside seconds before flames burst from the opposite dark cavern and covered the human female. Roaring with rage, Vigholf jerked forward, but Rhona grabbed his forearm, held him back.

"*What are you doing?*" he demanded.

"Look."

"Why would I want to see—"

"Just *look*."

He did—and he saw Annwyl. Not a burned-to-a-crisp Annwyl, but a perfectly untouched Annwyl. Even her clothes were fine. But Vigholf didn't understand. That burst of flame could have wiped out an entire human battalion.

"The Dragon Queen," Rhona murmured. "I'd heard she'd blessed Annwyl with this gift, but I've never seen it in action before. A dragon's flame can never hurt her now."

Annwyl shook her hair back and said, "Ready to talk? Or are we going to keep playing these games, Rebel King?"

And, from that dark cavern, the Rebel King stepped out.

He was younger than Vigholf thought he would be. Much younger. Not even two hundred winters, Vigholf would guess. His scales the color of steel, his size that of any big Northlander dragon, his white horns curving around until the tips nearly touched his mouth. Long, steel-colored hair nearly reached the floor, different from the way most Irons wore it, and an eye patch covered the hole where his right eye should be. A scar that stretched from his forehead to where his snout began telling the tale of that loss. And the King wasn't alone—a platoon of well-armed humans and dragons stood behind him, ready to defend him to their death.

"The Mad Bitch of Garbhán Isle," the Rebel King growled. "Come to die?"

"No. But you won't be the first one to try. To succeed even." She grinned and even in the pale light of the torch Izzy still held as she returned to Annwyl's side, they could all see the cocky and crazed smile of the royal. "But I'll only come back anyway. . . ."

Rhona dropped to the ground behind Annwyl, and Vigholf behind Branwen and Iseabail. The Rebel King studied their small party. "Three dragons and a human girl? That's all you bring to fight me?"

"I'm not here to fight you. I'm here to secure your assistance."

"I know of your war, Southlander. I know your mate fights Thracius in Euphrasia and you fight Laudaricus in the Western Mountains."

"You know of it, but you do nothing to help either of us. To end this war and take Thracius's rule. But if you help me, you can be emperor of the Provinces. Or king. Or whatever you call yourself."

"That does sound nice, doesn't it? Tragically, though,

not something I can do at the moment. But because I'm feeling benevolent, I'll allow you and your friends to leave alive. Now go."

Rhona felt a brief moment of elation, but it was quickly squashed when Annwyl re-sheathed her swords and followed the Rebel King into the dark cavern he'd just come out of. She pushed past his human and dragon soldiers, ignoring them all in her pursuit.

"Shit," Vigholf muttered, watching Iseabail and Brannie follow right after their queen.

Sure, they could walk away. But they wouldn't. It wasn't in their nature. Their stupid, stupid nature. So they followed after the mad queen and the evil king.

"You can't just walk away from this," Annwyl told the dragon's back.

"I can, human. And I am."

"Why? Are you afraid of Thracius? Is that it? Are you weak?"

King Gaius's tail slammed down right where Annwyl was standing. Thankfully, she was spry, managing to jump out of the way before it landed.

"I find you irritating, human. You don't want to irritate me."

"Why? What will you do? You won't even fight your uncle. Because you're weak."

"You grab Izzy and Branwen," Vigholf whispered. "I'll grab the nut."

The Rebel King spun around, Iseabail and Brannie ducking his long, spiked tail.

"Do you really think you can play this game with me, Queen?"

"I have nothing to lose at this point."

"Don't you?"

And that's when human soldiers grabbed Iseabail, a dragon in human form grabbed Brannie, and Rhona and

Vigholf were surrounded by well-armed dragons and humans who came at them from behind.

"If you don't think I'll kill them all, human, you're sadly mis—"

"She's hurting her, you know," the queen said.

Confused, Vigholf glanced at Rhona, but all she could do was shrug, exasperated.

"Every day," the queen went on. "Every day she hurts her more and more. And soon she will be so broken . . . it won't matter if they let her go. Because she might as well be dead anyway." Annwyl stepped forward, moving closer to a dragon who clearly didn't like her. "And whose fault will that be, Gaius, the Rebel King? Whose fault?" She smiled, but it wasn't one of her pleasant, slightly off ones. It was a mean smile from a very mean royal. "It'll be yours because you've done nothing to help. You'll have killed her because you're sitting on your fat ass in these stupid caves doing *nothing*. Tell me, Iron, how will you live knowing all that when they send her crucified body back to you?"

It was a low rumble, like an oncoming earthquake or one of the volcanoes near her father's home just before it erupted.

And gods, did the Rebel King erupt.

Roaring in rage and pain, he grabbed hold of a startled Annwyl and flung her to the ground. Vigholf dashed forward, barely catching her before her brains and body could be decimated against the cave floor. Then the king sucked in air and Rhona yelled, "Izzy! Move!"

The human girl dove behind her cousin seconds before they were hit with a blast of flame so mighty it shoved Rhona and Vigholf back, knocking Annwyl from his arms, and Brannie into Izzy, both young females squealing.

Annwyl flipped across the cave floor, landing face-down. The Rebel King marched forward, shifting as he did, his eye patch adjusting to his human size. Gaius Domitus snatched a spear out of one of the human soldiers' hands and stalked over to the queen. Vigholf tried to stop him, but dragons held him back, and another two held Rhona, so that all they could do was watch.

King Gaius raised the spear above Annwyl as she lifted her head, flipping her hair back. "So that's it then?" Annwyl asked, grinning. "You're just going to let her die?"

"*Shut up!*"

"You're going to let your own sister die at the claws of Vateria?" Annwyl got to her feet. "I'd heard you were smarter than that. Smart enough to know an opportunity when you see one." Annwyl moved a bit closer. "Let me get her for you. Let me bring your sister back."

The king's body jerked a bit, his arms lowering. "What?"

"I'll get her. I know *you* can't. None of you can. They know who you are. They know your scent. They took her because keeping her controls you. But once Thracius is back—she dies. But they don't know me. I can free her. I can bring your sister back to you."

"You? You go into the heart of the Provinces, into the Overlord's palace, and release my sister from their dungeons? You?" he said again.

"Why not me?"

"You can't just waltz in there and save her."

"What's your alternative? To hope to see her on the other side when your time comes?"

His hands tightened on the spear. "And if you fail, human?"

"And if I don't? As it is, if you don't get her out now—you might as well go ahead and build her funeral pyre. Because *you* killed her."

Rhona only had a moment to roll her eyes, knowing how she would respond to someone saying that to her about her siblings, before the king rammed the spear at Annwyl. But the queen, a true warrior, caught hold of the spear's shaft with her left hand, yanked the king's human form close, and punched him twice in the face with her right. Then she unsheathed one of her swords and had it against his throat before he had a chance to register pain from her punching him, or his soldiers even had a chance to move. Clearly Annwyl's madness only affected her mind, not her battle skills.

"I've been fighting dragons like you for years," Annwyl told the king. "Warriors that'd be using the bones of you and yours for toothpicks by now. So think hard and long on what you want to do, Rebel King. Leave your sister to die? Or let me get her out and give yourself a chance at Thracius's throne?"

She released the spear and stepped away from the king. "But choose quickly. Because time is running out for those I love and for the one you love."

The Rebel King stared at Annwyl for a very long time until he finally stated the obvious. "You truly are as insane as everyone says."

"I prefer the term persistent. It has a nicer ring, don't you think?" Then she grinned and everyone in the cavern took a cautious step back.

Chapter 27

There were times in Gaius Lucius Domitus's life when he'd wished things were different. That he was different. That he could simply sit back and accept his uncle's completely brutal and vicious rule like everyone else in their bloodline. Or that he could overlook the way his kind abused the humans they shared their lives with. Or that keeping someone, anyone, enslaved was something he could completely overlook. If he was different, none of these things would bother him in the least.

And, as he'd stared into the crazed green eyes of a human queen with absolutely no boundaries or sense, he realized this was one of those times he wished he was that kind of dragon.

Gaius had heard about Annwyl the Bloody. Hell, *everyone* had heard about her. She was the half-dead queen who fucked dragons and somehow managed to have offspring with them. Something that, as far as anyone knew, had never been possible between dragons and humans before. There were those who said that on top of being crazy, Annwyl the Bloody was cruel, violent, cold, murderous, nasty, whorish, and a host of other things that made her one of the most reprehensible beings on the planet.

And yet she'd come here herself, risking an unbelievable amount of danger to reach him. She could have sent a messenger, or one of her soldiers. All of whom Gaius would have sent back to her in pieces. Instead she'd come with three dragons and a girl, all of them sneaking through the tunnels under the mountains. Tunnels that most Sovereigns and Irons would never attempt to travel through, which was why Gaius and his troops used them.

"What are you thinking, old friend?"

Varro Marius Parthenius was the son of Laudaricus Parthenius, Thracius's human leader-representative. Although father and son had never gotten along, Varro had given up much to fight by Gaius's side. They weren't merely friends or comrades in arms. They were brothers, species differences be damned.

"I'm thinking the Southlander is right. About Agrippina."

"She's insane, Gaius. How can you believe anything that woman says?"

"Because Aggie's my sister. We came from the same egg. And every day I feel her dying. Bit by bit. Inside. So that even if she walks out of our uncle's dungeon one day, she'll just be a walking corpse. She won't be my Aggie."

"Then we attack. Now. Tonight."

"And we never get past the front gates and Vateria will crucify Aggie in front of us. The gods know Vateria's been waiting to. But she also knows keeping Aggie alive is the only reason I haven't made a move while Thracius has been gone for five years." Gaius shifted to human and, after pulling on leggings and boots, sat down beside his friend.

"There is another option," Varro said, his voice nearly a whisper from the shame of the words he was forcing himself to speak. "We now have something Vateria wants. Needs, even."

Gaius shook his head. "I'm a bastard, Varro. But I'm not that big a bastard."

"Yes, but—"

"To turn Annwyl over to Vateria will be giving that snake exactly what she wants. I can't do that. I won't."

"Not even for Aggie?"

"I'm doing it for Aggie. There are some things she simply won't forgive me for. Giving Vateria *anything* is definitely one of them."

"Then what do we do, old friend? The mad queen is not leaving."

The pair stared at each other. Then they leaned far over so they could see past the cave wall and into the cavern in which the queen and her guards were waiting. They watched the royal as she sat quietly, staring off at nothing in particular. Around her, her guards chatted, looked worried, concerned, anxious. But the queen didn't seem to have any of those emotions. She just sat there.

Then, all of a sudden, she slowly turned just her head and looked at Gaius and Varro. All Gaius could see were vibrant green eyes scowling at him from behind a stringy mass of light brown hair. The friends immediately sat back.

"She's what we've always heard, Gaius," Varro warned. "She's crazed."

"Shit."

"What?"

"She's coming in here."

And she did, forcing her way past Gaius's guards and into his private chamber. "Well?" she demanded, folding her arms over her chest.

"Well what?"

"It's a simple enough deal, Rebel King. I get your sister. . . . You help me stop Thracius. What are you not grasping? Gods, are you slow? No one warned me that you were slow."

Gaius gripped the sword lying next to him, but Varro caught his hand and held it.

The queen looked at their joined hands, then them. "You two together then?"

"Together? What?"

She focused on Varro. "Can't you talk to your mate? Get him to see reason?"

Gaius snatched his hand back and jumped to his feet. "Out!" he roared.

Annwyl pursed her lips. "I'm not going anywhere."

"Gaius—"

Ignoring the warning in Varro's voice, Gaius stalked up to the queen. "Get out. Now."

She stared up at him, then asked, "How did you lose that eye?" Startled by the question and then by Annwyl reaching up to lift his eye patch, Gaius slapped her hands away. So she slapped him back. They were slapping and kicking and shoving each other until Varro got between them.

"Stop it! Both of you!"

Fed up, Gaius headed toward the exit, pushing past his own troops and the queen's guard. Behind him Annwyl followed.

"I'm not leaving!" she yelled at his back. "I'm staying right here until I get what I want!"

"Then I guess you're going to die here, female. Because you'll get *nothing* from me!"

"You handled that well," Izzy muttered, and Annwyl turned on her, pointing her finger in her face.

"Don't start with me, little girl."

"Not starting. Simply making an observation, my liege."

"Just like your mum with that *tone*."

"So what are we going to do now?" Rhona asked, proving she was the sanest of the group in Vigholf's estimation.

"I'm not leaving." Then Annwyl screamed at where the king had walked out, "*Ever!*"

"Gods deliver us," Rhona muttered, walking away from the queen.

"So we're just going to stand here?" Vigholf asked. "Until the king you just pissed off comes back in here and changes his mind? That dragon's never changing his mind."

"Why not?"

Vigholf frowned and replied, "He hates you."

"Everyone hates me at some point or another. They get over it."

"I haven't," Rhona snapped.

"Annwyl," Vigholf cut in. "We have to get back to Euphrasia. We have to help our troops, our kin."

"If we leave now . . . we lose. Don't you understand that?"

"No. I don't."

"Do not question me, foreigner!" Annwyl bellowed, but just as quickly it seemed the fight went out of her. She rubbed at her eyes with her fists. "I can't talk about this now."

The queen walked off, and Izzy motioned to Branwen. "Keep an eye on her."

The She-dragon followed after the royal and Rhona's pretty human face turned red. "Why is my cousin taking orders from *you*?"

"That wasn't really an order, but if it was, she'd *still* have to listen to me. I'm the Queen's Squire."

"In what world does a squire outrank a private?"

"In Annwyl's world. Now do me a favor and get off my back." Izzy stepped away.

"Don't walk away from me, little girl."

Izzy spun back to face Rhona, her finger pointed at her. "I am *not* a little girl. And I don't report to you, cousin."

"Not my cousin. Not by blood you're not."

Vigholf flinched at that direct hit, and he wasn't surprised that Izzy's laugh was bitter.

"Good to know," the girl sneered.

"Where are you going, Izzy?" Vigholf asked her as she walked away.

"To get us a place to sleep and some food. And, if we're lucky, a lake to bathe in."

"I don't think we should separate."

"Well, you can't expect me to stay here," Izzy snapped before she disappeared down an alcove.

"What the hells are you doing?" Vigholf demanded.

"You're blaming me for this?"

"You attacked her!"

"She seems to think she's a Cadwaladr. Then she should be raised the Cadwaladr way and be given a good thrashing for being such a pain in the ass!"

Vigholf pulled Rhona around until she faced him. "Nothing you do or say is going to change what happened between Izzy and Celyn. In fact the only thing you really have to worry about is pissing off Annwyl because clearly she's protective of Izzy on this. And, personally, I'd really like to avoid pissing off Annwyl if we can."

"You think I'm being unreasonable."

"No. I think you're being the Babysitter. But blaming Izzy for what happened . . . it just doesn't seem fair to me."

"She shouldn't have gotten between cousins."

"She didn't. What she did is get laid. Good and proper from the sound of it."

Gasping, Rhona thumped him on the chest. "Vigholf!"

"What? Can you tell me I'm wrong?"

"That's not the point."

"Then what is the point? I mean other than you holding a grudge against something a nineteen-year-old *human* girl did with your nearly hundred-year-old cousin that pissed off another nearly hundred-year-old cousin because he didn't have the balls to go after what he wanted in the first place."

"You've never liked Éibhear."

"That's not it. I just know what I saw. And Izzy was the long-legged bone caught between two pit dogs. Don't blame her for that."

"So you want me to blame them instead?"

"I don't want you to blame anyone. In fact . . . I think you should mind your own gods-damn business."

"Oy!"

He tightened his grip around her waist so she couldn't walk away from him. "Just hear me out. In order to grow up in this world, you sometimes have to do really dumb shit. Some of us do dumber shit than others." He pointed at himself, making Rhona chuckle. "Some of us never have a chance to do really dumb shit." He pointed at Rhona. "And some of us wallow in dumb shit until it blows up in our face."

"And that would be Éibhear and Celyn?"

"And Izzy. But they'll have to learn the hard way because they're so bloody hardheaded. Trust me when I say there's nothing you can do about that. But what you can do is not treat Izzy like some treacherous whore out to destroy those two idiots. If for no other reason than we need her focused and ready for whatever ends up coming our way. Not worrying that all her kin have turned against her."

Rhona closed her eyes and let out a breath. "You're right." After dealing with Éibhear and Celyn for five long years, it had been easier to blame it all on Izzy—since the girl wasn't there and Rhona had to live with the other two—than it was to simply chalk it up to bad decisions on all their parts.

"Hey." Vigholf tilted her chin up with his finger. "Look at me." She did. "There's no blame here. None. Let's just try to make it out of this alive."

"You can't really think we're going to—"

"Positive. You must think *positive*. Like me."

Vigholf winked at her and Rhona went up on her toes, her hand around the back of his neck, bringing him in for a kiss. She was beginning to adore this dragon and she had no idea what to do with that. Then again . . . if they got killed tomorrow, it wouldn't really matter.

Their lips touched and that's when they heard, "Ooops. Sorry!"

Rhona pulled away from Vigholf and watched Branwen back out of the cavern. A moment later, they heard her announce, "Oy! Iz! You owe me that ale. Told you these two were fuckin'."

"See?" Vigholf teased. "Positive."

"Yeah, positive. I'm positive every one of my kin is insane."

Chapter 28

Briec the Mighty felt like he'd been stuck in this boring place for *years*. Nothing to read. Nothing to do but sit. Gods, he was so bored!

He looked off and he could see land, but he could never reach it. Under one sun, he could see dragons enjoying themselves. Eating and drinking and, from the looks of it, fucking.

And here he sat . . . trapped.

"And bored!" he yelled out. "I am so *bored*!"

The parchment floated from the sky and landed right by him. Briec picked it up. It wasn't, as he'd hoped, a letter with instructions telling him exactly how to get out of here or, at the very least, directions that led over to the more fun-looking place with all the dragons having a good time. But it did have something at the top he recognized.

Written very carefully was: *For My Daddy.*

Briec smiled. When posts were still getting through, he'd often get sweet little drawings from Rhian with always the same message at the top. Yet this . . . this was different. She usually drew horses or birds or the castle she lived in. But this was just . . . symbols.

Why was she drawing him symbols? Symbols that he vaguely—very vaguely—remembered.

He smoothed out the parchment on the ground. Yes. He did recognize at least one of the symbols. From his Dragonmage training days, when he thought that immersing himself in books and Magicks would be his entire life. But the call of the Dragonwarrior had overshadowed it and that was the way he'd headed. Yet he still remembered things. Like this symbol. It was incredibly old. And, if memory served, incredibly powerful.

"Where? Where do I know this from?"

Briec took his talon and followed the patterns on the parchment. The drawings looped and swirled around the page, and as Briec's talon moved over the images, they began to lift off the parchment. They came alive, growing in size and swirling around him. He watched in fascination, the images moving faster and faster while growing brighter and brighter until Briec could no longer stand to look at them. Until he could no longer see. Until the screaming had him sitting up straight with a roar.

Panting, he opened his eyes and looked straight at his brother.

"Fearghus?"

"Briec?"

Briec looked around. He was no longer on that lonely piece of land. He was in the cave, the sounds of an ongoing assault from siege weapons a welcome sound to his bored ears.

"Thank the gods. What a shit dream." He smiled, but his brother just kept staring at him, saying nothing. Then Ragnar ran in, several of the healers behind him. And then they all stared at him, too.

"What? Why are you all looking at me?" When no one answered, he stood, which made them all gawk at him more. "*What?*" When they *still* didn't answer, he shook his head.

"I'm getting something to eat. I'm hungry." He eased past them, not sure why they were all gawking, not sure he even wanted to ask. He could find out later . . . when they all regained the power of speech.

Fearghus pointed at where his brother had laid, near death, and then at where he'd just walked out. "How . . . ?"

Ragnar shook his head. "I don't know. You saw him, Fearghus. His back was . . . was . . ."

"Fucked. That's the terminology we use among our kin. His back was fucked."

"Yes. I didn't think he'd survive, much less . . ."

"Walk. But then how . . . ?"

"I don't know," Ragnar told him gravely. "And perhaps we don't want to know what dark forces have your brother healed and walking as if nothing had happened."

Rhian released her cousins' hands and smiled. "That was fun!"

"That was boring," Tally complained. Then she glared at her cousin. "And we still don't have our swords."

"I said I was sorry!"

"But that doesn't bring back our swords!" Tally pointed a warning finger. "And don't you cry, ya big baby!"

"I am *not* a baby!"

The door to the small room they were in on the top floor of the castle opened and Ebba walked in. She scowled down at them. "How . . . when did you . . ." She stamped her foot and whispered, "How do you keep getting away from me?"

Rhian and Tally just stared at Ebba, and Talan . . . well,

Talan yawned and was asleep before his head landed comfortably in Rhian's lap. Either someone's lap or some dog's back were usually his favorite places for naps.

Annwyl didn't sleep that night. Then again, she didn't sleep much anymore. No matter how exhausted she was, the task of closing her eyes and sleeping was lost to her.

She missed sleeping. She missed shutting everything in her mind off for a few hours. Yet somehow her body kept going, though she didn't understand how that was possible. She should be dead on her feet, but she kept going.

Then again, she was being pushed, wasn't she? Always pushed.

When she heard people and dragons moving about, she guessed it was morning and went in search of some place to bathe. Izzy, after handing her some bread and cheese, told her she'd found an underground lake, but Annwyl had just nodded at that. She hadn't been in the mood to find it. She hadn't been in the mood to feel water on her skin. Instead she stood in the middle of that big cavern and waited. Waited for the Rebel King to do what she needed him to do.

Yet when morning finally came she still hadn't gotten her way. So with time quickly running down, Annwyl searched out that lake. She was vaguely aware that, as she walked along, human and dragon alike moved out of her way. No one wanted to get near the "crazed queen."

There was a time Annwyl would laugh at that kind of reaction. She was only as crazy as she needed to be to get the job done, she'd often tell her mate. But these days, Annwyl was beginning to feel as crazy as everyone thought she was.

Probably the loss of sleep. She was pretty sure one needed sleep, a good sleep, to function properly. How could she expect to function properly when she couldn't sleep? When they wouldn't let her sleep. Why wouldn't they let her sleep?

Annwyl found the lake and stripped off her clothes and dived in. She scrubbed her scalp, realizing she still had bits and pieces of the Sovereign soldiers who'd taken her stuck in her hair and on her body. Her original plan had been to kidnap the commander of one of the Sovereign units and find out the information she needed to track down Gaius, but she had to allow herself to be taken instead. That's what she'd been told to do.

She was tired of being told to do things.

Dragging her body out of the water, Annwyl sat on the edge of the lake naked and soaking wet, her arms wrapped around her raised legs, her forehead resting on her knees. She began to rock back and forth. She tried not to do that—it seemed to upset everyone when she did—but it felt soothing to her somehow. So she rocked and she tried to think. But her mind . . . it was so tired.

It was usually when it got this bad that he showed up. He did what he always did. Laid down next to her, pressed his head against her.

"He won't help," she told him. "Your Rebel King that you were so sure about. He won't help." She began to rock more, harder. "I could just go there myself without him." And she knew she was babbling—again. But she couldn't stop. "I could just go there and kill everyone. Everyone in the Provinces. I could kill them. The soldiers, the guards, the women, the children. I could kill them all until I get what you want. Until I kill the one you want. You just want the head, right? I could bring that to you. I could stab and stab until I get the gods-damn head! I could—"

He licked her. Giant, wet, disgusting tongue, slathering across her forehead.

She leaned away from him, but then she blinked, and

everything sort of came into focus. She stopped rocking. She stopped babbling.

Annwyl looked at what sat next to her. "You should have come sooner," she said, calmly. "I'm relatively certain I've destroyed any hope we had he was going to help."

She took a breath. It felt so good to think again without all the screaming that went on inside her poor brain. "Look, if all you need is for me to kill—"

He pressed his snout against her cheek and that's when Annwyl heard that voice in her head. He only talked to her like this. Probably because he was a big, shaggy wolf-god. The one time he'd softly "moofed" around her, Annwyl's ears had bled for days. She thought for sure she'd be deaf forever. So he did this instead. Told her things in her mind and she listened. She had no choice.

Because Thracius had a god on his side, too. Helping him fight and win, unless Annwyl did something. Unless Annwyl went against everything she believed in and gave her soul to a god. At least she liked dogs. That helped.

"All right," she told him when he'd finished telling her what to do. "I'll suggest it. But when this is over"—she looked at the god lying beside her—"I want my life back."

He nodded, then pushed his body into hers.

"Is that really necessary?" she demanded. "I'm not some whore who will just do things on command. I'm a bloody queen!"

But her protests were ignored and he pushed her again.

Sighing, Annwyl got to her knees. "I'm doing this," she said, "But if you ever tell Fearghus—I'll find a way to destroy you."

With a quick glance around to make sure they were alone, Annwyl gripped the wolf-god, Nannulf was his name, on either side of his head behind his ears and proceeded to dig her fingers in and scratch and scratch and scratch.

The wolf-god rolled to his side, Annwyl's hands still on him, his tongue hanging out, his eyes closed, and a low growl rumbling from his chest that managed to shake the cave walls.

"Shameless, ya are," Annwyl told him, even as she couldn't help but smile a little. "Bloody shameless!"

Rhona was getting dressed when the cave walls shook a bit. She glanced over at Vigholf. "Earthquake?" she asked.

"Sounds like it. But minor." Finished pulling on his boots, he stood. "I'm—"

"Yes. I know. You're starving." She laughed, shook her head. "Go, find food. I'll be along in a minute."

Vigholf left and Rhona closed her eyes and sent out her thoughts to her sisters. Any of them. Then her brothers. She still heard nothing back and she tried hard not to panic.

But gods, how could she not? Annwyl told them the siege had begun—and Rhona didn't really want to think much on how the royal had known that when she'd been off in the Western Mountains before they had—and yet here Rhona was. In the Septima Mountains with a bunch of worthless rebels—hiding! A Cadwaladr hiding! Gods, what she'd come to.

"Have you seen Annwyl?"

Rhona opened her eyes and looked up. Izzy, freshly bathed and with clean clothes on, stood in the entrance to the private alcove Rhona and Vigholf had made their temporary home. The Rebels hadn't seemed to care what they did. It was like they didn't exist for them because their king was ignoring Annwyl.

"No," Rhona replied. "I haven't."

"Okay. Thanks." Izzy turned to go.

"Izzy."

She stopped, faced Rhona again.

"What I said to you last night about not being my cousin . . . I'm sorry. You are kin and like most of them you've really pissed me off. But that was an unfair hit, even for me." She cleared her throat. "I sounded like me mum."

Izzy let out a breath and stepped farther into the alcove. "You were just trying to protect your own and . . . I understand that. I still don't think it's your business," she felt the need to add. "But I do understand it. And I'm sorry if I snapped."

Rhona got to her feet, picking up the chain-mail shirt her father had made for her. "Now you see, Izzy, that's what makes you stick out in this family. You actually apologize. You *feel* real regret. How can you fit in with the Cadwaladrs when you do all that?"

Izzy chuckled.

"I can assure you that those two idiots ain't apologizing for a gods-damn thing. Instead they just fight. Constantly."

Shaking her head, Izzy said, "I didn't mean for them to. . . . I was never going to tell. . . . I was just going to . . ."

"Enjoy?"

She flinched. "Yeah. I guess."

Rhona pulled her shirt over her head. "I will say that you shouldn't have expected any Cadwaladr male to keep his mouth shut about a conquest. That was, I think, your only real mistake here."

"No one told Éibhear. He sort of . . . saw us."

"Oh. Well, that's awkward."

"And then he went round the bend. Beating up poor Celyn."

Rhona snorted. "Poor Celyn, my tail. I don't feel sorry for either one of them. And you shouldn't either." She stood in front of Izzy. The girl was as tall as any She-dragon in human form, as wide too. A powerfully built female with a pretty smile. *Gods. Those two idiots don't stand a chance.* "Do you love Celyn?"

"I love him . . ."

"But you're not *in* love with him, yeah? And Éibhear?"

Now she snorted. "I'm trying *not* to love him at all."

"Well, I'm going to tell you what I'd tell one of my sisters. Think of your own life, Izzy. Think about what you want. Now. Don't let them two throw you off course. They've got some growing up to do, and so do you. Do that first and then worry about the rest of it."

"Iz!" Brannie called out. "Annwyl's back."

"Let's go and deal with our mad queen."

"Thanks, Rhona."

"Yeah, sure. Now go on. I'll be right out."

Izzy walked out and Rhona grabbed her weapons, putting them on before she followed. Vigholf stood outside the alcove, eating a turkey leg and grinning down at her.

"Eavesdropping, Northlander?"

"Just listening to someone handle an awkward situation brilliantly." He grinned. "Babysitter."

"Oh, shut up with that."

Varro walked around the corner and that's when he came face-to-face with the crazed queen.

"Where is he?"

"If you mean King Gaius—"

"Look," she said, dropping her hands onto his shoulders. "I don't have time for games. Where is he?"

Varro pushed her hands off him and walked around her. "Gaius made himself perfectly clear yesterday. I can assure you that nothing has changed since then."

"The open games are tomorrow, aren't they?"

Varro stopped walking and slowly faced the queen. "What?"

"Today they have games of all the well-known fighters.

But tomorrow is the open games. Anyone with coin and the willingness to die in the arena can sign up. Yes?"

"Yes. How did you—"

"According to my mate's father," the unstable female—although she looked much saner at this moment than she had the evening before—put her arm around Varro's shoulders, "I'm a right little brawler. So let's have some fun with that, eh?"

Rhona was in the middle of her meal when Annwyl crouched in front of her. The queen looked different . . . clear-eyed. Rational. Well, as rational as she had looked before the war against the Irons.

"I've been told you're an excellent blacksmith," Annwyl began with no preamble. "Is that true?"

"Did my father tell you that?"

"No. He just said you were missing your true calling. I heard from someone else."

"Who?"

"Can we discuss that later? Are you a blacksmith or not?"

"Well—"

"She is," Vigholf volunteered for her. "A really excellent one who's considering coming back to the Northlands with me when this is over so she can make weapons for my brethren."

When the two females looked at him, he grinned. "Just trying to help."

"You must be *really* good," Annwyl said, "if you've got a Northland *male* singing your praises."

"Northlanders don't sing," Vigholf felt the need to say.

"I can help you, Annwyl," Rhona said, before Annwyl and Vigholf got into a heated discussion about what Northlanders do and don't do. "Tell me what you need."

* * *

"You can't be serious," Gaius argued.

"She's the one being who could possibly get Aggie away from Vateria. A mad bitch against an evil one. This plan . . . it could work."

"Or we could just be giving Vateria what she wants. Then she'd have Queen Annwyl *and* my sister."

"Gaius—"

"No, we're not doing this."

"Why not?" Startled, they both looked up to find the queen standing at the cavern entrance, watching them.

"Because no matter what the world says about me," Gaius explained, "I'm not that much of a monster to turn a female, any female, over to my cousin. She especially likes females to . . . play with."

"You may not be that much of a monster"—Annwyl grinned—"but I am." She walked into the cavern. "First off . . . I'm sorry about what I said yesterday." She shrugged. "My head hurt."

Probably from all those voices screaming in there. But Gaius only said, "I understand."

"You know . . . I have twins. Talan and Talwyn. All they do is fight. Constantly." Her smile was warm. "But don't try to get between them. Or, even worse, don't hurt one and think the other will let you get away with it. Talwyn can be clear across the castle grounds or on a different floor, and she'll know when Talan's in trouble. She feels it. I know she does."

Annwyl stood in front of him, her hand reaching out, calloused fingers cupping his cheek. "I understand how much you hurt, Gaius. And how scared you are for her. But you can't let that fear stop you from taking this chance to get her out. We have to get her out."

"Why? Why do you want to get her out so badly?"

"It's complicated. But to do what I need to do, to get what I need, I have to help you first. Let me."

"I send you in there, Annwyl, I'm sending you to your death. And that's if you're lucky."

"I stopped fearing death a long time ago. You know . . . after I actually died. It changes your perspective." She frowned and added, "Vateria's destroying your sister as we speak. So I help you. . . . Then you help me. An alliance, of sorts."

"You control the entire Southlands, and yet you're willing to risk your life doing this?"

"Because I'll do whatever it takes to protect my twins. And we both know that if Thracius wins, they won't live long."

Gaius glanced at Varro, but his friend was leaving it all up to him. But before Gaius could agree—and they all knew he would because he'd run out of choices—he noted, "You seem different today, Annwyl."

"Yeah. The wolf licked my head."

The two friends looked at each other again, but this time there was definitely more panic involved.

"What?" Gaius asked.

"My head always feels better after he licks it. Although I'm hoping that won't be necessary anymore once I get some real sleep."

"And do wolves always . . . lick your head?"

"No. Just this one. I'm hungry," she sighed and walked away. "Hope you don't mind," she tossed back at him. "We're using your forge."

"At this point," Varro admitted, "I usually tell you that it could be worse. But honestly, I can't even . . . there's just no . . . I'm at a loss!"

So was Gaius, but as king, he couldn't really say that out loud.

Chapter 29

Edana saw them too late. Somehow they'd slipped past them all and made their way to the tunnels.

When she realized, she charged after them, Breena and Nesta following without question. She was able to trip one with her tail, then bring down her broadsword, splitting his spine.

She followed after her sisters, who'd kept after the other three Elites. They were nearing the exit, and Edana didn't want to lose them in the forests.

"Stop them!" she yelled at her sisters. "Don't let them out!"

Nesta tackled one of the Elites from behind. Once on the ground, she used a dagger to open his throat. Breena flew over the head of another and met him head-on with her knife.

But the last one . . .

Snarling, Edana went after him. He was nearing the exit and she didn't think she'd reach him in time. But she saw her cousins near the exit. The problem was . . . it was Celyn and Éibhear. And they were gods-damn fighting again!

"Éibhear! Celyn!" she called out. But her cousins were

too busy shoving each other, poor Austell once again trying to separate them.

"*Éibhear!*" she screeched, still running, still trying to catch up.

Her cousin turned, looked at her.

"Stop him!"

Confused, Éibhear blinked, but then he caught on. He and Celyn dove at the Elite, but the Iron slipped past them and shot out the entrance.

"No!"

"We'll get him!" Nesta and Breena yelled, the pair charging after the Elite.

Fed up, wishing Rhona was here, Edana turned her attention to the two idiots who'd been—once again!—fighting while everything fell apart around them.

Getting to his claws, Éibhear quickly apologized. "Edana, I'm so—"

"I don't want to hear it. From either of you!" she said before Celyn could add his apology. "That is it."

Nesta and Breena returned, shook their heads.

"They must have been waiting for him," Nesta said. "Once he took to the skies—"

"—arrows rained down. No way we could get through that to get to him," Breena explained.

"Sorry, Edana."

"You didn't do anything wrong. It was these two!" she accused her cousins.

"Edana—"

"I don't want to hear it." She began to pace in front of her cousins. "Do you see what you did with all your fighting? *Do you?*" She stopped in front of the two males. "This centaur shit ends here. Do you understand me? Or I swear by all the unholy gods that when Rhona gets back—"

"When Rhona gets back from where?" another voice asked from behind her.

Edana briefly closed her eyes at the sound of that voice. *Damn*.

She did try lying, though. "Oh, Mum, yeah, Rhona just—"

Bradana yanked Edana by the neck of her chest plate and pulled her close.

"Where is she, girl? And don't you *dare* lie to me."

After spending all day at the forge, Rhona was glad for a break. She washed off in the lake that Annwyl showed her and then returned to the alcove she was sharing with Vigholf. As soon as he saw her, he smiled, surprising her with his tenderness.

"Here," she said, handing him his hammer and ax. "It didn't need much work, but after that time with the wyvern, figured it couldn't hurt."

"Thank you." He examined the weapons, nodded. "Excellent. What did you do for Annwyl?"

Rhona tossed her own weapons to the floor and sat down on her bedroll beside Vigholf. "I did as much as I could for her, trying to remember everything new my father showed me when we were at Garbhán Isle. And Annwyl seemed happy with what I came up with."

"But?"

"But what if it doesn't work? What if it fails her just when she needs the damn thing most?" She shook her head. "I wish my father was here. He could have done so much better."

"Centaur shit. I know you made something wonderful."

"Such faith in me."

"I know what I've seen. I have faith in that." He put his weapons aside. "What is it, Rhona? What's bothering you?"

"That we sit here, planning what's sounding more and

more like a suicide mission, while our kin . . ." Rhona closed her eyes. "I haven't been able to get in touch with the triplets. Or any of my siblings." She smirked. "Didn't bother with Mum, though."

"I haven't been able to reach any of my brothers or Meinhard either. Or my mother. I doubt that means the worst, though."

"I know. But the triplets are alone, yeah? On their own. Who's going to watch out for them?"

"They don't need anyone to watch out for them." Vigholf leaned in, looking her in the eyes. "Have you not watched them, Rhona? Have you not seen the skill with which your sisters kill? You've trained them well. Better than anyone else."

"We should still be there, by their side."

"But we're here."

"And we'll be dead before the suns set tomorrow."

Vigholf lifted Rhona onto his lap, his arms around her waist. "That's not a positive outlook."

"How can you talk to me about positive anything?" Rhona lowered her voice and added, "Rumor is that Annwyl is going around telling people a wolf licked her head."

"What?" Vigholf asked on a laugh.

"That's what she said. That she felt better because a wolf licked her head. And that's who we're following into the Provinces tomorrow."

"Was it a big wolf? Or just a good-sized dog?"

Rhona tried to get off Vigholf's lap, but he held her in place.

"I was just asking," he insisted.

"No. You were making fun, but that woman scares me!"

"She scares everyone." He thought a moment, then added, "Except Izzy. She doesn't scare Izzy."

"If you knew Izzy's life story before she came to Briec

and Talaith that realization wouldn't make you feel *any* better."

"So you're just going to give up?"

"I can't give up. I'm a Cadwaladr. We foolishly push on until our last breath. Like most diseases . . . it's in the blood. You know, like idiocy."

He frowned. "Idiocy isn't a disease."

"It is to me."

Bradana paced in front of her twins . . . er . . . triplets.

Damn girls. Protecting their sister without thinking about the consequences.

Bradana was no fool. She knew the loyalty of her offspring was with their eldest sister. And Rhona had earned it. But the one thing none of them could say was that their mother wouldn't do everything and anything to protect every last one of them. Even her stubborn eldest child!

"We're sorry, Mum."

"Yeah. Really sorry."

"But Rhona said she wouldn't be gone long. Drop off Keita and Ren and she'd be back."

"And that was the last you heard from her?" Bradana asked.

They nodded.

"But," one of them added, "no one here has heard from a blood kin past the Euphrasia borders. We haven't heard from Daddy in weeks."

"Royals ain't heard nothing yet either," Bradana admitted. "They usually hear from the queen on the regular—but nothing."

"So Rhona's probably okay, yeah?" one of them eagerly asked, needing to hear her sister was alive and well. "We're all just cut off somehow."

They were cute when they were that age. Full of hope and a positive outlook. But Bradana knew it wouldn't last.

"You going after her, Mum?" one of them asked.

"No. Your sister made this decision, chose this path. . . . She wants to go it alone, she can."

"Mum—"

"I won't hear it . . . uh . . ."

The child's shoulders slumped. "Nesta. Me name's Nesta."

"Right. Nesta. I know," she quickly added. She waved them away. "Go. Get out of my sight. We'll discuss this later." Much later.

"But, Mum . . ." The girl pointed at herself. "Edana."

"I know! What, Edana?"

"The Elites that were in here . . ."

The one thing that Bradana did know was that if her Rhona was here, not one of those bastards would have made it out of here alive. "What about them?"

"It's just . . . we don't think them Elites came from the outside."

"What?"

"They suddenly came out of the alcove. Near the tunnels. But how could they get past all of us?"

"And we have every entrance in this place covered," Nesta added.

And the one she assumed must be Breena said, "No way they just come in and no one notices."

Her girls were right. "You three set up a search party. Scour this place, see if you can find anything. But leave whoever's on the tunnels there. We need to get that blasted thing done."

"Right."

They headed out and Bradana tossed after them, "And good work."

Once they were gone, Bradana tried contacting Rhona, but she knew it wouldn't work. But now, instead of assuming she was just blocking her—as the girl sometimes liked to do—she was assuming that Rhona had been . . .

No. She wouldn't think that. Not about her girl. Not about her Rhona. Soldier that she was, Rhona was also a survivor. A scrapper. She'd be fine.

And Bradana would have to believe that if she hoped to make it through all this.

"I just hope," Vigholf said, "that you're not going to spend what, according to you, is our last day on this planet sitting around sulking."

"Well . . . that had been part of my plan. The other part was to feel resentful and angry."

Vigholf pressed his forehead against her cheek to stop himself from laughing. "And what if I have a more entertaining plan than that?"

"More entertaining than sulking? I know of nothing like that, Northlander."

"Then clearly you need to get out more," he teased, stroking his hand down Rhona's back, kissing her throat.

Vigholf was moving in to kiss her when she said, "I'm sorry."

"Sorry? For what?"

"For getting you into this."

"You didn't exactly invite me along. I came of my own accord."

"I know, but—"

"And," he cut in, "no matter what happens tomorrow, Rhona. I've been honored to fight by your side."

Rhona pulled back a little, brown eyes peering at him. "Do you mean that?"

Vigholf took her hand in his and lifted it to his mouth.

He kissed the back of it, then turned it over and kissed the palm. "When it comes to war, death, and battle, I never say what I don't mean."

He could have said a lot of things to her. Told her how pretty he thought she was. How much he liked her eyes. How nice she smelled after a bath. How he didn't find her scars disfiguring in the least. He could have said any of that, but none would have meant more to her than what he did say. Because he meant those words. She'd earned his respect and he'd earned her trust. And with that respect and trust came loyalty.

Rhona slipped off Vigholf's lap and while on her knees, faced him. He watched her with that I-need-to-eat expression again, and it only became worse when she pulled her chain-mail shirt off, tossing it into a corner.

Vigholf scrambled to his own knees then, yanking his shirt up and over his head. He hurled it away, then reached for her, slipping his arm around her waist and pulling her in close. He kissed her, his tongue teasing hers, one hand on her breast, squeezing and tugging the nipple.

Rhona nearly had her arms around his neck, but Vigholf lifted her up and stretched her out on the floor. He stripped the rest of her clothes off, his hands running along her flesh while his avid gaze followed. Rhona reached for him, but Vigholf pulled back, and lowered himself until he could bury his face against her.

Rhona groaned when Vigholf's tongue slid inside her, licking her out, and only stopping to tease her clit with the tip. He did it over and over, making Rhona's body writhe beneath his, her hands gripping the back of his head.

Vigholf took hold of her legs, pushing them back and spreading them wide. He held them down while he feasted on her. Rhona's eyes closed, and she bit her bottom lip.

When her body began to shake, he latched his lips around her clit and suckled.

Rhona barely held back her scream by shoving her fist against her mouth and biting down on her knuckles. As the first orgasm swept through her, Vigholf continued sucking her clit while he pushed first one, then a second finger inside her. He stroked those fingers in and out and tugged on her clit until she came again, her body nearly twisting out of his arms.

Groaning, tears in her eyes, Rhona realized Vigholf had moved away from her, but just as quickly he was back, only now he was completely naked. Still dazed, she let the Northlander lift her up and turn her away from him. He pulled her onto his lap and pressed his hand against her back until her upper body was stretched out, facedown on her bedroll. He pulled her back a bit more and she felt his cock nudge against her.

Rhona took hold of the bedroll, biting down on it, seconds before Vigholf rammed himself inside her.

She choked on a sob, his big cock filling her, taking her. He held her tight with his hands while he rocked her back and forth. He moved over her, his tongue gliding up her spine, teasing the back of her neck and all while he was still inside her. He kissed her cheek, her throat, until his lips pressed against her ear. He was panting hard, but she knew he was saying something. She tried to focus away from the next orgasm working its way up her spine to hear him. To hear what he was trying to say to her.

"Everything, Rhona. You are everything to me."

And that's when that next orgasm hit, ripping in and through her, leaving Rhona lying there covered in sweat, exhausted and unable to move.

Vigholf grasped her hands in his, held them as he came hard, his whole body tight around hers until he collapsed against her back.

* * *

Vigholf forced himself to roll off Rhona before he crushed her. Her arm reached out, stretching over his chest. He pulled her close until she lay on top, her head resting against him.

They stayed like that for a long time, Vigholf's hands stroking up and down her sweat-soaked back, his eyes locked on the cave ceiling.

"You know," he said into the quiet, "at some point we really must do this while we're dragon." He grinned. "I'd love to see what you can do with that delicious tail of yours."

When Rhona didn't answer, Vigholf assumed she was asleep. But she moved up until she could rest her arms around his shoulders and bury her face against his neck. Her head lifted a bit, and she said, "I've grown ridiculously fond of you, and I'm not sure I can ever forgive you for that." Then she pressed her hand to his cheeks. "And you've become everything to me, too."

Closing his eyes, Vigholf immediately wrapped his arms around Rhona, holding her close.

He finally had what he wanted, but now he'd have to find a way to keep them both alive in order to have even a hope of enjoying it.

Chapter 30

Rhona brushed his hair off his face and Vigholf opened his eyes. Even though they were deep underground, he knew it was morning and Rhona was already dressed and ready for what they had to do.

"It's time," she said.

Vigholf nodded and sat up. "Do we have a plan?"

Rhona sighed and headed out of the cavern. "We have something."

Vigholf didn't like the sound of that.

They dressed in cloaks provided by the Rebel King's men that would help them blend better. Since Brannie would be the one retrieving the king's sister, he gave her a necklace and a small vial of liquid. "Show the necklace to my sister. If she sees this, she'll know I sent you. Then get her to drink what's in the vial."

"What's it do?" Rhona asked.

"You need my sister awake and alert to help you get out of there. The effects won't last long, so you'll need to move. But once she drinks this, she'll be strong enough to help you help her."

"A squad of my men and I will show you the way to the city gates," General Varro said. "But you'll be walking in alone. Avoid the city guards. They have a tendency to question suspicious-looking outsiders."

"And you five look very suspicious," the king muttered.

"If you are stopped, let the Northlander do the talking. They're more accustomed to seeing your kind and more likely to let you go. But a Southlander of any kind—you're in trouble." He glanced at the king. "Anything else?"

"Not that I can think of."

Annwyl walked up to the king. One monarch talking to another. "You're doing the right thing."

"I hope you're right."

As promised, General Varro and some of his men escorted them about ten miles from the main gate. With surprising ease, they slipped into the sea of travelers flowing into the city. As the king had also promised, with so many coming and going at that time of the day, especially with the monthlong games in progress, it was incredibly easy for them to pass the guards and soldiers without being questioned. Although they did have their stories ready should they be stopped.

Once in, they followed the crowds to the stadium, a large, circular building filled with stands that looked down over a fight-ready arena and was connected to the royal palace.

Instead of the front entrance that paying customers were going into, however, the five of them went to the side entrance that led into the dungeons, and got into the long line.

While they waited, Rhona turned to her cousins. "Are you ready for this?" And when Izzy didn't answer right away, Rhona snapped her fingers in her face.

"Huh?"

Good gods. "I said are you ready for this?"

Izzy frowned. "Ready for what?"

Rhona curled her hands into fists.

"Oh! You mean . . . oh, yeah. Yeah. I'm ready."

Unable to help herself, Rhona felt the inherent need to lecture the girl. "You have to pay attention, Izzy. You can't be daydreaming or thinking about your next meal. You have to be here. In this moment. Understand?"

The girl nodded. "Aye. I understand. I'm here. I'm ready."

"Good." Rhona focused on Brannie. "And you?"

"I'm ready."

Finally, their group reached the entrance and the table where masters and sponsors offered up the services of their fighters. Here, men would check in those willing to fight to the death for money. If the fighter won, glory and riches could be theirs. If they lost, their bodies were dumped in a trash heap and burned at the end of every month. Amazing to Rhona how many of them thought it was worth it, even though they would be fighting against the empire's greatest pit fighters.

Rhona waited behind Vigholf as he stood at the table. An Iron in human form took one look at him and shook his head. "No dragons today. Only humans."

"I got humans. Me own private stock."

Vigholf grabbed Annwyl and Izzy and pulled them forward. He yanked the hoods of their cloaks off their heads. "Pretty, yeah? And big tits on this one," he said about Annwyl.

Brannie abruptly looked down at her feet, her shoulders shaking. But Rhona didn't see what was so damn funny.

The Iron looked up, eyes narrowing in calculation. "Women?" He sniffed a little. "Not worth much if they die quick. Need someone with actual skills, actual tal—"

Vigholf clicked his tongue against his teeth and Annwyl caught hold of the guard closest to her. She yanked him down and snapped his neck by twisting her hands once.

When he fell, his comrade rushed forward. Izzy broke his leg with her shield and, while he was on the ground, Annwyl finished him with a dagger from her boot.

The Iron grinned, feeling absolutely no loss at the human guards. "Yeah. All right. We'll take 'em."

And with that—the game had begun.

Chapter 31

The tunnels were filled with fighters and the ones who controlled or owned them. Annwyl and Iseabail were quickly noticed, the idea of women fighting getting everyone's instantaneous attention. They were given the standard short sword used by all the soldiers and the short, dark red tunic to wear. On top of that a fancy but rather weak—in Rhona's estimation—breastplate made of strips of steel and brass fittings that tied in the front, was also added, along with a sword belt, and army sandals. They were also allowed a second small weapon of their choosing. Izzy chose her dagger and Annwyl a small useless-looking steel stick. The guards laughed at her over her choice, but stopped when she glared. Not that Rhona blamed them. After all that, the pair were allowed no helmets and they were told to wear their hair down. In other words, the ones running the fights wanted the audience to see that Izzy and Annwyl were women.

By late afternoon, they were up. The guards who managed these fights yanked Annwyl and Izzy away from Vigholf. When he tried to follow, he was shoved back, and stared down by an Iron in human form.

Vigholf held his hands up. "Yeah. All right. But I better get something if the bitches die. They weren't easy to find."

The Iron sneered at him as only an Iron could and walked away. As soon as the announcement was made that females were to fight, the crowd's roar escalated tenfold, and Vigholf, using the hand he held behind his back, motioned for Rhona and Brannie to go.

It really wasn't hard to slip away; as the king had said, all attention was on the two women entering the arena.

With a last look at Vigholf, his eyes on her as she moved through the crowd of men and dragons trying to see out the steel grates, Rhona took her cousin and did one of the stupidest things she'd done in a long while.

Izzy and Annwyl were seconds from stepping out into the arena when someone grabbed their arms and steel manacles were placed on Izzy's right wrist and Annwyl's left. The manacles were locked, a thick, three-foot steel chain stretched between them.

Annwyl snarled, "You son of a—"

"Enjoy, ladies!" The guard laughed and shoved them out into the arena, slamming the gate behind them, trapping them.

They stumbled, their eyes trying to adjust to the bright sunlight they hadn't seen since they'd entered the tunnels, their ears trying to handle the screams and cheers of the crowd.

"You all right, Iz?" Annwyl asked her.

"Yeah. Don't worry about me."

They walked out into the middle of the arena, Annwyl looking up into the crowd.

"There," Izzy murmured. "Over there."

Izzy motioned at what had to be the royal seats. They were high above the ground, but without anything blocking the view of the carnage below. The seats were upholstered in velvet and silk, servants hovered nearby, and everyone had fresh fruit, wine, or both.

"I bet that's her," Annwyl said. "I bet that's Vateria."

It could be. Izzy really didn't know. Although she was certain the female was a She-dragon in human form. She wore a tunic of the finest silk draped around her in the fashion of the Provinces, gold and silver flowers entwined throughout her perfectly sculpted silver-colored hair. But still . . . she could be just any royal, couldn't she?

"Don't assume, Annwyl. Please."

The queen laughed, not making Izzy feel any better. But she abruptly stopped, both of them realizing at the same time that not only was the crowd cheering louder, but there was something standing behind them—breathing.

They looked over their shoulders, and up, Izzy forced to squint because of the suns.

"Oh," she said on a breath. "An ogre."

Annwyl quickly counted. "Eight of them, actually."

"Well, you fought Minotaurs before—and won."

"True. But I was a bit more . . . *angry* then."

"Then perhaps you should get angry now."

"Nor was I chained to you."

"What does that mean? What's wrong with being chained to me?"

"Nothing. I'm just—"Annwyl shoved her back, the spiked club the ogre swung over its head slamming into the ground where Izzy had stood. But the power of the swing broke the chain that bound them.

"Nice," Izzy teased.

Annwyl grinned, winked. "Now," her queen said, pulling the short sword, "start running for your life."

* * *

While her guests clapped and cheered in excitement at the sight of female combatants, Vateria studied the women closely. After a moment, she looked at Junius, who sat several seats over and a row back as protocol dictated.

"Junius? Is that . . . ?"

"I believe it is, my lady."

"Oh," she gasped, clapping her hands together and returning her focus to the arena. "She will be *quite* the entertainment in my dungeons."

"For safety, my lady, you may want to send guards down to the dungeons in case she's up to something else as well."

"Very good idea," she said, motioning to one of the guards.

"And do you want me to stop the ogres, my lady?" Junius asked.

"No, no. Not yet. Let them have some fun. Then, when they're nearly done"—Vateria grinned—"*I'll* have some fun."

Rhona slipped down the stairs and around another corner. General Varro had given her exact directions. He, like Gaius, had grown up in this palace before they'd raised an army in an attempt to overthrow Thracius's Empire.

She really didn't know if retrieving the Rebel King's sister would actually change anything, but they'd come this far. . . .

They reached the end of the hallway Varro had directed them to. According to what she'd been told, she should turn left and go straight until she reached the last dungeon alcove that had several caged chambers.

Pressed against the wall, Rhona motioned to her cousin. Brannie crouched low, and leaned over, trying to see around the blind corner. After a moment, she leaned back.

Held up all of her fingers. Ten? Ten guards for one royal's sister? Then Brannie made a fist and again flashed ten fingers.

Twenty? she mouthed to her cousin.

Brannie nodded.

Wonderful. Well, there was nothing to be done about it now.

Rhona shrugged. *You ready?* she silently asked.

Brannie nodded again. But in mid-nod, her gaze slowly moved to a spot behind Rhona.

"They're more behind us, aren't there?" Rhona asked, out loud this time.

Her cousin winced. "Uh-huh."

Rhona let out a breath, her head dropping forward. This day was getting more and more difficult.

Vigholf hauled several human males out of his way so he could watch Annwyl and Izzy through the steel-barred windows.

"Ogres?" He looked at the man standing next to him. "They're making them fight ogres?"

"Yeah, well . . . ogres really like the girls." The man at least had the grace to grimace a little. "You know. They don't usually kill them right off."

Vigholf took a deep breath and focused on the powerfully built, ten-foot-tall monsters towering over his friends. "Wonderful."

He stepped back, examining the hallway he was in. He wondered if he could destroy all this if he shifted. But with just one glance, he knew that a building built by or under the direction of dragons would ensure that foreign dragons couldn't destroy it all at their whim.

The crowd roared and Vigholf rushed back to the grate. Annwyl was on her back, the sword kicked from her hand, one of the ogres over her, a club raised. Izzy was running from three of them, two of them were wandering around and drooling, and two were trying to escape by digging through the wall.

And just when Vigholf didn't think it could get any worse, he saw guards at the end of the tunnel run by and head off in the direction Rhona and Brannie had gone in.

His instincts, of course, were to find Rhona and protect her. Gods! It was to protect all of them, but especially Rhona. Yet he couldn't, could he? As difficult as it was for him, they were soldiers on a mission. He couldn't suddenly treat Rhona or the others as weak females who couldn't take care of themselves.

So he returned his focus to the pit fight and the ogre slamming its club down again and again, trying to hit a rolling-and-dodging Annwyl.

"Your girl," the man next to him said, "she's not doing too good."

"She just has to . . . get her bearings." He hoped.

Rhona impaled another throat and slashed another chest. "Brannie, move!"

As it was on the battlefield when fighting the Irons, the soldiers just kept coming, backing Rhona and Brannie into the hallway. Rhona pushed her cousin by the shoulder, then used the butt of her weapon to fend off another advancing soldier, and unleashed her flame.

The human soldiers screamed and tried to put the flames out, running off or dropping and rolling on the ground. But the ones who weren't human, she faced herself.

"Get her, Brannie. Go."

Rhona let her weapon extend a few more feet and faced

the soldiers. "Come on, lads," she told the dragons. "Let's get this over with."

Knowing her cousin was holding the line, Brannie charged down the hallway toward the last alcove, striking the guards who stood right outside the steel gates. She cut the arms off one and the head off the other. The one without the head had the keys, so she snatched it off his belt and quickly unlocked the door. She stepped inside but instead of finding multiple chambers, she found only one. One big chamber with only one captive. The She-dragon was in her human form, naked, a gold collar around her throat, long silver hair framing her face and covering her shoulders and breasts. She'd been chained to the wall, and cuts, sores, and burns—old and new—littered her human flesh, both eyes swollen shut, nose broken.

Remembering what Annwyl had said to the Rebel King, Brannie now knew her queen to have been right. Vateria had made this dragoness her plaything. Her toy. A fellow dragon. In fact, now that Brannie thought of it—her cousin! How could Vateria do this to her own cousin?

It always amazed her how some dragons could be no better than the lowliest of humans. Harming others simply for their own amusement. Brannie would kill a body in battle or if threatened or hungry. But just to watch others hurt? That did nothing but piss Brannie off and, thankfully, it pissed her kin off as well.

She went to the She-dragon's side, lifted her chin with her gloved hand.

"My lady? Can you hear me?" She pulled out the glass bottle King Gaius had given her. "You need to drink this." The royal turned her head, groaning, but Brannie heard a bit of a snarl and that gave her hope. "Please, my lady. It'll give you strength until we're free of this place."

"Never free," she muttered. "Never."

"You need to be strong. Please. For your brother."

Somehow the dragoness forced those swollen eyes open and gazed at Brannie. "Southlander."

"Your brother sent us. Oh!" Brannie pulled out the necklace King Gaius had given them before they left. She showed her the stone pendant at the end. "Here. He wanted me to show you this."

"Gaius."

"He sent me. But you need to drink this. Now. My cousin can't hold them off forever."

The royal jerked her head a bit and opened her mouth. Brannie poured the contents of the bottle in.

"Now swallow that down and I'll get you out of these chains. Gods," she went on while she tried the keys on the royal's manacles. "Treating your family like this. I don't understand it. Yeah, sure. We'll beat the shit out of our kin if they're asking for it, we Cadwaladrs will. But that's it. We'd never do *this* to each other."

None of the keys she held worked, so Brannie used her ax. With two hits, the chain broke and she helped the royal to her feet.

"Can you walk?"

In answer to that, the royal went down, her hands grasping at the gold collar. Brannie realized it must be one of those mystical ones that could keep a dragon in human form. Only this collar seemed to be doing more than that. Now that the royal was loose from her bonds, the damn thing seemed to be choking her to death.

"Shit," Brannie said, crouching before the royal and gripping the collar. She knew absolutely nothing about Magicks and such. She left that to the witches and mages. Too much reading and thinking for Brannie's tastes. But then how was she going to deal with this thing if she didn't

even know what it was? At the very least she had to deal
with it before it killed this female.

Brannie studied the thing while desperately trying to
ignore that the royal's human face was turning blue. From
what she knew, never a good thing. With a quick glance,
she realized that there was a small lock in the collar that
needed a key. Too bad she didn't have the key. None of the
ones she had were small enough to fit. She had nothing.

Desperate, Brannie left the royal's side and went back to
her cousin.

"The royal!" she yelled.

"What about her?" Rhona yelled back, fighting off three
and four dragons at a time.

"She's got a collar. I can't get it off!"

"So?"

"It's killing her!"

Rhona snarled. "Shit and piss!" She tossed her spear to
Brannie. "Take over!"

Thankful to be back to what she understood—fighting—
Brannie followed orders.

Rhona ran to the royal's side and quickly saw that what
Brannie had said was true. The She-dragon's face was blue,
her hands desperately gripping that gold collar. That bitch
Vateria wanted to make sure the royal didn't escape even if
King Gaius had been able to rescue her himself.

Rhona crouched over the royal and pushed her hands
away from the collar. She felt around the metal and saw the
small keyhole, which meant there was a key. A key that
probably only Vateria had. But no matter because Rhona
was the eldest daughter of Sulien, which was meaningful
for two reasons.

She forced her fingers between the collar and the royal's
neck, hoping to relieve some pressure. Rhona opened her

mouth and unleashed molten lava into her free hand. She spread the lava around the collar before it had a chance to cool and chanted the appropriate words. She watched as the collar changed from gold to steel to glass.

Rhona broke the collar then and the royal began to gasp as she took in big gulps of air.

"That's a good lass," Rhona said, patting the female's shoulder. "Think you can stand?"

The royal nodded and Rhona helped her to her feet. But they were halfway across the room when the female began to shake and shudder. It took Rhona a moment, but she quickly realized the She-dragon was having a seizure.

The shaking became worse and Rhona was forced to set her down, stretching her out on the floor, and pressing her hands against the female's shoulders. Gods, she hoped the She-dragon didn't shift. These dungeons had not been built for a dragon to shift to natural form.

"Rhona, come on!" Brannie yelled. Rhona could hear that her cousin was still fighting in the hallway around the corner.

"Hold the line!" Rhona ordered Brannie. "We'll be right—"

A strong hand closed around Rhona's throat and squeezed, cutting off her air and risking bones she'd become rather fond of.

Rhona punched at the hand and arm holding her, but the royal ignored all that as she slowly got to her feet.

The female studied Rhona like some offending mouse she'd found in her room, looking her over from head to foot.

"My brother sent *you* to rescue me?"

Rhona, unable to get this female off her without cutting her open from belly to throat—which would only make the whole trip a bit of a waste—pointed toward the exit.

The royal's head turned a bit and she listened.

"You're not alone. Good."

She dropped Rhona to the ground and stepped over her as if she was someone else's trash on the street. Gods, Rhona never thought she'd find royals more ungrateful than her own, but she'd been quite wrong.

Rhona jumped to her feet and went after the royal, ignoring her sore neck.

The She-dragon walked down the small hallway until she reached the turn where Brannie was doing an excellent job of keeping the guards at bay.

She was fighting off four at once when the royal walked up behind her, caught Brannie by the hair, and yanked her out of the way.

The royal stepped in front of the Irons, her back straight, her swollen eyes open and clear.

"*You*," one of the Irons whispered. Then he screamed, "*Gods above, she's free!*"

Rhona didn't like the sound of that, but there was nothing she could do now as the She-dragon smiled a bit, took in a small breath, and while still in human form unleashed the most brutal and widespread flame that Rhona had ever seen. Sounding like hurricane winds coming in off the sea, the white-hot blast filled the room and, Rhona could see, melted stone and metal while covering the Iron dragons in the hallway. The flame was so bad that Rhona instinctively grabbed her cousin and covered her with her own body.

When the sounds of those flames died, Rhona lifted her head. The She-dragon stood there before the remains of dragons whose armor had been melted into their human forms, killing them instantly. As fellow Fire Breathers that should never be a problem when dealing with flame.

The royal looked at Rhona over her shoulder, and Rhona yanked her spear from Brannie's hand and faced her while still protecting her cousin.

The She-dragon ignored that and said, "Come. We must

go. And quickly. Before this lot starts shifting back. I've damaged the stone columns. . . . The base will crumble now and cave in the entire arena."

"I have to get my comrades."

"Comrades?"

"Aye. In order to distract Vateria so we could get you, our friends are fighting in the arena."

"Trust me. That won't distract my cousin for one bit, which is why we need to go now. Besides, your comrades are a lost cause if they're in the arena."

From behind her, Brannie said, "I'm not leaving Izzy, Rhona. She'd never leave me."

The royal stopped. "She? You put *females* in the pit?"

"They were the only ones among us that were human."

"I see." The royal began walking. "Then, if they haven't already been raped to death and eaten, I suggest we go get your friends now."

"Uh . . . Rhona?"

"I know, I know. But we follow the plan. We follow our orders."

"Doesn't the royal outrank us, though?" Brannie whispered.

"She's not *our* royal. Now come on. We need to give Vigholf the signal."

Vigholf tried again to get the gods-damn bars off the gods-damn grate, but they weren't moving. So, like some wretched human male, he was forced to watch as Annwyl got tossed around the arena like a toy and Izzy earned boos because she was a fast runner and dodger. But how much longer could they keep it up? And where the bloody hells was Rhona?

Annwyl was backhanded and sent flying. She hit the arena wall and slid down. One of the ogres picked her up and dragged her back to the center. He threw her down, flat on her back, and raised his club over her.

"Now!" Brannie barked as she ran past him, hard-charging right for the exit so she could begin clearing the way of soldiers.

"Now!" Vigholf yelled into the arena, unable to do anything but watch that club, already in mid-swing, come down at Annwyl's head.

Annwyl heard Vigholf's yell and relieved because she was fed up with playing nice, she rolled to her side. The club slammed into the ground beside her as Annwyl got to her feet.

The ogre, not the brightest of breeds, stared at her, mouth open and ew—there was drool. Annwyl hated when things drooled! Disgusted beyond all reckoning, Annwyl quickly pulled the small steel stick Rhona had made for her, prayed the blacksmith's daughter was as good as Vigholf had bragged, and watched the stick extend into the long-handled ax she'd thought of.

Pleased, Annwyl brought the ax up and over, burying it into the side of the ogre's neck. It screeched and Annwyl put her foot on its chest and pushed, while yanking the ax out. Another ogre came at her from behind, but she quickly spun and hacked off its head, spun back, and finished off the other one by splitting its skull into two.

"Izzy!" Annwyl called out to her squire. "*Kill 'em all!*"

Izzy stopped running and turned. A club swung at her and she ducked, the heavy spiked weapon crashing into the wall. Izzy slammed her hands against the ogre's arms, breaking them both as she pinned them. She snatched the club from the ogre's hands and used it to crush its head in. Then Iz went about crushing the rest of them with that club she seemed to be enjoying way too much.

Gods, but the girl was strong. Really, *really* strong.

And while Izzy did what she did best—kill stuff—Annwyl focused on the raised dais that Vateria sat upon.

Because to get this far, this close to ending the war for good, Annwyl had made an agreement. A price she must now pay for such goodwill from the gods. Nothing was for free it seemed, even when the god had paws and liked to be scratched behind the ears. So, ignoring the guards sprinting at her from the three entrances in the arena—and *any* common sense—Annwyl ran right for the dais and the ones on it.

Vateria laughed a little. "Oh, look, Junius. The human queen is going to try and assassinate me. Isn't that cute?"

Junius nodded. "I believe she is, my queen. Would you like me to have her killed for you or just incapacitated?"

"Incapacitate is fine, but in a moment. I want to see how far she gets."

"Her little friend seems to be having quite the time with the ogres," her sister noted.

"That she is. Although I was hoping for something a little different there."

Vateria and her guests laughed as Annwyl the Bloody used her ax—*where did she get that from anyway?*—to cut down human soldiers that got too close. Vateria's dragon guards hit the woman with flame as they ran toward her, but that didn't affect her at all. Vateria glanced back at Junius, and he suggested, "A spell of protection, my lady. Probably from the Dragon Queen."

"Ah, yes." Although why any dragon would give a human that kind of protection was beyond Vateria. It was knowing that the Irons could destroy them and those they loved that kept the Sovereigns in line.

Vateria watched with a smile when the scarred little

wretch skidded to a stop in front of the dais, her arm going back, the ax in her hand changing somehow to what looked to be a much smaller throwing ax of some kind. Fascinating.

"Junius," she said calmly so as to not concern her guests.

"Of course, my lady."

Junius raised his hands and Vateria felt the Magick he unleashed wrap around her like a protective cloak. And Vateria smiled as the human threw her weapon, but—she realized too late—the little bitch wasn't aiming for her.

Vateria looked to her mage, screaming, "*Junius!*"

Hearing the warning, Junius turned, raising his hands to block the weapon, but it was too late. The ax rammed into his head with unbelievable force, splitting his skull down to his nose. His body flew back, crashing into the guards behind him, and Vateria stood, screeching in rage and pain and abject loss.

She turned toward the human queen and—gods-damn the cuntish whore to the very pits of hell—Annwyl laughed at her. At her! She laughed, turned, and took off running, heading toward the fighter entrance.

Behind Vateria her mage shifted back to his natural form, pillars crumbling from his dragon body pushing into them.

Those that were dragon simply shifted and took to the air. But those humans whose dragon masters didn't remember to take their pets and slaves with them were crushed.

Vateria shifted and dove toward the arena, her claws reaching out, talons ready to catch the worthless human who'd killed what belonged to her.

The human looked over her shoulder, saw Vateria, and screamed out, "Shit!" before leaping into the arms of some Northlander. He unleashed bolts of lightning at Vateria, but she was too angry to feel the pain from it. Too angry to care. She just kept coming even as the Northlander shoved the human queen and her big-muscled girl-soldier into the tunnels.

It had been some time since Vateria had killed a Northlander. First him, then—

Vateria's wings jerked forward and back, halting her in mid-flight as that bitch walked past the Northlander from the fighter's entrance. She was still naked, still in her human form.

Vateria roared at her cousin. She roared and unleashed her flame. But Agrippina merely shook it off and opened her mouth. . . .

That's when Vateria made a run for it.

Rhona grabbed the royal's arm. "Leave her!"

"*She's mine!*" the royal bellowed.

"Not now!" She pulled, but the royal wouldn't move. "Vigholf!"

He ran out and swept the female into his arms, tossing her over his shoulders as he ran. "Go!" he ordered Rhona. "Now!"

They made it out of the crumbling arena, the bodies of the dragon Annwyl killed and the dragons the royal had killed below destroying the coliseum from within. They rushed through the tunnels while behind them more soldiers charged at them. They made it to the exit and ran into the streets, Vigholf pushing them along.

Once outside, Vigholf lifted his head and unleashed long bolts of lightning that reached high into the air. Seconds later, they heard the battle cries from the Rebel King's human cavalry. They breeched the gates on horseback, riding into the crowd and sending them panicking and screaming, running anywhere and everywhere, it seemed.

Rhona pushed through the crowds, but the Sovereign soldiers, some of the most well trained she'd ever come across in her life, were not confused by Gaius's men. Instead, they surrounded the small group, their focus on one thing and one thing only.

"Hand her over," the commander said, pointing at the royal Vigholf had over his shoulder. "Hand her over or we'll kill—"

The commander's eyes suddenly widened, his mouth opened, and a blade pushed through his chest from behind. When he fell forward dead, Rhona wouldn't say she was surprised to see Annwyl standing behind him, but she was relieved. The soldiers quickly snapped out of their shock at the loss of their commander and they went on the attack. Annwyl dove in sword first, as was her way, Izzy and Brannie fighting by her side.

"Take the royal," Annwyl ordered Vigholf. "Take her and go. We'll be right behind you!"

Rhona motioned to Vigholf. The strength that the Iron royal had a few minutes before was quickly waning, and if she died, Rhona would prefer it was in her brother's arms rather than theirs. "Go, Vigholf. Take her."

"And you?" he asked, gazing down at her. Doing something she didn't think he ever would—trusting her to protect herself.

Rhona smiled. "Don't worry. I'll be right behind you."

Vigholf stroked her cheek with his hand. "You better be," he warned. Then he swung his hammer and battered his way through the soldiers surrounding them.

Chapter 32

It was the abrupt silence that worried him. For days it hadn't been quiet. Not with boulders constantly slamming into the cave walls of their stronghold.

But now?

Now there was nothing, and Meinhard the Savage didn't like that at all.

By the time Meinhard made it to the cave entrance that faced the Polycarp Mountains, Ragnar was already there, staring out.

"Get everyone ready," his cousin ordered.

"Already done."

"The Fire Breathers?"

"Ready."

Meinhard waited for his cousin to give the next order, but Ragnar didn't move.

"What is it?"

"I don't know. Something's not right. It's too quiet. It's too—"

The entire Valley rumbled, cutting off Ragnar's words.

"Ragnar?"

He shook his head. "I don't know. I—" Ragnar braced his claw against the wall, the first explosion rocking everything around them. Then the second explosion came and the third. The pair watched as the Polycarp Mountains began to fall, one after the other, after the other. Until there was nothing but dust, dirt, and level ground. Now there was nothing separating them from the Irons. It would be a straight, head-on battle. Irons against Northlanders and Fire Breathers.

"Get all our troops up here, now."

Meinhard nodded, turned to go. But one of the Fire Breathers ran toward him.

"Meinhard! Coming from behind. Sovereigns."

"They're closing in around us," Ragnar murmured. "Any sign of Annwyl's army?"

"Scouts just got back. They're coming in from the Eastern Pass, moving fast, but they don't know about all this."

"They'll find out soon enough." He looked at Meinhard. "We'll let Annwyl's army deal with the humans. And I want everyone who's in that bloody tunnel out. Now."

Meinhard nodded. "Done. And Annwyl's troops?"

"We hope they get here before it's too late. Now go, cousin," Ragnar ordered as they both heard the sound of advancing Irons. "Because we've just run out of time."

Brastias rode along beside his troops, using the Eastern Pass as Morfyd had suggested. They'd made good time this way, but still, the men were restless. Not simply because they wanted this fight over with, but because they hadn't seen Annwyl. The fear and gossip that the queen had deserted her troops was spreading through the ranks. Although how any of them could believe that she'd desert them out of fear or boredom or some monarch pique, did nothing but make Brastias very angry. So angry that he'd had anyone spreading those rumors flogged for insubordination.

True, Annwyl had left them, but not because she'd run

away. No. Not his Annwyl. She'd done something even more stupid. She'd gone right into the enemy's den. But what she was facing there, he had no idea.

Brastias's horse, a veteran of many battles like his rider, suddenly reared up, only Brastias's skill keeping him seated. Then almost all of the horses reared or backed up, colliding into the horses behind them, the ground beneath them shaking and shuddering.

"Earthquake?" Danelin, Brastias's second in command, asked.

"No. I don't think so. It's something else." The rumbling continued on, the land beneath them rolling. Until, finally, it stopped. "It's begun," he said.

"Are you sure?"

"Aye. I'm sure."

Brastias turned to two of his messengers. When they were on the march, it was these mounted soldiers who spread commands when time was short.

"We cut off on that path up ahead, then we cut the Sovereign snake in half. Now go!"

"You sure the Sovereigns are already in the Western Pass?"

"The Irons wouldn't move until they were. They're there, and we're going to kill them all."

"And Annwyl?"

"I've never doubted her before, Danelin," he said, spurring his horse to a gallop. "I won't start now."

As Vigholf made his way to the gate, he wasn't surprised to see the Rebel King walking through. He was in human form, the hood of his cape covering his face, but it was him.

While the royal's gaze searched the panicked crowd,

Vigholf carefully pulled his sister off his shoulder and carried her in his arms to the Iron.

"King Gaius."

The king turned and saw his sister. First, he seemed stunned. Unable to do anything but stare. But as Vigholf moved closer, the king reached for her and took her into his arms.

"Agrippina?" He dropped down to one knee, cradling his sister. "Aggie?"

The royal opened her eyes, reached up, and pressed her palm to his cheek. "Gaius."

The king laid his forehead against his sister's. "Aggie, I'm so sorry."

"No. Don't. You apologize for nothing." She turned her head, looked over at the city she'd just left behind. "It was her. I want *her*."

"Our army is right outside this gate. One word—"

"She's gone. Slithering snake that she is. She's slithered away. We could burn the city to the ground and we won't find her."

"Then I'm getting you out of here."

He stood and carried his sister out of the castle gates.

To be honest, Vigholf didn't think much about it until Annwyl ran up to him a few minutes later. "Where's the royal?"

"Her brother took her."

"They're gone?"

"Well—"

Snarling, she ran off after them.

"Annwyl!" When the royal didn't stop, he looked over his shoulder at the still-battling females. "Rhona, come on!"

He didn't wait, assured they could take care of themselves. It was the lunatic he was concerned about.

Vigholf followed, catching up to Annwyl as she cleared

a hill. On the other side stood King Gaius's army. And they were, in a word, vast.

"You promised!" Annwyl was saying to Gaius's back.

The king stopped and slowly faced the Southland queen. "I'm not leaving my sister."

"You wouldn't have your sister if it wasn't for us."

"What's she talking about, Gaius?" Lady Agrippina asked.

"Nothing."

"You promised!" Annwyl insisted.

"You're irritating me again."

"I don't care."

The king's sister motioned to the ground. "Put me down, Gaius."

"You're not well enough—"

"Don't argue or we'll be here all damn day. Just put me down."

Gaius put his sister on the ground but kept an arm around her waist, letting her lean against him while Varro covered her naked body with a cape.

"Now tell me," she ordered. And it was an order.

"You!"

A hand gripped his tail and Nannulf was tossed back and into the side of a mountain, moving the mass several feet. "Worthless little beast dog! How dare you interfere with my people!"

The wolf got to his paws and bared his fangs. He didn't like most other gods, but he especially didn't like this one. Chramnesind, the sightless one. An angry demon god whose only desire was to become the one and only god everyone worshipped. The only one everyone turned to when in need.

Something that Nannulf found completely unacceptable!

"Do you think you're stronger than me, *dog*? Do you think you can really stop me?"

Nannulf didn't know, but he was always willing to try. He charged Chramnesind but even without eyes, the bastard still saw well enough, and he was fast. He caught Nannulf by the throat, slammed him to the ground, and held him there.

"It's too late," Chramnesind told him. "It's much too late. Without your help, they'll never get there in time and Thracius will destroy them. But you . . . you will pay for what you did to my mage. He was mine! Mine!"

A sword slid under Chramnesind's chin and a soft voice asked, "What do you think you're doing to my friend?"

Chramnesind hissed, his tongue—a forked one—slashing across Eirianwen's cheek, flesh burning.

Eir, the goddess of war, reached down and grabbed Chramnesind by his throat, lifting him to his feet.

"You," she snarled, "dare challenge *me*?"

Chramnesind pulled his sword and slammed it into Eir's belly. They both looked down as her guts poured to the ground.

And that's when Eir pulled back her arm and shot-putted the demon god away from her.

"*From my sight, you worthless bag of flesh!*" she roared, her voice booming across the land. "*Or I will wipe your existence from this world!*"

Chramnesind hissed at them again and dug into the ground, disappearing under the dirt.

Eir took in several breaths to get control of her rage; then she faced Nannulf.

"And you . . . what the fuck were you thinking?"

Nannulf shrugged.

"I protected you from Rhy, you know. Lied to him! Told him I had no idea where you were or what you were up to. But he'll know now, I can promise you that, because everyone will tell him. Och! And don't look at me like that. This is all your fault and you know it. You should have stayed out of it!" Eir spun away from him and marched off. "Well, come on, you idiot! Let's see if we can fix this!"

"You promised!" Annwyl said again while she and Izzy removed their ogre-blood-splattered tunics and army sandals and put on their own clothes.

"Would you stop saying that!"

"What did you promise?" the king's sister asked again, but it was Annwyl who answered.

"He promised me that he'd help me defeat Thracius."

"Thracius?" Lady Agrippina leaned back a bit and studied Annwyl. "You're the Southland Queen? You're Annwyl?" Her nose wrinkled. "You?"

"What were you expecting?" Annwyl demanded, tugging on her boots.

"From what I'd heard . . . someone hideous."

Annwyl smiled. "Awww. Thanks." Then she frowned. "Wait. You heard I was hideous?"

"Annwyl?" Rhona pushed, hoping to get her to focus. Gods, she was as bad as Izzy. But at least Izzy had youth and inexperience as her excuse.

"I'm not leaving my sister," the king said again.

"Yes," Lady Agrippina told her brother. "You are."

"Aggie—"

She stepped away from her brother, but she was still weak. Still unable to stand on her own. Rhona caught hold of her, held her up. The She-dragon nodded at her in thanks. She was much more polite when her brother was around, it seemed.

"You have to go, Gaius."

"You can't even stand. How do you expect me to leave you now?"

"Because this is our chance. To end this. To end *him*."

The earth around them shook, and Rhona realized that Vigholf had moved a boulder close so that Lady Agrippina could sit. He smiled at Rhona, quite proud of himself and she knew in that moment—she loved him.

Lady Agrippina sat on the boulder, and gave Vigholf a nod of thanks. Then she focused again on her brother.

"I want him dead," she said plainly. "And I want you to do it. At the very least be there to see it."

"I won't leave you here alone, and you're not fit to travel."

"Leave a battalion with me for protection. Take the rest. I want this done, brother. I want Thracius. And then, when I'm ready, that little twat he spawned is mine." She glanced at Annwyl. "Besides, we owe her." She grinned. "She killed Junius."

Gaius, stunned, looked at Annwyl. "You did?"

"The wolf told me to."

King Gaius frowned. "The wolf that licked your head?"

Vigholf stood next to her and said low so only Rhona could hear, "I never know how that head-licking thing is supposed to help us."

"That's because it doesn't help us."

"It will take us days to get there," Gaius argued, but Aggie didn't want to hear it.

"I don't care if it takes you eons. I want Thracius's head!"

"Aggie . . ."

"I'm all right, I'm all right." She tried to control her breathing, tried to calm down. She was running out of energy and fighting with her brother wasn't helping. When she felt she could speak without panting, Aggie raised her head. "Look—" she began, but then the woman appeared out of nothing and, at first, Aggie thought she was seeing things again. Since her time in that slit's dungeon, she'd been seeing lots of things. Some good, some a nightmare. To be honest, she enjoyed the nightmares more. It took a little more out of her every time she realized that blur walking toward her was not her brother or Varro.

Yet Aggie quickly realized that the woman walking toward them this time wasn't a hallucination because everyone else was staring at her, too.

She was brown of skin, like one of Aggie's rescuers and like the humans of the Desert Lands. She was dressed like a warrior and wounded like one, too. Wounded like a dead warrior, though.

"Annwyl the Bloody," the woman said to the human queen.

Annwyl pointed at the woman's stomach. "Did you realize that someone disemboweled you?"

"That'll heal," she said, walking around Annwyl. "My traveling companion says you need to get somewhere quickly. I can help with that."

A god. This woman was a god. They were chatting with a god. Things certainly had become interesting since Aggie had been rescued from her incarceration.

"Could you at least tuck your organs away?" Annwyl complained.

"You kill things all day."

"But I don't stand around talking to them afterward, their guts pouring out while I do."

"So sensitive."

Annwyl rubbed her eyes. "I'm tired. I'm very tired." Now that battling the city guards was over, the Southland queen did look tired. Exhausted. Aggie knew that kind of exhaustion.

"Yes. I see that." The god studied Annwyl. "Too tired for this?"

Annwyl brought her fists down. "I will end this. But I

can't do it from here. Send me or piss off. I'm tired of talking. Or send the wolf to deal with me. I like the wolf. He doesn't bore me with talk."

The god crossed her arms over her chest, leaving that gaping wound even more exposed. "I saved your life once. You could be a little more respectful."

"You saved my life after your mate took it. And that was after he used *my* mate to knock me up without our permission. So don't look to me for respect. I'm tired of you. I'm tired of him. I just want this over with. So send us or don't—but just. Stop. *Talking.*"

While the god and Southlander glared at each other, Aggie looked to her brother. "*This* is who you sent to rescue me?" *A lunatic who argues with gods?* she finished in his mind.

"I'd run out of ideas, all right?" He shrugged helplessly. "Cut me some slack."

"You think you can win against Thracius?" the god asked.

"I think I'm willing to kill anything in my way." The human queen tipped her head to the side. "Are *you* in my way?"

"Perhaps. So let me move out of your way." And with a flick of the god's wrist—Annwyl the Bloody was gone.

They were evacuating the tunnel, nearly out the exit, when it started again. The arguing. Always with the bloody arguing. And, as she'd been doing since Rhona left, Nesta's sister Edana got between the two idiots along with poor Austell. The arguing this time, though, was more vicious, more physical. Like it was before Rhona threatened both Éibhear and Celyn. Maybe they knew the war was almost over. Knew they wouldn't have much more time to fight because *all* of them would insist the pair was separated. For their own good and the good of others.

Éibhear caught hold of Celyn by his breastplate, yanking him close, and slamming his fist into the dragon's face. Nesta looked at Breena and her sister could only roll her eyes and shake her head.

Austell, clearly fed up with all of them, pushed himself between the pair, slamming his claws against their chests.

It was what had been happening a lot. There was only one difference this time—the human who suddenly appeared in the middle of all this. And Nesta didn't mean Izzy and the proverbial wedge she'd shoved between the cousins. But an actual, living, breathing human.

Nesta and Breena looked at each other and then back at the human. They leaned in a little closer.

"Annwyl?" Breena asked.

The human queen looked around, snarled as only Annwyl could, and roared, *"That bitch!"*

They pushed the Irons back again, but Briec stopped. Looked around. Something wasn't right. A trap? He turned in a circle, using his tail to bat off any Irons who got too close.

He expected some attack to come at them from either flank, but there was nothing. But still, the Irons were being pushed back too easily. Perhaps another attack with their siege weapons?

"Hold!" he called out to his troops. Then, to his brothers, "Fearghus! Gwenvael!" He motioned to them with his shield. "Pull back. Now!"

Fearghus responded immediately, but Gwenvael was impatient. "Why?" he demanded. "We've got them."

"Don't be an idiot," Fearghus snapped. "They're pulling us away from here."

"But—"

"Do you want to take a little longer to return to your

mate, or do you want to go back to her without important parts of you intact?"

Gwenvael didn't even have to think on that. He began moving back, calling his troops with him.

And, instead of retreating, the Irons again moved forward. They attacked again. But what they were trying to lure them from, Briec really didn't know.

"*No!*" Izzy bellowed, jumping forward to where Annwyl had been.

Rhona caught her, held the girl in her arms while they all gawked at the spot the human queen once stood in.

"Bring her back." Izzy pulled away from Rhona and faced the goddess.

"You think you can order me to—"

"Bring her *back*!"

"So much emotion," the god chastised. "I see why I like dealing with Dagmar more."

And then the god was gone.

"*No!*" Izzy screamed again.

"You have to go after her," Lady Agrippina ordered her brother. "There's no arguing over this."

"It'll take us days to get to Euphrasia. By then . . ." King Gaius shook his head, glanced over at Izzy, whose roar of pain was so gut-wrenching that no one could look at her for long.

"Rhona," Vigholf said in a low voice. He jerked his head and Rhona looked in front of them. It was a wolf. A wolf just sitting there. An enormous, freakishly sized wolf, but a wolf nonetheless.

Vigholf shrugged. "A wolf licked her head and made her feel better. He's a wolf."

Rhona frowned in confusion; then her brown eyes grew wide.

"You," Rhona said, pointing at the wolf. "You can send us to Annwyl, yeah?"

"To Euphrasia," Vigholf clarified. A good idea since who the hells knew where that pissed-off goddess sent Annwyl.

The wolf looked at King Gaius. The Iron glanced at his sister, then said to the wolf, "Let us end this. Send us. We're ready to fight."

The god nodded once—and they were flying.

Aggie made the mistake of blinking. That's how fast they were gone. With no more than a nod from the god, some Southlanders, a Northlander, her brother, and Gaius's entire army were gone with just a thought.

She heard her cousin's soldiers moving through the trees toward her. Except for the cape Varro had given her, Aggie was naked and alone. But she wouldn't go back to that dungeon. She would never go back.

The first group of thirty burst through the trees into the clearing. They saw her sitting on that boulder and the captain smiled.

"My lady," he said.

"Captain." Aggie forced herself to her feet, amused when the soldiers flinched.

"Now, now, my lady," the captain said, "let's not be hasty."

"I'll not go back. You know that."

"I know you'll fight, but you won't be able to stop us. Look at you . . . every second you're getting weaker and weaker. All we have to do is wait for you to drop." And Aggie felt real fear at the captain's words, but the wolf, now much smaller than he had been before, stepped in front of her, facing the soldiers. That's when Aggie realized she'd gone deaf. She could hear nothing. Not the soldiers laughing at the wolf or the wind in the trees or even the sound of her own heartbeat. She heard nothing, but she could see well enough. She saw the wolf bark. Once. And although Aggie could hear nothing, the world around her shook. Trees falling, boulders rolling, and the ground cracking open beneath the soldiers' feet. The men opened their mouths—she assumed they were screaming—their hands grabbing their heads, blood pouring from their ears and through their fingers.

When they were dead on the ground, the wolf walked back to Aggie's side, pushing into her with his body. She could hear again now that the danger had passed, so she nodded at him. "Thank you."

He pushed her again. He was offering to escort her home, and she silently accepted. If for no other reason than how many times in her life would she be able to claim a god had walked her home?

With one last look at where her brother had stood and with a silent prayer that he would be safe, she headed home, the god by her side.

Chapter 33

"That conniving, evil, whore of a god!"

Éibhear heard a voice he hadn't heard for five years but knew so well. Annwyl's voice. But when he turned to look at his brother's mate, Celyn punched him in the face.

Snarling, he returned his focus to his cousin. Annwyl and why she was in these tunnels could wait.

A horn he knew was not a Southland horn sounded in the distance and Edana, who'd been trying, with Austell, to separate him and Celyn, abruptly stopped.

"Edana?" Breena asked, and Éibhear heard the warning in his cousin's voice. The fear. That's when the ground shuddered beneath them and Edana caught hold of Éibhear *and* Celyn by the neck of their breastplates, her tail whipping out and wrapping around one of the old cave rocks that jutted from the ground. Not even a second later, the ground opened up. So stunned by this, they all dropped. But Edana held him and Celyn. Breena caught Annwyl, and Nesta caught Breena, yanking both onto firm land. But no one, absolutely no one, caught Austell. And the drop was so short, even if he'd thought about it, his wings would have been of no use. Besides. It wasn't the drop that killed him—it was the row after row of planted, sharpened steel stakes that did.

Éibhear only had a moment to realize his friend and many of his comrades were impaled on those stakes before Irons flew out of the opening that ran the entire length and width of the tunnel. All these months while they'd been building the tunnel, the Irons had been building one right underneath. Waiting for this moment.

"Everyone out!" Edana screamed. "Out! Move!" She threw Celyn and Éibhear and the pair spread their wings, went up. But for Éibhear all he could still see was Austell. The weight of his friend's body dragging him down that stake, his wide-open eyes glazing over as he tried twice to breathe, then stopped trying altogether.

"Éibhear!" Celyn yelled. "Come on!"

An Iron charged, ramming a steel spike at Éibhear. But Éibhear caught it and with one claw, bent the metal.

And that's when a rage he'd never known took over.

Like it had a few hours ago, the ground beneath Gwenvael's claws shook. He looked down, expecting to see the ground beneath him cracking or for something to explode, as the Irons had done to the Polycarp Mountains. But there was nothing. At least nothing around them. Then he heard one of his younger cousins screaming from the entrance to their cave.

"The tunnels! They're coming in from under the tunnels!"

Gwenvael looked at his brothers and they all thought the same thing at the same time. *Éibhear.*

But then the Irons they were fighting suddenly charged, pushing them all back.

* * *

Breena still held the royal in her arms while her fellow troops who'd been working on the tunnel—but hadn't fallen into the death trap below—were pouring into the cavern. Their older sister Delen was trying to get everyone under control so they could assemble a counterattack. But they were young recruits. Mostly privates and unseasoned. For some it was their first real battle and they were panicking.

"Put me over there!" Annwyl ordered her. "On that boulder."

Breena did as she was told and Annwyl with a bellow that could shake the walls called out, *"OY!"*

Every private and corporal, used to being yelled at and ordered about by superiors, immediately came to attention.

"Calm down!" the monarch ordered. "Now. You don't have time for all this. You—" She pointed her sword at Celyn and several of his siblings. "Get back in there and help Éibhear. He's in there fighting alone." When they only stood there, gawking at her, "Don't just stand there, you twats! *Move!*" They did.

"You—" She pointed at Delen. "Get your mother. Get Ghleanna. Get them all! Tell them what happened. Tell them the Irons are coming in through the tunnels."

"But—"

"They'll overwhelm you lot, break through, and destroy our army from the inside out. We can't afford that, so *move!*"

Edana stepped forward. "What do you need from us, Annwyl?"

"The Cadwaladr triplets." She grinned. "You're all coming with me."

Fearghus dodged an Iron spear to the face and blocked a sword to the gut. One of his cousins came in from behind and shoved her broadsword into the back of one dragon while he took out the legs of the other.

"Fearghus!" Delen dropped next to them. "Where's Mum? Ghleanna?"

He pointed with his sword. "A mile that way. Why?"

"The Irons." Delen shook her head. "They tore open our tunnel, are pouring in through it now. Annwyl says—"

Fearghus faced his cousin, ignoring the Iron at his feet trying to drag himself off without legs. "Annwyl? Annwyl's here?"

"Aye. She went off with the triplets." Delen shook her head. "We're overrun in there, Fearghus."

"Briec! Gwenvael! Go!"

"What about you?" Briec asked. Gwenvael was already calling his troops to follow him.

"Don't worry about me. Éibhear's in there," he reminded him. "And Mum will have our asses if we let anything happen to that little bugger."

Colonel Ampius sat on his horse beside Lord Laudaricus Parthenius.

"How much longer?" Parthenius asked Ampius.

"Soon, sir. Overlord Thracius has the Southland dragons trapped between his armies and the Hesiod Mountains. And we're holding off Annwyl the Bloody's army in the pass entrance.

"Good. Once Thracius gives the order, we move in to crush what remains of the queen's army."

"Yes, sir."

Another commander leaned over and warned, "More dragons, sir."

"Use the spears."

"Yes, sir."

The other commanders called out Laudaricus's orders,

allowing him to sit back and watch. The soldiers pulled the giant catapult around, several twenty-five-foot wood spears already loaded into the mechanism.

The dragons flew closer, dodging the arrows shot at them from the ground.

"Hurry up with those spears, you worthless bastards!" Ampius yelled out.

The order was given and the spears unleashed. They were near their target when the three dragons turned at the same time, the spears shooting past them. It was strange, how the three dragons moved at the same time, in the same way. Usually at least one dragon was struck when the others scrambled to avoid the spears.

The dragons continued toward them.

"Get the spears ready again," Parthenius ordered.

The spears were quickly re-loaded and aimed. The three dragons were close now. Nearly over them. If they moved lower to attack them directly, the spears or arrows would definitely take them down. But instead the one in the middle tilted to the side, something falling from its back.

"What the hells is that?" Parthenius asked him.

"I don't know, sir, but—" Ampius's words stopped, his mouth open as a woman landed on the back of Parthenius's white stallion, two swords slamming into their leader's shoulders and into his spine, killing him instantly.

The woman yanked her blades out, and pushed Parthenius's body off the restless horse, settling into the saddle.

Grinning, she looked at the men surrounding her.

"Hello, lads." Her grin widened, and Ampius felt real fear for the first time in a long time. "Name's Annwyl."

Fearghus and Ragnar stood side by side now, fighting their way through the Irons pushing in. But with his brothers' troops in the caves, they were quickly becoming overwhelmed and they both knew it.

"Pull back!" Ragnar yelled after a nod from Fearghus. "Pull back!"

Their troops pulled back, but the Irons pushed forward, the call for a charge made.

"Shit," Ragnar muttered.

"Yeah. I know." But to the troops he yelled, "Shields!" Their troops lined up, shields locked. "Hold the line!"

The Irons crashed into their shields. "Hold the line!" Fearghus yelled, slamming his sword into the Irons trying to push them even farther back.

Moments from calling the order to retreat—something he was loath to do—a light flashed and Fearghus watched as dragons and human soldiers from . . . somewhere, he didn't know, crashed into the Irons, battering and crushing them.

The Iron troops who'd been advancing turned toward this new attack, rushing forward to assist their comrades.

From the pile of dragons and humans a figure rose. What looked to be an Iron, all steel-colored but with long hair like Southlanders wore, and a patch over one eye, he stood tall, glaring out of that one good eye at everything around him.

"Who the battle-fuck is that?" Fearghus asked.

"I think that's the . . . wait. Is that Izzy?"

Fearghus leaned forward, squinting. And, yes. Yes, that was Izzy, climbing onto the back of Branwen, the pair taking off.

"What the hells—"

The Irons were rushing back into formation, their commanders getting them organized. But the Iron with the eye patch didn't seem to be in the mood to wait. He gave the order and the Irons with him went on the attack. But they didn't attack the Southlanders, but the other Irons. Thracius's soldiers.

In the midst of it, Fearghus saw two other dragons get to their claws. "It's Rhona." He grinned. "And your brother."

Ragnar put his head down, briefly closed his eyes. "He's alive," he said softly. "He's alive."

"And somewhere around here is Annwyl. Killing someone or something I'm sure."

Brannie landed behind some trees, their view of the fighting clear. "Let's find Annwyl," she told Izzy.

"No."

"No? What do you mean no?" Brannie had assumed that would be the one thing, the *only* thing Izzy would want to do.

"Look over there."

She followed where Izzy pointed. "Yeah?"

"That has to be him, right? Look at that armor . . . and the way he's standing high up on that hill, giving out orders. That's gotta be him."

"That's gotta be who? What are you talking about?"

"That's Overlord Thracius."

"So?" When Izzy said nothing, Brannie exploded. "You have lost your mind!"

"Hear me out—"

"No!"

"They'll never expect us."

"There's a good reason they would never expect us. Because I'm a lowly private and you're a squire."

"I'm not saying we should kill him."

"That's good because we can't."

"But maybe we can wound him. Make it so Gaius can

get to him. Finish him. Otherwise he's going to fly away and this won't end."

"You're as crazy as Annwyl."

"But she's been right. Crazy, but right." She pressed her hand to Brannie's shoulder. "All we need to do is wound him, Bran. Then we run for our lives."

"You promise?"

She patted her. "I promise. I have plans! Can't be promoted to general if I'm dead."

"Yes. That eases my concern, cousin."

And Izzy's laugh . . . did not make it any better either.

"There had to be an easier way for him to do that," Rhona complained, trying to wipe the dirt off her scales from where she'd slid into the ground.

"Be glad you shifted back before we got here." Vigholf winced. "Some of Gaius's human troops didn't fare so well."

She looked around, nodded. "At least we're here. We're back. I need to find my sisters."

Rhona started to walk off, but Vigholf caught her claw. "Be careful. We have much to discuss when this is over."

"Aye," she agreed. "We do."

He nodded and said, "Behind you."

Using her spear, she turned and impaled the Iron that had been running at her. She dragged him around and Vigholf brought his hammer down, cracking the bastard's skull, and finishing him up.

They smiled at each other for a long moment before Rhona unfurled her wings and took to the skies, spearing Irons as she went along.

Letting out a sigh and trying to ignore how hard he'd become just watching her do that, Vigholf turned and came snout-to-snout with his brother.

"So . . . you're alive then?" Ragnar asked.

"Last time I looked."

"And that dragon over there? With what I'm sure Keita will refer to as the 'sexy eye patch'?"

"Gaius. The Rebel King."

"So Annwyl did it then?"

"Did you really have any doubt?"

Ragnar shook his head. "Not really."

Vigholf hefted his weapon, resting it against his shoulder. "Let's get this done, brother. We've got an overlord to get rid of, I've got a female to Claim, and we have some Tribesmen to stomp out at Garbhán Isle."

Ragnar sighed. "So much bloody work. Can't wait to take a proper holiday."

"We're Northlanders. We don't take holidays."

"Oh, for the love of the gods, shut the battle-fuck up."

Brastias breathed a bit easier when he saw an aerial assault in the form of three She-dragons. They were smallish, but that seemed to only make them faster—and a wee bit meaner. They tossed the Sovereigns around like toy soldiers and happily destroyed attack weapons aimed at dragons.

One of them flew down to Brastias, slamming her back legs down and crushing several soldiers he'd been fighting with.

"Go!" she ordered, pointing toward where the army had been headed. "Annwyl's there. Fighting alone!"

Shocked, Brastias stopped a moment to stare at the She-dragon.

"Well, don't just stand there, you clod! Move!"

He whistled over his horse and mounted. "Danelin! Call the troops to me! We go to Annwyl!" He couldn't help but smile a little at his second in command. "We go to our queen."

Rhona came around the corner to find Annwyl decimating what looked to be Sovereign commanders while on horseback and Annwyl's troops pouring out of a side pass to engage the Sovereign soldiers.

"Rhona!" a trio of voices screeched and then the triplets were there, hugging her, squealing like little hatchlings.

She hugged them back, so glad to see them well and strong.

"I'm so glad you're back, Rhona," Edana said. "To be honest, we don't know how you do any of it. Running everything. It's a bloody nightmare, it is."

"Edana was busy trying to be you," Breena teased.

"We laughed at her," Nesta admitted.

"I'm glad you're all okay. Where are we?" Rhona asked.

The triplets immediately turned serious, and Edana spoke first. "They set a trap for us, Rhona. They built a trap right under our bloody tunnel."

"We started to find them inside the caves a day or two ago, but we thought there was just another entrance we missed. But they were under us the whole time."

"They were waiting for the time to strike," Breena added. "And they did, this morning. Leveling the Polycarp Mountains first, drawing us out."

"How many did we lose?" Rhona asked, never one to shirk from real numbers and real information. Even when every fellow soldier they lost cut her like glass.

"A few of the recruits," Edana replied. "We were all evacuating the tunnels when they struck. Took the floor out from under us in one fell swoop."

Nesta looked down, her pain evident. "We lost Austell,

Rhona. They had stakes built under the tunnel and when it went—"

Rhona raised her claw, cutting her off. "Austell's dead? Where are Éibhear and Celyn?" Austell was never far from those two. So if he was in those tunnels, chances were high that so were her stupid, stupid cousins.

"Fighting the Irons coming through the tunnel."

"But they'll send their Elites that way. Those two can't handle—"

"Celyn went back for Éibhear," Edana explained. "Éibhear wouldn't leave. He's angry, Rhona."

And the triplets said together, "Very, very angry."

"I think he blames himself," Nesta said softly. "For Austell."

"I don't know about now," Edana went on, "but for a while, Éibhear was the only thing keeping the Irons back until Gwenvael and Briec showed up with their troops."

Breena nodded and said, "Meinhard's there too."

"So what do you want us to do, sister?" Edana asked.

"I need you to get the word out. We've got the Rebel King here, helping us defeat Thracius."

"Who?"

"I'll explain later. He and his troops are Irons and Sovereigns too, but they're no friends of the overlord. The dragons wear their hair long and the humans are in black and silver, not the red and gold our enemies wear. I need you to get the word out to all the commanders. All of them." She sighed a little. "Especially Mum. They have to know Gaius and his troops are part of the alliance. They're not to be purposely harmed by us. Especially Gaius. He may be the only one who can kill Thracius. Now go tell everyone."

Once her sisters were gone, Rhona dropped down beside Annwyl.

"Annwyl! Are you all right?"

The monarch pulled her sword out of another corpse. "I'm fine. Feel great! How are we doing?"

"I don't know yet. It was a trap, Annwyl. The Irons came up through the tunnels. I want to go and check in with the troops still inside."

"Go. I'm fine." She grinned and motioned to her army riding in from the pass. "My troops are here. And look, Morfyd's arrived." She waved her swords to get Morfyd's attention, forcing Rhona to lean far back so she wasn't hit with the damn things.

"Morfyd!" the queen screamed out. "Oy! *Morfyd!*" When Morfyd was heading toward them, Annwyl waved Rhona away. "Help the others. I'm fine."

Rhona nodded and was about to lift off when Annwyl said, "Oh! And by the way. The triplets were great. You taught them well."

Surprised, Rhona stuttered, "Oh, uh . . . thank—"

"Go. Let me finish here, then I'll see if my troops can help Gaius."

"Thanks, Annwyl."

"No." And, for a brief second, Rhona saw the real Annwyl. The sane one who loved her offspring and mate and adored her people, was willing to die for them. More than once. "Thank you. For everything." Then that crazed smile returned, and Annwyl said, "Now go. I've got so many heads to take before the day is over."

Morfyd slid to a stop in front of them after dragging her claws through a few of the Sovereign troops.

"Morfyd!" Annwyl cheerfully greeted her Battle Mage.

"You cow!" Morfyd snarled in return.

Annwyl gasped. "What are you yelling at me for? What did I do?"

"What did you do? You left! That's what you did, you impossible female! With no word to me! To Brastias! And you took my ridiculously impressionable niece and young cousin with you!"

"Don't you dare yell at me, Princess! I'm queen. I rule! And if I want to go off on a suicide mission with or without your niece and cousin, I can! Because I'm queen!"

"You are the most foolish, insufferable, intolerable female I've ever known!"

"And you're a whiny royal! There! I said it! Now everyone will know the truth!"

Not about to get in the middle of this, Rhona unfurled her wings and took to the skies, heading toward the caves and whatever nightmare awaited her there.

Chapter 34

Word quickly spread among the Southland and Northland troops that the Irons with the long hair and black sashes over their breastplates, were in fact Rebel troops. Vigholf would have to say he was impressed, too, by the way they fought. The Rebels were brutal and merciless to what was once their own. But that could be because they and those they loved had been treated so heartlessly.

Yet none of them had been able to get near Thracius. And, with a glance, Vigholf could see that it was driving the young king mad to see his uncle so close but still out of reach. Gaius must long to get his claws around the male's throat and squeeze the life from him after what he allowed his daughter to do to Gaius's sister. The king kept trying, though, flying up and over the fighting masses. But each time he was taken down by the Iron troops before he could get close enough. The Irons hadn't managed to kill the young dragon—although they continued to try—but they were successfully halting his efforts to reach their overlord.

Ragnar caught Vigholf's arm, pulled him in close. "I pulled Meinhard's troops from the tunnels. They're coming in from the right. Take your troops and circle around to the left. Fearghus and I will push the Irons back. Understand?"

He did. It would be like catching a rat in a pincer and squeezing.

Vigholf let out a low whistle, and without making a fuss, he and his troops moved into position.

Rhona flew into the mountain cave they'd called home for the last five years. A home now filled with the bodies of comrades and enemies.

Snarling, pissed at herself for not realizing what the Irons had been planning all along, she headed toward the tunnel, pushing and impaling her way through the battling troops. She came around a corner but quickly brought up her shield, a broadsword slamming into it seconds before it would have cleaved her head open.

"Rhona?"

Rhona lowered her shield. "Mum."

She expected her mother to rail at her about sneaking up on her rather than just apologizing for nearly killing her eldest. But, instead, Bradana the Mutilator pushed Rhona's shield aside and . . . uh . . . she hugged her.

"Mum?"

"Your sisters kept lying to me and then when they finally told me what they knew . . . and I just heard you'd been with Annwyl. Gods, girl, we could have lost you forever!"

"I'm fine, Mum. Really." And, because she was just in that kind of mood, Rhona added, "And I'm in love!"

Her mother tensed. "In love? With Annwyl?" Her mother shrugged. "Well, you know, I've always thought . . . it doesn't matter. The thing is she's with Fearghus."

"No, Mum." And Rhona fought her desire to slap her own mother in the head. "Vigholf."

Bradana stepped away from her. "Vigholf? That . . . that . . ." An Iron tried to run past Bradana from behind, but

Rhona's mother turned, hacked the Iron into two pieces, yanked her broadsword out, and again faced her daughter, sneering, "That *Lightning*?"

"Aye." Rhona patted her mother's cheek with the tips of her talons. "That Lightning. Now if you'll excuse me, I've got to help the others."

"Don't you fly away from me, little girl!"

"It'll have to wait, Mum! Killing to do!"

Rhona flew through several caverns, striking at Irons where she could. When she reached the cavern where the tunnel was, she saw Celyn and flew to his side.

"Celyn!"

"Rhona!" He slammed his shield into the face of the one he fought, knocking the Iron out. "Thank the gods you're here. It's Éibhear."

"Where is he?"

"Still in the tunnel."

"You left him there?"

"He wouldn't leave." He ran back to the tunnel entrance, Rhona behind him.

They both stopped right outside the entrance, Rhona taking in the sight of all those Irons. Well . . . their corpses anyway. Elites that had been smashed and sliced and basically turned into mangled messes their own mothers wouldn't recognize—but that *her* mother would be proud of.

"See?" Celyn asked.

"Éibhear did this?"

"Just look."

She stepped over or around the bodies and looked into the tunnel. Éibhear was still at it, hovering over the collapsed tunnel floor and the rows of spikes beneath, while he used someone's warhammer and a bare claw to kill, well . . . everyone.

"He blames himself for Austell," Celyn explained behind her. "But, if anything, it was both of us."

"Don't worry about that now. Watch my back, I'll talk to him."

"I'm right behind you."

Rhona flew into the tunnel, her wings keeping her hovering over the collapsed floor. She could see Austell's body and her heart ached for her cousins. There was no pain like the first time one lost a comrade. And, even worse, she knew Éibhear well enough to know that he'd put the blame for his friend's death right on his own shoulders. If there was time, she'd sit down with him, talk to him. She'd make him understand that in war, they all had to watch out for each other, but there was always the risk comrades would be lost no matter what. That's what she would tell him, if she had the bloody time—but she didn't.

"Éibhear? Éibhear!"

The Blue, busy crushing the snout he had in his claw, slowly turned to face her. When the Iron he held stopped moving, Éibhear released him, letting the body fall. Rhona flew a little closer and that's when she saw the full number of Irons that hadn't made it past Éibhear to fight the rest of the troops outside this cave. And that number was . . . impressive.

"You were right, you know," he said to her and Rhona could see how much he really hurt. "You warned me and I didn't listen. Now my friend is dead."

"Éibhear, stop. You didn't kill Austell."

"Of course I did. I wouldn't stop. I wouldn't stop and now he's dead and it's my fault."

"Éibhear, it's not your fault. It's not Celyn's fault."

"It is. It's my fault."

"Éibhear, stop this. Right now. Look, if you just want someone to blame, then blame Thracius."

Éibhear blinked, studied her. "Thracius?"

"Aye. If it wasn't for him, none of us would have been here in the first place. But we can't run around looking for who to blame, we need to—Éibhear, *no!*"

Rhona watched as her cousin began to use the warhammer on the cave wall, battering it with big sweeping hits. Celyn flew next to her, but she caught him before he could make any attempts to stop Éibhear.

After several hits Éibhear flew back, unleashed his flame, and charged forward—and straight out a millennium-old cave wall that had withstood everything but the rage of a Cadwaladr male. Because, at the moment, that's exactly what Éibhear was.

Vigholf and his troops were closing in around the Irons from one side, while Meinhard was closing in from the other. Fearghus, Ragnar, and Gaius were pushing them back from the center. And although this battle was turning, it would still be a challenge to get to Thracius. He was surrounded by a mighty legion of Elites and it wasn't like he couldn't fly away if he wanted to. They would give chase, of course, but that didn't mean they'd catch him.

But none of that mattered. Right now it was about stopping the overlord here and now.

They kept moving forward, fighting off the Irons, pushing them back. They were near Thracius, and Vigholf could see that Gaius was readying his attack. Yet Thracius motioned to his guards, ready to move to a new location or run completely, his wings unfurling.

But that's when Vigholf saw her. The young She-dragon casually easing her way into the midst of Thracius's protective guard. She wore no armor. Had no weapons. And was female. She'd gone out of her way not to be seen as a threat. And it seemed to have worked. No one noticed her at all—until she suddenly made a mad dash and threw herself at

Thracius's back, her black-scaled forearms reaching around his neck.

"Good gods," Vigholf whispered. Then he yelled out, "Branwen! No!" But Thracius merely grabbed the She-dragon and tossed her off him. She went flipping head over tail into the other soldiers. And Fearghus ordered his troops to move in to help his young and very foolish cousin.

Vigholf motioned to his troops to move in as well when he realized that what Brannie did was nothing but a distraction. Because the real problem for Thracius—who was busy ordering his soldiers to "kill the insolent whelp!" he'd just tossed aside—was still on his back. A brown-skinned woman raising some dragon's large and extremely cumbersome battle-ax above her head and bringing it down where Thracius's wing met his spine. Blood spurted from the overlord's wound and he roared in pain. But, he was also unable to fly away. Now he was trapped.

Vigholf raised his shield, about to give the next command to strike the overlord now, while he was at his weakest point, when they all heard the explosion. Rock and debris flew out and over them from a cave wall; fire burst from the opening. Vigholf briefly thought that the Irons had set up more explosions within their cave and that the Hesiod Mountains would meet the same fate as the Polycarp Mountains. But there was something rushing at them from that cave opening. Something that broke free of ancient and mighty cave walls and was moving fast.

"Vigholf!"

He heard Rhona's voice and looked to the newly created opening she was flying through. "Stop him! Stop him!"

Vigholf looked back and that's when he realized what that something was. It was Éibhear. And Vigholf knew from experience—there'd be no stopping him.

But Izzy . . .

"Iseabail!" Vigholf screamed out. *"Iseabail! Move!"*

Whether she heard him or not, Vigholf didn't know, but she dropped the ax, bolted up the raging dragon's back, over his head, and dived off his snout and onto the back of another dragon before sliding off and disappearing into the battling crowd.

Thracius looked moments from going after her, but he heard the roar—they all did—and turned in time to see Éibhear the Blue ram into him, the pair tumbling off the hill Thracius had stood upon and right into the heat of battle.

Vigholf flew up and he saw the pair fighting on the ground. Rhona sped toward them, Celyn behind her, but Vigholf caught her and held her. Celyn automatically stopped beside them, and they watched as Éibhear got the overlord onto his back. First he struck him, several times, with the warhammer he held. But he got bored with that and tossed it away, taking the sword Thracius had barely managed to brandish and slamming it into the overlord's skull. He pulled the sword out and rammed it in again. Then again. Then a few, oh, dozen times.

And they all stood or hovered there. They all watched. Northlander, Southlander, Sovereign, Rebel—they all watched.

After some time Éibhear tore the head from the overlord's neck, lifted both the head and body high into the air, roared in rage, and tossed them in separate directions.

Panting, he looked out over the waiting armies, his talons curling into his claw, tight fists shaking with unused anger. He may have just killed the overlord, but clearly the pup wasn't done. And that's when Ragnar yelled out, *"Attack!"*

Vigholf released Rhona, pushed her away from him. "Kill them all. Leave none to remember this day." He grinned at her. "We'll remember it for them."

With that, they separated and they all went to work.

Chapter 35

Izzy and Brannie collapsed by some cave, both panting and barely able to move.

"Of all your ideas," Brannie told her, "definitely the most stupid."

"It worked, didn't it? He was only going to fly off before they could kill him. I don't know about you, but I'm ready for something new to kill."

"That bitch Vateria's still out there, cousin."

"That's not our problem. Gaius and his sister will have to deal with her."

"Yeah, well, you just better hope our—"

"Parents don't hear about it?" a voice snapped at them.

Izzy and Brannie flinched and looked up to see Ghleanna and Briec standing over them, glaring, more than a little pissed off.

Izzy tried her sweetest smile. "Hi, Daddy."

"Shut up."

Well, clearly her sweetest smile wouldn't be working today.

* * *

Fearghus made his way over to the Eastern Pass. That's where he found the Southland human army, his sister, and Annwyl . . . arguing with his sister while she simultaneously killed every enemy around her. How she managed to do both at the same time said much for her skill.

"If you're just going to sit here and yell at me while doing *nothing*"—Annwyl screamed at Morfyd—"then you can just go the fuck home!"

"Don't order me around! And after what you did? You're lucky I don't flay the skin from your bones!"

"Lovely, isn't she?" another voice said beside Fearghus. "My Morfyd."

Fearghus rolled his eyes at Annwyl's general and Morfyd's mate, sitting on his horse, gazing lovingly at Fearghus's sister.

"How did we do?"

"Most are dead," Brastias told him. "I sent a few squads out to track down any runners."

"No prisoners?"

"You know Annwyl hates prisoners. She'd rather just kill them all. Besides"—he shrugged—"we don't have to worry about feeding anyone and we'll only have to kill them later. So it's a waste of time to keep them alive now."

"Do me a favor, Brastias. Get Morfyd for me."

"Of course." The general smiled. "You have no idea how grateful I am to see you alive and well, Lord Fearghus."

Fearghus laughed. "Really? I never thought you'd have cared one way or the other."

"Oh, I care. The entire Queen's Army cares whether you live or die, my lord. Trust me, it would have been a dark day for me and mine if anything had happened to you. A dark day indeed."

Brastias spurred his horse forward and rode over to the still-arguing females.

"Morfyd?" the human called up to his mate, not seeming

intimidated by her much-larger dragon form. "Love? Can I talk to you for a moment?"

"Yes! Rescue me from this ungrateful wench!"

Morfyd stomped away and Annwyl flicked her middle and forefinger in his sister's direction before she went back to the rather mindless task of finishing off the enemy soldiers who were already dying but hadn't quite crossed over yet. She used a spear and was efficient in ending the men, severing the spine from the head. Probably taught to her by Ghleanna.

Fearghus watched his mate a moment longer. It had been five years since he last saw her. Five years since he last touched her, kissed her, fucked her, saw her smile, told her to calm down, yanked a weapon from her hands before she hurt someone, or stopped her from getting in a pit brawl with her own daughter. It had been too long since he'd done all that and it was a bit overwhelming to be here now, so close to her after all this time.

Annwyl slammed her spear into another Sovereign, then leaned against it, wiping her brow with the back of her hand and looking out over all the bodies she and her troops had left behind.

She looked rather proud.

Deciding he could wait no longer, Fearghus walked toward her, his claws stepping on corpses but he didn't really care. Most of them were the enemy anyway.

When he was close, he said, "Annwyl."

Her whole body tensed and, slowly, she faced him. He saw the new scar that cut across her entire face. He found it disturbingly sexy and couldn't wait until they were alone and he could lick the damn thing from one end to the other. Yet Annwyl gazed at him for so long, Fearghus became concerned. Why hadn't she said anything?

But then, suddenly, Annwyl the Bloody burst into tears. Not simple crying, but full-on sobs. Sobs so hard they racked her entire body, dropping her to her knees, her hand still clinging to that spear.

Fearghus shifted and went to her. He reached down and lifted her to her feet, removed the spear from her hands and tossed it aside.

He pulled her into his arms and held her. She clung to him, her arms around his waist, her head against his chest, her tears dripping down his body to mingle with the blood on the battlefield.

As they held each other, there in the middle of all that carnage, Fearghus whispered, "I missed you too, Annwyl."

"King Gaius?"

Gaius pushed one of his uncle's soldiers off his sword and faced the dragon behind him.

"Ragnar of the Olgeirsson Horde. Brother to Vigholf."

"Yes. Vigholf save my sister," Gaius admitted. "I owe him and the others much. Is that why you're here, Lightning? Payment?"

"No. But how much were you thinking?"

Gaius stared at him until the Northlander smiled. "I'm kidding. I'm actually here to talk alliance. Thracius is dead, but his direct bloodline lives on."

"Like my cousin Vateria, you mean?"

"Do you think she's a real threat?"

"Although she may not be as schooled in military strategy as her father—she's a serious threat."

"Then let's talk."

"Fine. But I can't stay long. My sister is alone and although it took us seconds to get here, we have a long way to travel back."

"Seconds? How did you get here?"

"It's . . . complicated."

"The gods sent you?" the Northlander asked.

"Oh . . . so not that complicated."

"Not to us, no."

Vigholf found Rhona sitting on the ground, her back against a tree. She drank from her water flask and tried to wipe blood off her chin with a dirty cloth.

"Why did your mother just call me a manipulative bastard?" he asked.

"Because you are?"

His eyes narrowed. "Why did your mother—"

"Oh, ignore her." She patted the ground beside her. "Sit with me. Things are just about to get interesting."

He sat down, moving in so his hip pressed into hers. "Interesting how?"

"You'll see."

"Where's Éibhear?"

"Off. Not willing to talk to anyone." She shook her head—Vigholf sensed a little sadness and a little awe in that one move. "When he finally snapped, he really snapped."

"He'll be all right," Vigholf assured her. "Just give him some time."

"I don't know. He seems truly devastated about Austell."

"We've all lost comrades in battle, Rhona. And we all handle it. He will, too. He's just young. It will take him some time. And the last thing he needs is more females babying him."

"I'm one female who has never babied Éibhear. I'm here to keep him alive, not be his mother." She patted his thigh. "Oh! It's about to start."

"What? What's about to start?"

Ragnar was standing not ten feet away, talking to Gaius. It was easy to see his brother was making another ally. He was good with that.

But stalking up to Ragnar and Gaius, looking quite

unhappy was Briec. Izzy was behind him, trying her best to calm him down, but it didn't seem to be working.

"Is this about Gaius?" he asked Rhona.

"No. Not at all." She offered him some dried beef and kept watching.

When Briec reached Ragnar and Gaius, he shoved Ragnar. "You smarmy bastard! No wonder my sister picked you for her mate!"

Vigholf winced. "Guess he found out about the Tribesmen attack on Garbhán Isle."

"And you would be guessing correctly."

"You told him, didn't you? About everything."

"He demanded a full report—I gave him one."

"But, Rhona—"

"He outranks me," she argued. "I have to follow orders."

Vigholf took a moment to eye the She-dragon. "Centaur shit, you vindictive harpy."

"After sending us off with Keita, involving us in one of her insane schemes—your brother deserves every bit of this."

"Your cold, inflexible heart makes me burn to be inside you."

"Charmer."

He laughed until he saw Fearghus and Annwyl walking up to Briec and the others, Gwenvael behind them.

"What's going on?" Fearghus asked his brother.

"Garbhán Isle has been under attack for days by Tribesmen. *Days!* And this idiot knew and he said nothing!"

"Does this mean we're going home?" Gwenvael asked, sounding eager.

Annwyl flinched and, after looking at Vigholf and Rhona, eased behind her mate's back. She'd known about the attack since they were at the Sovereign camp and yet she'd decided to go on and get Gaius. But she'd been right. They'd needed Gaius and his soldiers or they would have been overrun by Thracius's troops. Of course, they all thought Gaius was there to kill Thracius himself . . . but that job turned out to be Éibhear's.

"How could you not tell us?" Fearghus demanded.

"So we're going home, yeah?" Gwenvael pushed.

"Look," Ragnar began, "Keita thought—"

"When exactly did our sister start thinking?" Briec shoved Ragnar again. "And when did you start listening, you twat?"

"If you push me again—"

"You'll what, barbarian? What exactly will you do?"

Rhona yawned and rested her head on Vigholf's shoulder. "I was hoping to get some sleep, but it seems like we'll be heading back to Dark Plains tonight."

"I think you're right."

"So where do we go from here?"

"I'm in love with you, Rhona. Wherever you go, I'm with you."

She raised her head, looked him in the eye, and smiled. It was the sweetest smile he'd seen in a very long time.

"And what are you two doing?" Briec snarled at them.

"Oy!" Rhona yelled back. "Back off, royal! I'm off duty!"

Gwenvael jumped between them. "Home!" he yelled. "We're all going home! Now! So let's make that happen. Right now! Everyone, move . . . *move!*"

Briec, Ragnar, and Fearghus backed away from their brother while Gwenvael walked off, ordering the troops to get ready to move out.

"Gwenvael *really* wants to go home," Vigholf observed.

"My cousin hasn't fucked a female since the last time he saw his mate. And that was what? Three years ago? No sex for Gwenvael is like no food. The dragon's starving and all he wants is his steak."

"Speaking of which," Vigholf glanced around. "While

everyone is breaking camp, maybe you and I can find a quiet place to—"

"Why aren't you two moving?" Gwenvael screamed at them. "Move, damn you! *Move!*"

Laughing, Rhona got up and brushed the dirt off. "Let's go before my cousin's mind explodes. Besides, you need to think of what you're going to tell Daddy when we get back to Garbhán Isle."

"Tell him? Why do I have to tell your father—with the enormously large arms, expert skill with all weapons, and the ability to spray me with lava—anything?"

"Because you love me and Daddy loves me. So you better find a way to keep him from pulling your head right off your body."

Vigholf stood. "All right. I will. But at least make it worth it for me, Rhona."

"Make it worth it?"

"Don't tease, female. Tell me you love me."

"I'll do better than that. I told me *mum* I love you. *My* mother. Bradana the Mutilator who has the horns of several Lightnings decorating her armor."

He grinned and they headed toward the troops to help those leaving with them in the next few hours get ready. "And what did she say to you?" Because he already knew what Bradana had to say to him.

"I don't really know."

"So you ran away."

"Not at all. I walked away . . . with purpose."

"Oh, well . . . that makes all the difference."

Chapter 36

"They're getting ready to strike," Rhiannon called out to the weak little humans. "Everyone inside. Quickly now." She had no idea she'd enjoy being helpful. But she did! She felt like a mother hen.

People were rushing into the castle for safety, but Talaith and Ebba ran out.

"What are you two doing out here? The Tribesmen are right outside. They're about to strike."

"The children," Ebba said. "The children are missing."

Rhiannon immediately sent a call out to Bercelak, who was with his kin, preparing an ambush from behind the advancing Tribesmen. "Where the hell are the Kyvich?" she demanded.

"Searching the castle, but Talaith and I don't think the children are inside."

"Wait." Rhiannon closed her eyes. "Let me search for them."

"Ladies," Dagmar called from the top of the castle walls. "I think all of you better come up here."

Talaith and Ebba ran up the stairs, pushing past soldiers and guards. Rhiannon quickly followed, but everyone moved out of her way. Together the four females stood at the rails and looked out over the Tribesmen army that stood no more than several hundred feet from their door. Rhiannon didn't count to see how many were left, but it was at least a legion's worth, she'd guess.

"Look below," Dagmar said.

The three of them leaned over the railing and down into the land right outside the castle walls. That's where her three grandchildren stood.

Talaith tried to jump over the railing to fetch the children, but Ebba and Dagmar caught her in time and held her.

"How the hells did they even get out there?" Talaith demanded. "They were standing right next to us!"

"I'll go," Ebba said. "I'll get the children."

Rhiannon grabbed Ebba's arm. "No."

"What are you doing?" Talaith nearly screamed. "Have you lost your mind?"

"If we move," she told them, "they'll kill them all."

The lieutenant and his commander stared at the three children. None of them saw when they arrived. One second there was nothing and the next . . .

But that was no matter to them. They all knew who the three children were. They were the ones everyone had been talking about. The one his tribe's priestess had described as a little one with brown skin and two others who were a male and female with unholy eyes. His tribe's priestess said to look for "The Three," as she had called them.

"Do we kill them, commander?" the lieutenant asked, because he knew that once the children were dead, they could all go home.

"Yes."

Nodding, the lieutenant motioned for the troops to ready their bows.

"No!" some woman on the castle walls screamed at them while the gates opened. He could hear the demon horses of those damn witches. They were coming out here, they would try to stop them. That's why his commander wasn't going to try to grab the children and perform a ritual killing later. Too much bother. So instead they'd kill them with enough arrows to destroy an entire army.

The commander, always enjoying giving these kinds of orders himself, raised his hand to give the signal that would tell the soldiers to unleash their arrows.

And that's when the smallest girl, the brown one, said into the anticipating quiet, "Daddy's home."

The commander looked at him, but before he could say a word, give an order, the large silver dragon dropped behind the girl, the ground beneath them all shaking. The dragon picked the child up in his claw and lifted her so that she rested by his neck, his talons holding her gently.

"See?" the little girl said. "Daddy's home."

"Commander?" the lieutenant prompted in the brief moment that followed. They'd been dealing with vengeful dragons for days. What was one more?

But there was more than one, dropping from the sky. Hundreds of them. Dragons of all colors and sizes. They'd already been in one battle it seemed, many of them still with healing wounds, broken limbs. Yet he could tell from their expressions they were more than ready for another fight.

"Commander?" the lieutenant pushed again.

"On my command, send in—" Something landed behind the commander on his horse, sword blades flashed and collided at the center of the commander's neck, his head popping off, falling to the ground, and sadly rolling a few feet away.

The woman pushed the dying commander's body off the horse and settled in to the empty spot.

"Hello, lads," the woman said. "Name's Annwyl."

Then she smiled, and the lieutenant knew he'd not live to see the end of this day.

Talaith ran down the stairs and into the courtyard. She watched with relief and something she was almost afraid to term actual joy as Briec the Mighty stomped his way through the gates, their youngest daughter happily riding on her father's neck.

The silver dragon stopped when he saw Talaith, the pair peering at each other. Talaith saw it, felt it, knew her mate was experiencing the same thing. That overwhelming flood of love and connection—and neither was ready for any of *that* sort of thing!

Using his tail to pull his daughter around and into his claws, the dragon snarled, "Explain to me why my perfect, *perfect* daughter was out there." He held Rhian out for Talaith to see. "Unsafe!"

Talaith snatched her daughter away from the monster she loved, quickly stepping away from the flames that came with his shifting, and growled back, "If you don't stop calling her that!"

"Don't chirp at me, woman!"

"Chirp? *Chirp?*"

"You put my perfect, *perfect* daughter at risk!" He pulled on leggings and boots handed to him by one of the servants and yanked Rhian back to him. "What exactly have you been doing here? Letting her run wild? Like a banshee!"

"I'll have you know—"

Izzy ran in through the gate. "Morning, Mum!" she cheered while running past and over to Sulien the Blacksmith. Without saying a word, he seemed to know what she needed, tossing her an extremely large battle-ax. "Thanks, Uncle Sulien!"

"Welcome, Izzy!"

"Iseabail!" Talaith called after her.

"I'll be back in a bit, Mum!" Then she was gone.

"Damn that girl!"

"Are you even listening to me?"

"No!" Talaith snapped, yanking her hysterically laughing youngest daughter back into her arms. "I'm not! I can't believe I spent even a moment of my time missing *you*!"

"I missed you too, you difficult, demanding female!"

"Difficult? I can show you difficult!"

"You do that with every breath you take!"

Fearghus entered the courtyard, not surprised to see his brother arguing with Talaith. He rolled his eyes, not in the mood to deal with any of that.

His mother, in human form, walked toward him, smiling.

"Fearghus."

"Mother."

"I'm so glad you're well." And he knew she meant it. He was so glad to be home.

"Well enough." He motioned to the children with a tilt of his head. "Take them, would you?"

Once his mother had Talan and Talwyn, he shifted and put on leggings, then some boots. He kissed his mother on the cheek.

"Should I ask," he murmured, "how they managed to get outside?" He knew well that the ones left to watch over the children would never have purposely let them wander around on their own during a siege.

"I have an idea, but . . ."

He waved that away, sensing it wouldn't be an easy answer. "Can it wait?" he asked.

"I'd prefer it did. They're fine. That's all that matters."

"Good. We need to talk about something else," he said.

"What?"

"Éibhear."

Rhiannon tensed. "He's—"

"Perfectly healthy. But we should still talk."

"Of course." She motioned to Ebba, and the centaur trotted over, the children immediately leaping from their grandmother's arms to Ebba's back.

"Don't take them far," Fearghus stated. "Annwyl will want to see them as soon as she's done."

"Of course." Ebba smiled at him. "It's good to have you back, my lord."

"Thank you, Ebba."

Once they were as alone as possible in a busy courtyard with a battle going on right outside the castle gates, Rhiannon nodded at her son.

"All right. Tell me everything."

The battle barely lasted an hour. The few Tribesmen left made a fast retreat with only a few of Annwyl's men in pursuit. Everyone was so tired and happy to be back that the Tribesmen who remained were of little consequence to any of them. Especially after fighting the Sovereigns and Irons for the last five years.

With her swords tied to her back, Annwyl walked back to her home, an arm thrown over Izzy's shoulder. They didn't say anything because there was nothing to say. Not between them. They'd been through too much together, seen too much . . . gods, they'd *done* too much to worry about what to say.

They entered the castle gates and Annwyl wasn't surprised to see Talaith and Briec well in the middle of an argument. It was like they had to make up for the last five years of no proper fighting. But as soon as Talaith saw her daughter, tears sprang to her eyes and she ran to her, Izzy moving away from Annwyl to meet her mum. They threw their arms around each other, both women sobbing and laughing, holding on to each other.

Annwyl winked at Briec, his smile warm as he watched the women he loved, and she patted his shoulder, stopping a moment to kiss sweet Rhian on the cheek. But Annwyl was nearly knocked on her ass when Gwenvael stormed past her, shifting from dragon to human in seconds, not bothering to put on leggings or even a robe.

Dagmar already stood on the Great Hall steps, but the welcoming smile faded from her lips when she saw Gwenvael, her eyes growing wide with a panic she rarely showed anyone.

Gwenvael took the stairs three at a time, picking Dagmar up along the way and dumping her over his shoulder like a sack of so much grain before he disappeared into the Great Hall.

Annwyl glanced up at Briec, but the Silver shook his head. "I won't discuss it. But let's hope it makes him less of a bastard. Because he's been a right bastard."

Shaking her head, Annwyl headed toward the Great Hall, but she slowly came to a stop when she saw them walk out the doors. She swallowed, feeling such a jumble of emotions at the moment, she simply couldn't suss one out from the next.

Unlike Fearghus, Annwyl had not been home since the day she'd headed into the west with her army. Then, her children had just turned two. They'd been cute and impossible, and she'd adored them like the suns.

But now they were five years older and scowling at her from the stairs, her daughter looking more like her grandfather now than any of them would want to admit and her son looking like . . . well, like Annwyl.

When neither moved, Annwyl did the only thing she could think of. She crouched down and opened her arms and, to her great relief, both her children ran to her, throwing themselves into her arms as if pitched by a catapult. She caught them and pulled them tight into her body, hugging them with all her strength. They put their arms around her shoulder and buried their faces into each side of her neck.

The twins had grown into a right pair of little brawlers, just like their mum. Strong arms held Annwyl, little scars from fights and hard play littered any exposed flesh she could see. They were dirty and probably even worse nightmares to deal with than they had been.

And they were hers. They were hers.

Annwyl didn't even realize she'd begun to cry until Fearghus's thumb wiped the tears from her cheeks. He now crouched in front of her and smiled at her with such love, she didn't know what to do, what to say. All she knew was that she was home, she was safe, she had her family, and the heads of Overlord Thracius and Lord Laudaricus had been planted on spikes outside her gates. Although that was temporary, since the troops she'd be sending off to help the Rebel King Gaius claim his empire would bring those two heads with them.

Standing, Fearghus took Talwyn and Annwyl kept Talan. Together, they carried their children inside their home and Annwyl knew that finally, she could get some sleep.

Chapter 37

Rhona wrapped her arms around her father and hugged him tight. "Hello, Daddy."

"My girl. I'm so glad to see you. I'm so glad you're home."

"Me, too" She sighed. "But . . ." She pushed her father back from the flap and farther into his tent. "Mum's on her way in. She's not happy."

"This isn't the Dragonwarrior thing again, is it? Because I won't listen to any of that centaur shit yet again."

"No, no." She looked away from her father's dark gaze.

Sulien chuckled. "Let me guess. It has something to do with that Lightning."

"He says he loves me."

"Of course he does. You couldn't tell?"

"Well—"

"Forget I ask. As bad as your mother." He kissed her forehead. "Well, you know I'll have to terrify him at least a little."

"I know. I think he's expecting it."

"That takes the fun out of it."

"Daddy," she laughed.

Her mother walked into the tent and Rhona stammered, "Well . . . uh . . . must go."

"Like a rat from a sinking ship!" her mum yelled after her.

"Made a run for it?" Vigholf asked. He stood next to the tent, patiently waiting for her.

"I didn't want to hear it." Especially since she'd heard "it" all the way back from Euphrasia Valley until Ghleanna had finally barked, "Pack it in already, Bradana! We're sick of hearing about it!"

Gods, she loved her Aunt Ghleanna.

"You know what?" Vigholf asked.

"You're hungry?"

"Starving."

She took his hand in hers. "Then let's go feed you, yeah? Before you *starve* to death."

"You're okay with this?" Bradana asked her mate.

"I don't have a problem with Lightnings. Of course, my people didn't try to systematically wipe them out either."

Bradana shrugged. "It wasn't systematic."

"And in answer to your question . . . yes. I'm okay with this. He makes her happy, he cares about her, and the dragon can wield a mighty warhammer."

"He'll take her back to the north, you know? To live with that Horde of his."

"So? I came with you, I'm no more the worse for wear."

Bradana examined the blades her mate had hanging from a rope. "You don't think she's leaving just so . . ."

"She can get away from you?"

She shrugged again. "I know I pushed her a bit. Expected more from her than the others. Maybe she's just doing this to get out from under, yeah?"

Sulien slipped his hand around the back of Bradana's

neck and pulled her close, kissing her cheek. "If there's one thing we both know about our oldest girl is that she'd never leave her siblings except for a dragon she loved. If she goes with him, it's because she wants to. Because she loves him. Not to get away from you or anyone else."

Bradana hugged Sulien tight, dropping her head against his shoulder. "I'll miss her when she's gone—the impossible little cow."

"Of course you will. Who will you complain about if she's not here? Ow! That was unnecessary, female!"

Ragnar stopped walking and sighed. Loudly.

"What are you doing?" he asked the She-dragon he loved, who'd wrapped her arms around his shoulder.

"Pummeling you into submission!"

"You're not very good at it."

"So everyone keeps telling me." She released his neck and dropped to the ground. Ragnar faced her and marveled at the fact that being caught in the middle of this siege on Garbhán Isle had not affected Princess Keita's dress code. Her blue dress glittered, her jewel-encrusted gold jewelry sparkled, and she still wore no damn shoes! Why wouldn't the female wear shoes when she was in her human form? Was there a moral reason? A fashion one? What was her problem with shoes?

"Why are you staring at my feet?" She raised a brow. "Do they arouse you?"

"Keita—"

"They do, don't they?" Pushing the toes of her right foot into the ground and raising the heel a bit, she said, "They are quite adorable. Just like me!"

"I missed you, Keita," Ragnar told her, all teasing aside. "Very much."

"Oh? That's nice to hear."

"Is that all you have to say?"

"What do you want me to say? What do you think I *should* say?"

"I don't think you should say anything. I was just asking."

"Well . . . all right. I'm going to see my brothers." She nodded, walked away, but she was heading away from the castle, so she stopped and turned, heading back. She walked by, got about ten feet, stopped.

Then Keita the Viper spun around and ran into his arms, hugging him tight. "This is all your fault!" she accused.

"What is?"

"How much I missed you! And I was shockingly worried about you. I actually cared if you were hurt or had been damaged in some way." She leaned back, squinted up at him. "You weren't, were you? Damaged?"

"Not so that I won't heal."

"Good." She rested her head on his chest. "Believe it or not, I don't know what I'd have done if something happened to you."

Keita abruptly pulled back from him and punched him in the chest. "What have you done to me, foreigner? Well, let me make it plain that you'll not trap me in your evil web of amazing sex and unconditional love! I'm stronger than that!"

And Ragnar sighed . . . loudly.

Rhiannon sat down beside her youngest offspring on the hill that overlooked the castle of Garbhán Isle and the surrounding grounds.

She'd known since his hatching that this time would come. For Fearghus and Briec it had come quite early. For Morfyd it had come quite late. And for Gwenvael and

Keita . . . well, it had never been. It was that point in a young dragon's life when he was no longer a hatchling, a babe. Yet being a full adult was still a few years out of reach. For most of them it wasn't a hard transition. They simply went from being filled with wonder to cynical pains in the ass seemingly overnight. But Éibhear had always been different. A little smarter. A whole lot sweeter. She'd always feared that the transition for him would not be an easy one.

And, based on what Fearghus had told her, it wouldn't be. Not for her sweet Éibhear. Not now that he blamed himself for something that could have happened to any of them. And, in some ways, had. As royals they all had to make decisions, had to do things that didn't always feel good or even right, but were necessary. Austell's death, while tragic, was the way of war. As a soldier in Rhiannon's army, that was the risk Éibhear took. The risk Rhiannon took by allowing her offspring to involve themselves in war, to risk their lives picking up a sword, an ax, a hammer and set off after her enemies. To keep her throne safe, her kingdom safe.

Really, what could she say to her son now that would make him feel better? What words of wisdom could she impart that would make him say, "Oh? Well, if it was to be . . ."

No. There was nothing to say. Nothing she could say or do that would make her son feel any better.

In fact, Rhiannon knew only one thing at the moment. She knew that she'd already lost the sweet hatchling she adored since she'd seen his handsome face grin at her after tumbling out of his egg, head first. And what dragon would replace that blue-scaled hatchling? Rhiannon still didn't know.

So with no words to ease what Éibhear was going

through, Rhiannon simply placed her arm around him and tugged until he rested his head on her shoulder. And there they sat, on that hill, staring off at the bodies of Tribesmen not yet cleaned up, wishing things could go back to the way they were, but knowing that would never happen.

Chapter 38

For five full days Queen Annwyl slept, and Izzy had never been so grateful. Annwyl had needed that sleep more than anyone could possibly know. At first, everyone tried to tiptoe around, Fearghus snarling at anyone making too much noise. But what Izzy knew and what everyone else eventually realized was that nothing could wake Annwyl. But when she finally did emerge, bounding down the stairs into the Great Hall, her long, light brown hair washed and a clean pair of black leggings, black boots, and one of her favored sleeveless chain-mail shirts on, Izzy couldn't help but grin. This . . . *this* was the Annwyl she knew. And gods, was she glad to see her again.

"Morning, Iz."

"Morning."

Annwyl dropped hard into a chair catty-corner from Izzy and put her feet up on the table. Izzy handed her a round loaf of bread.

"Sleep well?" she asked Annwyl.

"Like the dead. It felt wonderful." Annwyl tore off chunks of bread and ate while looking around the room. "Where is everyone?" she asked between bites.

Have no idea. Everyone's been rather scarce since our
urn. I think they're all shagging."

Annwyl laughed, her humor back, eyes bright. "I think
you're probably right." She glanced around and whispered,
"And you?"

"And me what?"

Annwyl made her eyebrows dance a bit.

"Gods, Annwyl!"

"Oh, come on. You've got both here."

"Yeah, right. Éibhear's sitting outside, staring pensively
off into the distance—who knows what's going on with
him—and Celyn's been avoiding me like I might fuck him
right here on this table during morning meal. Tell me, my
wise queen . . . why do we bother with any of them?"

"We both like cock."

Mortified, Izzy still laughed. Out of everyone, Annwyl
remained the one being who wasn't Brannie who could
make Izzy feel like everything—eventually—would be all
right.

"So what do I need to know?" Annwyl asked her.

"Violence is back and safe. I put him up in his stables,
got him a couple of sexy mares to keep him company. I
think he's a wee pissed at you that you went off without
him, though."

"He always gets that way when I leave him for too long.
He'll get over it. I'll go see him after I eat."

"Are you going to take him out? Because I haven't had
a chance to clean your saddle yet and it's absolutely caked
in blood—"

"Ralphie will take care of it."

"Ralphie?" Izzy lowered her spoon into her bowl of
porridge, her heart plunging. "Your old squire?"

"He's still fat, but Violence likes him."

"But—"

"Now don't get upset. But honestly I don't really need a

fit, fighting squire right now. I'm taking some time off.
Going to be a proper queen for a bit and order others to kill
for me. Just like your grandmum."

Izzy sat back in her chair. "So it's back to formation
then? Just like that?" Gods! Where was the loyalty for
duty served?

"Now don't pout. And don't whine. Besides," the queen
added, dropping her feet on the floor as a servant placed a
steaming bowl of porridge on the table in front of her, "I
don't know any squire that has a rank of corporal. It would
be unseemly. Nor do corporals go stomping around in formation, either."

"Corporal?" Izzy sat up straight, eyes wide. "I'm . . .
I'm a corporal?"

"You are now. Promotion effective immediately."

"Brannie—"

"Her, too, but your grandfather is telling her. It's all that
Dragonwarrior stuff. And keep in mind, they'll probably be
sending her off to Anubail Mountain for that training of
theirs in the next few years. You'll need to make some other
allies for when she's gone. Brastias will let you know what
your orders are in the next day or two." She lowered her
voice to a whisper. "I'm pretty sure, though, you're going
to be named team leader of one of the four-man units going
east in another month or two. But let Brastias tell you that
and make sure to look surprised." Her voice returned to
normal. "And don't worry about your mum. She'll blame
me anyway, and now that I've had some sleep, I think I'm
up for a good, old-fashioned, verbal argument that doesn't
end with me taking anyone's head." She glanced off. "It'll
be a nice change."

Izzy scrambled out of her chair and dived at Annwyl,
almost knocking them both over, hugging her tight.

"Thank you, Annwyl!"

"You've earned this, Izzy." She pushed Izzy back until

she crouched in front of her. "I don't know what I would have done without you, especially these last couple of years. You protected me, protected your comrades, and fought like one of the gods of war. You stuck with me when everyone else thought I'd completely gone round the bend and made sure I got back here alive and well to my children . . . to Fearghus. So thank you, Iseabail, Daughter of Talaith and Briec. Thank you for everything."

"Annwyl—"

Brannie screaming Izzy's name out in the courtyard cut off her next words and her queen grinned at her. "Go on. I'm sure your grandfather's spoken to Brannie, and I know you two have some girlish squealing to do that will only manage to set my nerves on edge."

Izzy nodded, then reached over and hugged Annwyl again, whispering, "I'm loyal to you until my last breath, my queen."

"Gods, let's hope that's not for a very long time or I'll never hear the end of it from your mother!"

Izzy laughed and Annwyl pushed her away. "Go. See Brannie before she pees her leggings in excitement."

With a nod, Izzy ran out the Great Hall doors, stopping at the top of the stairs. Brannie stood at the bottom, the pair staring at each other. They'd been through much together and Izzy knew that over the next few years they'd be separated, sent off on different assignments, different missions. But they'd been a team that no one could touch and nothing would ever take away all they'd gone through.

At the same time, they both squealed and Izzy leaped down the stairs, slamming into Brannie, knowing the She-dragon was one of the few females who could handle that. Spinning in a circle while managing to jump up and down, they squealed more than seemed right that early in the

morning. They squealed and squealed until Izzy heard her
mother ask, "What's going on?"

At that point—they stopped squealing.

Annwyl was digging into her second bowl of porridge,
trying desperately to ignore the squealing from outside
when Dagmar made her way downstairs. Poor thing, she
looked exhausted as she sat down across from Annwyl, the
servants putting a large cup of tea in front of her.

"Morning, Dagmar." Annwyl's Battle Lord blinked, and
squinted across the table at her. "Your spectacles," Annwyl
prompted.

"I must have forgotten them upstairs."

"Actually, they're on top of your head, luv."

Dagmar reached up, touching the small round spectacles
she wore except when she was asleep or reading. "Oh . . .
there they are." She placed them on, yawned.

"You all right?"

"Fine. Why?"

"Because you look like I guess I looked nearly two
weeks ago." She leaned in a bit. "Gwenvael missed you,
didn't he?"

"More than seems reasonably possible."

Annwyl laughed, licking her spoon. "I think it's cute and
rather romantic."

"And that's why you can shut the battle-fuck up, my
queen."

Laughing harder, Annwyl reached into a bowl of raisins.
She leaned her head back to drop a few into her mouth, and
that's when she saw Talaith standing next to her, seething,
arms crossed over her chest.

Annwyl held out her hand. "Raisin?"

Talaith slapped the raisins from her hand. Honestly, no one respected royals anymore.

"You made that stupid, stupid girl a corporal?"

"She deserved it. Your daughter is one of the best soldiers I've ever had the honor of—ow! Let go my nose! Let go my nose!"

"You vicious, horrible, female!" Talaith slapped her own hand off, which hurt Annwyl's nose more than she thought possible since it was still a bit sore from being broken only a few days before. "I thought we were over with this insanity! That she'd come home—"

"She has!"

"—and that she'd stay for good."

"Oh . . . yeah, that's not happening. Ow! Let go my nose!"

"Talaith," a new voice interjected, "you had to know this was going to happen. Izzy's a natural."

They all looked down the length of the table at Keita.

"How long have you been sitting there?" Talaith asked, releasing Annwyl's nose.

"Since you started yelling at Lady Insanity."

"That's an unfair title. . . ." Annwyl muttered. "Mostly."

"Gods, I'm starving." Keita crinkled up what she referred to as her "adorable" nose. "I don't want porridge, though." She motioned to one of the servants. "Have any meat?" She whispered loudly, "Perhaps a little dog?"

"Don't make me kill you," Dagmar warned around a yawn. "I have no qualms about killing you."

"Speaking of which," Annwyl cut in. "Where are my dogs?"

"In their own kennel." Dagmar glared at her. "They'd become unruly under your handling. They're worse than your horse."

"Because they know they're better than everyone else."

Morfyd walked into the Great Hall from the courtyard. "How wonderful!" she announced. "Izzy just told me the good . . ." Her words faded off when she saw Talaith glowering, and she finished with ". . . horrible, terrible news about her promotion. Just horrible."

"That was smooth," Keita sneered.

"Quiet, lizard!"

Dagmar pointed at Annwyl. "Do you realize that you have a big scar right across your face?"

"Yes."

"Just going to leave it there, eh?"

"Why shouldn't I? I think it's stylish."

"My father would like it," Dagmar admitted. "Which does nothing but horrify me."

"I like your father."

"And that horrifies me more."

"Is it true," Talaith snarled, pulling the chair beside Annwyl out and dropping into it, "that you took my daughter with you to see that murdering lowlife scum lord?"

Keita grinned. "We just call him daddy."

"Not that murdering lowlife scum lord," Talaith snapped. "Gaius Domitus."

"I did." Annwyl looked at Dagmar. "He'll make a good ally. His sister, though . . ." She shuddered a bit. "She makes me look forgiving and benevolent." She leaned forward. "Her flame is so hot . . . it can melt the scales of other Fire Breathers. It melted *stone*."

Morfyd rested her hands against the table. "Are you sure?"

"That's what Rhona told me. Double-check with her."

"Why does it matter?" Dagmar asked.

"I've just never heard of that before. Unless she's a witch."

"Not that I know of." Annwyl ate a few more raisins. "Rhona also said that once the sister was released, the other Irons were terrified of her."

"If she can melt the scales of other Fire Breathers . . . they should be afraid."

"Yes, yes. That's all quite fascinating, but . . ." Keita sat up a little taller, fluffed her hair a bit. "Notice anything different?"

"Your hips getting wider?" Morfyd asked, which got her punched in the leg. "Ow! You viper!"

"Anything else?" Keita pushed them. "Anything new about me?"

They all shook their heads, not sure *what* the royal was talking about.

"This." She smoothed her hand over the bare, unmarred flesh above her left breast, where her bodice slipped low.

"What about *that*?" Morfyd snapped. *Back five minutes and the pair already going at it like pit dogs.*

"Can't you tell?"

"Tell what?"

"This is where I'm going to allow Ragnar to put his Claim brand upon me . . . when I'm ready to allow him to do that . . . in a few years or so."

"Years?" Annwyl asked.

"Uh-huh. Don't you think this spot is perfect?"

They all stared at the smiling royal, their mouths slightly open, until Dagmar turned back to Annwyl and said, "So this Rebel King . . . a right bastard or is all that just legend?"

"A little of both, I think. And he's young . . . for a dragon."

Keita threw her hands up in the air as they all went about ignoring her because it amused them to do so.

Annwyl wouldn't say it was right what they did—but it was fun.

"Good morn to my lovely family!" Gwenvael happily announced from the top of the stairs. He looked his old self

again, Annwyl thought. No more scowling and so bloody
cheerful. "How is everyone this glorious morning?"

Dagmar rolled her eyes and muttered under her breath,
"Oh, piss off."

"Now, now, my love," he said to his mate, completely
missing the fact that Fearghus and Briec were walking up
behind him—and not one of the females bothered to warn
him. "Have no fear. I won't be leaving you anytime—
aahhhhhh! *You heartless bastards!*" Gwenvael yelled after
his brothers tossed him over the banister and he landed on
the floor.

Damn but it was so very good to be home!

"Rhona!"

Rhona, busy pulling on her boots, watched the triplets
run up to her.

"What?" she asked once her boots were on. "What's
wrong?"

"Nothing! Look. Look!"

They forced a piece of parchment at her and she opened
it and quickly read the words, lifted her gaze to her sisters.
"Did you tell Mum?"

"Not yet," Edana said. "We wanted to tell you first."

"I . . . I can't believe they're taking you so early."

"You're upset," Breena guessed.

"No, no. I'm . . ." She was overwhelmed. The triplets
would be heading to Anubail Mountain. They would be
trained as Dragonwarriors. Just like all Rhona's other siblings. Just like most Cadwaladrs.

"You're crying," Nesta accused.

"Of course I'm not!"

"Then what's that leaking out of your eyes?"

"You *are* upset," Breena insisted.

"No. It's just . . . just . . ." Unable to hold it in anymore,

Rhona burst into tears and sobbed out, "I'm losing my babies!"

"Awwww!" Her sisters surrounded her in a group hug, now all of them crying.

"You'll never lose us," Edana insisted.

"What's going on?" Vigholf asked from behind them, his mother next to him. Rhona had left the pair alone to talk while Rhona put on her boots.

"What's wrong?" he demanded when he saw that they were all crying.

"See?" Edana said. "You have him now. And he's not half bad."

"But he's not you lot."

"But now you can have your own hatchlings . . . not just Mum's." Breena wiped her eyes and sized up Vigholf. "He looks like a right good breeder."

Both mother and son's eyes grew wide at the turn in the conversation.

"But I'll probably just have males," Rhona complained. "They never breed females in the Northlands."

"You're a Cadwaladr, luv. The Cadwaladrs always have females. We're sure of it." Nesta motioned to Vigholf. "Tell her you'll have female offspring." When Vigholf did nothing but gawk, Nesta snarled, "I said *tell her*."

Shaking his head, Vigholf took his mother's hand and walked away.

Rhona didn't actually blame him for doing that, though.

When his mother doubled over in laughter, Vigholf finally had to stop walking.

"It isn't funny. They're *all* like that."

"But . . . but . . ."

"Mum! It's not funny!"

"Oh, yes it is." She wiped tears from her eyes and gazed at her son. "She's the perfect choice."

"She hasn't agreed to anything."

"What more of a sign do you need?"

"She didn't say the words, 'I'm coming with you, Vigholf. I will stay with you forever, Vigholf.' Just discussing my breeding capabilities does not mean much with this group, Mum."

"Och!" His mother waved her hand at him. "You always have to hear specifics."

"When we're talking about the rest of my life and future happiness . . . yes! I do!"

Briec walked into the room his daughter shared with her twin cousins. Ebba stood next to the window, staring out, probably watching the bonfires of bodies they'd had over the last few days to get rid of the dead.

Without even looking at him, Ebba turned to the twins and said, "Come. I believe Sulien has something for you both."

The twins, apparently knowing that Sulien was a blacksmith, ran out of the room screaming. Ebba followed, closing the door behind her, and Briec sat down on the bed beside his baby girl.

She was drawing on parchment, but when he sat down, she reached over and began braiding his hair.

"You sent me a gift while I was away, didn't you, Rhian?"

"Uh-huh."

"Do you know what kind of gift it was?"

Fearghus had finally explained to Briec how bad his injuries had been from that boulder to the back. And Briec had seen enough battle wounds to know that he *never* should have survived what his brother had described to him. But Briec had survived, which made him realize that his strange dream—not really a dream.

"It was to make you feel better."

"And it did. Very much so. Thank you."

"You're welcome." She smiled up at him, and he ignored his desire to just pick her up in his arms and hold her.

"Did someone give you that?" Briec asked. "The thing you sent me to make me better?"

"No."

"How did you know it would help me?"

"I just knew."

Interesting and a bit terrifying. "What else can you do?"

She shrugged. "I can draw." She held up the picture she was working on. It was a drawing of a horse and it wasn't half bad.

"Yes. You can. Anything else, though? Can you do anything I couldn't do? Or your mum? Or your cousins?"

She looked up, squinting her eyes. Her "thinking" face he would guess. "I can go places."

Briec's heart dropped. "Go places?"

"Like Lord Ren. I can travel. Sometimes I can send things away. Like those bad men. Didn't tell Mommy about them, though. She'd have been upset." Well, that was most likely an understatement.

"You didn't tell her about the bad men?"

"Uh-uh." She went back to working on her drawing. "They were here to hurt me and the twins."

"So you sent them away?"

"Uh-huh. Afterward."

"After . . . what?"

"After the twins were done."

Briec flinched. This was getting worse and worse.

"After they were done doing what?"

"Stopping the bad men from hurting us."

"How did they do that?"

"With their swords."

Aye. Worse and worse.

"And then you sent the bad men away?"

"Back to the other bad men beyond the gate. I knew if Mommy saw them lying there she'd be sad and I hate when she's sad."

"So do I."

"But Tally was mad at me because I sent the swords with them and now she doesn't have her sword."

"I'm sure Sulien will give her and Talan new swords."

"Good, because she still complains."

"The twins talk to you?"

"In my head."

Gods. It had taken him and his siblings years to hone the skills necessary to communicate with each other simply by thinking. For Rhian and the twins to be able to do it after only a few years . . .

Briec picked his daughter up and sat her in his lap, lifting her chin with the tip of his finger so she looked right at him.

"I need you to do me a favor, Rhian."

"Not tell anyone about what I can do?"

Smart girl. "Aye."

"Because they won't understand?"

"Aye."

"All right."

"You're not upset about that?"

"No. Sometimes people and dragons are stupid. Why should I help them be even more stupid?"

Briec chuckled, knowing that he was so blessed to have been given such amazing daughters. "Has anyone told you how brilliant you are?"

"Mommy has, but then she says 'But don't tell your daddy because he'll just say'"—and his daughter's voice dropped amusingly lower—"'Of course she is! She's *my* daughter.' Then Mommy smiles." His daughter looked up at him with eyes so much like his own. "She missed you every day you were gone."

"She told you that?"

"No. I felt it. She likes it when you argue." His daughter smirked. "You like it too."

"I do. But sssssh. Don't tell. It's our secret."

"All right." She twirled his hair around her small fingers and asked, "Will I grow up and argue with someone I love one day, Daddy?"

"As part of this family, Rhian? Absolutely."

They rested against the fence surrounding the training field, passing a warm loaf of bread back and forth between them. Rhona's father stood next to her, his elbow on the fence, his chin resting in the palm of his hand.

The sounds of steel crashing against steel rang out over the courtyard, luring other Cadwaladrs to the fence. Some were eating their first meal, bowls of hot porridge in their hands, and others were simply watching. How could they not? It wasn't every day one could witness two children, not even nine winters yet, who could sword fight like that. Uncle Bercelak finally walked away from the twins and motioned to Vigholf. "What's *that* doing here?" he asked Bradana.

"And a happy hello to you, too," Vigholf said with enough cheer to choke a pig.

Bercelak gave one glare at the Lightning, then looked back at his sister. "Well?"

"Well, what?"

"Isn't it bad enough we have one around?" And Ragnar, standing next to Ghleanna, waved. "Now we've got two?"

Bradana suddenly stood tall, glaring at her younger brother. "He's with me Rhona, ain't he? So you watch how you talk. Ya ain't too old to tear the wings off of, Bercelak the Black."

"Fine then. You deal with him."

"I need to be dealt with?" Vigholf asked softly, but Rhona bumped him with her hip to shut him up. Her mother just defended Rhona and her choice of mate to Bercelak. This was a monumental moment in her life and she wouldn't have it ruined by gods-damn Lightnings!

"I got enough to deal with," Bercelak was saying, "training these two."

"Nice work on those swords and shields, Daddy," Rhona said, smiling at him.

"They're all right, I guess," Bercelak muttered and nearly everyone cringed when Sulien's eyes narrowed on his mate's brother. "Heard you did some nice work on Annwyl's weapon, though," Bercelak said to Rhona, surprising her that he'd already heard.

"Of course she does nice work," Bradana snapped. "What did you expect? My daughter has talent, she does."

And at that point they *all* turned to Bradana, gawking at her, Bradana's offspring with their mouths open.

"What are you all looking at me like that for?"

"Well—" Rhona began, but Vigholf covered her mouth with his hand.

"Let's just enjoy this moment, shall we?"

Rhona nodded in agreement until he yanked her back, the small sword Rhona's father made, flipping end over end past her—aimed right for the head of the monarch walking up to the training ring.

But a steady hand caught it before it reached its destination. The newly promoted Izzy glaring at her young cousins. "Oy!" she snapped.

"Give me that!" Annwyl growled, snatching the sword out of Izzy's hand and marching over. "No more training for you two! In the house!"

The twins stood in the middle of that ring, staring at their mother. It had been five years. Rhona remembered well the reaction of her siblings when their mother would return home from a battle, trying to order them around, and none of them responding until Rhona gave the signal. It seemed like it would be that kind of moment now until Rhona remembered this was Annwyl they were dealing with. Not Bradana.

The queen, seething that her children weren't jumping at her commands, suddenly slammed her entire, well-trained, muscular body into the sturdy and well-built wood fence of the training ring. The wood splintered and she rammed into it again, destroying the section. She pushed the pieces out of her way, pointed at her children, and roared, "*Get in the house!*"

Eyes wide, the twins took off. When they ran past her, Annwyl added, "And every time you use my head for target practice, you lose weapons privileges!"

Annwyl stalked after them, but she stopped long enough to add while pointing at the sword, "Nice work, by the way." She said it to Sulien casually, no longer angry. And that somehow made the whole thing . . . scarier.

Everyone wandered off after that, and Vigholf told her, "I find your kin *unbelievably* entertaining."

"That's good," she said, "because they will visit . . . often. And for long periods of time."

"What's long?" he asked her as she walked away from him. "A few days? A week? Perhaps we should start discussing what's long and what's *too* long . . . wait. Are you saying you're coming back with me? Well, that's a rude gesture! It's a valid question, female!"

Vigholf grabbed Rhona around the waist and carried her into the closest stable.

"Great," he muttered. "More horses."

"Annwyl's horse, Violence. Isn't he cute?"

"No." Vigholf turned Rhona to face him. "You need to give me a straight answer."

"About what?"

"You are a cruel, heartless tease, Rhona the Fearless! Just tell me."

"My sisters' discussion over your breed-worthiness wasn't a clue?"

"They're not you, Rhona. I need to hear it from *you*. Tell me. Is this tail mine or not?"

"This tail belongs to me, Vigholf the Abhorrent." She stepped closer to him, put her arms around his shoulders. "But my heart . . . my heart is yours from now until the end of time."

Vigholf grinned, a weight he didn't know had been there lifted from his shoulders. He kissed her then, holding her close.

"Oy!" The couple pulled back and gawked at the horses. "Could you two do that somewhere else? We were here first."

They walked over to the empty stall beside Violence and leaned over the top.

Rhona shook her head in disgust. "Gwenvael!"

"What? I'm making up for lost time."

"Lady Dagmar," Vigholf said, giving her a wink as the poor woman tried to hide her naked body and embarrassed face under her mate.

"You," Rhona told her cousin, "were appalling as a hatchling and you're worse now! Anyone could have walked in. We did!"

"Piss off!"

"I'm telling your mother!"

"Like always! Blabbermouth!"

Vigholf caught hold of Rhona's hand and dragged her outside, closing the stable door.

"The stables?" Rhona asked, disgusted. "They're doing it in the stables? Those poor horses!"

"And who knows what's in that hay."

"Eeeww."

Laughing, Vigholf took Rhona's hand in his own and dragged her away. "Come on. I'll find us a nice, *clean* place to fuck."

"You know, that's all I've ever asked!"

Chapter 39

There were three weeks of official mourning in the Southlands. A time to remember those who'd died in order to protect the kingdoms and the reigning monarchs. At the request of Celyn, Austell's body was brought back to Garbhán Isle and a funeral pyre built to honor him. His kin attended, along with the Dragon Queen and her offspring, and the Cadwaladr Clan. The event was sorrowful but necessary.

When the mourning period finally ended, the Cadwaladrs had a feast at Garbhán Isle. It was to celebrate many things: the end of the war; that they'd won the war; those who'd earned promotions, including Branwen and Izzy to corporal; the oncoming end of winter; the upcoming return of spring; and anything else they could think of that would warrant a feast.

And as Garbhán Isle readied for the celebration it was obvious that some things had changed for longer than just the duration of the war.

The Kyvich did not leave simply because the war ended, much to Talaith's annoyance. The barbarian witches planned to stay until the twins reached their eighteenth year, still guarding the gates and surrounding territories even while everyone toasted to a new time of peace.

Ren of the Chosen would be heading back to the Eastlands at the request of his father. He had every intention of returning to the Southlands, but no one, not even Ren, knew when that would be.

Keita would be returning to the Northlands with Ragnar, although she still refused to call him her mate. Rhona also would be going back with Vigholf, but she seemed more than happy to call him her mate.

Meinhard, probably because he feared being made to dance, had already headed back to the Northlands with his troops, escorting the Northland females who had no desire to stay for the feast, including Ragnar and Vigholf's mother.

And now, as the hour grew late and the ale flowed more freely, Izzy stepped out the back door and away from the castle. The moon was full and the air crisp and cold. She should have worn her fur cape over her dress, but she'd slipped away from the party, not wanting to be seen.

As she walked past the Kyvich on guard duty at the back gate, Izzy had to smile a bit. She loved hearing her family happy and together again. Hearing the music, seeing them dance. Even her grandparents were dancing! Both of them ecstatic their offspring were home and safe, but neither willing to simply say the words out loud.

The music faded behind her as she trudged through the trees and, after about a mile, up Rose Hill. She reached the top and sat down on the ground, gazing out over the land she and so many others had fought hard to protect. The bonfires that went on for several days to dispose of the Tribesmen's corpses were gone, and Dagmar had taken care to rid any signs of what had happened there. If Dagmar had her way, by springtime, there would be nothing but tall grass and flowers down there. Izzy wouldn't be here to see that, though. In another week, she would be shipped out again. Her mother was not happy, but Izzy, to her own surprise, was. After the last five years, she thought she'd want to take the next year off before returning to the life of the troops—barely tolerable army food, sleeping on bedrolls, and taking orders. But gods, she longed for the army life. She loved it. Even after everything that happened, she absolutely loved it.

Izzy let out a sigh and asked the male she'd sat down next to, "Are you going to stay out here all night—looking maudlin?"

"I'm not in the mood for a feast," Éibhear told her. He was polite, but she could hear from the way he clipped his words, he'd rather not be. "But don't let me stop you from returning to the party, Izzy."

"You going to hate me forever?"

"I don't hate you at all. Or Celyn," he said before she could ask.

"So it's just yourself you hate then?"

"I don't hate myself. I'm a Southland dragon and a prince of the House of Gwalchmai fab Gwyar—I don't think I'm physically capable of hating myself." And Izzy had to look off so he couldn't see her smile. "But if you're asking me if I'm disappointed in myself and crushed at the loss of a good friend . . . then sure. Why not?"

Sure? Why not?

Frowning, Izzy said, "I'm so sorry about Austell." She'd only met the red dragon once, but he'd been very sweet. Besides, no one should die on the end of a stake. "But it's the risk we all take as soldiers. He knew that. You can't blame yourself—"

"Please go."

And she felt the coldly stated words like a knife to her chest, cutting through flesh and muscle and bone, right into her heart. But she didn't argue, simply stood.

She brushed off the back of her dress. "I'm sorry, Éibhear."

"For what?"

"That you lost a friend. That you feel such pain for it." Izzy let out a breath. "And I'm sorry that you found out about me and Celyn."

His soft laugh was bitter, cold silver eyes looking up at her. "Really?" he asked. "That's what you feel sorry for?"

"Aye. I'd never intended to tell you or anyone because what happened between me and Celyn was between us."

"Do you really think he would have kept that quiet? Do you really think he wouldn't have eventually told me on his own? That what you had between you was so desperately precious?"

"That's between him and you and, to be honest, not my problem. But I never wanted you to be hurt by—"

"I'm not hurt," Éibhear said, slowly getting to his feet. She was tall, but he absolutely towered over her when so few did. "In fact," he shrugged. "I don't feel anything. About you. About Celyn. Not even about Austell. Not anymore."

"Then I feel sorry for you because no one should go through life like that."

"Right. I should stumble along instead, feeling nothing but pain for everyone. Like a walking open wound. That does sound like fun."

"With the bad comes the good, Éibhear."

"You're amazing," he said, shaking his head. "After all that you've been through, all that you've seen and lost. Everything that you've killed. With what the gods did to your mother and Annwyl—to *you*. Marking you like chattel," he said, gesturing to her shoulder, where the mark of the god Rhydderch Hael had been branded into her flesh so many years ago. "After all that, you can still walk around talking about feelings? About caring for others' pain?" He laughed and it was like having knives thrown at her. "That's quite . . . astounding."

And with that, Éibhear the Blue headed off down the hill, away from the castle and his kin. Izzy had the feeling he wouldn't be back. That he was going to try to catch up with Meinhard so he could start his new life in the Northlands, away from everyone and everything that he'd known.

And she knew she was right when he said, as he disappeared into the darkness, "Good-bye, Izzy. And good luck."

After he was gone, she stood there until Brannie came up behind her and stood next to her.

"You all right?" her cousin asked.

"Well enough."

"I wouldn't let what he said bother you, Iz. He's just—"

"Is it supposed to be this bad?" Izzy asked about the change every young dragon was supposed to go through as they got older. "Honestly?"

Brannie shook her head. "When Fal went through it, I mean we all do, but he mostly just whined about the misery of his soul and read dark poetry. The pub girls loved it. But he was never this . . ."

"Empty?"

"Well . . . I was going to say bitter, but you always were more dramatic than me." Brannie tugged on the dress Keita had chosen for Izzy. It was a very dark blue and it sparkled. "Do you want to go for a walk, Iz? So we can talk?"

Izzy briefly closed her eyes, let out a breath. "Brannie, my friend, my cousin, the *last* thing I want to do is talk. I want ale, and I want to dance, and I want to forget that Éibhear the Miserable ever existed."

Brannie put her arm around Izzy's shoulders and steered her back down the hill and toward the castle. "I can help you with those first two, dead easy. But you're on your own with that last one."

"Yeah," Izzy sighed. "Yeah, I know."

* * *

A week after the feast ended, about one hundred leagues from Garbhán Isle, Rhona sat by the lake as human, trying to see over her shoulder at the mark that Vigholf had branded her with, Claiming her.

Unlike her own kind, he'd used lightning to brand her with that mark and she'd never say it out loud, but . . . ow!

"Here," Vigholf said, crouching behind her and carefully placing ointment on the area. "This should help with the pain."

Gods, he was just so sweet, but not what she was used to. Fire Breather males usually let the pain linger for a while, so their females knew who they belonged to. At least that was their logic. The females gave it back to them in full, though, when their turn came.

"That feel better?"

"It does. Thanks."

They'd split off from Ragnar, Keita, and their troops so they could get some time together alone. Once they made it back to the Northlands, they'd both be busy. The civil war in the Provinces was heating up and Vigholf would be taking his troops in to join Gaius's while Ragnar and Meinhard's troops would be dealing with the Ice Land dragons who'd crossed borders during the Horde's absence. Rhona would be making weapons for the troops in the Northlands and then in the Provinces. The few days they'd have alone now would be it for quite some time. So they planned to enjoy it.

Once he'd taken care of her mark, Vigholf grasped her face between his hands and gazed into her eyes.

"I love you so much, Rhona."

Rhona went up on her knees and kissed him hard. Her body still trembling from the way he'd just taken her, she still knew that she'd more than happily let him take her again. And again.

"I love you," she said when she pulled back a bit.

Vigholf petted her cheek, smiled at her, then announced, "I'm starving."

Rhona crossed her eyes. "Of course you are."

"Want to hunt something down out here or go into town?"

"I don't really . . ." Rhona smiled and stood.

"What? What's wrong?"

"Look." With real happiness, Rhona walked over to the white mare standing a few feet away. "Hello, you," she said. "I'm so happy to see you again."

The mare nuzzled her and Rhona stroked her forehead.

"Wait," Vigholf said from behind her. "If she's here, where's that mean bastard of a stall—arrgggh!"

Rhona glanced over her shoulder to see that the chestnut stallion had run over Vigholf, slamming him to the ground. Then he galloped back and began to pummel the dragon with his hooves.

"Honestly," Rhona said to the mare. "They're both so pathetic." Rhona leaned in and whispered to her equine friend, "But by the gods, I do love him more than I could ever say." They briefly watched the males. "No matter how astoundingly ridiculous."

"You deceitful bastard!" Vigholf yelled at the stallion, shoving him back with a well-placed fist.

"Oh, would you two stop it," Rhona chastised, focusing again on the mare, the two of them bonding over their love of two idiots.

"You two? He started it!"

Did you miss the other books in G. A. Aiken's fabulous dragon series? The magic begins with

DRAGON ACTUALLY

It's not always easy being a female warrior with a nickname like Annwyl the Bloody. Men tend to either cower in fear—a lot—or else salute. It's true that Annwyl has a knack for decapitating legions of her ruthless brother's soldiers without pausing for breath. But just once it would be nice to be able to really talk to a man, the way she can talk to Fearghus the Destroyer.

Too bad that Fearghus is a dragon, of the large, scaly, and deadly type. With him, Annwyl feels safe—a far cry from the feelings aroused by the hard-bodied, arrogant knight Fearghus has arranged to help train her for battle. With her days spent fighting a man who fills her with fierce, heady desire, and her nights spent in the company of a magical creature who could smite a village just by exhaling, Annwyl is sure life couldn't get any stranger. She's wrong . . .

[And just wait until you meet the rest of the family . . .]

ABOUT A DRAGON

For Nolwenn witch Talaith, a bad day begins with being dragged from bed by an angry mob intent on her crispy end and culminates in rescue by—wait for it—a silver-maned dragon. Existence as a hated outcast is nothing new for a woman with such powerful secrets. The dragon, though? A tad unusual. This one has a human form to die for, and knows it. According to dragon law, Talaith is now his property, for pleasure . . . or otherwise. But if Lord Arrogance thinks she's the kind of damsel to acquiesce without a word, he's in for a surprise . . .

Is the woman never silent? Briec the Mighty knew the moment he laid eyes on Talaith that she would be his, but he'd counted on tongue-lashings of an altogether different sort. It's embarrassing, really, that it isn't this outspoken female's magicks that have the realm's greatest dragon in her thrall. No, Briec has been spellbound by something altogether different—and if he doesn't tread carefully, what he doesn't know about human women could well be the undoing of his entire race . . .

WHAT A DRAGON SHOULD KNOW

Only for those I love would I traipse into the merciless Northlands to risk life, limb, and my exquisite beauty. But do they appreciate it? Do they say, "Gwenvael the Handsome, you are the best among us—the most loved of all dragons?" No! For centuries my family has refused to acknowledge my magnificence as well as my innate humility. Yet for them, and because I am so chivalrous, I will brave the worst this land has to offer.

So here I stand, waiting to broker an alliance with the one the Northlanders call The Beast. A being so fearful, the greatest warriors will only whisper its name. Yet I, Gwenvael, will courageously face down this terrifying . . . woman? It turns out The Beast, a.k.a. Dagmar Reinholdt, is a woman—one with steel grey eyes and a shocking disregard for my good looks. Beneath her plain robes and prim spectacles lies a sensual creature waiting to be unleashed. Who better than a dragon to thaw out that icy demeanor?

And who better than a beast to finally tame a mighty dragon's heart?

LAST DRAGON STANDING

I know what they see when they look at me. The charming, soft-spoken dragoness bred from the most powerful of royal bloodlines. A disguise stronger than any battle shield that allows me to keep all suitors at tail's length. A technique that's worked until him. Until Ragnar the Cunning, handsome barbarian warlord and warrior mage from the desolate Northlands. Unlike those who've come before him, he does not simply submit to my astounding charm and devastating smile. Instead, he dismisses me as vapid, useless and, to my great annoyance, rather stupid!

Yet I'll allow no male to dismiss me. Soon he'll learn my worth, my many skills, and the strength of my will. For this one challenges me enough to make me want to ruthlessly taunt him, tease him and, finally, when the trap is set, bring him to his knees.

Don't miss SUPERNATURAL, a fabulous
paranormal romance anthology, available now!

*Desire comes in many forms . . . some dark,
some dangerous, all undeniable . . .*

In this tantalizing collection, four *New York Times*
bestselling authors invite you into the alluring worlds
they've created in the Demonica, Guardians of Eternity,
Nightwalkers, and Dragon Kin series. Each mesmerizing
page will leave you craving more . . .

SUPERNATURAL

"Vampire Fight Club" by Larissa Ione

When a wave of violence forces shape-shifter Vladlena to go undercover, her first stop is a haven of vice—with a dangerously sexy vamp in charge. Both Vladlena and Nathan are hiding something, but they can't conceal the lust that simmers between them . . .

"Darkness Eternal" by Alexandra Ivy

After being held captive by one vampire for four centuries, Kata had no intention of taking another one to the underworld with her. Yet even in the pits of hell, there's no ignoring the intoxicating desire awakened by his touch . . .

"Kane" by Jacquelyn Frank

Kane knows Corrine was meant to be his . . . just as he knows that truly possessing the lovely human is forbidden. But on the night of the Samhain moon, the beast in every demon is stronger than reason, and Kane's hunger is more powerful than any punishment . . .

"Dragon on Top" by G. A. Aiken

Escorting the highborn Bram through deadly Sand Dragon territory will try Ghleanna's patience . . . and her resolve. For Bram is determined to enhance the journey with a seduction no female could resist . . .

A RIVETING ZEBRA MASS-MARKET PAPERBACK!